Peter Hunter and the Minions of Mara

BOOK ONE OF FREELANCE EXORCISTS

By Janie St. Clair

freelanceexorcistsbooks.blogspot.com

FreelanceExorcists@gmail.com

Cover art by Mackenzie Zimmerman

Contents

To Eileen Dailey, my resident Buddhist;
Aunt Jennifer, the best aunt in the world;
To Frances Blake for her amazingly brilliant editing;
and to Sr. Paula Jean Miller, F.S.E
.

"Greater in battle than the man who would conquer a thousand-thousand men, is he who would conquer just one — himself."
The Buddha, Dhammapada, 103

Prologue

Silas watched from the alley shadows as a young woman laughed with her friend on the steps of a city gym. After this exercise class, she would go home to an empty apartment.

PLING!

His phone rang with a message from Penny:

"Can you get milk and diapers on your way home?"

She was probably wondering why he was working so late. If she ever found out, he'd be in for it.

"If I don't kill her first," he thought.

He stopped himself.

I don't want to kill my wife. I don't want to kill anyone.

"But I will," he thought. *"There's no stopping now."*

His thoughts had been running wild for weeks. He wanted to stop stalking the young woman, but something wouldn't let him. Something pulled him like a magnetic force he couldn't fight.

"I don't want to fight it."

The young woman waved goodbye to her friend and walked toward her car alone. She fumbled with her keys. It was the perfect moment.

Then Silas felt a strong grip on his shoulder.

"Excuse me, sir," a man said. "Do you need some help?"

Silas studied the man. He had a bright smile with successive dimples and large white teeth that almost shone against the darkness of his skin. His black dreadlocked hair had golden ends and was pulled into a high half ponytail.

"This idiot isn't even worth my time. Just get away from him."

Silas grumbled, "Whatever you're peddling, I don't want it."

"What I have to offer you is free," the man replied.

"This is a trap! He knows what you were planning!"

Silas rubbed the spot above his eye where a headache was developing. "I don't need a Lord and Savior," he grumbled.

Silas felt an odd shudder that made him feel like throwing up.

The man's smile remained as he said, "How about a Buddha?"

Silas felt another shudder.

"Run, you idiot! Forget the girl and just run!"

Silas closed his eyes, trying to squint the headache away.

Then the man made a weird shape with his hand, holding his two middle fingers down and extending his index and pinky. At the same time, he started chanting some strange sounds in a deep, resonating voice:

"SABBE SATTE SUKHI HONTU."

The man repeated the same phrase over and over again. The vibrations seemed to shake the entire alley. Then Silas realized that he was the one shaking, not the alley. His whole body rocked in slow, isolated convulsions. He thought he would explode at any moment.

When the convulsions stopped, Silas was paralyzed. He couldn't move. He couldn't speak. He couldn't think. Yet, his body moved.

First, he heard himself laughing. *"You are no match for me!"* another voice spoke with Silas' mouth. *"I have existed for untold ages! I have orchestrated the destruction of countless vermin like you. I will tear you apart and feast on your flesh!"*

The alley erupted in flames, but the mysterious man seemed unfazed. He continued to chant:

"SABBE SATTE SUKHI HONTU."

"You are nothing!" the other voice roared above the fire and the chanting. *"You are a rodent! A worm! You cannot defeat me!"*

"Maybe," the man paused his chant. "But I did bring a friend."

Silas felt his spirit shiver. The man started glowing with a green light that hurt Silas' eyes. He wanted to scream out in pain, but he couldn't manage a single sound.

Instead, flames exploded from his mouth, shooting towards the man. The man dodged, waving his hands through the air and conjuring a wall of transparent green water. The flames sizzled into vapor.

The man raised his hands in the air and the water followed, rising into a curl that filled the alleyway. Silas fell to his knees as the wave came crashing down on him, leaving him dry, but weak.

The man then pressed his folded hand against Silas' forehead and said, "May you be washed clean."

Immediately, Silas felt like he had been gutted. He heard a piercing howl erupt from his mouth. The last thing he saw was the pavement getting closer as he blacked out.

Silas awoke to someone shaking him. He opened his eyes to a blurred scene.

Where am I? He wondered. *Some downtown alley?*

"Hey, you feeling alright?" a man asked.

Silas studied the young man. He had a bright smile with successive dimples and large white teeth that almost shone against the darkness of his skin. His black dreadlocked hair had golden ends and was gathered into a high half ponytail.

"Yeah, I just…" Silas stopped when he saw that the man had four huge slashes over his chest in a diagonal line. Blood stained his shirt.

The entire situation made Silas nervous. He quickly sat up and patted his pockets for his phone and wallet. The man looked hurt, like maybe he thought Silas didn't trust him, but that was ridiculous.

I trust this man with my… life?

"You passed out," the man told Silas. "You think you can get home alright or do you need me to call a cab?"

"I feel great actually," Silas said. His mind was clear for the first time in weeks. He stood up. "You should worry about yourself," he told the man, pointing at the gashes on his chest.

"I got this," the man smiled. "Just take care of yourself. Okay?"

Silas walked out of the alley, read the cross streets, and started on his way. He felt light, as if he could skip all the way home.

Oh, yeah, he thought. *Penny needs diapers and milk. I'd better get moving or she'll get mad. Don't want that.*

Chapter 1: Just a Black Eye

Peter sat in the principal's office, tapping his toes impatiently. He studied the clock.

TICK … TOCK.

Ten impossibly long minutes had passed.

He looked at his dad sitting next to him. His gray eyes were fixed on some imaginary spot in front of his thick glasses as he ran his fingers over his sandy hair. Peter usually appreciated his calm nature, but now it only made him nervous.

Peter focused on the freckles that dotted the backs of his hands. He had freckles scattered all over, just like his mom. When he was younger, she would concoct stories, matching each new freckle to an important event or a personality trait.

If she were here now, Peter imagined she would say, *"Look at this new freckle. It must be a 'you're grounded forever' freckle."*

The principal's door opened and Jeremy Matthews came out with an ice pack on his eye and fake sniffles. Jeremy looked like one of those artist sketches where a human is drawn in simple shapes: he was all rectangles. Even his too-small-for-his-face nose was a tiny rectangle.

"I expect you to clear this up soon," Mrs. Matthews threatened.

She scowled at Peter before raising her nose in the air and ushering Jeremy out. As they passed, Jeremy flashed a rectangular smirk that made Peter want to hit him all over again.

Mr. Sullivan, the principal, took a deep rumbling breath as he massaged his forehead. "Alright, Mr. Hunters," he sighed. "It's your turn."

Samuel Hunter gave a gentle, nonthreatening smile. Peter trudged into the office after his dad and sat with his back slouched and arms folded.

"Mr. Hunter, are you aware of your son's actions today?" Mr. Sullivan asked.

Mr. Hunter studied his son. "Only the cursory explanation I've heard so far," he responded calmly. "Perhaps Peter can enlighten us."

Both men eyed him expectantly.

Peter rolled his eyes and said, "He was throwing rocks at Stacey."

"Stacey Sanders?" Mr. Sullivan asked. He had the start of a condescending smile. "And do you have a crush on Miss Sanders?"

Peter looked at him like he was crazy. Sure Stacey was pretty, but she spent too much time giggling about boys, makeup, and gossip. Peter found most girls boring or annoying.

"Do I have to have a crush to not want someone to throw rocks at her?" he asked incredulously.

Mr. Hunter let a miniscule smile curl the very edge of his lip.

"No, I suppose not," Mr. Sullivan replied. "Regardless, your actions were inappropriate. Jeremy will most likely have a black eye."

Again, Peter looked at him like he was crazy. He had seen plenty of bruises and scrapes over the years. Black eyes healed. They healed cleaner than an injury from a rock.

"But it was on his right eye," Peter pointed out.

"Yes…" Mr. Sullivan said carefully. "You struck him on his right eye. What does that…?"

"That means I used my left." When Mr. Sullivan still looked confused, Peter took in a frustrated breath. "I'm right-handed, so I used my non-dominant hand. And I used a front jab," Peter demonstrated, "not a reverse punch, aimed for his cheek, not his temple or his jugular. If I didn't *just* want to stop him, I could have used a million other techniques that would've stopped him for good."

Mr. Sullivan's eyes grew wide. Peter's dad looked wary.

"He was throwing rocks at a girl!" Peter repeated.

"What disturbs me," Mr. Sullivan cleared his throat, "is that Jeremy was hurt while you sustained no obvious injuries."

"So I'm stronger than Jeremy," Peter said. "That disturbs you?"

Again, Mr. Hunter let a smirk escape.

"No one saw the fight," Mr. Sullivan explained sternly. "It's your word against Jeremy's. He's the one with injuries while you are unscathed. Now, this is your first offense, we can let you off with one day of at-home suspension. But this is your eighth grade year. Your actions have lasting consequences now. You need to refrain from using violence on school grounds. And you'll be lucky if Mrs. Matthews doesn't press charges."

Peter's lips tightened. Somehow, he knew that Jeremy wasn't getting the same sentence.

"And I strongly suggest you consider switching hobbies," Mr. Sullivan added. Peter's head jerked to attention. "Perhaps martial arts is too dangerous for someone with Peter's… personality."

Peter cast wide, offended eyes at Mr. Sullivan, then his dad, then Mr. Sullivan again.

Mr. Hunter nodded with a pensive expression. "We'll consider it," he promised. Peter's jaw dropped. "And I think Peter can promise you that he won't use violence on a classmate again."

As they left, Mr. Hunter and Mr. Sullivan exchanged a few pleasantries while Peter seethed, barely hearing their words. He was stiff all the way to the car.

Why doesn't dad believe me? he thought.

Then the car slowed to a stop in front of an ice cream shop.

Peter turned to look at his dad. "What are we…?"

His dad smiled as he pulled the key out of the ignition and said, "It only seems right that you get a reward for defending an innocent girl."

Mr. Hunter let Peter vent his anger while they ate their ice cream.

"And the worst part was when Hazel told Stacey that Jeremy probably likes her. As if that made it all okay! You like a girl so you throw rocks at her? Is it the same when you get married? Do you hit mom because you like her? That's crazy, right? Right?"

"Yes, it's crazy," Mr. Hunter agreed.

"And then I get in trouble for defending her? You know I talked to him first and I only threw that punch after he threw the first three. But he couldn't even touch me."

"I can imagine."

"And the punch I threw was barely a tap. I'll be surprised if he even has a black eye. And the nerve of Mr. Sullivan saying I should stop karate! If I didn't have the training I had, I could have really hurt him in my anger!"

"'I aimed for his cheek, not his jugular,'" Mr. Hunter repeated Peter's words. "You certainly inherited your mother's mouth."

"I would never hurt someone unless it was in defense!"

"I know, son. I know. And I'm proud of you. And you won't be stopping karate classes unless you want to."

"Then why didn't you yell like Jeremy's mom did?"

Peter's dad thought a while, taking a few bites. He was always slow and careful to respond. Sometimes it drove Peter crazy.

Finally, he spoke, "There are some fights you fight. Like when someone is throwing rocks. And some fights it's better to concede."

"Shouldn't you always fight for what's right?" Peter challenged.

"Yes. In most cases," he nodded. "But maybe I should say that there are other ways to fight. People tend to think that whoever is loudest wins the argument. But I think whoever is most controlled is the true winner."

That night, Peter came out of his bedroom, lured to the kitchen by the smell of chocolate chip cookies. Jody Hunter held an adamant belief that desserts lost all their celebratory power unless they were only baked on special occasions. In fact, Peter had been charged to keep the ice cream shop a secret.

"What's this for?" he asked her.

She smoothed her brown bob behind her ears. Then she told him in a storyteller's voice, "This, my son, is from underdogs, the down-trodden, and persecuted girls everywhere."

He chuckled and grabbed a cookie. "Thanks, mom."

Suddenly she looked gravely serious and fixed her eyes on his forehead. She ran around the counter and smoothed his hair back with both hands while she studied the skin just beneath his hairline.

"What?" Peter worried with his mouth full.

"It's a new freckle," she breathed. Peter rolled his eyes. "But hey, this is a special one. You get something like this for acts of extreme valor."

"Mo-om!" he complained, batting her hands away. "I'm thirteen. I'm too old for the freckle thing. I'm not a kid anymore, you know."

She stepped back and assessed him seriously. "No, you're not. You've grown up in one short day. Today, you are a man, my son."

DING!

The chimes rang as Peter opened the door of a small karate studio nestled in a strip mall. Moms watched from benches while the class of children was finishing. Peter sat, too, and waited for his class to start.

"Tyler," Sensei Rob called out jovially to a younger boy hiding in a corner. "My main man. Come and join us, buddy."

The little seven-year-old didn't budge, but Peter knew this wouldn't last. Sensei Rob's ability with people was like a superpower.

Rob, the owner of the karate dojo, was a charismatic teacher and a powerful black belt. He had dark skin and black hair gathered in dreadlocks with bleached tips. He had a huge smile with successive dimples and bright white teeth.

Rob crouched down to get on Tyler's level and whispered softly. "I know you're upset about not winning that race earlier, but let me tell you something. Do you think I'm strong?" Tyler nodded. "You wouldn't believe the competitions I've lost. And each and every time I lose, I want to crawl into a tiny ball and never come out. But should I?" Tyler shook his head. "No. I'll never improve that way. If you want to be strong and feel absolutely great about yourself, you have to keep trying until you get it."

Peter could see Tyler starting to come around.

"Now, all we have left of class is a few small exercises. If you can join us and throw all your energy into them, I can guarantee you'll end this day feeling better. What do you say, Tyler man?"

Tyler nodded and got back into place.

"That's my man!" Sensei Rob praised him.

As they finished class, Tyler's kiaps were louder than anyone else's. And he wore a self-satisfied grin as he and his mom left the dojo.

When all the younger kids were gone, Peter started stretching in the dojo area, waiting for his class to start.

"Heard you put some kid in the hospital," Sensei Rob teased.

Peter huffed. "I didn't put him in the hospital!"

"Right," Sensei Rob wagged his finger. "You broke his legs."

"I just punched him. One tiny little jab and the school goes crazy!"

"I'm just teasing," Rob assured him. "You had good intentions."

"Still got in trouble for it," Peter grumbled. "It doesn't make sense. I defend a girl with no thought of reward and *I* get in trouble."

Sensei Rob studied Peter for a few moments. "Let me show you something," he said. "Try to hit me. Go full out. Forget form and technique and just try to hurt me however you can."

Peter threw a punch at Sensei Rob's gut. Sensei didn't react. Peter might as well have punched a wall.

"Again," Rob ordered.

Peter used his most powerful kick, straight to Rob's ribs. Again, Sensei Rob let it hit him without a reaction.

"Do you feel big and powerful?" Sensei asked.

"No. I feel weak and frustrated. Thanks a lot by the way," Peter used his most sarcastic tone. "I appreciate you trying to cheer me up."

"Where do you think a bully gets his power from?" Rob asked.

"From rocks?"

Rob laughed. "From your reaction. You hurt me, but if I had let you know that, you would've felt more powerful. When I didn't react, I took your power away. Imagine an angry guy throwing rocks at a river. Does the river care? Do the rocks change anything about the water?"

Peter thought a moment. "Are you telling me to take a punch?"

"You could handle it," Sensei Rob said. "But I'd just say that you don't have to react. Can you imagine how this kid would've felt if he yelled at you and you just smiled back? Or if you dodged while he got red in the face trying to hit you?"

"Actually, that's fun to think about," Peter admitted.

Peter was the last student in the dojo when his mom pulled up. He started to leave when he was distracted by a rattling noise. A small Buddha statue fell off a shelf on the wall.

Peter looked at it.

Nothing else had shaken or fallen. When he turned back to ask Sensei Rob about it, he noticed that Rob's face looked tense.

"See you next time," he said as he pushed Peter toward the door.

"Hold up. How did that fall?" Peter asked.

"Don't worry about it. Your mom's waiting. Bye."

Rob shoved Peter through the door and locked it. Peter gave him a confused look through the glass and Rob simply waved back.

"Good lesson?" Mrs. Hunter asked as he got in the car.

"Yeah…" His eyes fell on the windows of the dojo. The lights were flickering wildly and in a flash of light, Peter swore he saw a dark shadowy figure looming over Sensei Rob. In the next flash, it was gone, though the lights continued to blink even as they turned out of the parking lot.

Weird optical illusion, he decided.

Then a strange thought hit him. "Hey, wait a sec," he realized. "Did you tell Sensei Rob about my fight with Jeremy?"

His mom shook her head. "No. I just dropped you off, remember? When would I have talked to him?"

"Then how did he know?"

Chapter 2: As Calm as a River

On Monday morning, Peter was chaining his bike in front of the school when he heard a loud and booming voice.

"Hey, Hunter!" Jeremy bellowed.

Peter rolled his eyes and started walking towards the school.

"Hey! I'm talking to you!"

Jeremy reached out from behind to grab Peter's shoulder, but Peter knew it was coming. He could almost feel the air shift in reaction to Jeremy's movements, like the sixth sense skill of that the popular superhero, the Arachnid Kid.

Sensing Jeremy's movements, Peter stepped to the side just in time. Jeremy had a confused expression as he stumbled forward and Peter tried to keep a straight face.

"Hey, Jeremy," he greeted pleasantly. "Sorry about what happened on Thursday. I just don't know my own strength. You feeling alright?"

Jeremy cracked his knuckles. "I'm about to feel a lot better."

He threw a punch, but Peter dodged effortlessly. A few onlookers let out oohs of approval.

"Get that stupid smirk off your face!" Jeremy threatened.

Peter couldn't help it. He had a particular smirk that graced his face whenever he was really proud of himself.

Jeremy threw another punch. Peter dodged again and watched Jeremy's fist swipe the air in front of his chin, missing the mark. Jeremy let out an intimidating grunt and threw both hands towards Peter's collar. Peter ducked under the grab and got behind Jeremy, forcing him to turn around.

"Stay still so I can hit you!" Jeremy howled.

Peter imagined Jeremy yelling at a river and smirked again. Jeremy threw a punch straight to Peter's gut. Peter stayed still this time, but tensed his muscles. Jeremy winced and shook the pain out of his hand.

"Hah, look at that," laughed one of Jeremy's friends. "He punched Peter, but he got hurt."

"I'm not hurt!" Jeremy yelled. "Fight me, Hunter."

"I just don't know," Peter shook his head regretfully. "I'd hate to hurt you again." The onlookers sniggered. "So go ahead, hit me as much as you need to. I can take it."

Jeremy was red from anger. He threw a punch at Peter's ear.

BAM!

Peter let it hit the side of his head. It stung, but he held in his reaction and gave Jeremy a simple smile.

"Jeremy Matthews!" Mrs. Sommers' voice startled them both.

They turned simultaneously to see the imposing figure of their homeroom teacher, watching them from the school steps.

"You have a lot of explaining to do," Mrs. Sommers barked.

Beside her stood one of Stacey's friends, Alicia Lisowski. She wore a self-righteous smile while she told Mrs. Sommers, "I saw the whole thing. Peter did nothing wrong."

"Thank you, Miss Lisowski," Mrs. Sommers smiled at her. "And you, young man," she addressed Jeremy. "You are coming with me to the principal's office. Now!" Then she softened her tone. "Miss Lisowski, can I trust you to take Mr. Hunter to the nurse?"

Alicia nodded, causing her blond hair to bounce on her shoulders.

"You'll regret this," Jeremy threatened as he passed Alicia.

"No, you will," Mrs. Sommers corrected him.

Alicia turned to Peter and casually glided down the stairs. Peter noticed how her hair sparkled in the sun.

"You didn't have to do that," Peter said. "I could've handled it."

She nodded with a hidden smile. "I think what you meant to say," she said slowly, "was, 'Thanks, Alicia. You are so amazing.'"

"Thanks, Alicia," he repeated robotically. "You are so amazing!"

She grinned. Peter could see why a lot of guys talked about her. When she smiled, it was as if the sun got brighter.

"You're a fast learner," she told him. She wrinkled her nose slightly and smiled again. "That's points in your favor."

"Oh, yeah?" Peter looked at her sideways. "What kind of points are we talking about exactly?"

She ignored his question. "Come on," she ordered. "I promised I'd walk you to the nurse's office."

"Nah, I don't really need to go."

Alicia rolled her eyes. "Peter Hunter, do I have to teach you everything?" she complained. "A pretty girl just saved your life…"

"I don't know about saved…" he contradicted.

"…*and* offered to walk you to the nurse's office. The correct response is, 'Gee, I must be the luckiest boy in the whole school.' Now, say it with me. 'Gee…'"

Peter smirked. "You're funny, Alicia."

"'Gee, I must be…'" she persisted.

“The luckiest boy in the school,” he obeyed, laughing.

“Good,” she gave him a nod of approval. “You pass.”

As they walked to the nurse’s office laughing, Peter started thinking that maybe not all girls were boring and annoying.

Peter was anxious to tell Sensei Rob all about his victory at his next karate class. He had to wait, however. Sensei Rob was in his office talking to a parent. His assistant teacher, Charlene, was helping a young girl in the dojo area.

Charlene was an impressive teacher. Peter thought she moved like a viper: fast, precise, and intensely focused. She had long hair that was only slightly darker than her golden brown skin and a smile that stretched across her whole face.

She had been teaching at the dojo for half a year and Sensei Rob was the only one who called her Charlene.

“He said what?” Charlie asked the student with a scandalized tone.

“That girls can’t be strong,” the girl, Zoe, answered.

Sensei Charlie looked personally offended. “When I was your age, I punched a boy for saying that,” she confessed.

“No!” Zoe’s eyes widened.

“And he never said it again,” she said with a victorious nostalgia. “Oh, but I got in so much trouble for that. Don’t do it.”

Zoe laughed, then sighed. “Did you ever worry that you were chasing the guys away by being into martial arts?”

Charlie smiled. “Oh, Zoe. I know what you mean. Sometimes I didn’t like that it scared boys away, but then I realized that it scared all the wrong boys away. It’s better to have no boyfriend than the wrong one. And it’s even better to be yourself no matter what. Now let’s see if you can take down the punch bag. Pretend it’s every boy who ever wronged you!”

They worked together as Sensei Rob and Zoe’s mom came out of the front office.

“Are you sure?” she asked Sensei Rob in a hushed voice.

“Of course,” he said. “I wouldn’t want her to miss out on classes right now. She needs the consistency.”

“She does.” The mother’s lips tightened to hold in her tears.

Sensei handed her a tissue.

"Thank you," she told him. "I'll pay you back when…"

"No," Sensei stopped her. "Pay whatever you can even if it's nothing. No strings, no debt, no IOUs."

The mom nodded and took a stabilizing breath. "Come on, Zoe," she called. "We need to go get dinner."

"Is dad going to join us?" Zoe asked as she bounded over.

Her mom's lips tightened again as she forced a smile. "I'm not sure. I guess we'll find out."

"Hi, Peter," Charlie greeted him as Zoe and her mom left.

"Hi, Sensei Charlie," Peter returned.

"You see?" she turned back to Rob. "The boy gets it. Every student gets it. So why can't you call me by my real name?"

"But your real name is Charlene," Sensei Rob retorted.

"That's an old lady's name. I have asked you so many times…"

"When you interviewed here, your resume clearly said 'Charlene.' Are you telling me that you lied on your resume?" He gave her a scandalized look that melted into a winning smile.

Then Peter noticed that Sensei's arm was in a sling.

"Hey, how did you get hurt?" Peter asked.

"Just dealing with my own bullies," Sensei Rob explained.

Peter wasn't sure if that was a joke or a serious description. He dismissed the thought, however, and told Sensei Rob his own story.

"I'm proud of you, kid." Rob shook Peter by the shoulder.

"I bet that took a lot of self-control," Charlie added.

"It was all thanks to Sensei Rob," Peter told her. "And my dad. He said whoever's the calmest is the true winner."

"He's a wise man," Sensei nodded. "Hey, I wanted to ask you something. Would you be interested in private lessons?"

"Ooh. Private lessons?" Sensei Charlie reacted.

"What for?" Peter asked.

"You have a lot of potential. I could see you doing great things. Maybe even the Olympics."

A few weeks later, when Peter entered the dojo for his first private lesson, he stopped still in his tracks. The place had been destroyed.

Chapter 3: Right View

It was an absolute mess. The decorations, paddles, blocks, and freestanding punch bags were all strewn about. There was a strong smell of incense and Peter could hear Sensei Rob in his office chanting, "OM MANI PADME HUM."

As Peter started cleaning up, he speculated all the possibilities: a freak wind storm inside the studio; a group of mafia members came to demand extortion money; Sensei had some hidden personality, like the superhero, the Big Green Lug, that exploded in a rage.

None of those seemed likely.

"Hey, Pete. Didn't hear you come in," Sensei Rob said as he emerged from the office with a large bandage on his forehead. It coordinated nicely with his sling.

"What happened here?" Peter asked.

Sensei simply said, "You probably wouldn't believe me if I told you. Anyway, thanks for helping."

All that was left was the Eastern paraphernalia Sensei kept on the shelves behind the front desk.

Peter handed Sensei a dagger and asked, "What are all these for?"

Sensei gave him a serious look. "They're not for fighting humans."

Peter snickered. Sensei Rob was the kind of person who picked up spiders in his hand to set them outside.

"They're all for warding off evil," Sensei said, as if that were a normal thing people usually talked about. "Let's get started. I want to talk about the way of the martial artist." He clapped Peter on the shoulder with his good hand and pushed him toward the mats. "It's not just about training the body. It's also about the mind and the heart."

Peter thought that sounded like a cartoon about magical ponies as he sat cross-legged on the dojo mats.

"So I'm going to teach you some Buddhist philosophy," Rob said.

"Is this going to be boring?" Peter asked with a smirk.

Sensei Rob chuckled. "Hopefully, it'll change your life. The Buddha said, *'Just as a candle cannot burn without fire, men cannot live without a spiritual life.'* Buddhism can give you that spiritual life."

"But Buddhists don't get to do anything, right?" Peter challenged. "I don't mind learning about them, but I have no plans to be a monk."

"There are many applications of Buddhism," Sensei explained with a smile. "And while Buddhist monks don't do a lot of things even other religions allow, the path of Buddhism offers true happiness in return. Buddhist monks are some of the happiest people on earth."

"Really?" Peter asked with a sideways gaze. It seemed unbelievable to him that someone could be happy without the simple joys in life like TV and junk food.

"Most people look to something outside themselves in order to be happy. How many times have you heard someone say that they'll be happy when they get enough money or when they get a girlfriend? How many of those people are actually happy when they get what they want? See, the world of our senses, of physical things, is impermanent. It's constantly changing, so it can't bring us lasting joy. So true, lasting satisfaction must come from somewhere else."

"Okay, I'll buy that," Peter agreed.

"Now, the way of Buddhism is called the eightfold path. Today, we're just going to discuss the first of the eight steps, which is called Right View, sometimes called Right Understanding. It means getting the right view of the world, an outlook, a belief system."

"Like religion or something?" Peter asked warily.

"It could be," Sensei Rob said. "It's more how you believe the world works. What's the purpose of life? What makes you happy? But first, there are many belief systems: Buddhism, Christianity, Judaism, and Islam. Why do you think it matters that you find the right one?"

"I don't think it does," Peter responded plainly.

"Why not?"

"Let's say your favorite color is green and mine is blue. It's not like one of us is right. It's not like I have to go to war with you to force you to choose blue."

"That's a great view. But let's say that because I like the color green, and I have more money, that clothing stores start selling only green shirts. Suddenly, there are no shirts in your favorite color."

"So what? I'd just wear green. And what idiot shirt maker would only make shirts in one color?"

"It's just an analogy."

"But it's a weak analogy."

"It was your analogy!" Rob laughed boisterously.

Peter thought a second. "Well, it wasn't weak when I said it."

Sensei shook his head. "Alright, let's try another one. Let's say you believe cows are sacred animals."

"But I don't."

"But the rest of America slaughters cows for food."

"Wait, do you think cows are sacred?"

"Beliefs determine actions! Okay?" Sensei Rob said quickly. "What you believe drives the choices you make. If a person has a worldview that money is the most important thing, he'll make choices to gain money even if it hurts someone. And if a person believes that people are the most important thing, he'll make choices to help people even if he loses money. Beliefs shape our actions and our actions shape the world. Get it?"

"You could've just said that to begin with."

Rob sighed. "So what do you believe in?" he asked Peter.

"I think people should be nice to each other," Peter thought aloud. "Like no stealing and killing."

"That's a start," Sensei nodded. "I want you to start thinking about it more. A lot of people think they can worry about what they believe later, when they grow up, but there's this thing called karma."

"I've heard of that," Peter interjected. "When you do good things, good stuff happens to you, right?"

"Yes," Sensei nodded. "And when you make harmful choices, it comes back to you. It makes sense, right? People will most often treat you according to how you treat them. So you see? Even if you're not worrying about what you believe and you're just having fun, there are still going to be consequences to all of your actions."

"So what am I *supposed* to believe in then?" Peter asked.

"Whatever you think is right."

"You're not going to tell me?"

"The Buddha said that part of having a right view is to base your beliefs on real world experiences, not on something you were taught by parents, teachers, society…"

"Or your sensei?" Peter asked with his smart-aleck smirk.

To his surprise, Sensei Rob agreed. "Exactly," he said.

Peter wasn't expecting that. Adults usually wanted him to subscribe to their beliefs and rules "or else."

"It's up to you to figure out what you believe," Sensei lectured. "But it's also up to you to keep your mind open. Really open. We should always be flexible, constantly observing the world as it *is*, not as you *think* it is or as you *want* it to be. I like to think about being like a river."

"You already used the river analogy a week ago," Peter joked.

"Well, I'm using it again. When a river meets an obstacle, like a rock, it doesn't blast through and annihilate the object. It finds a course that incorporates the rock. Our pursuit of the truth should be the same. Instead of fighting challenges to your beliefs, let the truth be what it is, as the river lets the rock be what it is. Alter your course if necessary."

"You really like water, huh?" Peter noted. "Should I start calling you Sensei Pocahontas?"

"Show some respect, punk," Sensei Rob teased. "Point is: your job is to challenge everything, including yourself. And that can be hard. Most people automatically accept beliefs from trusted authority."

"I'm a teenager," Peter countered. "We don't like authority."

"Maybe not parents and teachers, but you accept some authority. There's music you're supposed to listen to, shows you're supposed to watch, and even beliefs you're supposed to follow. Your job is to challenge everything. Challenge yourself to see things as they really are and form your opinions based on the reality of your experiences. Even the Buddha told his followers not to just take his word for it, but to challenge themselves to come to their own conclusions about the world."

"I'm liking this religion," Peter commented.

"Now, the Buddha developed his right view that all Buddhists follow. Think you can handle listening a little while longer?"

"I can listen," Peter attested. "I'm a great listener."

Rob gave him a skeptical look, then went on with the lesson.

"Buddhism is based on the Four Noble Truths." He held up his fingers as he listed them. "One: suffering is a part of life. Two: the source of suffering is wanting or craving. Three: the cure for suffering is to control your cravings. And four: the way to control your cravings is through meditation and self-discipline, or the eightfold path."

"That's it?" Peter asked, surprised. "Like, no god or gods?"

Rob shook his head. "Buddhism is more about the inner workings of the human mind. The Buddha himself grew up Hindu, so sometimes he talked about spirits and gods. And sometimes Buddhism merges with other religions, but some Buddhists are even atheists."

"I guess it's flexible like the river, huh?" Peter poked.

Sensei Rob smiled. "So, this week, I want you to challenge all your beliefs. Observe the beliefs of the people around you, too."

"That sounds fun. I'm really good at challenging things."

"Yes. You. Are," Sensei agreed wholeheartedly.

Somehow, Peter wasn't sure that was a compliment.

That night at dinner, he talked about his class with his parents.

"That's great," his mom said. "I think learning about different faiths and cultures can really strengthen you as a person. Your dad and I have studied some faiths. We never found one that we wanted to join, but every one we studied seemed to follow a natural law. You know, don't steal, and don't kill. Be kind and patient."

Peter knew his mom could go on all night. So he pretended to think she was finished, and asked, "What about you, dad?"

"I think it all comes down to the golden rule," his dad replied.

"I also think people should do what's right regardless of what others think," his mom added. "Even if a teacher or a political leader tells you otherwise. Follow that gut feeling, that conscience."

"But respect your parents, of course," Peter's dad winked.

"Yes, always respect your parents," Mrs. Hunter agreed. "And always eat your vegetables."

"And clean your room," his dad jested.

Peter's mom counted on her fingers, "Wake up on time. Do your homework. Do the dishes and laundry. Take care of your parents in their old age."

Mr. and Mrs. Hunter laughed as they continued. When the rules started getting outrageous, Peter walked away rolling his eyes.

The next day at school, Peter found himself studying his friends and wondering what they believed. He wasn't usually a fan of homework, but this task was more applicable to his life. Plus, no one would be grading it. At the end of the day, Peter decided if he was right or wrong. And so far, he had an A.

Jeremy was across the blacktop bullying someone. He obviously believed that if he wanted something, he could do anything to get it. Alicia was sitting under a tree with her friends, Stacey and Gina. Peter overheard their conversation.

"Did you know it's been over fifty years that China took over Tibet by force?" Alicia was lecturing passionately. "And people still haven't done anything to stop them!"

Peter chuckled, remembering the many times that Alicia had tried to spread awareness of some world crisis.

His friends Chris and Harrison were talking as they passed a basketball back and forth.

"So then Gina said she likes smart guys," Harrison said.

"Dude, you like Gina?" Chris jeered. "As in Gina Salvatore? How can you like her when Alicia is always next to her?"

Gina was an awkward girl with curly, out-of-control hair. She also had an unashamed personality with a mouth full of braces, but no filter.

"I can like more than one girl at a time," Harrison explained. "So anyway, now I have to pretend to pay attention in class."

He attempted a complicated dribbling technique that failed easily.

Another boy, Ethan, stole the ball and switched the topic, "Did you guys see that video of the dude trying to make a basket while riding his skateboard? He slammed right into the garage door. It was hilarious. Peter, you saw it, right?"

Ethan passed to Peter.

THUD!

The ball hit Peter's shoulder. "Hm? Saw what?" he asked.

"Earth to Peter," Ethan joked. "What are you staring at, dude?"

Peter picked up the ball and bounced it. "Have you guys ever noticed that what you believe determines your actions?"

They all looked at him for a beat.

"Are you on drugs?" Chris asked with mock seriousness.

"Just trying to figure out what I believe in." Peter stopped the ball in his hands. "What's our purpose? What gives us real happiness?"

"I believe funny videos give us happiness," Ethan joked.

Peter laughed and passed the ball hard at Ethan.

"Nope. It's girls," Harrison corrected, looking at Alicia, Gina, and Stacey. "They are God's gift to the world."

"I'm serious," Peter persisted. "What do you really believe in? What do you think is right, what do you think is wrong?"

"Everyone's going to have a different answer," Chris said, grabbing the ball from Ethan, shooting at the basket, and missing. "Truth is different for everyone. What's right for me may not be right for you."

"But that can't be completely true," Peter challenged him. "I mean, something has to be right for everyone."

"No, man, it doesn't work like that," Chris shook his head. "Nothing is true for everyone. Truth is relative."

"But that doesn't make sense," Peter argued. "You're saying that sentence like it's true for everyone. But it can't be true for everyone if nothing is true for everyone."

"Dude, seriously, what drug are you on?" Ethan laughed.

"Take Jeremy," Peter pointed across the blacktop where Jeremy was still pestering someone. "He thinks it's okay to bully everyone. But no one wants to hang out with him because of it, right?"

"So?" Harrison asked.

"So I'm saying that things are going to have consequences."

Chris shook his head. "You are so full of…"

"Wow, that's a really deep conversation," Alicia commented as she, Gina, and Stacey walked by with the forgotten basketball. "I like when guys think deep like that." She tossed the ball to Peter.

Each of the boys watched in silence as the girls walked off.

"Religion is so cool," Ethan said in a trance.

"My family's Christian," Chris admitted loudly. "We go to church every Sunday. Never miss it."

"I'm Jewish," Harrison informed. "It's a really important part of my life. I had my Bar Mitzvah and everything."

As the boys continued their conversation with a new set of opinions, Peter laughed to himself that maybe Alicia had a superpower just like Sensei Rob.

Chapter 4: Right Thought

The last parent and child were leaving the dojo as Peter entered for his second private lesson. Rob and Charlie were at the front desk, looking at a picture on Rob's phone.

"It must have gotten into a fight with another animal," Rob was telling her. "It had open wounds all over."

"And you nursed it to health on your back porch?" she asked.

Rob nodded. "He was so sweet, too. You could tell he was grateful. See, he let me pet him." He swiped to the next picture.

"Aw," she said with a smile. Then she narrowed her eyes. "But you're aware that's a raccoon, right?"

"Raccoons need love, too," he defended.

"Only you, Rob," she laughed.

"Hey! Pete's here," Rob smiled. "Let's get started." Then he explained to Charlie, "I started teaching him about the eightfold path of Buddhism."

"I love Buddhism," Charlie said as they all sat on the mats.

"Really?" Rob studied her. "I knew I made a good choice hiring you."

Peter rolled his eyes.

"Alright, so Pete," Rob turned to him, "tell me what you thought about Right View over the last few days."

"It was fun to challenge everything," Peter admitted. "I thought mostly about what makes me happy. Usually, I like to relax by watching TV and browsing the internet. But I end up wasting hours, and never feel relaxed."

"That's an awesome start," Sensei congratulated him. "Keep it up. Now, the second step in the eightfold path is Right Thought, sometimes called Right Resolve or Intent. And it's all about how you earn good or bad karma through your thoughts as well as your actions."

"Whoa. Hold up. Even our thoughts?" Peter balked. "I won't be judged for my thoughts, will I? I can't control what I think."

"It's not really about being judged," Charlie interjected. "That's what I always liked about Buddhism. There's no one judging you or punishing you. It's all about consequences, cause and effect."

"Exactly," Rob agreed. "The Buddha said, *'What we think, we become.'* Our thoughts transform us. Think about someone you don't like. Maybe that Jeremy kid, from school. There. Look in the mirror."

Peter noticed his reflection over Sensei's shoulder. His face had contorted into a scowl just at the thought of Jeremy Matthews.

"See?" Sensei asked. "But even if you could control your face, there would still be other consequences. The Buddha said, *'You will not be punished for your anger. You will be punished by your anger.'*"

"I love that quote," Charlie said.

"It's great, right?" Rob smiled.

Peter rolled his eyes again.

"The more you entertain negative thoughts about this kid," Rob continued, "the more likely you'll notice what you don't like about him. The more you don't like about him, the more you'll want to hurt him, perhaps even justify it. The more you want to hurt him, the more you'll make choices that will cause him harm."

"I wouldn't do that," Peter argued.

"Are you sure?" Rob asked.

Peter thought a moment. He had already punched Jeremy and really enjoyed it. "No," he admitted.

"See? Your thoughts have consequences."

"Also, how does it feel physically when you think about him?" Charlie piped in. "Does it feel pleasant? Or do you feel knots in your stomach?"

"Knots," Peter admitted. "But how do I change that? I can't control the thoughts I have."

Rob clapped his hands excitedly. "First, let's distinguish that there are two types of thoughts. There's the wandering thoughts which naturally pop into your mind. They're spontaneous and you can't directly control them."

"Hah! So I was right!" Peter congratulated himself.

Rob held up a hand to stop him. "Then there's the cultivated thought. These are the ones you can control. It's like, if you think 'I want to punch Jeremy,' then you stop yourself and think, 'I will respect Jeremy.' The more you choose thoughts that are non-violent and compassionate, the more you'll change your wandering thoughts. So: hah! I was right."

"Boys, it's not a competition," Charlie scolded them.

"Controlling your thoughts sounds exhausting," Peter complained.

"Maybe at first," Rob admitted. "But like muscles, your thoughts can be trained. See, in karate, you spend time in classes, practicing your moves. And through meditation, you can practice your thoughts."

"Meditation?" Peter groaned. He was already tired of sitting.

“It gets easy,” Sensei Charlie told him. “You can start out small, maybe five minutes at first, but then it’ll grow with time.”

Rob turned to Charlie. “You meditate?” he asked her.

She nodded. “I meditate or pray every day.”

“See?” Rob turned back to Peter. “Sensei Charlene agrees.”

“Charlie,” she corrected him.

He ignored her. “The idea is to let your mind settle. Think of waves on a lake. When the water’s too agitated, you can’t see to the bottom. When the mind is too busy, you can’t see your own thoughts clearly enough.”

“Again with the water?” Peter raised an eyebrow.

“The more control you have over your thoughts, the more control you’ll have over yourself and your world. In fact, there’s a story about the Buddha just before he attained enlightenment. He sat down to meditate and Mara, –for all intents and purposes, the devil– came to distract him. He assembled all his minions, thousands of demons, and they threw spears and shot arrows. The Buddha kept his thoughts focused and the weapons turned into flowers and sparkles.”

“Flowers and sparkles?” Peter asked warily.

“Then Mara sent his daughters, right?” Sensei Charlie asked.

“Yes,” Rob nodded. “They tried to distract the Buddha by dancing, but he remained focused and in control of his thoughts.”

“Did the girls also turn into flowers and sparkles?” Peter asked.

Charlie snorted.

“The point is,” Rob continued, “your mind is so powerful, it can even defeat the forces of evil and temptation. And meditation is how you get there. Humor me. Let’s try some right now.”

“Meditate? Right now?” Peter asked unenthusiastically.

“There’s this form of meditation where you let your mind relax and take in the moment without judgement. You’d be surprised how much we judge everything. ‘It’s too cold;’ ‘It’s too hot;’ ‘Sensei Rob is annoying!’”

“Can you read minds?” Peter joked.

Rob continued, “The best way to train your nonjudgmental thoughts is by focusing only on your breaths, nothing else. Try that for one minute.”

“Just breathing in and out?” Peter said. “Because, I don’t want to brag, but I’ve been breathing in and out this whole time. My entire life, in fact.”

Charlie snorted again.

“Try to focus all your concentration on only your breathing,” Rob reiterated. “Silence all other thoughts. I’ll time you. One minute. Go.”

Peter reluctantly closed his eyes and tried to concentrate on his breaths, instead of how awkward it felt. As he breathed, he felt all his muscles relax. He felt more at peace than he had all day, like he could slip off into sleep if he wasn't careful.

His head seemed to clear, too. When they were sitting and talking, his mind had been foggy. Now, it felt like a wind had swept through, leaving the air clear and calm.

"Alright, time's up," Sensei Rob announced.

Peter opened his eyes and refused to admit how much he had enjoyed it.

"What did you think?" Rob asked.

"Eh. It was alright," he bluffed.

"Just alright?" Charlie eyed him suspiciously.

"It was a lot of hard work," he complained. "All that relaxing."

Both senseis chuckled.

"Some would argue that the reward is worth it," Charlie said.

"But that's all meditation is?" Peter asked. "It's not that new-agey stuff like 'become one with the universe'?"

"It can be," Rob said. "But in essence, it's just calming down the mind and gaining control over your thoughts. So another thing you can do while meditating is to pay attention to the thoughts that occur naturally and use them to understand yourself better. Then, you can concentrate on choosing thoughts that will generate good karma. Try that a few times this weekend."

After that, Peter was relieved to start the physical lesson. They worked on new techniques at the punch bag, but after about ten minutes, Rob suddenly shivered, like someone had poured ice water down his back.

"I just remembered something I need from my car," he said quickly. "Sensei Charlene, can you take over for a while?"

"Sure," she agreed.

Rob ran out the door quickly and Peter and Charlie continued the lesson. After about fifteen minutes, Sensei Rob still hadn't returned. Peter and Charlie glanced at the door sporadically, both obviously worrying.

They stopped still, however, when Rob stepped out of the bathroom.

Chapter 5: Right Speech

"Sorry about that," he apologized breathlessly.

Peter and Charlie exchanged a confused look.

"I thought you went to your car," Charlie mentioned.

"What?" Rob started. Then he adopted a calm and casual air. "Oh. Yeah. You didn't hear me come back in?"

"I guess we were distracted," Peter said slowly.

"I guess so," Charlie agreed with a sense of doubt.

"Let's get back to the lesson," Sensei Rob rubbed his hands together. "I want to see all that Sensei Charlene taught you."

She was about to correct him, but seemed to give up.

When Peter arrived at the school in the morning, Jeremy was tormenting a lanky boy with shaggy dark hair and tan skin.

"Go back home!" Jeremy yelled as he kicked the boy, who was already on his hands and knees. "We don't need terrorists here." Jeremy's friend pulled a paper lunch bag from the kid's backpack. Jeremy opened the bag and gagged. "Gross. What is that?"

He turned the bag upside down, spilling the food all over the pavement. The boy looked like he was biting back tears.

Peter felt anger rising up inside him. He wanted nothing more than to practice all his latest moves on Jeremy. He stopped that wandering thought, however. Instead, as he got closer, Peter called out, "Good morning, Mr. Sullivan. How are you today?"

It worked like a charm. Jeremy and his lackeys scattered like roaches. They didn't even pause to make sure Mr. Sullivan was there.

The kid picked up his books and ruined lunch with a sniff.

"Hey, first day?" Peter handed the boy a notebook. The boy nodded. "Well, I see you already met the welcoming committee." The boy let out a quiet, bitter laugh in response. "I'm Peter."

The boy nodded, "Zahid."

"Cool name. What is that, Egyptian or something?"

"Arabian," he said softly.

Peter figured he was probably expecting some more name-calling. He was glad to disappoint.

"Cool. So where are you from?"

"Syria," he said softly. "Then Jordan. Now here."

"Wow," Peter said slowly. He wasn't sure of what else to say, so he resorted to his usual sarcasm. "Well, that *might* have prepared you for tolerating Jeremy. Maybe." Zahid laughed again. "But he's not that bad when you learn how to deal with him."

"How do you deal with him?" Zahid asked as he slung his backpack over his shoulder.

"Mostly with avoidance. So where are you headed?"

Zahid studied a paper and responded, "Mrs. Sommers' class."

"What a coincidence. Follow me. And my mom always packs way too much in my lunch. If you can handle her cooking, I'll share."

Mrs. Sommers led Zahid to the empty desk behind Peter and told him to introduce himself when the class started. In the meantime, Peter's friends made a circle around his desk.

"So where are you from?" Harrison asked him.

"The Middle East," Zahid answered hesitantly.

"Dude, are you from an area with fighting?" Chris asked eagerly. "Can you tell us what it's like?"

"I'd rather not talk about it," Zahid said softly.

"You're not here on a secret mission or anything, are you?" Ethan asked with an adventurous gleam in his eye.

Zahid looked down and Peter slapped Ethan's shoulder.

When class started, Mrs. Sommers told Zahid to stand up.

"I'm Zahid Nasir," he said softly.

Jeremy pretended to cough and said, "Terrorist!"

A few sniggers matched his joke. Mr. Sommers glared a threat at Jeremy. "Go on, Mr. Nasir," she encouraged Zahid kindly.

Zahid stared at his desk. "I look forward to learning alongside all of you," he said before sitting down quickly.

Peter had never been more ashamed of his class in their "welcome" of this poor kid. He silently hoped he would be there to personally witness karma come back to bite Jeremy.

"Can anyone volunteer to show Mr. Nasir around today?" Mrs. Sommers asked.

Peter saw his classmates look down at their desks and out the window. Gina Salvatore started to raise her hand when Stacey batted it down. They had a silent battle of facial expressions.

"I will," Peter raised his hand.

"We're surrounded by negative speech," Sensei started the next private lesson. "Whether it's bullies at school, angry parents and teachers, or even advertisers telling you that your life isn't good enough without their product. Too much negative speech can affect us. And we gain karma, good or bad, through our own speech. Words of dishonesty, insults, gossip, and sarcasm…"

"Whoa, hold up," Peter complained. "I don't have to give up sarcasm, do I? Because I'm really good at it."

"Some sarcasm is okay," Charlie clarified. "But if it includes an insult, it's negative. And if you think of it, your speech will flow naturally from whatever you're thinking. So if you're making sure you have kind thoughts about everyone, your speech will mirror that."

"Sensei Charlene is completely right," Rob said.

"Charlie," she corrected him.

"If you think about the people you want to be around," Rob added, "you'll notice that their language is kind and respectful. If you think of the people you don't want to be around, chances are their speech is full of insults and anger."

"Okay, but I can still be sarcastic, right?" Peter persisted.

Rob smiled. "Just pay attention and try to choose words that are kind, non-abusive, and honest."

"And, you know, maybe try to call people by the correct name, too," Charlie added.

"Yes," Rob agreed. "Good point, Sensei Charlene. Now, words can be spiritually powerful, too. Most religions have prayers to be recited aloud or even sung. In Buddhism, too, we chant mantras."

"Are they, like, magic spells or something?" Peter asked skeptically.

"No," Rob said emphatically. "The word mantra actually means the 'mind's protection'. They help us focus our thoughts and calm our emotions. Your words have the power to transform your mind and choices. All Buddhist practices are just tools to help us be more focused, compassionate, and self-disciplined. The second we start thinking they're magic is the second they become superstitions."

"It's the same with the prayers of most religions," Charlie added. "It's supposed to transform you into a more loving person. It doesn't mean a thing unless it does that."

"Exactly," Rob agreed. "It's all about making positive choices. Chants and prayers only work if they help us do that."

As they continued the lesson into drills and exercises, Rob had to run out again, leaving Peter in Charlie's hands. After class was finished, Charlie and Peter waited for Mrs. Hunter to arrive.

Peter was sitting on the bench by the door, putting his shoes on, when Sensei Charlie presented him with a question. "Peter," she asked. "Do you ever notice anything weird about Sensei Rob?"

He looked up at her, leaning on the half-wall partition that divided the benches and the dojo area and staring at the office with a worried expression. Peter thought of all the unexplained things he had seen over the years. He had tried to dismiss it, but lately, it seemed the strange stuff kept adding up.

"I think you mean is there anything *not* weird about Sensei Rob," Peter joked.

Charlie smiled dimly. "You know, when he hired me, he said it was because of some on-call job that sometimes makes him have to leave the dojo, but he won't tell me more. Do you know anything?"

Peter shook his head. "I've been here since I was five. He's skipped out on classes every now and then, and he's always had someone helping him, but I never knew why." He paused a moment, then decided to tell her, "This one time, I came in and found the place destroyed. Stuff was knocked off the walls, equipment was thrown all over and he was just chanting some Buddhist mantra in the office."

She leaned forward and met his eyes with an unblinking gaze. "No way," she spoke in a hushed tone. "That's happened so many times since I've been here. The whole place reeks of incense, too." She sighed. "Maybe I should've taken that other job instead."

Peter studied her worried expression and decided to try to make her laugh. "It could be mafia or gang-related," he speculated. "But I'm pretty sure we'd know if that were the case."

Charlie chuckled. "Yeah, I don't think it's that."

"The place could be haunted," Peter conjectured.

“Hm. Maybe,” Charlie considered it. “But can ghosts cause injuries? And do they even exist?”

“Fight club?” Peter continued. “Or underground cage fighting for extra money.”

Charlie laughed. “But that wouldn’t explain why the dojo gets messed up.”

“Maybe,” Peter whispered playfully, “he’s a superhero.”

Charlie let out a snort of laughter. “That is perfect. I can just see him, ‘I’m the champion of justice!’”

“’And the Buddhist way!’” Peter added.

They laughed together at the thought, perhaps a little too hard. Peter figured that they were both more worried about Sensei’s secrets than they cared to admit. They were interrupted by the telephone ringing.

“Hello?” Peter answered. “How can I help you?”

Sensei Rob’s voice responded from the other end, “Hey, Peter. Sorry I had to run out like that.”

“No problem, Sensei,” Peter exchanged a look with Charlie. “Is everything okay? We were both worried.”

“Just an emergency,” he said. “I’ll tell you about it sometime.”

Peter was surprised to find that he was actually annoyed. Sensei Rob had ditched class, confused and worried the both of them, and he didn’t think it was necessary to give them an honest explanation.

“You have the runs?” Peter asked. “That explains everything.”

There was silence on the other end of the phone.

“Charlene’s listening, isn’t she?” Rob said at last.

“You think it’s contagious?” Peter turned to Charlie with a scared expression. “Like we might have it now?”

“It wasn’t the runs,” Rob said quickly. “Tell her it wasn’t the runs. I am in peak physical condition and very healthy.”

“Explosive? Geez that is just too much information, Sensei.”

Charlie snorted as Sensei Rob yelled at Peter from the other end.

“Give me the phone,” Charlie said in a playfully stern voice.

Peter handed her the receiver and stepped out of her way.

“You poor baby,” she told Rob.

Chapter 6: Party at the Library

When Peter entered the classroom in the morning, he stopped behind Zahid's empty desk. It was covered in insults drawn in thick permanent marker. His muscles stiffened when he saw Jeremy and his friends snickering.

In a bold statement, Peter switched his desk with Zahid's, then sat down and opened a comic book of the Nocturnal Ninja. Suddenly, the book was ripped from his hands.

"Nice comic, Hunter," Jeremy said.

Peter controlled his face to a pleasant smile. "It's a good story," he told Jeremy, "about a man who uses his strength to protect people from bullies. I think you'd like it."

Jeremy sneered, making his nose look miniscule. "You think you're a hero? You hang out with a terrorist."

"What exactly do you think a terrorist is?" Peter questioned.

Jeremy slammed his hands on Peter's desk and leaned forward. "Someone who uses violence to control others."

"Okay. I'm just going to let that one hang in the air a bit."

"What are you talking about?" Jeremy scoffed.

"You know what?" Peter lowered his voice. "I actually agree with you. Completely. He's the worst bully I've ever met."

"Wait, you agree?" Jeremy looked taken aback.

Peter nodded seriously. "He's always threatening me. He's beat up people for stupid reasons, too. Like looking at the wrong girl or getting better grades than him."

"Dude, he's done that?" Jeremy looked scandalized.

Peter nodded solemnly. "And then, this morning, he found this totally nice kid who hadn't done anything wrong and destroyed his desk, right before stealing another kid's comic book."

Peter let that sink in as the teacher entered the classroom.

Jeremy showed his teeth when he figured it out, but with the teacher present, he was forced to go back to his desk. He had kept the comic book out of spite.

When Zahid entered, he saw Peter's desk and must have figured out that the insults had been meant for him. His cheeks flushed and he looked down. Peter tried to make casual conversation, pretending like nothing was wrong.

Alicia and Gina came over with tissues and hand sanitizer. "Hey, boys," Alicia smiled.

Gina waved at Zahid, but Zahid didn't look happy about it.

"What's this?" Peter asked.

"The alcohol in the sanitizer breaks down the chemical bonds of the ink and then you can just wipe it away," Gina lectured. "Dry erase markers and nail polish remover work just the same." Alicia stared at her. "What?" Gina rolled her eyes. "I have a nerdy cousin who told me about it once and I just kind of remembered."

They poured their hand sanitizers on the desk and helped to wipe away the marks.

"Wow, that's like magic," Peter said. "Thanks."

Peter noticed Jeremy was watching them with his face twisted in anger. It was no secret that he had his eyes on Alicia.

Who can blame him? Peter thought.

Alicia was easily one of the prettiest girls in class.

"So Zahid," Gina asked. "Where exactly are you from?"

Zahid got up suddenly. "Excuse me. I need to use the restroom."

Gina bit her lower lip as she watched him leave. "I love his accent."

"I don't think he likes to talk about his past," Peter told them. "He said he came from Syria and Jordan, so you know, I get the feeling he's seen some messed up stuff."

"Thanks for letting us know," Alicia said. "We'll try to be more sensitive." She slapped Gina to get her attention.

"What? Ow!" Gina complained.

"Speaking of Zahid," Alicia whispered conspiratorially, "you should know that everyone's talking about you hanging out with him."

"What about it?" Peter asked defensively.

"You know," she lowered her voice, "that he's… a foreigner. I mean, Jeremy's not the only one that feels that way."

"Aren't you Polish or something, Lisowski? And Gina, aren't you Italian? At one time, just about all of us were foreigners."

"You don't have to tell us," Alicia reassured him. "I know all about the horrible things happening in Syria."

Peter realized that she probably did know all about it.

"Anyway, we're not worried," Alicia told him.

"Yeah, we think he's… interesting," Gina said with a smile.

Alicia rolled her eyes. "I just wanted to warn you that being friends with him might cause you problems with other people."

"I'll take my chances," Peter said.

"I think it's just that most people haven't taken the time to get to know him," she explained. "So, I have an idea. I'm throwing a party on Saturday. Maybe you…"

"And Zahid!" Gina interjected.

Alicia rolled her eyes again. "You and Zahid should come. Everyone will see that he's a cool guy, you're a cool guy…"

"Well, he's a cool guy," Gina told Peter. "You're nice and all, but you're kind of boring."

"Thanks, Gina," Peter blinked.

"Anyway," Alicia glared daggers at Gina, "think it over. I was also going to say that someone special might go out of her way to spend time with you if you show up."

"Oh, really now?" Peter raised his eyebrows.

Alicia was known for her way with words. That was part of the reason why so many guys liked her. Peter was almost sure she meant nothing by it, but her words had worked a magic on him.

The girls walked back to their desks as the bell rang. Peter looked at his now-clean desk and back at Alicia. She smiled and waved from her seat. Her smile made him pretty happy. Of course, seeing Jeremy glare as he watched, helped as well.

At lunch, Peter mentioned the idea of the party to Zahid.

"What do Americans usually do at parties?" Zahid asked him.

"There's food, loud music, talking, maybe a few games."

Peter's enthusiasm waned. He usually felt awkward in big groups.

"I've heard stories of alcohol and immoral games," Zahid mentioned cautiously. "Will there be anything like that?"

"Depending on the party," Peter admitted, "sometimes."

"Is this that kind of party?"

"Maybe." Peter found himself liking the idea even less.

Zahid looked nervous as he said, "I'd rather not go."

Peter felt relieved. "Then do you want to do something else this weekend?" he asked. "I could show you around town or something."

Zahid's back straightened quickly and his eyes lit up. "There is this one place I really want to go," he confessed in a hush.

That weekend, Peter took Zahid on an inaugural ride on the city bus. There was a stop near Zahid's house and the information seemed to inspire wonder and excitement in him. That morning, they boarded the bus headed for the nearest library.

When they got there, Zahid disappeared among the shelves while Peter got bored and fell asleep at a table. He awoke with a start when Zahid dropped a pile of books on the table.

Peter lazily wiped the drool from his face and blinked the sleepiness out of his eyes. He watched Zahid eagerly reading a large book from a pile of other large books.

"Who goes to a library for fun?" Peter complained.

Zahid kept his gaze on the book as he said plainly, "I imagine my superior intellect must be intimidating."

It took a while for Zahid's words to register.

"Wait, did you just insult me?" Peter asked.

Zahid looked up suddenly. "I'm so sorry," he explained quickly. "My little brothers and I often tease each other like that, but I don't think I'm superior. Even Einstein said that there are multiple forms of intelligence and if you judge a fish by its ability to climb a tree, you'll think it's an idiot. But I don't think you're an idiot."

"It's okay," Peter chuckled. "You're just usually so quiet."

Zahid shrugged meekly. "We have a saying in Syria: the smarter you are, the less you speak. And you know," he added slowly, "you tend to talk a lot."

Peter looked at him, astounded again. Zahid gave in to laughing at his own joke and Peter couldn't help but laugh with him.

"Hey, I get good enough grades," he argued playfully. "I just don't like reading or sitting still for long. I need to move."

Zahid smiled kindly. "I'm just teasing. Education is a big part of my culture. If you're educated, you can do anything. But I know here in America, there are plenty of jobs that don't require reading. I've even heard that at some fast food restaurants, the employees only have to press buttons with pictures on them. Perhaps you could do that when you graduate."

Peter narrowed his eyes. If he hadn't just woken up, he'd be able to keep up with the game.

"All joking aside, though," Zahid said, "there're a lot of differences in the quality of education here and back home. Or at least, how it used to be." He got a sad, faraway look for a moment, then shook his head. "Here, let me teach you something all Syrian children know. It may shock you. Even my little sister knows it."

"What is it?" Peter asked.

Zahid flipped the book around and pointed at the print.

"You see this?" Zahid asked. "It's the letter A, the first letter in the English alphabet and it sounds like, 'Ah.' Can you repeat that?"

Peter pushed the book back as they both laughed.

"Why don't you check these out?" Peter asked. "Then we can go do something that's actually fun."

Zahid looked down and seemed sad again. "I don't know if I can get a card, not with my… circumstances."

"All you need is an ID card and a… permanent address."

Zahid shrugged dismally and buried his head in the reading.

"Be right back," Peter said.

He went to the circulation desk and filled out the paperwork for his own library card. When he came back to the table, he slid the laminated card over to Zahid.

"What's this?" Zahid asked breathlessly.

"It's in my name, but you can use it. Just return everything on time and pay any fines if you don't."

Zahid picked up the card carefully and studied Peter. "What will you do if you want to check out books here?" he asked.

Peter couldn't imagine even one situation where he would need that. "I'll manage somehow."

Zahid admired the newly issued library card in his hands and even caressed it gently.

"Maybe you should take that card out on a date or have it meet your parents first," Peter teased.

Zahid laughed. "This changes everything," he told Peter. "Thank you."

Chapter 7: Rob's Secret

Peter had almost forgotten about Sensei Rob's strange behavior until he walked into the dojo for his private lesson. But the sight of a large bandage on Rob's forearm reminded him right away.

"How many stitches?" Sensei Charlie asked him.

"Only five or six."

"At least you're free of the sling now. Oops," she said as she looked at the clock. "I need to get going. Hey, Pete. I have a friend's birthday tonight. You boys have fun without me."

"You're leaving me alone with that guy?" Peter joked.

"Hey, now!" Sensei Rob complained. "I'm right here."

"You'll be fine," Charlie smiled. "Unless of course," she stopped and whispered, "if Super Buddhist tries to recruit you into being his sidekick, I think you should refuse. He's enough weirdness for the whole dojo."

Peter laughed heartily.

"What?" Rob asked. "What was that? You're not supposed to have inside jokes about me. That's against your job description."

Sensei Charlie smiled as she raced toward the door and slipped into her sandals. "Bye, Sensei *Bert*," she said as she slid out the door.

"What did she say to you?" Sensei Rob asked eagerly.

"How did you get hurt?" Peter asked. "Does it have something to do with where you disappeared to on Thursday?"

"Dodging the question with another question? Crafty." Then Rob narrowed his eyes. "Alright, let's get on with the lesson. We're going to talk about karma tonight."

"Karma?" Peter asked. "We already covered that."

"But you forgot that karma is inescapable."

"Inescapable?"

"You can't run, you can't hide," Rob warned. "It will find you wherever you go. The Buddha once said, *'Nowhere in the world is there a place where one may escape from the results of evil deeds.'*"

"Okay, but why bring it up now?" Peter asked.

Rob glared and said, "You opened a dangerous door, my young friend."

Peter remembered the phone call after Thursday's class and laughed.

"I'll get you back some day," Rob vowed. "When you least expect it."

"Maybe," Peter smirked. "But it was worth it. Come on, what was the real reason you bailed? Are you sure you didn't have the runs?"

"You really want to know the truth, huh?" he regarded Peter for a moment. "Okay. I think it's time I told you. Get comfortable."

Peter suddenly felt very uncomfortable.

"I'm going to need your complete, undivided attention," Sensei continued as they both sat. "Are you distracted by anything?"

Peter shook his head.

"No thoughts of school or home or anything else?"

Peter shook his head again.

"Good. For the next thirty minutes, I need you to listen to what I'm going to say without interrupting. Judge later, listen now. Got it?"

Peter nodded tentatively.

"Do you believe in spirits?" Sensei asked him.

Peter felt a shiver up his spine. "Like ghosts and stuff?" he asked.

"Almost every world religion has some belief of spirits either good or bad, who interfere with our lives. Even in Buddhism, there's Mara and his minions, called the asuras. They tempt humans to make choices that distract them from the way of enlightenment. Do you believe any of this?"

"I'm open to the possibility," Peter answered, "but honestly, I haven't given it much thought. Why?"

Sensei Rob took a breath. "When I was younger, I took a year to study in India. While I was there, I met this guy. A Tibetan shaman or guru, like a spiritual expert. I witnessed him perform a ritual and save someone's life. Afterwards, he told me that the spirits don't just tempt people. Sometimes they take over their bodies."

A fresh wave of goosebumps prickled Peter's skin and he sincerely wished Sensei Charlie were there.

"Are you talking like demonic possession?" Peter gulped.

I don't believe in all this paranormal crud, Peter reminded himself. *Why am I getting freaked out here?*

Rob nodded. "The guru, –Yeshe was his name– said he could cast the asuras, the dark spirits, out of people and exorcise them."

"And you," Peter paused, "believed him?"

"I wouldn't have, if I hadn't seen it for myself. When a dark spirit takes over a person, you can tell. I mean, weird stuff happens, but it's more than just that. You know it's wrong. It reverberates within you, freezes you to the core. You can't really say what it is, you just feel the darkness. I saw Yeshe expel the spirit from the person and then he went back to normal like it had never happened."

"So what are you…?"

Sensei Rob held up a hand to stop him. "Asuras are spirits who bear ill will towards humans. They want to cause us pain. Yeshe said he had made a pact with a good spirit, called a deva, a spirit of positivity and kindness. This deva would act in him and through him and help him expel the bad spirits. It was really a lot to take in, as I'm sure it is for you right now. But then, the strangest thing happened."

"Stranger than everything else?" Peter asked dryly.

"Yeshe told me that I had been chosen to be his successor."

Peter felt another chill up his spine.

"He said there was a deva waiting to make contact with me. If I accepted the mission, I'd be able to save people from the asuras, too. So I let him train me to be an exorcist. And that was about fifteen years ago."

"So are you saying…?" Peter started.

"Shh," Sensei Rob said sharply. "Then when I returned to the states and settled in this town, I became the exorcist here. The devas position at least one of us in designated areas. So when someone's possessed by an evil spirit and they're ready to be free, I rush out to help them. Sometimes it's an easy fight and sometimes I get injured." He pointed to the bandage on his forearm. "It's not an easy job, but I know I'm helping people. That makes it rewarding. So there you have it. That's why I had to leave suddenly last time."

Rob paused. Peter waited for him to say something.

"Oh. Am I allowed to talk now?" Peter asked.

"Yes, you're allowed, punk."

"Okay," Peter bluffed a calm and disbelieving attitude. "Assuming this is the truth, why are you telling me?"

"Because you're next."

Another shudder seized Peter's senses.

"Uhhh… What now?"

"My deva told me that you've been chosen to be my apprentice exorcist," Rob said, as if that were something completely normal that completely normal people say.

Peter sat still for a while.

Was this why he wanted to teach me private lessons?

The thought made him feel manipulated. And creeped out. Thoroughly creeped out. He figured he should back out of the dojo now, run as fast as he could, and never come back.

"Do I have a choice?" Peter asked slowly.

"Of course," Sensei Rob said. "If you accept, it'll mean a lot of hard work and you'll see into the dark world of the asuras, which will change you forever. If you don't accept, there will be a vacuum and I don't know if it'll be filled right away. People may go without the help they need."

"Not to mention things will be awkward between us," Peter speculated.

"Nope," Sensei shook his head. "It's a decision only you can make and I won't force or even coerce you into anything. In fact, to prove my point, I won't bring it up again. If you have any questions about it, just ask me and I'll tell you. But otherwise we'll continue with your lessons normally."

"Really?" Peter eyed him suspiciously. "Just like that? We'll just pretend you never said any of this?"

"I know *I* can handle it," Sensei shrugged. "Since I'm so mature and in control of my emotional disposition. But it might be harder for you."

Peter glared at him. "Alright, let's get to the lesson."

Sensei Rob immediately switched back into instructor mode. He taught Peter a few new techniques and nit-picked details, making Peter practice repeatedly until he showed precise improvement.

The trouble was that Peter realized how great of a teacher Rob was. Under his instruction, Peter knew he could become a great master of martial arts. It was going to be regretful that he had to stop these lessons for good and run away to Canada.

No, Canada's not far enough. Mexico. Or maybe Australia.

When the lesson was over, Sensei Rob shook Peter's hand.

"I hope I haven't alienated you," Sensei told him. "You're a great student and if you don't want to accept the calling, I hope I can continue to teach you. At any rate, will you promise to think it over and tell me your decision whenever you come to it?"

Peter nodded and quietly went to the parking lot.

"Hey, sweetie," his mom greeted cheerily. "How was class?"

"Different," Peter stared into the darkness outside the car.

It was a few moments before he realized that his mom was waiting for him to buckle his seatbelt.

"Everything okay?" she asked.

"What do you think of Sensei Rob?"

"Did something happen?" she asked gravely.

He was too jittery to tell his mom the truth. And he knew if he spoke it aloud, he wouldn't be able to deny that it had happened.

“Forget I said anything,” he decided.

“Oh, no.” She shook her head. “You can’t say something like that and just expect me to drop it. Spill. What happened?”

Peter thought a moment about how to describe it without freaking his mom out as much as Sensei had freaked him out.

“It’s just that he offered me a sort of job,” he said at last.

“A job?” she questioned. “You’re only thirteen.”

“He called it an apprenticeship.”

“Wow. He must really have a lot of faith in you.”

He forced a smile. “I guess so.”

“So what’s the problem?”

“It would be a lot of work and just… different. But if I turn it down, things will be awkward with Sensei.”

“Oh, Peter,” his mom laughed as she shifted into drive. “Is that all? You can always depend on Sensei to be patient and levelheaded. Geez, you had me thinking something dramatic or scary had happened,” she laughed. “But this is nothing to worry about.”

Chapter 8: Troubling Thoughts

Peter didn't sleep much that night.

He realized that Rob's story would explain everything weird that had happened over the years, but Peter refused to believe it.

Now he struggled with the decision of whether or not to switch dojos. Sensei was a great teacher and Peter thought of him as an uncle. But he couldn't continue classes with someone who was crazy and wanted to convert him to the same brand of craziness.

And as his mind flipped in circles, his thoughts would always return to the same nagging question:

What if he was telling the truth?

The next day at school, as Peter picked at his lunch, he asked Zahid, "Do you believe in spirits?"

To his surprise, Zahid said, "Yes. In Syria, we believe in jinn, the unseen creatures and the shayateen, who whisper in our minds to tempt us to sin. And angels, too."

"Do you believe spirits can possess people?"

"I do."

"Have you ever seen it?"

Zahid got a faraway look in his eyes. "I've seen a lot of evil."

"Hey, Zahid," Gina greeted as she sat down. "And Peter," she added with much less enthusiasm.

Alicia sat down next to Peter. He felt the glare of a number of guys in the cafeteria. "Missed you on Saturday," she said with a playful pout.

"We aren't really into parties," he explained regretfully.

"We went to the library instead," Zahid added.

Alicia looked angry. "You skipped my party for the library?"

"Good-looking and smart," Gina said playfully. "Not you, Peter. You're neither."

"Thanks, Gina," he responded dryly.

"So what are you guys talking about?" Gina asked.

"I was asking Zahid if he believes in spirits," Peter said.

"Whoa," Alicia reacted.

"I totally believe in them!" Gina said, leaning forward and whispering. "My Nonna, when she was a little girl, apparently someone was jealous of her hair. We Salvatore women have great hair." She fluffed her massively curly hair and smiled at Zahid. "Anyway, so this girl was jealous of her and totally put the evil eye on her."

"What's the evil eye?" Alicia asked.

"It's this curse. When someone's jealous of you, like super jealous, they can put a curse on you, even without knowing it."

"And you believe that?" Alicia asked condescendingly.

"Totally. So listen. My Nonna, all of a sudden, started sleeping all day. She could barely keep herself awake."

Alicia sighed. "Like she had mono or something?"

"No," Gina shook her head. "They took her to the doctor and he couldn't find anything wrong with her. Then, her mom took her to this local holy woman who did this ceremony. See, you drop olive oil in a bowl of water and if the oil forms one big clump in the middle, that's proof that you have the evil eye."

Alicia laughed. "That's just a bunch of…"

"No, listen. There's more!" Gina interrupted. "The oil formed a clump, then the woman said some prayers and it spread out all on its own. That's how you break the curse. After that, my Nonna was cured."

"Gina, you're crazy. There is no such thing as spirits."

"Shh!" Gina crossed herself. "They'll hear you!"

"Look, it's all just in people's minds," Alicia argued. "It's a symbol of the demons and angels inside us all."

"I think it makes sense that there would be something we can't see," Zahid argued calmly. "There's only a small section of light visible to us. There are radio and microwaves, gamma rays and UV rays. But even though we can't see them, we still know they exist because of the effects they have."

"That is so deep," Gina said dreamily.

"What do you think, Peter?" Alicia asked.

"That's what I'm trying to figure out."

At dinner that night, Peter asked his parents about their beliefs.

"Hm," his father said as he rubbed his chin. "I've never had a personal experience of spirits, so I can't say."

"I think there's something to it all," his mom said. "Maybe it's our way of explaining something we haven't figured out yet. But when you were a baby, every now and then I would see something like a human shape, but glowing blue, standing over your crib."

"Whoa, really?" Peter felt his hairs rise.

"I remember you talking about that," his dad noted.

"I thought it might be your angel or something, but it usually happened when I'd check on you in the middle of the night, so you know, I was half-asleep and exhausted. Anyway, it's all fun to talk about, but I really don't think there are any spirits. If there were, I think we'd all have more stories than a blue glow watching a baby."

Peter intended it to be his last karate class. His mind was made up and his resolve was firm.

As the previous class filtered out, Sensei was still speaking with an angry parent.

"I understand your frustration," Rob told him patiently. "Some studios pass out belts based on time, classes, or even money paid, but we have a different policy here. I don't pass students unless they show mastery over their material. And Max didn't."

"And who's fault is that?" the dad demanded.

Sensei retained his composure. "I'm not sure, but I know that other students did show mastery."

"Are you saying that my son is slow?"

"Not at all. He shows great promise, but if I give him the next belt before he's ready, I'd be doing him a disservice in life. What I can do is give you a list of the moves so he can practice at home."

Peter was amazed at how calm Sensei Rob was. It would be hard to find another teacher as great as he was.

Only without the psycho qualities, he thought.

"You saying it's my fault?" the father exploded. He jabbed his finger into Rob's shoulder. "It's *your* job to make sure he passes to the next level! Not mine!"

Then the father's body shook in strange slow convulsions.

Peter ran towards them. "Sir, are you okay?"

Sensei Rob put his hand out between the man and Peter. "Peter," he barked, "get behind me. Now!"

Before Peter could ask why, Max's dad held out a hand and Peter was thrown by an invisible force. He slammed against the wall and fell to his hands and knees, gasping for the air that had been knocked out.

"No need for that," Rob told the man. "I can help you."

"You can help by dying!" the father blustered.

There was something wrong with the man's voice. It was deeper and seemed to echo within his body.

"I'll not be sorry to disappoint," Sensei Rob cracked his knuckles. "Wait," he thought a moment. "Did I say that right?"

Max's dad lifted his arms and all the equipment and decorations started to shake. Sensei waved his hands back and forth, like a fast-paced tai chi move, and, to Peter's disappointment, nothing happened.

Then, as the objects started flying, one by one, straight at Rob and Peter, they fell to the ground as if they had hit an invisible wall.

Rob started chanting something in another language and the father let out a piercing screech. He swiped a claw through the air, directed at Peter but Sensei jumped in front of it.

Peter didn't see anything, but something pushed Sensei backwards. Soon, he was bleeding in stripes across his forearms.

Sensei swiped his hands through the air as if he were spinning a large merry-go-round. The man was pulled off the ground by a few inches. The unseen energy spun him in a circle, rapidly growing in speed as Sensei moved his hands in front of him.

Then Sensei paused his hands and the man stopped, too. Sensei placed a hand on top of his head. The man gnarled and sneered, but his arms were pinned to his sides by an invisible something.

Sensei Rob folded his other hand into an odd formation with just the pinky and index fingers extended. He took a deep breath, closed his eyes, and said, "May you be washed clean."

The man howled as if a fatal blow had been struck. Peter was afraid the sound would shatter the mirrors and the windows. Then the man's body went limp as it slowly lowered to the ground.

Everything grew calm and still. Peter knew that the spirit, or asura, had left the dojo. He felt as if all was right with the world and that evil had never visited the dojo that day.

Sensei Rob breathed in deeply and said one final sentence in the strange language. Then he turned to Peter and offered a hand.

"You okay?" he asked, as calmly as if Peter had only fallen in the middle of performing a technique.

Peter stood on his own and studied the blood on Sensei's arms where he had absorbed the attack that had been meant for him. He looked at the mess and the man lying in the middle of the dojo's mats. They were the unmistakable proof that Peter had not been hallucinating.

Sensei chuckled, probably enjoying Peter's speechlessness. Then he walked to the man and touched his shoulder. "Sir? Are you alright?"

Max's dad blinked his eyes open and looked around. "Where am I?"

"You're at the karate school," Sensei Rob told him. "You wanted to talk to me, and then you fainted."

Peter marveled that Rob had spoken the truth, but had left out quite a few details about what had happened in between.

"Do you need me to call someone?" Sensei asked the man.

"I'm fine, I think," he said, pulling himself up with less difficulty than Peter expected. "I must have low blood pressure."

Sensei held his arms out in case the man needed assistance. "Are you sure you can get home safely?"

"Yeah. Yeah," the man looked around the messy studio with utter confusion. "By the way, Max loves it here," he told Rob. "Thanks for teaching him."

Then, as simply as anything else, the man smiled broadly and walked out the door.

Sensei Rob turned back to Peter with the slightest hint of a smirk. "I think that guy could've used some meditation to control his angry thoughts, am I right?"

Peter just gawked. It was real. Everything Sensei Rob had said was real. Peter knew that fighting these creatures came with great sacrifices, but he felt a tug at his heart, or his gut. After feeling the evil in the room and seeing his sensei vanquish it completely, he knew the answer. It resonated within him and it just felt so right.

"I'm in."

Chapter 9: Devils and Devas

"Great!" Sensei rubbed his hands together. "We'll get started right away." With that, he turned and walked toward the office.

Peter paused a moment, then followed him. "Hold up," he complained. "Aren't you going to explain what just happened?"

"Already did." Rob rifled through his desk, pulling out a first aid kit. "Bad spirits, good spirits, people get possessed, I help."

"You didn't say you had superpowers!" Peter exclaimed.

Sensei studied him. "That's not why you agreed to this, is it?"

"No," Peter shook his head emphatically. "Those things are evil. They need to be stopped. But am I going to get powers, too? Just tell me it won't be flower-sparkle-power."

Sensei took the medical supplies to the main dojo area again, with Peter at his tails. "When you meet your deva, –which is like a spiritual guide– its power will flow through you in a unique way. There's no telling what shape those powers will take."

He put the first aid kit on the partition and started cleaning and bandaging his wounds.

"Hold up. Again," Peter said. "Deva? Like devil?"

Sensei chuckled. "Nope. Different word, different creature. Some call them emanations of the Buddha. Other cultures might call them gods or angels. All I know is they're spirits of positivity and loving-kindness. And yours will help you fight the asuras."

"Is it like possession, just with a good spirit?"

"Different, again. Your deva works *with* you and *through* you. It doesn't possess you. You'll always be in control of your actions."

"So if there are spirits, are there gods, too?" Peter asked.

Rob shrugged. "I don't know for sure. I've had experiences where I felt a connection to the source of all consciousness, which is what most people seem to mean when they say 'God', but I don't know for sure. The Buddha, however, always stressed inner discipline over deities. In fact, he said, *'Better than worshipping gods is obedience to the laws of the righteous.'* As a result, Buddhists are flexible in their supernatural beliefs. But I do know that Mara, the devas, and the asuras exist."

"Where do these spirits come from?"

"The devas come from the celestial realm. And the asuras come from their own asura realm. Then the negative spirits under them dwell in the realm of Naraka, basically super-hot and super-cold caverns of torment."

"Is Naraka like hell then?" Peter asked.

"Sort of, except something that makes Buddhism unique in its world view is that hell, heaven, earth, none of these places are permanent. You always have the ability to change your choices, change your karma, and change your reincarnation."

Peter felt like his head was spinning. "Okay. Naraka is Hell. Asuras are like demons. Devas are like angels," he summarized.

"Eh, more or less, yes."

"But if they're spirits, how did that one throw things?"

"Spirits are entities of pure energy," Rob explained. "They can mess with electronics, throw stuff, start fires, make people sick, and anything else pure and powerful energy can do."

"Geez, I still can't believe this is all real," Peter breathed as he collapsed onto a bench.

"Almost every major world religion believes in spirits," Rob said. "It's not so odd when you think of that."

Peter mulled it over pensively. This was a lot to take in: new names, new terms, and an entirely different world view.

"So how do I start?" he asked. "How do I meet my deva?"

"Good question," Rob wagged his finger. He closed the first aid kit and leaned forward on the partition. "See, devas want to help us, but they are beings of awesome goodness and extreme loving-kindness. You have to get close to their level in order to be compatible with them. You have to do a lot of meditation, sacrifice, and self-discipline before you're ready to even meet them."

"The eight-fold path?" Peter realized.

"Yes. It's very important. See, the asuras will do anything to stop us from reaching enlightenment. And they are tricky and clever. If you don't perfect yourself through the eight-fold path, but then open yourself to invite a spirit in, an asura could come to you, disguised."

"You mean they'll pretend to be a deva and then try to possess me?"

"Yes. The closer you are to enlightenment, the more compatible you are with celestials; and the further you are from enlightenment, the more compatible you are with asuras."

"Okay. Then I really need to work on the eightfold path," Peter decided. "So what's the next step?"

"Go home," Rob smiled. "Your mom's here."

"What? No!" Peter looked out at the parking lot to confirm it, and then back at Sensei Rob. "At least give me homework."

"Peter Hunter is begging me for homework?" Rob laughed. "Alright. Your homework is to start meditating and exercising every day. And build up good karma. The Buddha said, *'Just as a storm cannot prevail against a rocky mountain, so Mara can never overpower the man who lives meditating on the impurities, who is controlled in his senses, moderate in eating, and filled with faith and earnest effort.'*"

"Huh?" Peter asked.

"Good choices, thoughts, and actions will be an armor for you. They'll also make you more compatible with your deva. But I have to warn you: it'll be a lot of hard work. Sure you can handle it?"

"Alright, where's the blender?" Mrs. Hunter hollered from the kitchen the next evening.

Peter came out of the laundry room with a basket of freshly dried towels. "Uhhh... under the sink," he responded tentatively.

"Why would you put it there?" she demanded.

"It seemed like a good place..."

"Under the sink is for chemicals," she lectured. "Under the counter is for appliances. And what's this?" she noticed the basket of folded towels and rushed over to him. "You folded them like... Ugh. Peter, this is not the way to fold towels."

She was over-pronouncing her consonants like she was trying to keep from yelling.

"There's a way to fold towels?" he asked.

"Yes. Here," she pulled a towel from the basket. "Look, you can see the edges. It looks awful."

Peter felt the burn of shame.

She should be thanking me for helping instead of attacking me for not doing it her way, he thought.

But he was trying to accumulate good karma. It wouldn't help if he got into a fight with his mom or even held resentment against her.

"I just wanted to help," he shrugged.

She studied him. "I changed my mind," she said. "I do believe in spirits after all. Since there must be a spirit possessing my son!"

Peter walked out of the school counselor's office studying a stack of brochures for service opportunities. He wasn't looking where he was going and bumped into someone.

"Sorry," he said.

He looked up and almost gasped when he saw it was Alicia, carrying a large empty cardboard box.

"What's got you distracted?" she asked, seeing the brochures.

"Volunteer stuff," he told her. "I don't know what to do first."

She smiled. "I didn't know you were such a thoughtful guy."

She leaned her head in as he showed her the brochures. He could smell a hint of vanilla, like someone was baking cookies.

"I just wanted to increase my own good karma," he told her. "In fact, I'll carry the box for you."

"Thanks. I think it's cool, what you're doing," she said as they walked to the classroom. "So many kids our age are blind to people in need."

"You're always talking about problems all over the world," Peter noted. "Do you do volunteer work?"

"My mom and dad are part of a few activist groups. We get emails all the time. Like, did you know there are children starving all over the world while the U.S. wastes about half our food?"

"Really? That much?"

They stopped at the front of the classroom and she took the box from him, placing it on the floor in front of the blackboard.

"Anyway," she said with a coy smile, "I think it's totally hot when someone cares about what's happening around them."

Peter froze. *Did she just say I was hot?*

Suddenly, he decided that he needed to participate in every service project on the brochures. And he should feed all those starving children while he was at it, too.

Then Mrs. Sommers called Alicia over to her desk and invited her to speak to the class as the bell rang.

"Hi, everyone," Alicia said. "So you know there was that awful flood just a few towns away. People lost everything. It's super sad. And there's this organization asking for clothing donations. If you have anything you can spare, please fill this box and my family and I will get it to the people who need it."

After class, Jeremy pestered Alicia at her desk. "You can have all my clothes," he told her. Then he picked at his shirt. "Should I put these in the box right now?"

She rolled her eyes at him. “Shut up, Jeremy,” she complained.

Peter sprang to her desk. “Hey, Alicia,” he said, squeezing in front of Jeremy. “When is the deadline for the clothing thing?”

“We want to drop it off by the end of the week,” she told him.

“I’ll clean out my closet tonight then.”

She smiled. “That’s awesome, Peter. Thank you so much.”

“Is there anything else I can do?” he asked.

“Yeah, check out this website,” she handed him a flyer.

“Someone’s trying to kiss up,” Jeremy mocked Peter.

“I just want to help these people,” Peter said. “If I wanted to impress her, I should just do what you’re doing, right? Since she obviously likes how you insult and annoy her all the time.”

Alicia giggled. Jeremy tried to punch him, but he dodged effortlessly and walked away.

“Hey, Zahid,” Peter called his attention when he approached his desk. “Want to come over after school today?”

Zahid looked up from his homework. “What’s the occasion?”

“I’m going to collect stuff for that clothing drive, but I thought I’d let you see if there’s anything you or your family need first.”

“I thought you’d want to give it all to the charity so you can impress a certain girl,” Zahid said knowingly.

Peter smiled unconsciously then shook his head. “I just want to accumulate good karma.”

“That seems paradoxical,” Zahid said, tilting his head. “Doing charitable things for selfish reasons. Does that cancel out the karma?”

“Is that a thing?” Peter worried. “I never thought about that.”

“How about this?” Zahid offered. “I’ll come over today, but then you have to come to my house for dinner over the weekend.”

“Charlene’s teaching a class at her gym today,” Rob told Peter as they sat for their next lesson. “So I thought I could go into more detail about Right Speech and chanting.”

Then Sensei Rob suddenly shivered like someone had thrown a bucket of water on his head.

“Whoa. You okay there?” Peter asked.

Sensei smiled. “Change of plans. How about a field trip?”

Chapter 10: House Call

Rob stood up and started walking toward his office.

"Hold up," Peter sprang to his feet and followed. "You're going out to fight an asura? Now?"

"Yep." Rob started filling a bag with eastern items from the shelf.

"And I can go with you?" Peter hastily put on his flip-flops.

"Of course," Rob said. "You're my apprentice. How else are you going to learn? Now prepare yourself. This can be a bit disorienting."

Rob put his hand on Peter's shoulder and the world blurred around them. Peter felt like he was being pushed along by a rip tide. After a few minutes, they came to a stop on the lawn in the middle of an older neighborhood.

"Whoa," Peter reeled. "That was amazing!" Then Peter looked at all the houses lining the street. "Wait, what if someone saw us?" he worried. "What do we say?"

Rob chuckled. "I've been doing this for fifteen years, kid, and no one has ever seen me." He thought a moment. "Or at least, they've never approached me about it."

Sensei started for the house in front of them with a "for sale" sign that included an additional: "price reduced!"

"The asuras and devas have this confounding ability to manipulate coincidences," Rob explained. "They can put thoughts into people's heads, and orchestrate a hundred people at once. Like right now, my deva could've coordinated all the people on this block to look away from their windows, get distracted by the TV or a phone call. Or maybe someone just realized they have to go to the bathroom."

"It works like that every time?" Peter questioned.

"The few who have seen me do something only see what they want to see or explain it away."

Peter thought of the times he had seen strange things around Sensei and dismissed it as exhaustion or an optical illusion.

Sensei jiggled the doorknob and found the house locked.

"So what are we dealing with here?" Peter asked eagerly. "Is it a haunted house? Are ghosts really just asuras? And what's with the book? Are you going to try to bore them to death with some reading?"

Rob laughed. "First of all, we don't kill anything. Even spirits."

CLICK!

Peter jumped as the door burst open on its own.

“Thanks,” Rob said to the air next to him. “Actually, I don’t even know if we *can* kill the spirits,” he said pensively. “Second,” he continued as they entered the house, “asuras often pretend to be deceased humans. It’s one of their favorite tricks. They love to show up at séances, sharing details that only the deceased person would know.”

The house was barren and the floorboards creaked beneath their feet. Peter felt a sense of dread like something was watching him.

“Now, that’s not saying that every medium only channels asuras,” Rob continued. “Or that people don’t have miraculous encounters of loved ones who have passed. But the asuras often mimic those experiences. They love to mimic everything good.”

“Wait, how do the asuras know the details?” Peter asked. “The ones that only the deceased person would know?”

Sensei Rob looked in each room as they walked. “Hm? Oh. Because they watch us constantly. Didn’t I tell you that?”

Peter shivered. “Like even now?”

“Yep,” Rob continued his slow procession through the house. “Once you connect to your deva, it opens up what Buddhists call the divine or third eye and you’ll be able to see them. They’re everywhere.”

Peter wasn’t sure he wanted his third eye opened.

“So what now?” he asked Rob. “Do we wait for some possessed dude to show up?”

“The asuras are already here,” Sensei said casually. “Can’t you tell?”

Peter was getting more than a little tired of Sensei creeping him out. He had thought the feeling of dread was just superstition and a spooky house at twilight, But now he couldn’t help but imagine the hate-filled creatures watching them from every angle.

“They’re here, without human bodies?” Peter gulped.

A door somewhere in the house slammed. Peter jumped.

Sensei Rob laughed again, “Don’t let them spook you. This is actually a simple case. I’m going to teach you to exorcise them with mantras.” He held up the book with excitement.

They came to a central living room and Sensei unslung his bag.

“Here, I have a gift for you.” He handed Peter a string of smooth wooden beads. “This is a mala, or prayer beads. It’s yours to keep.”

“Thanks,” Peter said as he took it.

“You can wrap it around your wrist, too, so you always have it with you.” Sensei Rob sat in the middle of the room and opened the book on the floor. He indicated that Peter should sit in front of him. “We’ll repeat the mantra one hundred and eight times, so use the mala to count. Some words might be hard to pronounce, but just worry about pouring all your positive thoughts into the recitation."

"Okay," Peter nodded apprehensively.

"Oh, and one more thing," Sensei Rob warned, making eye contact. "Beware of whispers and strange thoughts."

Another shiver ran up Peter's back. He wondered if, since they had entered the house, Sensei had said anything that was *not* creepy.

"The spirits can speak into our thoughts," Sensei said as he placed a wooden bowl next to the book and filled it with water from a bottle. "It'll seem like random thoughts that pop into your mind, it might even sound like your own inner voice, but they'll be distracting or destructive thoughts. So stay guarded and focused." Then he smiled at Peter. "No worries."

Riiight, Peter thought. *Nothing to worry about at all.*

Rob put the bottle in the bag and Peter noticed the small dagger with tassels and strange carvings from the shelf in the dojo, resting in the bag.

"The mantra is in Palī," Rob continued, "the sacred language of Buddhism. It means, 'may all beings be free from enmity and danger.'"

Sensei Rob took a deep inhale and said each recitation on a single, monotonous exhale.

"SABBE SATTA AVERA HONTU..."

Peter stumbled over the phrase at first, but as they repeated the mantra, the words became more natural.

It didn't take long for the spirits to react. First, the lights flickered erratically. There were scratching noises on the walls. More thuds resounded and the house seemed to vibrate beneath them.

Sensei continued his chanting like he didn't even notice the paranormal activity. Peter's eyes fluttered around the room, watching the shadows for a glimpse of their threat, though he still wasn't sure if he wanted to see them.

Then, without warning, a hidden force pushed into Sensei Rob, knocking him to the side. He tried to continue chanting, but more unseen hands attacked him. Rob jumped up and waved his hands through the air. A blast of power, not wind, but pure force, pushed against Peter like a wave breaking over him.

"Chant for me, will you?" Sensei said.

Peter turned the book around and looked at the foreign language. "But I don't know how to read this!" he complained.

"It'll be fine," Sensei said quickly. "What's important is the intention. Focus all your good will into the words."

Sensei Rob swiped his hands through the air as if he were performing some new age, liturgical dance. If Peter had not been so freaked out by the otherworldly screams that echoed through the air, he might have laughed at the sight.

He reluctantly tore his eyes away from Sensei and focused on the book.

"SABBE SATTA AVERA HONTU," he chanted, trying to control the shakes in his voice.

"What did I get myself into?" Peter thought. *"I should just kill myself."*

The thought startled Peter and he halted his chants. He never thought about killing himself or anyone else. He tried to focus himself on the chanting again.

"I really should kill myself," he thought. Then his inner voice started singing, *"Die! Die! I should die!"*

Peter remembered that Sensei had warned him about this. The thoughts were not from his own. The realization hit Peter with a fresh batch of shivers down his spine. He wondered how often the asuras had whispered thoughts into his mind over the years without him even knowing it.

Peter poured all his focus into the chanting and tried to ignore the voice. Sensei Rob fought furiously in his peripheral, but Peter held his eyes in place, looking at the book.

Then, out of nowhere, Peter thought of the dagger in the bag. It was like a vision, superimposed over his normal vision. He couldn't stop thinking of the dagger.

"I wonder how that dagger would feel," the voice taunted him, *"if I struck it straight into my heart. This could all be over. I could stab myself just to see what it feels like."*

Peter gritted his teeth while he chanted. He would never follow this voice, but it was so grating against his concentration.

If it continued, or if he had lived in this house with this asura whispering in his ear every day without knowing what it was, he could imagine how it would have affected him. He could see the constant banter weighing on him and wearing down his will to resist.

Did this asura drive its victims mad? Peter wondered. *Did it drive them to violence? To suicide?*

"The dagger is right there," the voice sang to him.

Peter saw a mental image of himself thrusting it into his heart. The vision-Peter pulled the dagger out and licked it gleefully.

No, Peter resolved. *I refuse to be influenced by this.*

Then Peter saw a new vision in his mind's eye. This time, he reached for the bowl of water in front of him and threw it over his shoulder.

Somehow, this vision felt different. Peter couldn't describe it, but it felt right. He knew he could try to figure out if the thought was a trick from the asura, a help from his deva, or a random idea from his own mind. Or he could just follow his gut.

He moved in a flash, grabbing the bowl firmly in both hands and splashing it over his right shoulder.

A howl pierced his ear, but he didn't move until he felt another wave of Sensei's power wash over him. Peter still didn't see anything, but he imagined a tremendous amount of water pouring into the entire house.

"It is washed clean," Sensei pronounced.

Peter felt like he could breathe again. All the oppressive sensations of doubt, dread, and danger had dissipated. The house was a regular empty house now and his thoughts were his own.

He sat still, adjusting to all the strange things he had experienced. He felt exhausted, like he had just had a match with a sumo master.

Sensei took the empty bowl from Peter and chuckled.

"Well, I was going to use this to bless the house, but looks like you beat me to it." Then he closed his eyes and prayed, "By the power of the truth of our words, may this house and all who dwell in it, ever be well." Then Sensei collected everything into his bag as he asked, "How did you know to use the water?"

Peter opened his mouth to talk, but ended up just shrugging.

Sensei laughed boisterously. "I could get used to this version of you. Now, let's get back to the studio before your mom gets there."

The strange traveling seemed to wake Peter up. By the time they came to a stop in the dojo, he had a million questions.

"So this travelling thing you do can make us go through walls? How is that even possible? And why did that water seem to hurt the asura? Was it like holy water? Also, that asura was inside my head. It was thinking for me, just like you said. But I wasn't possessed, right?"

"Nope. That level of activity is called oppression or attachment. Everyone experiences it from time to time."

"It was scary," Peter lowered his voice, "it told me to kill myself."

Rob got a pensive look. "I got the sense that the spirits there were focused on violence, especially self-harm. Maybe that's why the house has been on the market for so long."

"But, not every case of suicide is possession or oppression, right?"

Rob shrugged. "I know surprisingly few details about all this. Maybe sometimes, a difference in the brain can lead to dark thoughts of self-harm and sometimes the thoughts come from an asura. Just like sometimes, you have a temptation that comes from your own heart and mind, and sometimes you have a temptation that comes from outside you. Every case is different, I'm sure."

Peter looked at his shaking hands while he thought it over.

"You did great," Rob called his attention as he placed the book the shelf behind the front desk. He pulled out the bowl and paused. "But seriously, how did you know to use the water?"

Peter shrugged again. "I just saw it," he said, staring into the distance. "I guess it was a vision or something."

Rob nodded pensively and placed it on the shelf.

They both noticed Mrs. Hunter stopping the car right in front of the studio, waiting for Peter.

"Well, that's our cue," Rob said.

Peter picked up his bag and headed for the door.

"Oh. And I should warn you," Rob stopped him. "When someone starts fighting the asuras, they fight back. You've seen how they attack me."

Sensei waved his hand at the dojo and Peter remembered the day he had found the it messed up.

Rob continued, "They're going to watch you constantly to find the thing you fear the most and use it against you. So you'd be prepared."

Peter gulped.

Sensei smiled brightly and slapped Peter on the back. "Sleep well."

Chapter 11: Right Action

When Peter arrived at the dojo for his next lesson, Sensei Charlie and Rob were in the middle of fancy dance moves. Rob pulled Charlie's arms behind her, sat down, and pushed his feet against her backside. She flipped over him and hollered in midair.

"That was awesome!" she laughed. "Okay. Okay. Next one."

Peter waited impatiently for them to notice his presence.

Charlie threw a punch at Rob. He grabbed it and pulled her around him in a circle. Then he held his arm against the small of her back as he swept her feet from under her. She spun over his arm and laughed again when she landed.

After a few more moves, they both started laughing so hard that Sensei Charlie was snorting and doubling over.

"Is that a snort?" Rob hollered. "Are you snorting? That's adorable." He stifled his laughter. "I mean, professional. We are both entirely professional."

Peter cleared his throat.

"Hey! Pete's here," Rob greeted boisterously.

"I should go," Charlie said, catching her breath. "I have to fill in for another teacher at the gym," she told Peter.

"I'll see you at the adult class in the morning, right?" Rob asked.

"Should I bring my dancing shoes?" she joked.

He winked. "Couldn't hurt. Good night, Sensei Charlene."

She rolled her eyes, though her smile still stretched to the edges of her cheeks. "Good night, Sensei *Bobby*."

Rob watched her leave with a goofy smile. His smile fell when he caught Peter's eye. "It was for class," he asserted.

"Sure it was," Peter pretended to agree. "So what's the lesson today?"

They took their seats on the mats.

"Today is about Right Action," Rob said. "Every belief system has a set of right and wrong actions. And most of the major world religions even agree on these rules."

"Like the Ten Commandments?" Peter asked.

"Right," Rob nodded. "The Buddha taught his followers five precepts: Do not kill, steal, or lie, avoid sexual misconduct and intoxicants, like drugs and alcohol. These things lead to negative consequences. Now, some of the other world religions will stress the fear of hell, but the Buddha took it a step further. He said, *'The evil-doer grieves here and hereafter; he grieves in both the worlds.'* In other words, he stressed that you'll feel the effects of karma in this life as well as in the next one."

"So don't drink, don't smoke. Stay in school," Peter recapped.

"But that's the easy part," Rob told him. "Mara and the asuras can use your emotions and senses to confuse you. See, most people would agree that hitting another person is going to have negative consequences, but you'll want to use violence if you're overcome by anger. So part of right action is controlling your emotions so the asuras can't."

"How do you control emotions?" Peter asked.

"Meditation helps, obviously, "Rob said, "but the real secret is to wait. Emotions are fleeting. You can simply acknowledge them and allow them to run their course. Then you can choose to act when the emotion has cooled."

"Acknowledge them?" Peter asked. "What does that mean?"

"For instance, if you're angry, you say to yourself, 'I feel angry, but I will choose what to do with this emotion.'"

"Talk to myself?" Peter challenged. "That seems real normal."

Rob raised an eyebrow. "About as normal as becoming a vessel for a good spirit so you can exorcise bad spirits?"

Peter paused. "Well, when you say it like that…"

Just then, Rob was seized by a shiver that made all his limbs dance.

"Whoa," He shook his head to recover. "Looks like I have a job to do." He stood and retrieved his bag from the office.

"Do they always call you like that?" Peter asked. "It seems painful."

Rob smiled as he put a hand on Peter's shoulder and the world blurred around them. They came to a stop in a graveyard. Immediately, Peter was filled with the same sense of dread that he had felt at the haunted house.

"Oh, this will be interesting," Sensei said gleefully.

Peter looked at him like he was insane.

"We're sending some ghosts home tonight," Sensei explained.

"Ghosts?" Peter shivered. "Are they different from asuras?"

"Ghosts, or bhuta, are humans who went to the bardo, –or the transition place between our world and the next ones– but they weren't able to move on. Maybe they were shocked by all the bad karma they had accumulated or maybe they were too steeped in negative emotions when they left this world. Now they're stuck in that bardo."

"How do we get rid of them?" Peter asked. "A mass exorcism?"

Rob shook his head. "Have I ever told you about Padmasambhava? He was an influential Buddhist in the eighth century. Some people even call him the second Buddha. He went around converting demons and composing the Tibetan Book of the Dead, which guides people through the dying process."

"So he was an expert in creepy?" Peter summarized.

Rob chuckled and knelt on the ground, emptying his bag. "You could say that. But the point is we're going to show these spirits how to move on by using compassion, good will, and chanting."

Peter sat cross-legged on the cold, wet ground.

"Just like last time, you'll do some chanting while I work," Sensei said." I'll help you get started, and then I'll go talk to everyone."

Peter's hair stood on end. "Everyone?" he balked. "Like…"

"Yep, we have company." Rob pointed a thumb behind him to the seemingly empty graveyard.

Peter could only imagine the ghosts that occupied the space.

Sensei opened his book to the right page, placed it on the ground in front of Peter, and showed him which passage to read.

Then Sensei slapped a hand on Peter's shoulder and said, "One more thing. Just like how the asuras can whisper thoughts into your mind, they can also play with your emotions. So make sure you're in control."

Peter gulped.

Sensei didn't wait for Peter to nod or agree. He sauntered over to a nearby gravestone and started talking to the invisible spirits. "It's okay," he announced, holding out his hands as if addressing an audience. "I'll get to everyone, so please be patient."

Peter ignored his goosebumps and started reading from something called the Atanatiya Sutta.

Geez, I can hardly pronounce the title, he thought.

Luckily, there was an English translation.

"Homage to the Buddha, possessed of the eye of wisdom and splendor," Peter recited. *"Homage to the Buddha, compassionate towards all beings. Homage to the Buddha, free from all defilements and possessed of ascetic energy. Homage to the Buddha, the conqueror of the five-fold host of Mara."*

Peter watched as Sensei held his hand up, giving a blessing and chanting something from memory. After a few moments, a gentle breeze swept through the area, as if signifying that the spirit had moved on.

Peter continued reading while Sensei repeated the same pattern at the next tombstone and the one after that.

Then, out of nowhere, Peter saw a memory flash before his eyes of Jeremy tossing small rocks at Stacey Sanders on the black top. She covered her head with her arms and complained each time, but he continued, all the while cackling.

Peter's heart rate increased and his breathing turned shallow. His fists balled as all the anger of that day flooded his mind.

He shook his head to clear it and continued. *"Homage to the Buddha who has shed all defilements, and had lived the holy life. Homage to the Buddha who is fully freed from all defilements."*

But the thoughts of Jeremy didn't leave him. Instead, they increased.

He say multiple times that Jeremy had stolen a comic book from him. He saw Jeremy saying horrible things to Alicia and tugging on her hair. He saw Jeremy beating up Zahid on his first day of school.

"Guys like that are poison," Peter thought. *"They shouldn't exist."*

SCHWOOORSH!

Peter was suddenly distracted as the sound of a massive wave accompanied by a cool sensation washed over him.

"Had an asura on you, kid," Rob told him from over by the tombstones.

Peter's eyes grew large as he looked over his shoulders.

Sensei must have been finished, because he started packing his bag as he explained, "When a dark spirit becomes attached to someone that attachment can continue after death. The spirit will keep them from moving on by trapping them in the moments of their darkest emotions. Sometimes violent hauntings are bhutas trapped by an asura. That's why graveyards can be dangerous places. The asuras here may try to attach themselves to the people that visit."

"What would've happened if you hadn't saved me?" Peter asked.

"It would've followed you home," Rob said as he slung his bag over his shoulder. "Kept you up at night with weird noises, broken things around the house, tried to make you or your parents go crazy."

"It could've done that?" Peter gawked.

"It's not that scary," Sensei told him with a slight laugh. "I mean, becoming an apprentice exorcist draws enough attention already. Remember what I told you? They're watching you all the time now, planning your downfall." Peter stopped breathing. Sensei read his reaction and tried to comfort him. "But again, you don't have to be afraid. You just have to figure out your biggest weakness before they do. No big deal."

Chapter 12: Right Livelihood

The next morning Peter stared out the classroom window, paused in the middle of a comic book while he waited for class to start. He was preoccupied by Rob's warning: *"They're watching you all the time now, planning your downfall."*

Right, Sensei, he thought. *Nothing to worry about.*

He had watched all week for poltergeists, hauntings, and nightmares, but so far, they hadn't attacked him.

He wondered what his biggest weakness was. The faults most people talked about were his sarcastic mouth, his restlessness, and his poor listening skills. But he didn't know how the evil spirits could use those to hurt him.

Suddenly, Jeremy snatched his forgotten comic book as he quickly passed by. Peter started to complain when Alicia sat in the empty desk in front of him. Suddenly, he didn't care about Jeremy or the comic book anymore.

"Hey," he greeted. "What's up?"

"I wanted to thank you for all your donations," she said. "I couldn't believe how much you gave."

He shrugged. "I had a lot more than I needed."

"What's with the bracelet?" she asked, daring to play with his mala. Her fingertips brushed against the skin of his wrist.

"A gift from my karate teacher." He took it off and held it up for her. "It's supposed to be for prayers and stuff."

She took them in her hand and regarded him. "Are you in monk-training?" she asked.

"Something like that. I mean, I'm not going to be a monk. But he's been teaching me about Buddhism."

She handed the mala back. "That's cool," she said. "So is that what you're sitting here thinking about so seriously?"

He nodded as he wrapped the mala back around his wrist. "I was wondering what my biggest weakness is. You have any ideas?"

"Biggest weakness?" she tapped her chin. "You have a lot actually."

"Oh, do I?"

"You're slow, for starters."

"I'm not slow," he contested. "I get B's."

She assured him very seriously, "You're slow. Believe me."

"Okay. So I'm an idiot. Is there anything else?"

She nodded. "You're a head case. Always staring out the windows and thinking about deep things."

"What's wrong with that?"

She wrinkled her nose. "Maybe you spend too much time looking out the window instead of looking at what's in front of you."

"And what's in front of me?" he challenged.

She laughed at him. "Man, you really are an idiot."

"That was number one," he argued. "We're on number three now. You said I had lots."

She looked off to the side, thinking a moment. "I would say your biggest weakness is your hero complex," she told him.

"How is that a weakness?" he questioned.

"You're always protecting people."

"Yeah," he nodded sharply, "like a superhero."

"Too much of anything can be a weakness. Maybe you ought to think of yourself every now and then."

"Geez, I feel great now." Peter laughed. "I'm an idiot, a head case, and apparently I have a hero complex. Thanks, Alicia."

She playfully patted his desk. "Me now. What are my flaws?"

He studied her for a few seconds, unconsciously smiling. "Besides calling me an idiot? No, I don't see any."

"Oh, I like you," she said. Then her face erupted into a blush. "Not like, like-you-like-you," she corrected. "Just, you know, I'll keep you around a little longer. See you later."

She got up quickly, and walked away. Peter started thinking that she was too good at this game.

"Hey, Pete," Ethan greeted as he, Chris, and Harrison approached his desk, "we're going to go see that Arachnid Kid movie this weekend. Want to join us?"

"Sure, but I had plans with Zahid. Can I invite him, too?"

Chris, Harrison, and Ethan exchanged glances.

"We were thinking it'd be just… the guys," Harrison said softly.

"Zahid's a guy," Peter said dryly.

Harrison sat in his desk, turning to face Peter, "Look," he whispered, "he's just weird, you know? And if you hang out with him, you'll be weird by association."

Peter was ready to argue when Zahid came rushing in.

"Peter!" he said with wide eyes. "Did you know that this card works on other libraries in the area, too?"

“Yeah,” Peter said slowly, feeling the judgment of the other guys.

“Do you know what that means?” Zahid asked as if he had discovered the secret to life. “The amount of books I can read! I can even go online and request them to be sent and placed on hold at the library nearest me! And I can keep a book for three weeks! *And* if that’s not enough, I can renew them and hold on to them for three more weeks! Isn’t this amazing?”

Peter noticed that the guys had all gone to their own desks. He started worrying that he was weird by association. Part of him wanted to ditch Zahid over the weekend and go to the movie instead.

But he silenced that wandering thought. Zahid was a good person. And Peter realized that, considering his latest hobby, he himself was no longer fit to judge what was “weird.”

“Yeah, that’s how libraries here usually work,” he told Zahid.

“How could you let me have this?” he exhaled. “It’s a treasure!”

“It’s just a library card,” Peter laughed. “No need to get all romantic with it.”

“Oh, and my parents wanted to make sure you’re still able to come over tomorrow,” Zahid reminded him.

Peter took a brief glance at the other guys, realizing that he was making a forced choice. But he thought the choice was pretty clear.

“Yeah, I’ll be there,” he told Zahid.

“They kicked her out of school for wearing a tank top,” Zoe was telling Sensei Charlie when Peter entered the dojo. “It’s totally unfair.”

They were chatting with another girl, Marisa, by the door while they waited for their rides.

Marisa scoffed. “Come on, she was asking for it. I wouldn’t have worn what she did. I don’t want boys looking at me like that.”

“I don’t know,” Sensei Charlie argued. “As women, we should try to be modest and we should protect ourselves. But the thing is, I don’t think it’s just our problem. There are tribal communities where the women wear next to nothing and no one’s distracted. At the same time, in the eighteen hundreds, seeing a woman’s ankle or shin was enough to get a guy distracted. Men can lust after women no matter what they’re wearing and they can respect women no matter what they aren’t wearing.”

“Ready for a fun lesson tonight?” Rob called Peter’s attention.

"What's the topic?" Peter asked.

Sensei Charlie waved goodbye to the girls and joined them on the mats:

"Right Livelihood," Rob answered. "Last time, we talked about how every religion has a moral code, but no matter how resolved you are to live a certain way, there will be temptations. So, Pete, what do you think is the best way to fight temptation?"

"With karate!" Peter joked enthusiastically.

Charlie snorted.

"No," Rob corrected. "What's the best way to win a fight?"

"Avoid the fight," Peter recited.

"Avoid the fight," Rob repeated. "So Right Livelihood is about setting up your environment to avoid the fight of temptation."

"It makes sense, right?" Charlie said. "If I'm trying to eat healthier, I'm not going to go to a fast food restaurant. If I'm trying to be an honest person, I'm not going to hang out with people who lie."

"Exactly," Rob affirmed. "A Buddhist will make sure to avoid jobs that would require him to go against the eightfold path. So he wouldn't sell weapons, which would be used to harm others. He wouldn't buy things that were made by slaves or indentured servants. He wouldn't work at a restaurant where they sell meat..."

"Hold up," Peter stopped him. "Am I not supposed to eat meat? Because... I mean... bacon."

"You don't have to be a vegetarian," Rob assured him. "Many Buddhists still eat meat. But the point of Right Livelihood is to think about making the right friends, choosing the right hobbies and career, and paying attention to how you spend your time and money.

"Now, speaking of non-violence," Rob switched gears. "The Buddha taught that all violence leads to negative karma, but sometimes, we need to fight to defend ourselves. So with the help of the lovely Sensei Charlene," he smiled, "I'm going to teach you how to redirect an opponent by using dance moves."

Rob and Charlie taught Peter the dance moves he had seen them working on a few classes prior. He learned to redirect and confuse an opponent through a combination of turns and lifts. They finished four or five different moves when Sensei Charlie's cell phone rang.

"I'm so sorry," she told Rob. "My friend's car broke down."
"You should go," Rob told her.
She turned to Peter and asked seriously, "Are you going to be okay all alone with Super Buddhist?"
Peter laughed. "I'll manage."
"Super who-now?" Rob asked.
As Charlie raced out the door, Rob suddenly shivered violently.
"Wow, that was good timing," Peter commented. "It's like Sensei Charlie knew it was going to happen."
"Remember how I said that the devas and asuras can influence little coincidences?" Rob said as he started collecting things in his bag. "It was seemingly chance that she was here the nights I had to leave and not here the other times with the house and the graveyard."
"So you don't schedule the fights with the asuras?"
Rob laughed as he packed the book of chants into the bag and gave it to Peter to carry. "I wish. No, see, we don't get called out until someone needs us and that's not something even the spirits can predict. But the second it happens, we need to hurry. You never know what the asuras are going to do."
Without another word, he placed his hand on Peter's shoulder and they traveled quickly, the world blurring around them. They stopped in the parking lot outside a small and rundown strip mall.
Sensei led the way toward a business with dark windows. He opened the door to a dimly lit lobby with an empty receptionist's desk.
Peter looked around at the candles, vases of flowers, and comfortable seating in the lobby. On the walls were pictures of women in sparse clothing and suggestive poses.
"Oh, no," Rob said. "It's a brothel."

Chapter 13: Rob Takes Peter to a Brothel

"A brothel?" Peter asked, disgusted. "Those things still exist?"

Rob let out a frustrated sigh. "If I had known, I never would've brought you here." He grabbed Peter's shoulder and gave him an intense gaze, "No matter what you see, guard your thoughts. Every woman here deserves our respect and our protection. Got it?"

Peter was appalled. "What kind of kid do you think I am?"

"Everyone can be tempted," Rob said.

"Look," Peter reassured him, "if I see anyone, I'll just ignore them and they'll turn into flowers and sparkles, right?"

Rob shook his head at Peter. Then he rang the desk bell. Peter noticed a photo album on the counter and moved to open it absent-mindedly. Sensei slapped his hand to stop him.

A woman in a button-down blouse, heavy makeup, and cascading hair greeted them with a nervous smile. "May I help you?" she asked.

"I hope so," Rob flashed his smile. "We were told about this place."

Peter laughed internally at Sensei's choice of words.

"Someone referred you?" she asked skeptically.

"Something like that. Can I speak with the manager?"

She looked hesitant, but went into a room behind the desk area. Rob and Peter could hear frantic whispers. Soon, an old and overweight woman with short curly hair appeared with a tumbler of amber liquid in one hand and a cigarette in the other.

She had bulging bags under her eyes, lips so dark they looked purple, and her mouth drooped in a scowl. Peter thought that there was no way to describe how ugly this woman was. It wasn't just that she was old and wrinkly. She could've looked like a movie star and still radiated ugliness.

She cleared her throat with a hacking cough. "How may I help you?" she asked in a scratchy voice.

"Oops," Rob said. "This is awkward. I don't think I'm here for you."

Then the woman opened her mouth and spewed fire. Actual fire. Peter let out an expletive as he jumped back.

Sensei countered with a swipe of his hands through the air and the fire was extinguished. Then the woman leapt onto the desk in a crouching, frog-like position. She jumped onto Sensei Rob and they started fighting.

Peter backed up against the wall watching. He quickly unraveled his mala but realized that he didn't know any chants by heart. He was about to reach into the backpack for the book when he was stopped by a vision.

He saw himself walking behind the desk area, into a messy office space, then into a long hallway with many doors.

While the fire-breathing woman and Sensei were distracted, he hopped over the counter and walked into the back office. He saw a desk piled with papers, old drink glasses, and used take-out boxes. There were towers of trash and a horrendous stench.

Then he heard a door slam and jogged into the same long hallway he had seen in his vision. There were multiple identical doors lining the hallway, but his focus fell on the fourth door. He felt pulled to it as if a strong gust of wind was pushing him from behind

From outside, he heard the receptionist's voice whispering, "Stay quiet and I'll give you that candy you like."

Peter opened the door quickly to a space set up like a hotel room with a bed and a couple nightstands. The receptionist closed a closet door behind her and looked like a deer in headlights.

"You're not supposed to be back here," she said nervously.

Peter put the backpack down as he said, "I'm pretty sure you're not supposed to be locking people in closets, so I guess we're both in trouble."

She giggled. "Oh, you're cute." She unbuttoned the top three buttons of her shirt slowly, revealing too much. "You're a little young, but maybe we could still have fun together."

"I'll never get a chance like this again," Peter thought.

The idea nauseated him, but after two similar experiences, he now recognized the voice in his head.

"Not interested," he declined easily.

Apparently, she wasn't really interested either. She pulled a knife out and charged at him. Peter blocked, twisted the knife from her hand, and swept her feet. Then his eyes were drawn to her opened shirt.

She giggled again. "If you wanted me on my back, all you had to do was ask." She batted her eyelids.

She lifted up as if she were going to kiss him and he backed away instinctively. She grabbed the knife as she sprang to her feet.

Peter scolded himself. The main point of any move against a knife was to always get the knife. But he had been too distracted. Even now, her shirt hung open and drew his sight.

Geez, she should try to be modest, he thought.

Then he remembered what Sensei Charlie had said earlier that day: men could lust after a woman no matter what she wore and they could respect a woman no matter what she didn't wear. He couldn't control what she was wearing, but he could control his own thoughts.

She ran at him again. He sidestepped and grabbed her around the neck. With his free hand, he twisted her wrist, wrestling the knife from her grasp. Then he tightened his arm, pressing on the nerves that ran up the sides of her neck. She struggled a few moments, and then went limp.

He laid her on the ground, feeling guilty about knocking her out. That is, he felt guilty until he opened the closet door. There, amidst towers of boxes, he found a skinny girl about the size of most kindergarteners he knew. Peter could only imagine what she was doing in a brothel.

"Hey, I'm here to help," Peter told her, crouching down to her level.

She shook her head quickly and retreated further into the shadows. "Kari said not to trust you," the little girl said in a quiet, shaky voice. "She promised me candy if I'm good."

"My friend and I can help you get back home," Peter promised.

"No!" she yelled. "I want candy!"

She started convulsing. Peter tried to reach out to her instinctively, but he stopped when she looked up at him with cold and calculating eyes as a twisted smile played on her lips. The look made Peter freeze.

She didn't move, but he felt like a sledgehammer had hit his chest. He flew clear across the room and smacked into the wall.

He landed on the bed, then rolled out of the way just as the little girl came crashing down on the spot, knees first. He stood firmly on the ground, studying the girl. Her eyes held a piercing animalistic quality.

"You are not a threat," she growled in a voice that sounded like a fifty-year-old smoker. *"But I'll still enjoy destroying you."*

Thankfully, he remembered the dance lifts he had just learned. As she leapt at him, he ducked, aiming his shoulder at her waist, and she flipped.

When she recovered, she ran at him. He spun around her and grabbed her arms from behind. He sat down, pulling her arms backwards. With his feet on her backside, he pushed her into a backflip over him. She landed on her feet and snarled as he picked himself up.

"You're just wasting time until I devour you!"

She ran towards him again. He grabbed her hand and spun her in a circle around herself, twisting her arm behind her back. He held on to her with both hands while he swept her feet. She fell into a dip just as Sensei Rob appeared in the doorway. In an instant, he had a hand pressed to her forehead. "May you be made clean," he pronounced.

Her body became weak and Sensei made a sweeping motion with his hands and Peter felt the wave of energy wash through the room.

Peter laid the girl on the bed. Sensei looked at the woman on the floor and eyed Peter suspiciously.

"I can explain," Peter said quickly.

He didn't know whether he should start with the fact that she was unconscious or nearly shirtless.

"Save it," Rob grabbed the backpack. "We have to book it!"

The fire-breathing woman appeared in the doorway and opened her mouth. Fire spilled out and Sensei Rob grabbed Peter's shoulder. They shifted out of the brothel, through the town, and back into the dojo.

Sensei went straight to the phone and called the cops with an anonymous tip about the business and the little girl.

"You didn't exorcise that woman?" Peter asked when Sensei hung up. "I mean, she breathed fire, so she was possessed, right?"

"Yep," Rob said. "She didn't want to be exorcized. We only have the authority to free someone who wants to be freed. Otherwise it would be like showing up to someone's party and throwing out their guests."

"Even if their guests are spirits of hatred and evil?" Peter challenged.

"Free will is a sacred thing. Even if someone makes the wrong choice, they're allowed to do so. No one can take their choice away."

Peter thought it seemed wrong to leave people in the clutches of evil spirits, even if it was honoring their free will.

"So?" Rob asked Peter.

Sensei had a scolding look in his eye and Peter remembered the scenes from the brothel.

"The woman was crazy," he said quickly. "She was trying to tempt me. But I wasn't tempted, I promise. She's like, my mom's age and anyway, I would never do that: take advantage of someone."

"I'm talking about the other thing."

"I didn't want to knock her out," he said, "but she had the little girl locked in the closet. I made sure she still had a pulse, though."

"I'm sure she'll be fine. I meant the other other thing."

Peter's mind was blank. "What other other thing?"

"You ran off," Rob chided. "I can't protect you if you're not with me."

"Oh. Sorry." Peter was relieved. Running off didn't seem half as incriminating as the other things. "It's just… it was like something was telling me to go," he explained. "It seemed right at the time."

Rob studied him for a while. "It all worked out, but it might not next time," he cautioned. "Remember, I'm responsible for you. How would I ever explain it to your parents if something happened to you?"

"I won't do it again," Peter said sincerely. "But geez. Was that girl kidnapped? And a brothel? How is that still a thing in this day and age?"

"How is racism still a thing?" Sensei countered. "But I can't tell you how many times I've been judged or mistrusted because of the color of my skin. How is slavery still a thing? But how many people think about where their clothes or cell phones come from? Temptation and evil acts will, unfortunately, always be 'a thing.'"

They both stared off into the distance. It felt strange to leave such evils unresolved, just like leaving the ugly woman un-exorcised.

"Oh," Peter remembered, "and can we talk about the crazy dragon lady? What was with her breathing fire?"

"That," Rob pulled out a book from the desk drawer and opened to a picture of a hunched creature with a potbelly and scrawny, boney limbs. "That was what they call a preta, or a hungry-ghost. Because of negative karma, they're doomed to crave something, usually gross or destructive, which will never satisfy them. When they possess people, they usually inspire some nasty and disgusting addictions."

"And they can breathe fire?" Peter asked. "I mean, you talk like this is a totally normal thing."

"You'll see a lot more than that in this job," Rob said. "Speaking of that, I have a present for you." He closed the book and handed it to Peter. "This book contains general information. It also has mantras in Palī and English. You can start trying to memorize them. They'll help with your own meditation and during fights."

"I have to study this?" Peter complained picking up the thick book.

"Some of the chants might also help you when the asuras start targeting you," Rob added. "They haven't started yet, have they?"

"Not unless it has something to do with my bad grade in science," Peter pondered seriously.

Rob laughed. "Believe me, you'll know when they start." Then his eyes fell on the parking lot. "Your mom's here."

At the door, Sensei Rob clapped Peter on the shoulder and said, "Oh, and, uh, not asking you to lie or anything, but it's probably not a good idea to tell your parents that I took you to a brothel. That would not be fun to explain."

Chapter 14: The Nasir Family

That weekend, Peter went to Zahid's house for dinner.

As soon as he rang the doorbell, he heard shouts of excitement in Arabic, and a rush of movement. A plump and smiling woman in a headscarf and an apron answered the door.

"Come in, come in!" she smiled. "Welcome to our home."

"Asalaam alaikum," Peter recited before entering, just as Zahid had coached him.

"Look at you!" Mrs. Nasir said, impressed. "Wa 'alaikum salaam," she responded.

Peter was then distracted by two younger boys –smaller versions of Zahid– who had also greeted him. They were speaking so rapidly, he couldn't tell if they were speaking Arabic or English.

Then a man with salt and pepper hair, a mustache, and a happy smile shook Peter's hand enthusiastically and pulled him to three quick cheek kisses. "Welcome, welcome!" Mr. Nasir said.

Peter was glad Zahid had warned him of the Syrian greeting, otherwise it would've been even more awkward than it felt. He was also glad that Zahid didn't greet him this way.

"Nice to meet you, Mr. and Mrs. Nasir," Peter smiled. "Thanks for inviting me."

"You've been so kind and generous to our Zahid," Mrs. Nasir said. "We had to have you over."

"It's really not a big deal," Peter dismissed.

Mr. Nasir placed a hand on Peter's shoulder and told him, "We don't have a lot that we can pay you back with, but what we have is yours."

Zahid's younger brothers were still speaking rapidly and now started tugging on Peter's sleeves to get his attention.

"Hassan, Ahmed, give him room!" Zahid ordered his little brothers as he came around the corner. "Sorry, everyone's a little eager," he explained.

"No worries," Peter assured him. "This is fun."

Hassan and Ahmed turned their attention to Zahid.

"Brother, judge our towers," Hassan, the older boy, begged.

They dragged Zahid to a coffee table where two block towers stood side by side. Zahid crouched down and inspected them critically.

"Those are our other boys," Mrs. Nasir explained. "And our little angel, Yara," Mrs. Nasir indicated a small girl Peter had completely missed. She had been hiding behind her mother.

She seemed too young to be in school and Peter thought back to the girl in the brothel with a tug at his heart. He hoped that little girl would be returned to a family as loving as this one.

"Nice to meet you," Peter said to Yara.

She immediately disappeared behind Mrs. Nasir's dress.

"You'll have to forgive Yara," Mr. Nasir said. "She's shy."

"You boys are getting better," Zahid told his brothers. "Have you been reading the book I brought you from the library?"

The boys nodded and started speaking over each other.

Mr. Nasir said, "Zahid told us about the library card. He checks out books for all of us, too. We really cannot thank you enough."

"No problem," Peter dismissed.

"Yeah, Peter has a terrible condition," Zahid joked. "It's called, 'library aversion.' I think he might be allergic to sitting still, also."

"I'm not allergic," Peter complained. Then he explained to Zahid's parents, "I've been doing martial arts for years, I like to move."

Ahmed gasped and asked Zahid something in Arabic. Zahid scolded him in Arabic.

"Peter, we are going to finish dinner," Mr. Nasir told him. "Please make yourself at home. We leave you in Zahid's care."

They went into the kitchen with Yara at their heels. Zahid and Ahmed were still arguing.

"Everything okay there?" Peter asked nervously.

"Yes," Zahid rolled his eyes as Ahmed yanked on his arm. "Ahmed was just going to ask you an annoying question."

"Come on, brother, please?" Ahmed tugged harder.

Zahid made angry eyes at his brother. "He's already done too much for us. We don't want to take advantage of him."

"Seriously, what is it?" Peter asked.

"I want to learn martial arts," Ahmed said before Zahid could stop him.

Zahid sighed. "He's been having trouble with a classmate."

"Geez, that's nothing," Peter said. "Come on, let's go outside so we don't mess anything up."

Peter taught Ahmed and Hassan some crucial self-defense moves and the two younger boys practiced on each other. Yara came out and watched from the steps to the back door.

"Yara, do you want to try it, too?" Peter invited.

She shook her head. "I'm a girl."

"Girls can do karate," he told her. "One of my teachers is a girl and she's amazing. You have to hold your own against your brothers, right?"

"My brothers will always protect me," she said. "They promised."

"That's right, Yara," Zahid patted her head affectionately. "We'll never let anything bad happen to you."

Watching their whole family interact almost made Peter wish that he had siblings.

"Boys! Yara!" Mrs. Nasir called. "Food is ready!"

They all rushed in to find the table filled with plates piled high with different foods. Peter was disappointed that he didn't see anything familiar. The smells and appearances were completely foreign to him. He was impressed, however, by the sheer amount of food. He could barely see the tablecloth under the plates.

"Is this a special holiday or something?" Peter asked, thinking that it looked like a thanksgiving feast.

"This is to celebrate the first person to welcome us to America," Mrs. Nasir said in a singsong voice.

Peter blinked. "This is just for me?"

He felt bad for being afraid of the new foods and vowed that he would try everything and declare it delicious no matter what.

"Now, before we eat," Mr. Nasir held up his hand, "it's tradition that I tell a story."

The boys all groaned.

"Dad, not a Nasruddin story," Zahid complained.

Mr. Nasir ignored him. "Peter, have you ever heard of Mullah Nasruddin?" Peter shook his head. "He's a very famous figure in the history of our people. There are a million stories of Nasruddin. He was at once a great fool and a great sage. His stories always have much to tell us about our own lives."

"Really, it's our version of dad jokes," Zahid added.

"So one day, a great and well-respected religious leader invited Nasruddin to dinner. It was a great honor and many were jealous of the wisdom Nasruddin would gain from eating with such a learned and holy man as this leader. Nasruddin also knew it would be a great feast, for this teacher was rather wealthy. So the Mullah went an entire day without food to prepare himself for the amazing meal he would taste that night. Then, when he arrived, the leader started lecturing Nasruddin with story after story of beautiful wisdom and teachings. He told tales of the many prophets of the ages and what we could learn from their amazing example. However, this wise leader didn't offer any food while he spoke. Finally, after hours and hours of stories, Nasruddin stops the leader and asks, 'Excuse me, sir. I was just wondering: did any of the people in your stories ever eat?'"

Peter chuckled politely while the rest of the Nasirs groaned.

"And with that, let us eat!" Mrs. Nasir announced.

Peter reached for his fork but paused when he heard the family recite together, "Bismillah, ir-rahman, ir-rahim!"

Hassan piled food onto Yara's plate, speaking to her in Arabic. She giggled as Ahmed cut the meat for her. Meanwhile, Zahid started explaining each food to Peter.

"This one's hummus," he pointed. "There's falafels, kofta kebabs, manoushi bread."

Zahid offered the plate of bread and Peter took one as Mr. Nasir continued the explanation.

"That one's tabbouleh," he said. "It's made with bulgur, mint, parsley, and tomatoes. That's called fattoush, which is like a salad of different vegetables. Freekah. Very tasty. Very nutty."

"I'm not going to be tested on these names, am I?" Peter joked.

Mr. and Mrs. Nasir laughed.

"No, no, of course not," Mrs. Nasir said. "And there's meatball soup, rice pudding, and kibbe."

"Kibbe is sort of like a meatball," Zahid told him. "Traditionally, you use many meats: beef, lamb, camel…"

"Camel?" Peter interjected.

"Don't look so scared," Zahid snickered. "There's no way we'd get camel meat here."

"Everything is fresh," Mrs. Nasir boasted. "Syrian food is always made with the freshest ingredients."

Peter tried dish after dish. The meat ones were especially good. When he tried the kibbe, he made involuntary sounds of delight.

"Geez, they're delicious!" he exclaimed.

Zahid laughed. "The look on your face right now is the same one Hassan had when he tasted his first hamburger."

"I had never eaten one," Hassan protested.

"He looked like he had tasted heaven," Mr. Nasir joked.

"He even whispered, 'Alhamdulillah!'" Mrs. Nasir added.

"That means, 'Praise to God,'" Zahid explained.

"I honestly feel the same way about burgers," Peter assured Hassan. "But this food is amazing. Mr. and Mrs. Nasir, you could open a restaurant." Everybody laughed. "What? What'd I say?"

"We hope to open a restaurant soon," Mr. Nasir told him. "We're still working out all the details, but we hope you will be there at the grand opening."

"I'll be there for sure," Peter said. "Especially if you're cooking this."

"I may not be able to hang out for a while," Zahid complained. "We'll be working hard to get everything ready. If you don't see me at school, you can assume I was buried under fallen boxes."

"Do you need more help?" Peter asked eagerly.

"No, Peter," Zahid tried to stop him.

"I can carry boxes and stuff," Peter offered.

"You really don't need to do that," Mr. Nasir said.

"Peter likes to take advantage of innocent, suffering people to work on acts of good karma," Zahid teased.

"Well, who are we to deny you?" Mr. Nasir joked.

When the evening was over, Peter felt almost exhausted by the loud and energetic conversation. As Mr. Nasir got Peter's coat, Mrs. Nasir loaded him with bags and boxes of leftovers. He felt fairly certain that he had made the right choice hanging with Zahid instead of going to a movie.

Chapter 15: Right Effort

Peter was more than eager for his next exorcist adventure when he entered the dojo. Unfortunately, Sensei Rob was absent.

"Super Buddhist ran out again," Sensei Charlie complained.

Peter tried to hide his disappointment. He couldn't help but feel excluded by the elusive spiritual world.

"Maybe you can teach me all the rest of the eightfold path," he suggested. "I'm ready to know it all. So what's the next step?"

"Right Effort," Sensei Charlie said with a smile.

"What's Right Effort? Is it applying yourself one hundred and ten percent? Because I got that."

"Actually, Right Effort is all about using the right amount of effort to make sure you don't blast through your energy and burn out."

"So I have to pace myself?" Peter asked, disappointed.

Charlie thought for a moment. "I have an idea. Get your gloves."

She brought the standing punch bag to the center of the dojo while Peter got his combat gloves from his bag.

"I'm going to teach you the secret to my speed," she promised.

"Is there a special training technique or something?"

She nodded. "Most people usually practice moves with resistance bands and weights. But the real secret to speed is relaxation."

"Relaxation?" he asked skeptically.

"When you're relaxed, your muscles move faster. So try this: as you punch, relax your arm." She moved her arm out slowly. "Then, at the last moment, snap all your muscles into place."

About a couple inches from the punch bag, she tensed her muscles and hit with enough force to make it wobble.

"That was amazing," Peter said. "How did you generate the force from that close?"

"It's all about focusing your energy and using it when it counts. See, most people try to give each move all their effort and strength, but you can wear out your stamina that way. If you use the proper technique, however, you won't have to apply as much effort and your attacks will be even stronger. Go ahead. Try it."

As they ran through the drills, Peter was surprised to see how well it was working. His punches and kicks were getting faster and it didn't even feel like effort.

He began to understand the lesson. Just like with karate, if he used too much effort at once in his spiritual development, he risked losing his endurance. At the same time, a small amount of effort, applied with the correct technique, could be even more powerful.

They finished the lesson and Peter left as Sensei Charlie locked up the dojo. He was grateful for her wisdom, but he still regretted missing the exorcism with Rob.

The next day after school, Peter came downstairs at the sound of his mom calling. Sensei Rob was at the door, smiling.

"You're doing odd jobs for the dojo?" his mom asked.

Peter exchanged a quick glance with Rob. "Very odd jobs," he agreed. "Sorry I didn't tell you."

"Boys never talk about anything," Mrs. Hunter complained to Sensei Rob. "Anyway, I don't mind, since it makes tuition free. Go work hard, but be home by dinnertime. Love you."

She kissed his cheek as he grabbed his bag and followed Rob.

"So I have a job now?" Peter asked Rob as they walked to his car.

Rob nodded. "You can answer the phone during some of the classes. And I'll be able to bring you along to more exorcisms."

"That was a clever way of telling my mom, by the way," he told Rob as they got into the car.

"Now just to be clear," Sensei shut his door and adopted a stern tone, "That was only out of respect for you. But you should tell her. Lying will accumulate bad karma. I'll leave that decision to you, though."

Rob started the car.

"I could probably tell my dad," Peter speculated, "but I don't think my mom could handle it. She can be pretty crazy and irrational."

Then the world outside the car blurred and Peter watched in awe.

"What? You can transport the whole car?" he marveled. "Why would you ever drive normally?"

"It only works when it needs to work," Rob told him.

They arrived at a remote area with woods on either side of the road. Rob stopped the car and they both got out.

"What are we doing here?" Peter asked.

Rob closed his eyes, then decided, "It's this way."

He led the way through the trees until they came to an open field where they saw a girl about Peter's age.

She had long, dark wavy hair pulled to a ponytail. She looked like a normal teenager in jeans and a t-shirt, but her frantic pacing and mumbling made Peter think otherwise.

Near the girl, a cat meowed nervously within its crate and Peter noticed that the girl was playing with a knife in her hands.

"She's about to perform a spell," Rob whispered.

"Don't tell me magic is actually real," Peter challenged.

Rob gave him a sideways glance, "Says the boy who's training to become an exorcist."

"Well, when you say it like that…" Peter conceded. "But spells really work?"

"It's just like the mantras. What matters most is the intent. The only difference is that I have a deva helping me and when people cast dark spells, they usually have an asura helping them."

"So is all magic bad then?"

Rob shrugged. "I'm sure there're people like us working with devas and people unlocking the mysteries of the human mind. But I only deal with things when they go wrong."

"I know," the girl argued with the air around her. "I know I have to make sacrifices, but I've already gone days without food and I've literally given you my blood. Do I have to give you Mr. Snuggles, too? Can't I kill any other animal?" She paused, as if listening.

"What the Naraka?" Peter whispered. Rob raised an eyebrow at him, but Peter went on, "She's going to kill the cat?"

"It's a ritual," Rob explained. "When you do magic with asuras, they often make you prove yourself by doing something you swore you'd never do. They like breaking us like that."

Peter studied the girl, shaking her head in defiance to some unheard voice. "No. I can't," the girl said. "I'm sorry, but I just can't."

Suddenly, the girl stumbled sideways, as if she had been smacked across the face. "No, please!" she pleaded.

Peter almost questioned whether she was suffering from some mental disorder when he saw her ponytail lift up in the air, grabbed by an invisible hand. The girl was yanked backwards.

She let out a scream and fell. The invisible force dragged her by the foot across the ground. She became suddenly still, apparently passed out from fright.

"Chant for me, will you?" Rob said as he sprang to action.

He waved his arms through the air and attacked what seemed to be nothing. That "nothing" swiped back and left a deep scratch across Sensei's nose. He reeled from the blow, but quickly recovered.

Under pressure, Peter couldn't remember a single chant, but Sensei had said what truly mattered was the intent.

"OM, OM, OM," Peter chanted while he forced his thoughts to focus on good intentions for Sensei and for the unconscious girl.

After a few minutes of fighting, Sensei traced a big circle with his hands, meeting them at his chest and said, "By the truth of these words, may all be well."

Peter realized that the intense dread he had felt upon arrival had evaporated. Sensei unlocked the crate and the cat darted off into the night as Peter came to meet him.

"Poor kid," Rob sighed as he studied the girl on the ground. "I bet the spirit was pretending to be her spirit guide or deva."

"What could make her do something like that?" Peter asked. "There are lots of things I want, but I'm not going to kill a cat for any of them."

Rob explained somberly, "Asuras do this often. They make you think the animal sacrifice will give you magical powers. Some ancient religions used to sacrifice animals and even people to their gods. But the Buddha said, *'One is not called noble who harms living beings.'* See, in order to hurt or kill anything, you have to silence that voice of compassion and sympathy inside you. It debases you."

They started walking back through the trees to the car and Rob continued the lesson. "In cases like these, the asuras try to make people do horrible things they would never want to do. The spirits convince them that spiritual development will only come with some great sacrifice. But the Buddha taught right effort."

"Sensei Charlie taught me a little about that," Peter said. "It's not burning yourself out, right?"

Rob nodded. "Did you know that the Buddha was a prince? He had every luxury there was, but he knew it wouldn't help him find enlightenment. So he left the palace and studied with these gurus who lived out in the wilderness, where he took on strict practices of self-denial. He did this for years, and in fact, almost starved himself to death. But still, he didn't reach enlightenment. It was after this, that he found enlightenment by what he called the middle way. Neither denying nor indulging yourself too much. But the negative spirits will try to convince you to follow a more extreme path in the name of magic or some asura pretending to be a deva."

They got in the car and Rob started driving back to the dojo. Then Peter shivered as he had a scary thought.

"How do we know our devas are really devas and not just asuras?"

"Well, one thing is that my deva has never asked me to hurt any living creature," Rob answered. "It's never promised me power, money, or fame. In fact, it most often encourages me to let go of those things. But I think the real way to tell is to look at the fruit."

"The fruit?" Peter asked.

"Yeah. When I moved into my house years ago, there was this citrus tree in the backyard, but I didn't know what kind it was. Citrus trees are tricky, because they all look alike. I tried to look up if it was a lemon, orange, or lime tree, but there was contradictory information. So I waited. I got excited, thinking about what it would be and looked up tons of recipes for each fruit. Then, as it turns out, it was a grapefruit tree, which is ridiculous, because I don't even like grapefruit."

He paused, as if the explanation were over.

Peter waited a moment, then asked, "And what does that have to do with the asuras?"

"Hm? Oh. Just like a tree bears fruit, the spirits will have an effect on us. They can manufacture a pretty convincing false love that's really lust, and a false justice like when people get self-righteous and judgmental. But they cannot manufacture peace. They cannot give you that feeling when you look at the world and you see beauty in every person, in every creature. And they will not encourage you to perform acts of good karma. So you can always tell what the spirit is by the fruit it produces in you."

Chapter 16: Right Mindfulness

A few days later, Sensei drove Peter to an exorcism in a neighborhood of spacious newly built houses. Rob led the way to the front door of one house that looked just like all the rest and whispered a prayer under his breath. The door clicked open.

"Excuse me?" Rob called out as he entered. "Hope you don't mind, the door was wide open." He winked at Peter.

A woman hurried into the entryway carrying a Bible and a wooden cross. "What are you…" she started to ask.

She looked like a normal woman, the kind you would see in a grocery store or at the bank, but her face was knotted in worry.

"Sorry to trouble you, ma'am," Rob smiled brightly, "but we were in the neighborhood…"

"This is not a good time," she shook her head emphatically.

Peter noticed something red on the tip of the wooden cross.

"Trust me," Rob told her, "it's just the right time. See, we were sent to help you with your current situation."

"How did you know?" she whispered. "Are you angels?"

"Not angels," Rob chuckled. "Just experts in this area. We'll have this taken care of in no time. First, while I see to the patient, can you get a first aid kit for my apprentice, Peter?"

Why do we need a first aid kit? Peter wondered.

"Peter? What a good Christian name," the woman remarked.

Peter nodded and smiled dimly. He figured he wouldn't tell her that his parents named him after the superhero, the Arachnid Kid.

Peter and Rob followed the woman into the kitchen where a teen girl was secured to a chair with duct tape. A cross shape had been cut into the skin of her forehead and hands. Her lip was busted and her nose was bleeding. She was shaking and sniffling.

The red on the cross, he realized.

He looked at the mom with disgust as Sensei started chanting.

"This is what should be done by one who is skilled in goodness, and who knows the path of peace," Sensei recited. The girl started struggling against her restraints. *"Let them be able and upright, straightforward and gentle in speech, humble and not conceited…"*

The girl started growling and the mother covered her mouth to hold in a sob. The girl looked up at Rob with an intense focus that sent shivers up Peter's spine.

"You can't stop us!" a deep voice came from the teenaged girl. *"We're more powerful than your pathetic words!"*

The mom screamed as the chair started hovering in the air.

Suddenly, kitchen items started flying on their own, mostly aimed at Sensei Rob. He didn't skip a beat in his chanting. When the sutta was finished, he held his hand in her direction and declared, "May you be washed clean."

The girl went slack and hung her head, passed out.

CLACK!

The chair fell to the floor.

But the storm of pots and pans, knives and forks continued. The woman threw herself on her daughter to protect her.

Sensei Rob reached out with both hands and swept the air around himself. Peter felt the invisible wave rush over him and all the objects fell to the ground. The kitchen became still and quiet.

Rob untied the restraints and laid the girl on the couch. Peter bandaged her wounds with a look of disgust on his face while Sensei Rob pulled the mom aside.

"I understand the fear you were dealing with," he told her gently. "And I know you had her best interests at heart, but you need to realize something. You see, the dark spirit that was possessing your daughter, it was merely sharing space. It didn't share a link to her body. It could animate her limbs and use her voice, but it didn't share her sensations. Do you understand what I'm saying?"

The woman choked on a sob and covered her mouth with both hands. "I was only hurting my Grace?"

"It's okay now," Rob assured her. "We got here in time. Your daughter will be fine. But next time, leave it to the experts. Okay?"

She nodded.

"I feel awful," the woman cried.

Good, Peter thought. *You should.*

"The spirit tricked you," Rob assured her. "It wanted you to hurt your daughter. But you know what really hurts them? Intense love and brave goodness. You can guard yourself and your daughter with simple loving-kindness. Her body will heal and, with enough love, so will her heart."

Peter was amazed that there was no condemnation, no judgement, and no anger in Sensei's voice.

"Thank you," the woman wiped a tear. "You must be angels."

“Just Good Samaritans,” Rob corrected her. “Remember, our job is to handle spirits, yours is to love as much as you can.”

“Okay,” she nodded fervently. “I will. Will I see you again?”

“Better not,” he shot finger guns at her with a charming wink.

Sensei Rob drove Peter back to the studio.

“It only gets worse,” Rob said, reading Peter’s thoughts. “In this job, you see the worst of what humans are capable of. Sometimes the darkness comes from the spirits and sometimes it comes from within the person.”

“Is that what a Christian exorcism looks like?” Peter asked.

“No,” Rob said emphatically. “From what I know, most sanctioned exorcisms involve prayer, no beatings. Christianity is a beautiful religion based on peace and love. Jesus exorcised spirits using words or a simple touch. He never condoned violence. But every walk of life has its confused zealots. Oh, and we should talk about your face.”

“What is this? A joke?” Peter complained.

“No,” Rob chuckled. “Though I am sorry I didn’t think of that. No, your anger and disgust were very clear today.”

“Can you blame me?”

“It’s not about blame,” Sensei shook his head. “But you have to understand: the asuras are always watching us.”

Peter instinctively glanced at the back seat.

“Think of that bully at school,” Rob said. “When he saw you get upset, he knew he had power over you, right? It’s the same with the asuras.”

Peter digested Sensei’s instruction. It was unnerving to think of his enemy watching his every facial expression.

“I couldn’t help it, though,” he argued. “That mom was pretty evil.”

“I wouldn’t say she was evil,” Rob countered. “Remember that asura at the empty house that whispered into your own thoughts?” Rob said as he parked at the dojo. “They can be really convincing. If you’re not being mindful enough, it’s very easy to listen to what they say.”

“Mindful?” Peter asked. “What’s that mean?”

“So glad you asked,” Rob said as he unlocked the dojo door. “Right Mindfulness just happens to be the next step on the eightfold path. See, when people make mistakes, they usually say, ‘I wasn’t thinking.’ But karma still accumulates whether you're thinking or not. So we need to pay attention to the choices we make and why we're making them."

Peter sighed and realized that he would like Buddhism a lot more without all the reading, meditation, and self-control.

"This religion is mentally exhausting," he sighed.

Rob smiled patiently. "But it's worth it. You've seen the dangers of not being in control of your own thoughts." Peter nodded. "So speaking of a lack of mindfulness," Rob said with the hint of a smile. "A whole bag of chips, huh?"

Peter didn't know what Rob was talking about at first. Then he thought to the night before. He had stayed up late and had absent-mindedly eaten an entire bag of chips in one sitting. But no one had known. His parents had been asleep.

"What the fresh Naraka?" he exploded. "Were you spying on me?"

Rob smiled smugly. "No. Your deva told my deva."

"Not cool," Peter pronounced. "Geez, not only are the asuras watching me all the time, but my deva, too? Do I ever have real privacy? And why didn't this deva just talk to me?"

"It says you're not ready to meet yet," Sensei shrugged.

"Fine," he rolled his eyes. "I ate the chips. I was tired from a crazy mental routine I recently adopted and needed a break."

"Did you?" Rob asked knowingly.

"Yes."

"Did you?" Rob asked again.

"Haven't you ever wanted a break?"

"Ah," Rob wagged his finger at Peter. "This time you said wanted, not needed. Tell me, Peter, did you *need* those chips?"

He rolled his eyes. "No."

"Did they bring you any satisfaction?"

He grumbled, "Definitely not now that I'm in trouble."

"You're not in trouble," Rob's tone softened. "But this is the journey to enlightenment, it's not easy. If you want to meet your deva and become an exorcist, then you have to discipline yourself."

"Fine," he harrumphed. "No more whole bags of chips."

"You can eat whatever you like," Rob told him, "as long as you're being mindful and aware of the consequences. But can you tell me what situations helped you make your mindless decision of that late night snack?"

Peter glared. He had tired of this conversation two minutes prior. "I was really hungry."

"You didn't have dinner?" Rob asked.

"I did," Peter replied. "But I ate dinner at like, six and then at midnight, I was so hungry it was keeping me awake."

"Maybe you could track your nutrients and calories," Rob suggested.

"Fine. I'll do that," Peter agreed quickly.

"But why were you up that late?" Sensei asked innocently.

Peter sighed and glared again. "I don't know. I'm a night owl."

"That could be it," Rob considered. "Unless you were also ingesting large amounts of caffeine in the late afternoon…"

Peter searched his memory.

"Bloody Naraka!" he exclaimed.

Sensei chuckled. "You think you're so clever with that, huh?"

Peter rolled his eyes again. "I had a couple sodas after school. I wasn't thinking about what it would do to me."

"You see there?" Sensei snapped his fingers. "That's my point. Many of us go through life not thinking, like we're on auto-pilot. It's okay to eat chips and drink soda, but as an exorcist, you need to be in control of your thoughts and actions at all times. Because if you aren't in control, the asuras could use it against you."

"So a bag of chips could be my downfall?" Peter asked sarcastically. "Geez, are you this hard on yourself?"

Sensei nodded seriously. "And I'll be this hard on you until you meet your deva. Then the deva will be this hard on you."

"That sounds really frustrating."

"Actually, I find a certain enjoyment in it," Rob smiled wistfully. "It's like we have a never-ending game of perfecting ourselves. See, if there's always some way to improve, we'll never be bored."

"You are so not normal," Peter told him.

Rob flashed Peter a bright smile. "Why, thank you."

Chapter 17: Right Samadhi

When Peter arrived at the dojo the next day, Sensei Charlie was teaching the class and Rob was nowhere in sight. Peter sat at the front desk and pulled out his homework.

He wished he had been there earlier to run out to some spiritual adventure. He had even given up chips and soda for that purpose, but apparently, it wasn't enough yet.

When the class was over, Sensei Charlie leaned against the partition and watched the parking lot.

She sighed. "So Super Buddhist still isn't back yet?"

"Must be a tough supervillain," Peter joked.

After a short pause, he heard her say, "You know something."

Peter snapped his head up. "What?"

She was studying him critically. "You're less nervous than the last time we talked about this. And you've been awfully chummy with him lately. What do you know?"

Peter kept his face controlled. "You want to know what I know? He's calm with angry parents, patient with annoying students like me, and he's generous with people who can't pay tuition. He's strong and selfless and self-disciplined. And he's been all that since I was five. Whatever his secret is, I know he's a nice guy."

She mulled it over. "You've got a point."

He's going to owe me for that one, Peter thought.

"I don't know many people as good as he is." She got a faraway look and smiled to herself.

"So how long have you liked him?" Peter asked casually.

"What?" she straightened. "I never… I… I didn't say…"

He gave her a cut-the-act look. "Then why were you smiling?"

"It was a joke," she said quickly. "I was just thinking of a joke I heard recently."

"Oh, yeah?" he narrowed his eyes. "What was the joke?"

They had a stare down for a few moments.

"Did you see that new karate movie that came out?" Sensei Charlie asked him defiantly. "I hear it was a *block-buster*."

Peter groaned when he got it.

"I mean, it was really *sensei*-tional!" she added.

Peter chuckled and shook his head.

DING!

"Hey, guys, what are you talking about?" Rob asked as he came through the front door.

"Sensei Charlie was just making a bad joke," Peter said.

"Oh! I've got one, too," Rob clapped his hands in excitement. "What do Christians and Buddhists have in common? They both want to know if you've been born again!"

Charlie giggled politely.

"Get it?" Rob asked Peter. "Because of reincarnation!"

"I don't know which one is worse," Peter rolled his eyes.

"Now, now," Charlie chided him. "I hear reincarnation is making a comeback."

Rob paused while the joke set in. Then he laughed like a hyena. Peter thought that they were perfect for each other.

"Okay, let's get to the lesson," Sensei urged them both to the mats.

"I can't tell you how much I look forward to this," Charlie said.

"I bet you do," Peter eyed her knowingly.

She scowled back.

"Right Samadhi," Sensei said as they all sat, "or Right Concentration, is the final step in the eight-fold path to enlightenment."

"So I reach enlightenment today?" Peter asked enthusiastically.

"Not that easy," Rob chuckled.

"If I recall, you should be reviewing the steps constantly," Charlie added. "You don't perfect Right View and then move on to Right Thought and so on. You work on them all at once, over and over again, all throughout your life."

"That's right," Rob agreed. "And this last one is the most difficult to explain and the most difficult to achieve. It's sort of focus and concentration, but it's more than that. Have you ever heard stories of monks and nuns that live in isolated monasteries in the mountains who seem to have super powers?" Peter shook his head. "There have been tales of people who could levitate, read and influence minds, or go months without food, just living off of meditation."

"Is that even possible?" Sensei Charlie asked skeptically.

"I'm not recommending that you try it," Sensei Rob said quickly. "But the ones who achieved these things talked about how miraculous, satisfying, and sustaining meditation is."

"You mean how exhausting it is?" Peter challenged.

"Well, that's the thing," Rob wagged his finger at Peter. "You haven't hit upon samadhi yet."

“Some-odd-what now?”

“Sum-ah-dee. It’s this place between thinking and sleeping,” Rob explained with a gleam in his eye. “It’s almost magical. It feels amazing and you end up craving it. It’s totally ephemeral.”

“Effeminate?” Peter asked precariously.

“Ephemeral,” Rob corrected. “Transcendental. Ineffable.” When he realized that Peter didn’t know any of those words, he modified. “Basically, you hit this awesome spot in your meditation that’s a state of incredible peace. It’s impossible to explain to anyone who hasn’t experienced it.”

“Like a trance or something?” Peter guessed.

“Sort of, but it’s where you have these epiphanies, these moments of clarity. It’s when you’re most likely to interact with your...” he glanced at Charlie and cleared his throat, “to discover wisdom and insight. And here’s the trick, you can’t make it happen. You can prepare yourself with meditation, but samadhi happens to you when it happens.”

“I can’t control it?” Peter asked.

“It’s like working out,” Sensei Charlie added. “Often you start a workout and you have to force it, right? Your muscles are tired, your energy is low. But then you hit this adrenaline zone where all the movements come so easily. You can’t control when you get in the zone, but you can’t get there by sitting on the couch.”

“That’s a great analogy,” Rob marveled, watching her intently.

Sensei Charlie seemed to blush under his gaze.

“So, that’s why we meditate every day,” Rob turned back to Peter. “To prepare ourselves for samadhi.”

Peter took in a long breath. Apparently, if he wanted to make progress as an exorcist, he needed to meditate even more.

The next day, at lunch, Peter took his food to the school courtyard. It had started to get colder, so Peter had the space to himself. He sat cross-legged on a bench and tried to calm his mind.

Instead, he was flooded with thoughts of the day, memories of his parents, teachers, and friends. Samadhi was starting to feel futile.

Finally, he gave up and rumbled a frustrated sigh. When he opened his eyes, he saw Zahid paused, about to sit next to him.

“Am I bothering you?” he asked nervously. “I can go back.”

"Sorry," Peter explained. "I'm just trying to clear my mind."

Zahid squinted. "I thought it was empty enough already." He flashed a smile and sat on the bench.

"Hah. Hah," Peter pretended to laugh. "No, I'm trying to meditate. So far, it's just another thing I suck at."

"Sitting still and not thinking?" Zahid eyed him. "You suck at sitting and not thinking?"

"It's not as easy as it looks, okay?" Peter complained.

Zahid looked around and asked quietly, "Would it be alright if I say some prayers while you try to meditate?"

"Sure," Peter shrugged. "No problem here."

Zahid took off his shoes and socks. Then he started singing in Arabic and going between standing, kneeling, and bowing. Peter didn't mean to stare, but it was hard to resist.

When it was over, Zahid looked like he was about to cry. He shook himself, put his shoes back on, and sat next to Peter.

"Do you pray like that every day?" Peter asked.

"We're supposed to pray five times a day," Zahid said. "I usually skip the afternoon one, because, well, it's hard at school."

Peter couldn't believe Zahid prayed five times a day while he could barely meditate once a day without going mad.

"What were you singing?" Peter asked.

"It's all praises to God. We say that God is the greatest and we ask Him to guide us and bless us."

"Have you ever had an experience where you felt really at peace or, like, in a trance during prayer?"

Zahid nodded. "Many times," he said.

"Is there any way to make that happen?"

"Not that I know of," Zahid shrugged. "We have a saying: the fruit of silence is tranquility. You can only have those moments if you're being silent. But I always thought it was a gift from God."

Peter wondered if it was still a gift from God if Peter didn't believe in God.

That night, Peter sat on his bed and tried meditating again. His concentration was dancing all over the place, but he was determined to keep at it until something happened. Then something did happen. He fell fast asleep and into a terrible dream.

Peter dreamt of the girl from the last exorcism he had attended: Grace. She was duct-taped to the chair. Blood and tears trailed down her face. She screamed in pain as she was beaten. The Bible and wooden cross pounded against her, leaving scrapes and bruises.

He was repulsed all over again, that someone could do this to another human being.

"Please," the girl coughed, spewing blood from the cut on her lip. "It hurts so much."

SMACK!

The book hit her across the face.

"Your lies won't work on me," Peter's voice threatened.

Suddenly he realized that he was the one doing the beating.

Chapter 18: Rob's Torment

After weeks of daily meditation and joining Sensei on exorcisms at least once a week, Peter had still barely made any progress in the area of samadhi. At least there were other benefits to meditation, however. He felt healthier and calmer. And surprisingly, his grades had improved.

Peter waited at his desk while the teacher returned a history test. When he got his back, he was amazed to see that he had received a ninety-seven and a note from the teacher praising his improved penmanship.

He turned around to face Zahid, about to brag, when he saw Zahid's score.

"One hundred and three?" Peter yawped. On top of that, Zahid's handwriting was even better than Peter's.

"I included too many details in the short essay," Zahid said calmly. "She gave me extra credit."

Peter was about to complain when he became distracted by Jeremy pestering Alicia at her desk.

"I'll show you mine if you show me yours," he said loudly, holding his test in front of her.

"Buzz off, Jeremy," she rolled her eyes.

"You know you want me. Stop playing."

"Playing what?" Peter interrupted. "Is it a game to see who got the best score? Let's see," he looked over Alicia's shoulder at her test. "Alicia, you got a ninety-six? That's almost as good as my ninety-seven. What about you, Jeremy?" Jeremy snarled. "Did I win the game?"

"Peter, you are so funny," Alicia giggled. "Did you come over here just to talk about the test," she stood and brushed his arm lightly, "or was there something you wanted to ask me?"

Peter had little memory of anything happening before she touched his arm. He searched his mind for any question he might have for her.

"Uh… what did you get for number seven?" he decided at last.

She giggled again and Jeremy retreated, seething.

"Geez, that guy is always bugging you," Peter shook his head.

He watched, in vain, as Jeremy stole a comic book from where Peter had left it on his desk.

"And you are always coming to my rescue," Alicia said as she picked up her books. "If you keep this up, a girl could get ideas."

Peter's brain went weak. "What kind of ideas exactly?" he asked.

She flipped her hair as she put her backpack on. "What kind of ideas do you want me to get?"

He gulped. "The kind of ideas that would make you happy and not creep you out or annoy you."

"You're definitely not a creep," she assured him. "And the only thing that's annoying is how it takes you forever to figure things out."

He couldn't take his eyes away from her. "I'm not the best at thinking," he admitted. "I need people to spell things out for me."

"I think someone is spelling it out for you," she chuckled. "Let me know when you get it." She walked ahead as the bell rang.

He stumbled slowly towards the door.

"Everything okay?" Zahid asked, handing him his backpack.

"Yeah, thanks. I'm just confused."

Zahid looked over Peter's shoulder at his test and responded, "The answer to number seven was the 'the judicial branch.'"

Out in the hall, Peter felt something like a breeze whispering past him. He stopped and held Zahid back.

"What?" Zahid asked.

"I don't know…" Peter said.

He wasn't sure how to explain it, but he felt a tug at his gut. He just knew that something or someone was right around the corner. He could feel the ill intent. It had a similar feeling to an asura. He knew that he and Zahid were in danger.

Up ahead, Alicia told Gina and Stacey that she forgot something in the classroom and rushed back. As she passed Peter and Zahid, she leaned in and whispered, "Jeremy's around the corner and he looks mad. You should take the long way around."

"I guess you're the superhero this time, huh?" Peter teased.

She leaned in and whispered right into Peter's ear. "Then are you the one getting ideas?"

He watched her leave a little too long.

DING!

As he entered the dojo, all the younger kids from the previous class were leaving and Sensei Rob was talking to a parent.

"Hey, Peter," Sensei Charlie greeted. "Everything okay?"

"Yeah. I just wanted to ask Sensei Rob something."

"Anything I can help with?" she offered.
Peter asked her quietly, "How can you tell if a girl is flirting with you for real or if she's just being friendly?"
"Aw," Charlie tilted her head and put her hands over her heart. "Tell me what happened," she prodded.
He told her the story of what Alicia had said and Charlie started laughing and snorting.
"Sorry, sorry, sorry!" she calmed herself. "But seriously? Peter? You're a smart kid. Are you really confused about this?"
He shrugged. "Maybe she was just flirting and didn't mean it."
"Look, here's what you do," she instructed. "You look her in the eye, tell her she's beautiful, and ask her to a movie."
"And that'll work?" he asked eagerly.
"Trust me," she laughed again. "Based on what you told me, I bet she's been waiting months for you to ask her out."
"You really think so?"
"I'm pretty sure," she said in a sarcastic tone that could have rivaled Peter's. "I'm going to go get dressed. Good luck."
"Thanks, Sensei Charlie."
Peter committed her advice to memory. Before long, Sensei Rob was finished talking and all the parents and kids had left.
"Let's get started," Rob clapped his hands together. "Sensei Charlene had to fill in for an instructor at her gym, so it's just you and me."
"Wait," Peter interrupted him, "I have a question."
"Shoot."
"Well, see, there's this girl…"
He stopped when the dojo started shaking.
"Oh, boy," Sensei stared wide-eyed all around him. "This usually doesn't happen unless I'm alone."
"What is this?" Peter asked, trying to keep himself steady.
The lights started flickering.
"Remember I told you they have a way of fighting back at us?" Rob said.
Objects started flying at Peter and Sensei, as if hurled by an invisible hand. Peter blocked himself and Sensei batted the objects away with lightning fast reflexes.
"This is it?" Peter asked, bluffing a calm attitude. "This doesn't seem all that scary."
"Give it time…" Rob's face suddenly dropped. "Charlene?"

Peter turned and saw Sensei Charlie standing in the dojo area. She had changed into workout clothes and was cowering with her hands above her head, watching the flying objects.

"I thought you left," Sensei Rob said. "What are you doing here?"

"What is this?" she asked in a quivering voice.

Rob was so distracted by Charlie that a picture slammed into the side of his head. He only reacted slightly. "I'm so sorry," he told her. "I never meant to get you involved in this."

She turned and gave him a look that was between fear and anger. "You?" she questioned. "You're doing this?" Her lips curled back in disgust. "What are you?"

"Charlene, I…"

"Stay away from me!" she shouted. "You're a freak!"

Peter could see the very moment of Sensei's heartbreak. It was the first time Peter had ever seen pain on his face.

"Sensei Charlie," Peter attempted, "this isn't Rob…"

"No! I don't want to hear it!" she hollered. "I never want to see either of you again!"

Peter noticed a plaque flying in her direction. In the span of a breath, Rob sprang to her and threw himself in its path. He grimaced in pain as the plaque's corner hit his shoulder.

"You… you saved me," Charlie stammered.

"Of course," Rob smiled.

She met his eyes and they both seemed to forget that they were in the middle of an evil, supernatural storm of dojo equipment.

"Rob." She took his hand in hers and leaned towards him. It looked like she was about to kiss him. Peter thought it was strange timing, but figured it wasn't his place to judge.

Then, she twisted his hand and took a bite into his forearm. He yelled out in pain and tore his arm from her. She pulled away, laughing while a trickle of blood spilled from her lips.

"Deliciousss," she hissed.

Chapter 19: Rakshasas

Charlie morphed into a billowing cloud of black smoke and reformed into a large, fat, misshapen human. There were horns protruding from its head of wiry bristle-like hair. Its eyes glowed red in contrast to the creature's black-as-night skin.

"Peter, find the book and read the Metta Sutta," Rob ordered.

Peter wasted no time. As Rob fought the monster formerly known as Charlie, Peter raced to the office and found the book.

He unraveled his prayer beads from around his wrist and shuffled through the pages until he found the right chant. He raced back out of the office and ran straight into his parents.

"Peter?" his mom said. "What the heck is this?"

"Mom," he said quickly. "I should've told you…"

"Is this what you meant about odd jobs?" she asked as she dodged a flying figurine. "You lied to me!"

"Now, now wait," Peter stammered, "I never lied."

"We trusted you," Mr. Hunter said with a disappointed tone.

Peter couldn't remember the last time he had disappointed them and now he had been caught in a huge lie. But then he remembered the asura's trick earlier, pretending to be Sensei Charlie.

He started chanting, "OM MANI PADME HUM."

His "mom" knocked the book from his hands with a snarl. Both his parents morphed into creatures similar to the Charlie-monster.

Peter continued to recite the mantra while he fought the creatures. Rob joined the chant, adding power and resonance to the vibrations. Then Peter heard Rob's voice falter. The monster had changed back into Charlie.

"Rob, please don't hurt me," it pleaded in Charlie's voice.

When he hesitated, it swept his feet. He landed on his back and the monster leapt at him, sitting on top of his chest and strangling him.

At the same time, the dad-monster grabbed Peter's arm and pulled him off balance. He fell forward, slamming into the mats. The mom-monster grabbed Peter by the collar and lifted him into the air. He struggled, dangling and flailing.

"I want the first bite," dad-monster said.

Then a wave of power washed over them all. Peter looked up and blinked in astonishment. He saw a distortion in the air like the heat waves on a hot day. The distortion was shaped like a huge wave and as it crashed over him, it felt cool and refreshing.

When Peter pulled himself up, he saw the three spirits trapped in what looked like whirlpools, made of the same invisible substance. They howled, shaking the entire building, and disappeared from sight as the celestial water swallowed them.

Then he looked at Rob and saw a large greenish glow around him. Peter had only seen it for a second then it disappeared in the blink of an eye. Now only Rob stood in the still and empty, but thoroughly messed up, dojo.

They caught their breaths, appreciating the calm. Rob stumbled to the front desk area and picked up the book, setting it on the partition. He rested on the wall, facing the parking lot with his back to the dojo. His knees seemed to buckle and he slid down to the ground. Peter ran to the office to retrieve the first aid kit and a bottle of water.

"Thanks," Sensei Rob said breathlessly.

He was shaking. Although the attack had been frightening for Peter, it had obviously been more frightening for Sensei.

"What the Naraka were those?" Peter asked.

"Rakshasas. Also known as man-eaters." Rob showed the wound from where rakshasa-Charlie had bitten him. He studied the injury closely. "I hope I don't need stitches. The ER docs know me by name at this point. Anyway, those creatures are the lowest of the low of the evil spirits, completely consumed by rage, blood lust, and every other vice you can think of. And they're masters of illusion."

"And you almost kissed one," Peter attempted a joke.

Sensei Rob laughed bitterly. "Don't remind me."

"Thanks for protecting me," Peter said.

"I couldn't let them hurt my apprentice." Rob ruffled Peter's hair with a slight smile. "Actually, wanting to help you snapped me out of my panic. We're stronger when we care about other people."

Peter disagreed. He never felt stronger when he thought of other people in danger.

"So what were you going to ask me earlier?" Rob asked.

Peter chuckled. It seemed unimportant now.

"I just have this crush. I wanted to know if there's something I need to think about before asking her out."

"Hah, if I had answered before all this, I would have said to just go for it. But now, well, you saw what happened. The spirits can use the people we care about to attack us or," he stared into the parking lot, "or we can put them in danger."

"But there's a way to protect them, right?" Peter asked.

"Maybe," Sensei shrugged. "But honestly, that," he pointed a thumb behind him, "has me wondering if maybe guys like us should be alone."

"Whoa. Hold up," Peter complained. "You never said I had to give up the hope of a girlfriend to be an exorcist."

"I'm not saying you have to," Rob clarified. "I'm just saying be careful. Take Charlene. She's beautiful and strong and funny and intelligent. She's everything I'd ever want in a friend, or a girlfriend, or more. But am I going to ask her out?" he sighed heavily. "No."

"Ugh!" they heard a frustrated grunt from behind them.

Rob jolted up and looked over the partition. Peter followed. Charlie was standing right in the middle of the dojo area in workout clothes. She had a look of shock and indignation on her face.

"Why are you still here?" Sensei Rob shouted frantically.

She shook her head with an intense glare and ran back into the changing room. From the sound of it, she was collecting her things.

Rob turned to Peter, "I should…"

"Yeah," Peter interrupted him. "You should."

He chased after her. "Charlene…"

"Charlie!" Peter heard her yell. "Char-lie!"

Peter was very grateful not to be in Sensei Rob's place.

"It's been more than half a year," she ranted. "Everyone else calls me Charlie. I have specifically, clearly asked you to call me Charlie multiple times and you still won't call me by my name!"

"But your name is Charlene," Rob said playfully.

Peter winced for Sensei's sake as he started picking up the mess.

"Stop it!" Charlie exploded. "I only tolerated that because I thought that was a cute, flirty thing you were doing. Did you know Ninja Zone offered me a job last month? For twice this salary? Twice! I turned them down because yes, I think this studio has integrity, but also because you were cute and I thought you were flirting with me."

"I thought girls liked it when guys flirted," Rob argued.

"Not if it doesn't mean anything! Not if you never plan on asking me out because of some weird secret hobby you and Peter have going on."

"Wait, wait, wait," Rob stopped her. "You saw all that and you're upset because I said I wasn't going to ask you out?"

There was a long pause.

"I don't know," she rebuffed. "I guess I should be upset about the other thing, but I always knew you were weird and hiding something. And anyway you can tell me about it or not, because obviously I don't mean that much to you."

It suddenly became very quiet and Peter saw through the doorway that Sensei Rob had stopped her with a kiss. He figured he should stop eavesdropping and should definitely stop watching.

"Charlene," he heard Rob say. "Will you go out with me?"

Peter decided that this was the answer to his own question. Even with the potential danger involved, maybe a relationship was still worth the risk. He decided he'd ask Alicia out the next chance he got.

Peter saw himself in a shadowy warehouse. The rows of shelves were packed with boxes and equipment. In between the shelves, he saw his father talking to a man with a clipboard.

"The product should be ready to ship," the man was telling his dad.

Peter reached out and touched a shelf out of curiosity and saw his hand pass right through it.

Must be a dream, *he thought.*

Then, while watching his father from the other side of the shelves, he felt a sinister grin on his own face. He focused on a large crate on the third shelf, directly above his dad. It started to rattle.

His father looked up just in time to see it fall over the edge. He hollered as it came crashing down on him.

Peter awoke with a startled scream, sitting straight up on the couch where he had taken a nap.

His mom was sitting on the next couch, staring at him. Her pen was paused in the middle of writing a sentence on a notepad.

"Were you having a dream or something?" she asked. Then she nodded knowingly. "Was it about sparkly unicorns?"

"What? No, I…" he shook his head, thinking that his mom could be so weird. "What's up?" He indicated the notepad.

"Nothing big." She waved her hand in the air. "Your dad got hurt at work and I need to meet him at the hospital."

"Dad's hurt?" Peter gripped the edge of the couch.

His mom studied him and laughed. "Chill out. It's nothing serious. Some big box fell and broke his foot."

Peter's stomach turned.

"No big deal," she continued. "You stay here and rest up."

"No, I want to come," Peter stood with her.

She looked him over with a sideways gaze. "Must have been some dream," she speculated. "Evil rabid sparkly unicorns?"

"Dad!" Peter rushed to hug him as soon as they got to the ER room. "Are you okay? I am so sorry."

"What are you sorry for?" his mom laughed. "You were sleeping on the couch and dreaming of unicorns."

"Unicorns?" his dad asked.

"I wasn't…" Peter stopped himself. "I'm sorry you're hurt."

"Just a broken foot." He pointed to the thick boot around his foot and shin. "I can even go back to work. And honestly, the pain meds are making me feel pretty happy right now." He pulled them both to a hug and squeezed. "This right here, surrounded by the people I love the most, this is what life is all about."

Peter couldn't help but think that his dream had caused his dad's injury. Then Peter had another thought that twisted his stomach.

If I started dating Alicia, would she be in danger, too?

Peter was trying to focus on his homework at the front desk of the dojo when Sensei Charlie sat on the corner of the desk.

"So what is it like to be Super Buddhist's sidekick?" she asked.

Peter laughed. "We don't go around in capes and tights, I promise."

"Do you at least proclaim to be heroes of the Buddhist way?" she asked dramatically. They laughed together. "I wanted you to know that your secret is safe with me," she assured him. "And I only think you're half as weird as Rob."

"Thanks for that," Peter said.

"So did anything happen with that girl?" Charlie asked with a playful smile.

"Ah," his smile fell. "I, uh, decided not to ask her out."

Charlie looked disappointed. "Aw. Why not?"

"Because of all this," Peter waved his hand. "I mean, what if they try to hurt Alicia because of me?"

"Ooh, so Alicia is her name? Is she pretty?"

Peter smiled automatically. "Yeah, she's pretty. But it's only a crush. I don't want to put her in danger over just a crush."

"Right," Charlie nodded seriously. "You only want to put her in danger if you really care about her."

"You know what I mean. Don't you worry about that? Isn't dating Rob dangerous? Or at least weird? I mean, you act like this is normal."

Charlie looked into the office door where Rob was talking on the phone. Her smile enveloped her whole face.

"Yeah, he's weird and it's kind of scary," she said. "But I think it's worth it."

"That's great," Peter said, "for you. But that's not a decision I can make for Alicia."

"I get it," Charlie said. "But I bet it'll drive her crazy that you don't ask her out."

"Nah, you don't know her," Peter shook his head. "She could date any guy she wants. She'll get over me right away."

"Maybe. Or maybe she'll wait until you're ready."

That would be great, he thought. *But it's too good to be true.*

Then he wondered if maybe it was for the best. He had a lot on his plate at the moment with school, karate, working at the front desk, and, of course, learning how to fight ancient spirits of negativity. He had enough to focus on without thinking about dating.

Then Charlie punched his shoulder, shocking him from his thoughts.

"Ow," he complained. "What's that for?"

"That," she pointed her finger at him with a playful glare, "is for not telling me about all this sooner. I thought we were friends."

Chapter 20: The Winds of Change

On a Saturday morning in May, Peter ran through exercises at a local playground. He did pullups on the monkey bars, reverse crunches on the parallel bars, and push-ups on a bench before finishing his workout by running an obstacle course around the park.

Then he sat on a bench for meditation. After months of practice, he could now last more than thirty minutes in one sitting. And although he still hadn't experienced samadhi, he had come to enjoy the peace of sitting still.

He chanted on his mala, "GATE GATE PARAGATE…"

Soon, Peter felt a light-headedness, like he was feeling buffets of wind, threatening to blow him over. He opened his eyes and noticed a swirl to the world around him. As his vision focused, he realized he could see the air. It looked like a huge Van Gogh painting, with strings of swirling patterns in variating hues of transparent blues and whites.

He held out his hand, spreading his fingers, and watched the air currents pass around them. He thought of how powerful and gentle the wind could be. It could level cities and disrupt the oceans. It could bring a soft, refreshing breeze and clear polluted air.

He realized that an exorcism was like cleaning a polluted spirit. And he wanted to do that for the people in need.

WHOOOSH!

The wind wrapped around itself in a small funnel and shot into Peter's mouth. It swirled inside him and he thought he might get sick. The wind emerged, bringing a gray cloud with it. The clean air swirled around the gray cloud in a mini tornado and rotated until the gray scattered in all directions.

Peter blinked, wondering if his eyes were playing tricks on him. Then he realized that he didn't feel the bench beneath him. He looked down and suddenly felt it again, as if he had just sat down.

I must be tired, he concluded.

A few days later, Rob interrupted a private lesson to bring Peter along for an exorcism. The sun was getting low towards the horizon as they entered a nursing home near Peter's house.

When they approached the front desk, the nurse was arguing on the phone. "No," she said adamantly. "I promise you it wasn't any of us here." She held up her finger to tell Peter and Rob to wait. "You're free to come by and take a look anytime you want. Fine. Bye." She sighed heavily and turned to Peter and Rob. "How can I help you?"

"We're here on official business," Rob started.

"Are you the guy?" she asked eagerly, standing up.

Rob paused a moment. "I'm the guy," he said with a smile.

"Thank goodness," she breathed. "We're all wound up. Everyone dreads getting scheduled for this shift. And the night watchman is always quitting. We just want it to end."

Rob nodded and said, "Why don't you tell me the details again?"

"Nothing's new from when we talked over the phone. Room 210 has been empty for years. Any time they've had residents in there, the electronics go haywire, so it just stays empty. The PA system turns on randomly and you can hear someone whispering or breathing, but there's no one operating it. Then the phone issue." Her eyes got big.

"The phone?" Peter asked.

"The police often get a call from room 210, hearing screams. Almost every night, they call us asking about it."

"Is this the guy?" an older male nurse joined them.

"I'm the guy," Rob repeated with a smile.

The man shook Rob's hand. "I don't usually believe in stuff like this, but when it started affecting the residents..."

"How is it affecting the residents?" Rob asked.

"They complain about seeing and smelling things all the time," the man explained. "I'm not a man of superstition, but when one of them talks about seeing something in their room, it's not long after that that they usually die with no obvious cause. It's like they just waste away."

"How about you show me the room," Rob suggested.

They led Peter and Rob down the hallway.

"Any guess what it is?" Rob whispered to Peter on the way.

Peter thought back to his random readings in the book but gave up and shrugged his shoulders.

"Pishacha," Rob told him. "An energy vampire."

Peter didn't like the sound of that.

"He's going to catch you," a voice called out from a room.

Peter stopped and poked his head into the room. There was an old man slumped in a chair at a small table. His hands shook as he tried to put a puzzle piece in its spot. There were bags under his eyes.

"I was in 'Nam," he said, not looking at Peter. He spoke at an unbearably slow pace, "I had a mission to dismantle an anti-aircraft gun. We moved into the area, only to find an ambush waiting for us."

The man's slow speech had a draining effect on Peter. He was hoping for an opportunity to end the conversation politely, but he had a feeling that would be impossible.

"We were trapped," the man continued at a snail's pace. "It was brutal. Years of torture. The only thing that got me through it was thinking of my Dolores. I escaped years later and worked on farms and doing odd jobs until I got enough for a boat and hitchhiking. When I finally got back home, Dolores had no idea until I rang the doorbell. Should'a seen the look on her face." He smiled in reverie.

"Uh, that's a great story…" Peter started to interrupt.

"She never gave up on me, even when she heard I was trapped." He took a breath, but before Peter could interject, he continued. "I was lucky to get out. I felt like an animal when they caught me. Now he's going to catch you."

"Who's going to catch me?" Peter asked slowly. He leaned out of the room but saw no sign of Sensei or the nurses in the hallway.

"The one that smells like death," the old man answered. He sounded like he was in a trance or talking in his sleep. "He's going to eat me. He said he'll catch you, too."

A million shivers prickled Peter's skin. "Oh. Well, that's cool. Um, do you know where he is?"

"Yep," the man said plainly and then paused for an excruciating amount of time. Finally, he said, "He's right here." He nodded his head over his shoulder at the empty air.

Peter took an unconscious step back. "Oh. Interesting," he tried desperately to control his reaction. "So, I'm going to go get my sensei," he said. "I'll be right back."

He ran from the room, feeling like he couldn't get out fast enough. He turned the corner, but couldn't see Sensei anywhere. Luckily, there was a night guard walking the hallways. Peter was about to ask him if he had seen Sensei when the man pointed to a room: 210.

"Thanks."

Peter rushed into the room, only to find it empty. He turned to head out and the door slammed closed.

He tried the knob, but he was locked in. The lights flickered. The buttons on the empty bed lit up and beeped. The TV turned on and randomly flipped through the channels.

First, a news anchor reported, “A man trapped in his house by a devastating fire…”

The channel changed to some soap opera with a man explaining to his lover, “I just feel so trapped…”

Next was a sports commentary show, “He didn’t stand a chance. They had him cornered and trapped…”

The room had grown so cold that Peter could see his breath. He remembered how Sensei had often opened doors with his deva’s help and wondered if he could do the same.

He held his hand up to the door and pleaded, “Please help me.”

CLICK!

He could barely believe it. The door popped open. Peter stumbled into the hallway and straight into the guard from before. “Whoa,” he breathed. “You scared me. Did you hear…?”

Peter stopped himself when he looked at the guard’s face. It looked otherworldly. He could smell something that could only be described as the smell of death.

The guard howled. His mouth opened farther than a mouth should open. Its eyes glowed red and its veins glowed underneath the skin with the same color.

It grabbed Peter by the shoulders, digging sharp claws into his skin. Peter felt like something was sucking his energy away. He sliced knife hands to the spirit’s wrists, but his hands went straight through like he was slicing through smoke.

Please, he prayed again, thinking of whatever had helped him with the locked door. *Please help me!*

He latched onto the first chant he could remember and poured all his good intent into the words, “OM MANI PADME HUM...”

A fierce wind ripped through the hallway and the spirit’s grip loosened. Peter seized the opportunity. He escaped and rounded a corner. He opened the first door he could find, a supply closet, and hid behind a shelf of toilet paper to catch his breath.

Then his phone rang. Peter thought he had turned it on silent before coming into the nursing home. Conveniently, the call was from Sensei.

"Where are you?" Rob's voice asked when Peter answered.

"I'm in a storage closet or something," Peter panted. "The spirit was chasing me and I couldn't fight him."

"Of course not. You're weak."

Peter questioned if he had heard Sensei right. "Wait. What?"

"Like a little weak monkey yipping at a fierce dragon."

Peter hung up his phone immediately. He kicked himself for answering. He knew that they could mess with electronics, but he would have never guessed that they could make phone calls.

Suddenly, a smoky form materialized inside the door. It was a humanoid figure with black skin, and the same bulging red veins and glowing red eyes. The smell of death was so thick that Peter coughed, rasping for air.

He could feel his life force being drained out of him, like he was aging years in just one moment. His muscles weakened and he couldn't hold himself up.

Just as he was starting to panic, the door flew open. Peter saw the outline of a wave wash over the spirit as Sensei Rob's chanting filled the air, mixing with the sounds of the creature's screams.

"Thank god you came when you did," Peter breathed.

"What did I say about wandering off?" Sensei scolded him. "Do you have any idea what that spirit could've done to you?"

"I have a few ideas," Peter said sheepishly.

They walked back out into the hallway in silence. When Peter passed the old man's room, he found the man staring at him.

"You're not dead," the man assessed calmly.

"Yep. You should be safe now, too," Peter told the man.

"Martin," he introduced himself. "You should come visit sometime."

"Maybe." Peter nodded.

He was fairly sure that he never wanted to come back to this place again. He ran and caught up with Sensei Rob as they neared the front desk, where a man was arguing with the nurse.

"I'm the paranormal investigator!" the man told her.

"My brother," Rob greeted the man with a handshake. "Good to see you. I got it all sorted out. You should be free of all your problems," he told the nurse.

"How much do we owe you?" she asked.

"How much do you usually charge?" Rob asked the man.

"Uh… I don't really," the man explained, confused. "But if they want to give a donation…"

Rob turned to the nurse. "Send any donation you feel like to my associate here. Have a peaceful night."

They left the nurse and investigator in a stunned silence.

"You didn't want the money?" Peter asked him.

Rob shook his head. "I make the world a better place. Isn't that reward enough?"

"So, that was a 'pizza cha cha?'" Peter asked as they got in the car.

Rob laughed. "Pishacha. It's an energy vampire. Have you ever been around someone who just zaps all your energy? The pishacha can also lead people to insanity." Peter nodded. "All of which you would know if you had been reading that book I gave you," Rob added.

Peter forced a smile.

At home, Peter relived the memory of the mission. Between the incidents with the door and the gust of wind. He hoped that he was getting closer to meeting his deva and unlocking spiritual powers.

He decided to test it out and stopped in front of the back door in his kitchen. He held out his hand, concentrating. To his great disappointment, nothing happened.

"What are you doing?" his mom asked.

He turned and saw her at the fridge, getting a drink.

"Uhhh… apparently nothing," he responded dismally.

"Looks like you're trying to use superpowers," she mocked.

"Something like that," he admitted.

She regarded him and asked, "Are you on drugs?"

"Mom! I'm not on drugs."

Her eyes narrowed. "Your grades are up. You seem mellow all the time. You help with the chores and the cooking."

"I'm just doing meditation," he assured her.

"Is that what they call it?" she raised her eyebrows. "Because I need to start paying for it. Heck, I'll alert the news stations so all the parents can get this 'meditation' for their kids."

Chapter 21: Field Day

That night, Peter dreamt that he arrived at school to find Jeremy terrorizing Zahid. He rushed into the fight, shoving Jeremy aside.

"Stop picking on him," Peter warned.

"What are you gonna do about it?" Jeremy challenged.

Peter threw a punch at Jeremy's eye.

He stumbled and cursed. "You think you're so great?" Jeremy taunted.

Then Peter started wailing on Jeremy. Punch after punch, kick after kick, Jeremy had no time to react. When Peter paused, Jeremy was laying still and quiet.

"That's what I do to bullies," Peter told him.

Then, with no mercy in his heart, he bent down and gave one last punch to Jeremy's swollen and bloody face.

Peter jolted awake, breathing heavily. The dream reminded him of the one with the girl tied to the chair. He had the same feelings of guilt and shame. Even with someone as horrible as Jeremy, he knew he needed to have patience and compassion.

Then he remembered what day it was and sprang from his bed. The memory of the dream faded to excitement. For once, he couldn't wait to get to school.

"It's the best day of the whole year," Peter explained to Zahid while their class wandered out to the field. "No sitting in desks, no studying, no tests. You're going to love it." Zahid gave him an apprehensive look. "Well, I'm going to love it," he corrected.

Zahid sighed. "I imagine this is karma for always dragging you to the library."

He and Zahid were on the same team for the first event, which was Frisbee football. As they donned their jerseys, Zahid asked, "So what's the object of this game?"

"Try not to get tackled," Peter answered. "And get the Frisbee to the goal over there."

"Sounds simple enough." Then he spotted Jeremy on the other team and gulped. "Except for that part about not getting tackled."

"Jeremy?" Peter asked. "He's powerful, but he's big and slow. Anyway, just pass the Frisbee to me if you're worried. He'll charge whoever has it so he can draw attention to himself."

Peter lined up at the front, facing Jeremy head on.

"You're going down, Hunter," Jeremy intimidated.

"Down in history as a great athlete?" Peter quipped. "Thanks."

Jeremy twisted his face. "You are so weird."

"You mean different from you?" Peter returned. "Really, you're too kind."

"This is my game," Jeremy warned him through gritted teeth. "This is my field. And I will destroy you."

Peter smirked. "Good luck with that."

It didn't take long before Jeremy was eating his words. Peter's daily meditation routine had transformed his mind. His daily workouts had increased his muscle control. And his occasional exorcism excursions had trained him to stay calm under extreme mental pressure.

He jumped, dodged, and swerved with unmatched speed. At one point, he even sprang into a forward flip that sailed him right over Jeremy's head. He landed effortlessly behind Jeremy and ran to the goal posts before anyone could react.

In the end, Peter had drawn so much attention that all the students watching had started chanting his name.

Next was an obstacle course. Peter dazzled everyone again. His stamina and dexterity won him the record for the fastest time.

After that came water balloon dodgeball. Zahid and Peter stood next to each other on one side of the field.

"If I stand behind you, I should stay dry, right?" Zahid asked.

Peter pretended to be shocked. "Was that a compliment?"

Across the way, Jeremy and his friends were making threatening gestures at Peter.

"Actually, you might be safer getting as far away from me as you can," Peter suggested.

After only five minutes, everyone on Peter's team was out except for Peter. He stood alone with his last two balloons facing Jeremy and his friends who somehow each had five balloons.

They stared each other down for what seemed like a moment stopped in time. Then the attack started. They threw their balloons at a rapid rate. Peter zigged and zagged. All the while, he carefully cradled his last two balloons.

Then he thought of a plan. If he could time it just right, he could hit the boys just as they were throwing. They wouldn't have time to dodge.

He watched their arms for the moment when they were about to rise and snapped his arms, throwing his balloons before they could.

SKOOOSH! SKOOOSH!

He heard the sounds and prayed that they hit their targets while he dodged the two balloons that had been thrown at him. He saw the two boys trudge off to the sidelines and realized that the spectators were chanting his name again.

But now Peter had no ammunition. Across the field, Jeremy laughed while he weighed his last three balloons in his hands.

Then Peter's vision shifted all of a sudden like it had during his recent meditation. The air swirled in spiraling patterns. In a flash, Jeremy threw all three balloons in rapid succession.

Peter watched as the balloons tore through the stringy wind currents, pushing the air aside in beautiful, clean curves.

He dodged the first balloon, then the second. Then, moving with the wind, he cupped his hand behind the last balloon. He gently brought it with him as he turned around himself and flung it back.

SKOOOSH!

It hit Jeremy right in his little rectangular nose. He had been so shocked by Peter's moves that he hadn't tried to dodge or block.

The entire class exploded in a roar of wild cheers and rushed at Peter while he stared incredulously at his hands. He couldn't help but smile as everyone shouted praises and jostled him.

The final event of the day was a three-legged race. Peter started towards Zahid when Alicia grabbed his wrist.

"I was wondering if you'd be my partner for the race," she asked sweetly, hooking her sparkling hair behind an ear.

He figured he looked like an idiot just staring at her, but he couldn't make his mouth work.

"You know," she said, shyly averting her eyes, "it's only because I want to win."

Peter smiled. "You're just using me for my amazing skills?"

"Yes," she nodded. "No other reason."

They both laughed awkwardly.

"Okay, go ahead, use me," he agreed.

As the teacher tied their legs together, Peter avoided looking at Alicia. Instead, he looked down the line of competitors.

Zahid looked less than thrilled to be paired with Gina who was currently chatting his ear off. And Jeremy was glaring daggers at Peter. Peter smiled and waved cheerfully, which made Jeremy even angrier.

"So how do we make sure we win?" Alicia asked.

"I'll try to match you," Peter suggested. "So just go as fast as you want and I'll follow your lead."

"Sure," she bumped his shoulder. "But what about the race?"

Peter was shocked silent.

"You know, the finish line is over there," she giggled.

He must have been blushing. Either that or he was coming down with a fever. In the final moments before the whistle blew, she slipped her hand around his waist and held on. He thought his chest might explode as he did the same.

The whistle shocked him out of reverie and he focused on matching her pace. She wasn't going fast enough to win, but Peter didn't care. As far as he was concerned, he had already won.

Alicia, however, seemed to think differently. Jeremy and his partner had just passed them when she shouted, "Come on, Hunter! If we win this thing, I'll kiss you!"

Jeremy stumbled, nearly tripping, but righted himself and charged forward. Peter, however, did trip. If he had been on his own, he could have easily found his balance. But instead, he fell to the ground, taking her with him. She let out a startled scream and fell on top of him.

THUNK!

He hit the ground hard. He rubbed the back of his head and looked up at her face. It was so close to his that he felt paralyzed. He watched her in a shocked silence as she scowled at all the other teams.

"Man, we lost," she pouted.

She sat up and started untying their ankles with sharp, angry movements. Peter still couldn't make his mind or mouth work.

She glared at him and said, "It's all your fault."

She stood and huffed away. He scrambled to his feet.

"Hey, hold up!" he said, matching her fast pace. "You're really going to pin this on me? You said... *that*... and you expect me to keep my focus and not trip over myself?"

She faced him with her nose held high. "I don't remember saying anything. I'd probably remember if we had won."

"I won a lot of games today," he said. "It only seems fair that I should get… whatever that prize might've been."

She put her hands on her hips. Peter saw a blush in her cheeks and a smile trying to hide in her pout.

"Sad to say, that particular prize was for this race only," she told him. "You'll have to wait until next year's field day."

"Really?" he laughed. "You expect me to wait a whole year for another chance at this… mystery prize?"

"Those are the rules."

A whistle interrupted them as the teacher started wrapping up the field day events. Gina and Stacey stole Alicia away into the crowd as they filed back into the school. Peter tried to chase after her, but he wasn't able to catch up.

He looked for her at the end of the day, too, but she ran from the classroom before he had a chance to confront her.

He couldn't figure out if she was shy or if she regretted what she had said, but he was sure of one thing: he only had one more week to work up the courage to ask her out or he'd lose his chance over the summer.

Chapter 22: Dreams of Summer

Peter saw Alicia walking alone in the school hallway. He twirled in front of her, causing her to jump. His heart rate picked up as he braced himself for the question.

"Hey, Alicia," he greeted. "I was wondering if you'd be interested in catching a movie sometime. You know, just us."

Her face darkened. "Stay away from me," she rejected him.

"Whoa. What's this about?" he panicked. "I thought, um, I was getting the idea that you liked me."

Alicia scoffed. "I don't even want to talk to you."

She started to walk away, but he had to know what he had done wrong. He grabbed her hand and she turned to look at him.

"What?" she asked sharply.

He had to ask why she was mad. He had to beg her to forgive him. Instead, he threatened, "Don't walk away when I'm talking."

"Let go, Peter. You're hurting me," she complained.

He smirked. "Quit playing hard to get. I know you want me."

She struggled, but he only tightened his grip. The sight of her squirming made him laugh.

Then she glared at him. "You're nothing but a creep," she told him, "and I'd rather die than be touched by you."

The words hurt Peter to his core. He never wanted to hear those words from her. But instead of letting her go, instead of pleading for forgiveness, he slapped her.

Peter woke with a start.

He stared into the darkness, trying to gather his thoughts. He took deep breaths, attempting to calm his emotions. As long as he was in control of his actions, he'd never choose to treat anyone so cruelly. Especially not her.

So why do I still feel so disgusting?

For the last week of school, Peter avoided even making eye contact with Alicia. Anytime he saw her or heard her voice, he instantly remembered his dream.

Then, on the last day of school, while all the students were buzzing around the classroom signing each other's yearbook, she surprised him by sitting in the desk in front of him.

"Hey, Peter," she greeted.

"Ahh!" he leaned back quickly.

She giggled. "Whoa. You okay there?"

He stammered, "Yeah, sorry. I just, uh, I'm just a little jumpy."

"Okay," she laughed awkwardly. "Do you have any plans over the summer?"

"I have a martial arts competition," he responded quickly.

"Ooh. I bet you'll win."

"Let go, Peter. You're hurting me."

He shook his head to stop thinking about the dream.

She drummed her fingertips on his desk while she rested her chin in the other hand. "So, I think you're the only one who hasn't signed my yearbook yet," she hinted.

"Yeah?"

She blinked and asked emphatically, "Do you want to?"

He looked at her offering her yearbook with goading eyes. "Oh. Yeah, sure," he agreed.

He took the book from her.

"I don't even want to talk to you."

He tried to ignore the memory as he wrote quickly and slid the book back to her.

"'Have a great summer'?" she read with a disappointed tone. "Really? That's what you went with?"

He shrugged. "What did you want me to say?"

"Quit playing hard to get. I know you want me."

She laughed. "Maybe something that proves we know each other. Here, let me show you."

"I'd rather die than be touched by you!"

She reached out for his yearbook and her hand brushed against his. He jolted back.

"Are you okay?" she asked, worried.

"No," he admitted. "I mean yes. I'm just..."

He wanted nothing more than to bite the bullet and tell her that he liked her. He wanted to ask her out. He wanted to at least see her over the summer. But his dream made him worry about what the asuras could and would do to her. He could never live with himself if he caused her to suffer.

He shook his head. "I'm sorry Alicia. I just… can't."

Her face changed quickly, from confused, to hurt, then finally angry. She glared as she told him, "Well, if you decide to get over whatever this is, let me know."

She rose quickly and walked away.

"Hey, Harrison," she smiled and put her hand on his arm. "What are your plans over the summer?"

Peter dropped his head to his desk, feeling stupid.

Peter walked into the kitchen while his mom was making breakfast over the stove.

"Hey, sweetie. Did you sleep well?" she asked warmly.

"Mm-hm. Can I help with breakfast?" Peter offered.

"Of course." She made room and gave him the spatula for the pancakes while she moved on to another task. "So what would you like to do on your first day of summer vacation? Maybe we could do something together. There's always hiking or rock climbing. We could go on a picnic, or to a movie. There's that new superhero one that just came out. I know you probably think you're too old to go to a movie with your mom, but I still want to spend time with you."

Then, without warning, Peter picked up the frying pan and swung it at his mom's head. She reeled backwards, slamming against the wall and holding her head with a look of fear.

"Do you ever stop talking?" Peter barked. "It's like you just can't shut up." He pressed the hot pan against her and she screamed.

Peter caught his breath as he sprang up in his bed. He assured himself that he'd never do that to his worst enemy, but he still felt so disgusting.

He tried to forget the dream as he stumbled into the kitchen, but he stood still in the doorway when he saw her flipping pancakes.

"Hey, sweetie," she repeated her own greeting from the dream. "Did you sleep well?"

"Can I help?" he offered before he could stop himself.

"Of course," she smiled warmly and offered him the spatula.

He looked at the utensil as if it were an offer for his very soul.

"You take the pancakes," he said. "I'll set the table."

She turned back to the stove. While they worked, she gabbed almost non-stop. He vowed to let her talk as much as she wanted. He even feigned interest as convincingly as he could.

"Alright. What's the deal?" she slammed the spatula on the counter.

He turned slowly to face her. "Uhhh… What now?"

She narrowed her eyes. "You're not rolling your eyes or interrupting me. What's up?"

He shrugged. "I was just listening," he explained.

She laughed derisively. "Out with it. Did you break something? Steal money? You want me to buy you something expensive?"

"I was just thinking maybe we could do something fun," he said as he poured drinks. "Maybe a hike or a movie."

"Sure," she said slowly. "But after that, you'll tell me what you've done with my real son."

"So what's the lesson today?" Peter asked Sensei as he burst into the studio. "I'm ready for anything."

"Someone's eager," Charlie chuckled.

"I just want to keep improving," he explained. "I've given up TV, video games, apps, and junk food. I've been meditating half an hour and exercising every day. I've been doing chores and helping my friend's family get their restaurant ready for an opening. But I've still barely made any progress. So what's next?"

"Ice cream," Sensei Rob said simply. "We're going out for ice cream. Charlene, do you mind watching the place for a bit?"

She sat back in her chair and grumbled, "So Peter gets ice cream while I have to work? Which one of us are you dating?"

Rob kissed her cheek, "I'll take you somewhere special tonight," he promised.

Rob and Peter walked to the end of the strip mall to a small ice cream shop. They sat down with their cones on the bench outside.

“In this line of work,” Sensei explained, “you see a lot of darkness. So you need to find something positive and burn that memory into your brain to help you get through the dark moments. That’s why the ice cream.”

“I can appreciate that,” Peter said, thinking of his dreams. “But I want to make progress. I don’t want any negativity left inside me.”

“I’ve been there, too. I remember feeling impatient. But the eight-fold path is a life-long path. You’re not going to master it in a few months. And remember Right Effort? This,” he indicated his ice cream “is part of it. You have to put forth enough effort to make progress, but too much can wear you thin. Think of kata.”

Peter groaned. In karate, there was at least one kata for every belt, a routine combination of moves to be performed in an agonizingly slow motion.

“I hate kata,” he exhaled.

“I know you do,” Rob chuckled. “That’s because you always wear yourself out going all out. But with kata, you have to focus your energy to make it last throughout the whole movement. It’s the same with spiritual development. If you tire yourself out working too intensely, you risk losing your motivation.”

“So is my assignment more kata?” Peter asked. “I shouldn’t have said I hate it. I’ll go through all my forms every day.”

“Your assignment is to relax and eat some ice cream,” Rob corrected him. “So, how’s life?”

“Um, fine, I guess,” he answered half-heartedly. “No complaints, really. Except for not meeting my deva yet. You?”

Rob smiled uncontrollably, showing every one of his dimples. “I’m really happy lately.”

“No duh,” Peter smirked, knowing why he was happy. “Are you going to marry her?”

“Probably. I wouldn’t waste her time if I didn’t think I could marry her,” Rob answered seriously. “Anything happen with that girl you like?”

Peter shook his head. “I totally choked on asking her out before the summer,” he admitted. “Now I don’t even know if we’re even going to the same high school.”

“That’s rough. Have, uh,” Rob lowered his voice, “have the asuras started messing with you yet?”

Peter thought a moment, but he remembered that Sensei had said it would be obvious when they started their attack.

“I guess not,” he shrugged.

Chapter 23: Preta Sick Birthday

Peter saw his father sitting in front of his boss' desk at work.

"Sam," the boss overpronounced every consonant, "did you or did you not tell the client that the T920 wasn't ready yet?"

"Yes, sir," Peter's dad nodded calmly. "Because it isn't."

The boss rubbed his temples. "I've been on the phone all morning doing damage control. All because of your mess up."

Peter's dad remained calm, but looked worried. "With all due respect, the machine didn't pass the last test. If the customer bought it, they'd be disappointed."

"But you don't tell the customer that," the man explained like he was speaking to a child.

"I don't feel comfortable lying, sir," Peter's dad declared.

"That's what sales is. It's all about how you spin it."

"Our customers rely on my honesty. I have to live up to that."

"Then do it somewhere else," the boss said firmly. "Clear out your desk within the hour."

Peter's dad walked out awkwardly.

Then the boss turned to Peter and his face changed into different features. He had dark hair styled flawlessly, thick eyebrows, and a strong, cleft chin. His eyes were brown, but in them, Peter saw all the fierce power and hatred of an asura.

"Should I tell him?" the man asked. "That he's only suffering because of you."

Peter's eyes snapped open and he realized that he had fallen asleep in his room. He wiped the drool from his mouth.

These dreams need to stop, he tried to convince his subconscious.

He walked to the kitchen and froze when he saw his dad sitting at the table with his mom.

"Remember Ned who left the company last year?" he was saying. "He might know of some work for me."

"What's going on?" Peter asked anxiously.

"Nothing to worry about," his dad assured him. "Just hiccups at work. I'll be looking for a new job."

“The only problem,” his mom said, “is that we may need to cut back for a while.” She grimaced, bearing bad news. “And we might not be able to get you something big for your birthday.”

“Geez,” Peter said. “I don’t care about that. I don’t need any presents or a party.”

Peter’s dad held up his hand. “No, it’s your fourteenth birthday. We’ll still do something. You can even invite Zahid if you like. We may not be able to do something big, but we can still celebrate our amazing son who’s brought nothing but joy to our lives.”

Peter forced a smile, but heard an echo from his dream:

“...he’s only suffering because of you.”

Peter jumped in excitement as all the bowling pins crashed.

“Strike number five!” he praised himself.

“You’re smirking,” his mom complained.

Peter smirked wider as he took his seat and Zahid got up to bowl.

Mr. Hunter threw his arm around Mrs. Hunter and said, “Aw, honey, it doesn’t matter who wins this game. As long as I have you, I’m the real winner.” Then he kissed her.

“Geez, I’m sitting right here!” Peter reminded them.

A new song started playing on the speakers and his mom clapped her hands in excitement. “Oh! I love this one!” she exclaimed. “Remember it was playing when we were dating and we went to that shady biker bar?”

Mr. Hunter chuckled. “Why did you ever choose that place?”

“I didn’t choose it!” she argued. “You did.”

He stood up and offered her his hand. She rose and they started dancing, right there for the entire bowling alley to see.

Peter was mortified.

“My parents do that, too,” Zahid said as he sat back down. “Though not in public.”

“And on my birthday!” Peter commiserated. He looked at the screen to see how Zahid had done. “Hey, pretty good for never bowling before.”

“I think we’d still be winning even if I were bowling… what do they call them? Gutter balls? Oh, here.” He handed Peter two boxes. “This is a gift from my whole family.”

Peter opened the small box and found a ring of wooden beads.

"These are prayer beads from our religion," Zahid explained. "My mom saw yours and thought you may need another strand. I told her you didn't. But she insisted."

Peter inspected them. He thought it was cool that other religions had prayer beads, too. "Thanks. And what are these?" He picked up the bigger box and opened it.

"Barazeh. They're sesame seed and pistachio cookies."

Peter didn't like the description, but he took a bite and was pleasantly surprised.

"Geez! Your parents can cook. Thanks, man." Then Peter noticed Zahid staring at the kid in the next lane. "You keep looking over at that guy. Everything okay?"

"Yeah, it's just…" Zahid tried to dismiss it, then looked at Peter pensively. "Promise you won't think worse of me?"

"Of course not."

Zahid whispered, "He has teeth like Gina."

Peter looked at the boy. "You mean the braces?"

"Is that what they're called?"

Peter smiled. "You've never seen braces before?"

Zahid shrugged. "Is it a serious condition?"

Peter laughed. "They're for straightening teeth. They didn't have braces in Syria?"

Zahid looked relieved. "I thought she was a cyborg!"

Peter doubled over laughing.

"It's the Hunters," a familiar voice interrupted them.

Peter turned to see Sensei Rob and Charlie.

"What are you guys doing here?" Peter asked. "Zahid, these are my karate teachers, Rob and Charlie."

"Hey, why don't you join us?" Mrs. Hunter offered eagerly. "Unless you wanted to be alone," she sang.

"I think it'd be fun," Charlie nodded. Then she turned to Rob. "What do you say?"

Rob pretended to consider. "I say someone has to take Peter down."

"You think you can?" Peter goaded. "Check out that score."

Rob's eyes narrowed. "Kid, I've been bowling since before you were born. I'm going to wipe that smirk off your face."

"Do I really smirk that much?" Peter complained.

"All the time," Zahid rolled his eyes.

They started a new game, though no one seemed to be taking it seriously. Charlie and Peter's mom talked up a storm and Rob and Mr. Hunter enjoyed their own quiet conversation.

Then, all of a sudden, Rob shivered and looked at Peter. "I'm going to get some snacks, want to come with me?"

"Sure," Peter said as he stood. "Gotta warn you though, the nachos here are disgusting. I think it's just melted plastic instead of cheese."

As they walked towards the snack counter, Rob said in a hush, "You know this isn't about snacks, right? I wasn't sure if you told your parents about being my apprentice yet."

Rob pointed and Peter saw the man behind the register pouring cheese sauce into a plastic cup and drinking it.

"Gross," Peter gagged. "I mean, that's *preta* sick." He smiled wide and Sensei Rob shook his head at the pun. "I mean, I'm guessing it's a preta," Peter recovered. "That's about the only way I'd eat that stuff."

The man started lapping the "cheese" sauce directly from the dispenser.

"And what chant would you choose?" Rob tested him.

Peter controlled his reaction to the man's choice of food and responded, "I'd choose a simple one like om mani padme hum."

Rob smiled. "Good choice."

Together, they started chanting while counting on their malas. The man turned and looked mortally offended. He opened his orange-covered mouth and fire shot out.

Sensei Rob swept his arms through the air. Peter could see the green outline of a wave that extinguished the fire and knocked the man off his feet. Sensei leapt over the counter and quickly held his hand against the man's forehead.

"Be washed clean," he declared.

As Peter continued chanting, he saw –for the first time– a dark smoky form peel away from the man. It took a shape, sitting on the counter like some half-human, half-frog creature.

It took all his concentration to keep chanting.

Sensei Rob thrust his hand out like a punch and Peter saw a stream of water hit the preta and knock it off the counter. It landed right in front of Peter. He forced himself to resist flinching. The creature looked up at him and Peter felt a chill. Its eyes were so full of anger and desperation.

A thin whip of water wrapped around its form and it was yanked towards Sensei Rob. Then the spirit was encased in a bubble of water and Peter watched as its form dissolved.

The water bubble burst into nothingness and Peter looked at his Sensei. When he blinked, he saw a flash of a green human-like form standing next to Sensei. In a moment, it was gone.

Then, Peter became aware of the outline of a form, glowing in a cool and calming blue, standing right beside him. In a moment, it was gone as well. He blinked.

Then Rob reached over the counter, picked out a candy bar, and put exact change next to the register. “Here,” he said as he handed the chocolate bar to Peter. “If I had known, I would’ve gotten you something bigger, but this’ll have to do. Happy Birthday, kid.”

Peter looked at the candy bar and back up at Sensei.

“I’ll cherish it forever,” Peter said sarcastically. “Or maybe for five minutes.” He took a bite. “Yep, here’s me cherishing.”

Chapter 24: Mr. Monster Matthews

That evening, Peter opened the front door, responding to the doorbell, and nearly jumped when he saw Alicia on his front steps. Butterflies exploded in his stomach.

She was holding a cupcake with a candle in it.

"I heard it was your birthday," she said with a smile.

"So is this my present?" he asked.

She wrinkled her nose. "No, this is just a cupcake. I had another present in mind for you."

She leaned in over the cupcake and kissed him. His heart pounded.

Then his smile turned into a sneer. "You really think I wanted that?" he mocked. "From you?"

He grabbed the cupcake and threw it on the ground.

"Hey!" she complained.

He gave her a slap. "Why would I want to kiss your ugly face?"

Peter woke with a start at the front desk of the dojo. He hadn't realized that he had fallen asleep. And now he wished he hadn't. He didn't understand how he could be dreaming such horrible things.

Then Rob emerged from the office with an eager smile. "Who's ready to fight an invisible spirit of unspeakable evil?" he asked cheerily.

"Me!" Peter jumped up.

Maybe fighting a monster would help him feel less like one.

They arrived in the backyard of a suburban house and looked through the window where a muscular man with a small nose was yelling at his wife. They looked familiar, but Peter couldn't remember who they were.

"Medium well?" the man bellowed. "I said medium rare!"

"I'm sorry," the woman quivered. "I'll get it right next time."

"I should kick you out," the man threatened, "so you can overcook someone else's dinner!"

"He's mad because she slightly overcooked food?" Peter whispered.

This is the perfect mission, he thought.

This man was worse than his dream-self.

"Wait," he noticed a dark sheen around the man and the woman. It was like the opposite of glowing. He had never seen it before, but he knew what it meant. "She's possessed, too?" he asked. Rob nodded. "If they're both possessed, why aren't they working together?"

"Technically, they are," Rob responded. "Remember, they want to drive us apart and make us hate each other. The only problem is that we're here for the wife and *not* the husband."

"So what do we do?" Peter asked.

The man yanked a toaster from the wall and threw it at the woman. She cried out as it hit her. Then she started convulsing.

"No time," Sensei said quickly. "Chant, and don't wander off."

The woman started laughing as she picked up a large knife from the countertop. Rob held his hand towards the back door and it flew open. He conjured a wave that knocked both the husband and wife backwards.

Peter stood in the doorway and chanted.

The woman held her hand towards a chair and it was hurled at Sensei. It broke as it hit him and left a gash on his arm.

Then she threw her knife. He deflected it with celestial water and it hit the man's shoulder. Peter jumped and expected the man to react. Instead, he calmly pulled it out.

The husband started stalking towards Peter while Sensei Rob was distracted by the wife. Peter backed up into the yard.

The man lunged with the knife, throwing a straight thrust at Peter's gut. Peter caught the man's arm and twisted it behind his back, peeling the fingers and stealing the knife.

"I'm warning you, get out of this man," Peter threatened.

The asura twisted, bending his arm unnaturally, and placed a hand on Peter's chest. Peter was repelled by an invisible force. He stumbled and fell on his back. He lost the knife in a bush.

"A monster threatens a monster?" the asura laughed.

"What?" Peter reacted, trying to get up.

But the asura pressed a foot into Peter's throat and taunted, *"You and this human, you're exactly the same."*

Peter felt a rush of emotions. "I'm nothing like him."

"We know you've had dark thoughts and dreams. You're destined to be like this man here. Why fight? Destiny is inevitable. Don't you want to have power? Power over that stupid bully at school? Power over that attractive blonde girl? You want to dominate her, don't you?"

No, Peter reassured himself. *I would never do those things.*

SHWOOORSH!

A curl of green water wrapped around the man and pinned his arms to his sides.

"Oh, darn," the spirit said sarcastically.

Sensei's whirlpool suspended the man in the air, while the asura snarled and roared. Peter pulled himself up quickly.

"Stay with him and chant for a while," Rob told Peter as he started for the house. "I think the wife is waking up."

He went inside. Through the open windows, Peter saw him help the woman stand.

Peter looked at the possessed man, just a few feet away and only separated by a nearly invisible swirl of water.

He gulped, but chanted, "OM MANI PADME HUM."

The man spat insults and threats at Peter, but he kept his focus on the chant. He glanced inside to see how Rob was doing.

The wife looked around at her kitchen and started crying. Sensei handed her a business card from his wallet.

"Here. This place can help you," he told her.

She shook her head. "I can't. He needs me."

"He needs you to teach him that people shouldn't be treated this way," Rob said firmly.

"But I have sons…" She covered her mouth to hide a sob.

Peter realized then how he recognized her. It was Jeremy's mom.

This explains everything, he thought.

Peter thought of all the people Jeremy had hurt and how it could all be blamed on the man trapped behind him. Mr. Matthews was a poison, infecting the world.

"The shelter will help you find a way to help your sons, too," Rob told Mrs. Matthews. "But you should go quickly."

"Thank you," she said through her tears.

She rushed out the front door and Mr. Matthews fell limp in the whirlpool of water. Sensei came out and cautiously pulled the water away.

"Be careful," he told Peter. "Either the man regained consciousness or the asura is only tricking us."

Mr. Matthews started stirring. "Marianne?" he asked as he pulled himself off the ground.

He held his head, wincing in pain as he stumbled around the backyard.

“I don’t get it,” Peter whispered. “Aren’t people usually better and happy when they get free?”

“He’s not free,” Rob answered in a hush. “The asura is only sleeping or hiding.”

“Where’s my wife?” Mr. Matthews asked, spotting Rob and Peter.

“She’s safe now,” Peter said, trying in vain to hide his disgust.

“She… she left?” he asked. Then he turned angry. “Did you do this?”

“Geez, get your act together.” Peter lectured. “None of this would’ve happened if you had just…”

“PETER!” Sensei Rob snapped, causing Peter to jump. “Go. Wait. For. Me.” He sternly pointed toward a tree a few yards away.

Peter hesitated a moment, feeling like a kid in trouble, then trudged off angrily and stood by the tree.

Why am I getting yelled at? he wondered as Sensei spoke softly to the man. *Even if I was maybe rude, I wasn’t as rude as, say, trying to beat your wife over food!*

After a few minutes, Jeremy’s dad threatened Sensei Rob and stormed into the house. Rob sighed heavily and came over to Peter. Then his face turned into a glare as his eyes met Peter’s. “Back to the dojo,” Sensei ordered fiercely.

He slapped Peter on the shoulder and they traveled quickly through a blurred scene until they came to a stop inside the studio.

“What?” Peter asked defiantly. “What’s your deal?”

“*My* deal?” Rob turned quickly to face Peter. “What’s *my* deal? Peter, the second you judge and start thinking you’re better than the victim is the second you become just like the asuras.”

“I was giving him a lecture!” Peter retaliated. “He was trying to beat his wife because she cooked the meat a little longer than he wanted!”

“Yes, his choices were regrettable,” Sensei conceded.

“‘Regrettable’?” Peter scoffed.

“Have you never made a bad choice before? Have you never been accused and yelled at because of a stupid mistake?”

“What? Like now?”

Sensei took a few breaths and softened his mannerisms. “You’re right,” he admitted. “I’m too angry to get into this right now. Go home. We will continue this discussion when I’ve calmed down.”

Rob turned sharply towards the office and Peter used his thickest sarcasm to say, “Okay, *dad*,” before grabbing his bag and storming out.

Chapter 25: Sensei's Confession

Peter didn't want to go to his karate class the next day, but he didn't know how to tell his mom: "Sensei's mad at me because I was judgmental with an abusive husband possessed by an asura, –a spirit of hatred and evil– that, hey, we happen to fight in our free time." So he went.

As soon as everyone from the previous class had cleared out, Rob and Peter stared each other down.

"So are we gonna talk now?" Peter challenged him.

Sensei Rob glowered. "You have this tone when you talk…"

"Now you sound like my mom."

"Just be quiet for one minute, would ya?" Rob gritted his teeth.

He pointed to the benches by the door and they both sat. Rob stared into the empty space of the dojo and they passed a few moments in a tense silence.

"So here's the deal," Rob said at last. "We don't know for sure what leads to possession. I can tell you what things open the door for a dark spirit and what things close a door. But you can't say, 'do a, b, and c and you'll get possessed' or even, 'do x, y, and z and you'll never get possessed.' It's a muddled, complicated existence we have."

"So?" Peter argued. "What that guy did was still wrong."

"Of course," Rob agreed. "But it's the action we judge, not the victim. When I see a victim's pain, anger, or hatred, I hurt with them because I'm reminded of all my own faults and weaknesses. And a great way to ignore that pain is to accuse; to start thinking that somehow I'm better than them. But that's just not true."

Peter thought of all the times he had seen Jeremy as the enemy when, he knew now, Jeremy had only been taught anger and abuse. Maybe Mr. Matthews had never been taught differently either.

And he had to admit that he had probably been so angry with Jeremy's dad because he wanted to ignore the feelings and thoughts his dreams had been conjuring.

Rob continued. "And the Buddha said, *'Conquer anger with non-anger. Conquer badness with goodness.'* In other words, anger and yelling will only add fuel to the fire; they won't extinguish it."

"Yelling and anger won't fix anything, huh?" Peter volleyed.

Sensei glared, then softened his features with a sigh. "I'm sorry I got mad at you," he said sincerely. "I should've been more patient. The truth is," he paused, "this is a touchy subject for me."

"What do you mean?" Peter asked.

Sensei Rob slouched over his knees and stared at the floor. "Remember how I said I randomly met Yeshe, my mentor, when he was exorcising *someone*?"

"No…" Peter said when he realized. "You?"

Rob nodded. "I was meditating a lot and, like I told you, once you open up to the spirits, you can meet the wrong kind of spirit."

"But you've always been a nice guy," Peter said.

Sensei chuckled. "The asuras aren't going to come up to you and say, 'hey kid, I'm a spirit of unimaginable evil. Wanna let me take over your body and wreak havoc on your life?' Instead, they're going to promise you everything you ever wanted. This particular spirit said it was my spirit guide, or deva, and it wanted to help me reach enlightenment. It wanted to reveal the secrets of the universe to me.

"Once I let it in, it even gave me powers. I thought I was special, magical. But then it started attacking me, like they did here. It started tempting me to break from the path of enlightenment, telling me that there was no right or wrong. It took over my body whenever it wanted, too. I had no idea how to save myself. If not for Yeshe, I'd probably still be possessed or worse."

"What was it like?" Peter asked softly.

"You know when you have dreams where you're running through water? It's similar to that kind of feeling of powerlessness. Sometimes you black out and have no idea what you did. Sometimes you're completely conscious and you can only watch as someone controls all your words and movements."

Peter could barely handle the nightmares and wondered how someone could endure that torture all day long. He felt a pit in his stomach, identifying too strongly with Sensei's description.

"I'm sorry," he told Rob. "I didn't know."

"I hope you never have to know. I don't wish it on my worst enemy. So that's the deal. These things are monsters and every human victim deserves our sympathy and our help, not our judgment. It's easy to look at a victim and think that it's their fault for making the choices they did. And it's more difficult to accept the truth: that we can all become victims of the dark spirits' tricks and our own dark desires."

Peter sighed and said, "I wish I could go back to when I didn't believe in spirits. They're worse than nightmares."

"Speaking of nightmares," Rob said, "apparently your deva told mine that you've been having some. Why didn't you tell me?"

Peter's head snapped up. "Whoa, how'd it know?" he asked. "I thought it was just the exorcist stuff seeping into my dreams."

"Maybe," Rob considered it. "But remember how the asuras can whisper into our thoughts? They can do the same when we're sleeping and our defenses are down."

Peter felt a shudder when he thought of evil spirits hanging out in his room and whispering in his ear while he slept.

"So do you want to talk about the dreams?" Rob asked.

"Not at all." Peter shook his head.

"Scary monsters?"

"Me," he confessed. "It's always me doing things I would never do in a million years. Please don't make me say more."

Rob thought a moment. "It's actually a good sign, if you think of it. Your resolve is too good for them to mess with your choices, so they have to try a different method. You didn't perform those actions, but it feels like you did. You get the illusion of negative karma."

"Can I stop it?" Peter asked desperately.

"Perhaps." Sensei grasped his chin while he thought. "This might just be how they attack you all through your life. But you could also try doing Tonglen."

"What's Tonglen?" Peter asked.

"It's a special discipline that many Buddhists swear by and it's very simple. As you breathe in, you imagine taking all the suffering from a specific person onto yourself. And as you breathe out, you focus on all the blessings you want for them."

"You think that would help get rid of the dreams?" Peter asked hopefully.

"Possibly. You'd be amazed by the life-changing power of loving-kindness."

Peter eyed him skeptically. "You realize you sound like a fairytale princess, right?"

That night, Peter practiced Tonglen for the Matthews family, including Jeremy. As he breathed in, he thought of all the sadness and pain that must be fueling their anger. And as he breathed out, he thought of all the virtue and love that he wished for them.

The most remarkable effect was the immense peace that washed over him. Before long, he slipped into a tranquil slumber. There were dreams, but nothing haunting.

The only disturbing dream he had was of riding a sparkly unicorn, but no one was hurt.

A few evenings later, Rob took Peter to a nearby bridge road, where they saw a man standing on a rung of the railing, leaning over at this waist. As they approached, Peter realized it was Mr. Matthews, still possessed.

"Sir?" Sensei called his attention calmly.

Peter could see the dark outline around him, but it seemed to vibrate in dissonance. He felt a tug at his gut, telling him that Mr. Matthews wanted to be free.

The asura put on a good show, however.

"You again!" Mr. Matthews thundered. "I should've known you'd be back. It wasn't enough that you ruined my life? You had to come and watch it end."

"I'm here to help," Sensei said earnestly.

"Like you helped my wife?" Mr. Matthews snapped. "And convinced her to abandon her family?"

Peter was amazed at how the Tonglen had transformed his thoughts. As he watched Mr. Matthews, raging at Sensei, he only felt compassion. He realized that the asuras had accomplished exactly what they wanted: to make Mr. Matthews and his whole family miserable.

"We only want you to help you find true happiness," Sensei Rob said.

He held out his hand for Mr. Matthews, but the man shook as if he were being electrocuted. Then his body rose from the railing, hovering in the air. Peter saw dark currents of wind spiraling underneath him, holding him up off the ground.

"You can't have this one," the asura said in a gravelly voice. *"He belongs to us. His death will be our entertainment and then we will work on his sons!"*

Peter thought Jeremy was in bad enough shape already, without the asura's help.

A sudden wind whipped around them and Sensei started to chant. Peter jumped when he saw a huge geyser shoot up from the river below the bridge. The water and Sensei were glowing green.

Mr. Matthews, still floating, darted towards Sensei with a snarling expression. Sensei waved his hand across his chest, as if pushing something aside, and the geyser changed direction. Mr. Matthews dodged midair and Sensei redirected the water again.

This time, it was stopped by an invisible wall of wind in front of Mr. Matthews. The asura let out a strange mix of growls and laughter as the water splayed out in all directions. Before Sensei could adjust his plan of action, the asura grabbed his hand.

CRACK!

The asura snapped Rob's hand sideways. Peter gasped when he heard the noise.

The geyser collapsed, but Sensei continued chanting through his clenched teeth. Peter saw swirling rotations in the wind patterns beneath Sensei's feet that propelled him upwards. It was the same dark wind he had seen underneath Mr. Matthews. Then the asura tossed Rob to the side and over the rail.

Peter watched in horror as Sensei plummeted down into the water below. "No!" he screamed.

Chapter 26: Boy Meets Deva

Peter ran to the railing and saw the evidence of the splash.

The asura laughed. *"You look sad, little monkey,"* it mocked. *"How about I send you to where he is?"*

Peter saw the same dark wind start to spiral beneath his own feet. He jumped back.

The asura moved Mr. Matthews' hands sideways through the air, sending a slice of dark wind at Peter. He dodged.

"So you can move quickly," the asura growled. *"But you can't dodge everything."*

It made an unusual motion with Mr. Matthew's hand, jerking it upwards from the elbow. Peter wondered at it for a split second until he felt the changes in the wind from behind him.

He ducked quickly and avoided the hit.

"You need to leave this man," Peter tried to argue. "His sons need him. They don't deserve what you're doing to them."

"Are you really trying to appeal to my sympathy?" the asura laughed again. Then Mr. Matthews' face darkened. *"I have none!"*

The asura crossed Mr. Matthews' arms then uncrossed them. The movement sliced sharp streams of currents in Peter's direction. He leapt into the air, rotating above the attack in a sideways flip, and landed easily on the pavement.

He felt a surge of victorious adrenaline. He had flipped before, but he had never felt this rush, speed, or height. He realized that he could see the wind currents like he had on field day. He wondered if he could control them, too, like the asura.

He imitated the same move with crossed arms and imagined gathering the wind currents like strings around his fingers. Then he whipped them out. Streams of blue and white sliced through the air in crisscrossing arcs.

The wind hit the asura and Mr. Matthews' body dropped to the ground, landing on a knee.

Peter then touched Mr. Matthews' head and, on instinct, said, "Be swept clean."

A massive gust of wind battered them from all sides and dark smoke exploded from Mr. Matthews, rendering him unconscious.

The asura formed into a giant horse in front of Peter. It towered over him with glowing red eyes. It was made of smoke, but as it stomped on the pavement, it left a giant pothole with a series of cracks.

All of Peter's confidence was suddenly sucked out of him. The horse-asura reared on its hind legs with a terrifying whinny.

Before its hooves came crashing down, Peter stumbled backwards and landed on his rear. The horse lifted again and Peter rolled out of the way and onto his feet. Then he tore into a sprint.

He felt sudden changes in the currents behind him, by his left shoulder. He spun to the right, just missing the giant teeth that almost snapped into him.

He turned sharply and ran underneath the horse-asura in the opposite direction, back to where he had started. He thought he could gain a few moments as the asura adjusted, but after a few paces, the asura materialized in front of him.

He stood stark still, staring into its eyes, full of hatred for hatred's sake. He resorted to the last thing he could think of as the creature grunted and picked at the ground.

If my deva is listening, he pleaded in his thoughts, *if you're here, please help!*

Suddenly, he was filled with a surge of energy and felt at one with the wind. In an instant, he knew the speed, the direction, and the formation of the air currents all around him. And he knew how to control them.

Peter punched the air and the currents formed a battering ram that slammed into his opponent. He raised his arms at the elbows, and the horse-asura rose into the air.

Peter gathered the wind with his hands and wrapped it around himself in a circle. Then he blasted it at the asura and its form scattered and disappeared.

Peter slowly lowered his arms and took in the quiet night. Mr. Matthews was still passed out a few yards away and a single car turned onto the road and Peter jumped to the sidewalk, out of the way. The car passed over the bridge and drove off.

Peter felt like he should have been exhausted, but instead, he was energized. He felt like he could run a marathon. He felt like screaming out in victory. He felt like he could fly.

He had a reeling sensation, like his feet were glued to the earth but his body was pulling into the sky. It was almost like he could feel the sensations of gravity and the rotation of the earth.

Then, he became aware of an apparition, floating in the air before him. The creature looked like a human, but a transparent, glowing human. The creature's hair and clothes looked like they were made of stringy air currents, billowing in wind. Its face was smooth and graceful, but Peter couldn't tell if it was a woman or a man.

Its power radiated outward and swirled around Peter, drawing him in. But he wasn't afraid. He felt a familiar sensation. He remembered the vision in the haunted house. He remembered the currents he saw on field day. He remembered the wind that saved him from the pishacha.

"Do not be afraid, Peter Hunter," the creature spoke. Its voice sounded like the whispers of the wind. *"You may call me Anuvata. You have grown strong and kind. I offer you a partnership. If you accept, we will work together to help many people in dire need."*

"So you're going to talk to me now instead of tattling to Sensei?" Peter asked. It slipped out before he could stop himself. He prayed the deva would not strike him dead.

To his relief, the spirit smiled. *"I will speak with you from now on. That is,"* its eyes narrowed, *"as long as you are listening properly."*

Peter gulped. "Oh. I'm not always good at that," he admitted.

The spirit smiled again. *"Don't worry, we have many other things to work on as well. Your sensei will be returning shortly. We will speak again soon. I am always with you."*

Then the deva faded just as Sensei Rob came blasting out of the river with a battle cry and a cyclone of water propelling him upwards. He landed powerfully on his feet, shaking the bridge, as water splashed all around him. It all looked very powerful and dramatic.

Peter quickly leaned with his back and elbows resting on the bridge's railing. He adopted a relaxed and nonplussed expression.

"There you are," Peter greeted. "I was starting to worry. Luckily, my deva and I had no trouble cleaning up your mess."

"Uh. Wait. Your…" Sensei looked all around, studying the scene and holding his injured hand.

"I can only imagine what you're going through right now," Peter said with contrived compassion. "You've been doing this for so long and then this young sarcastic hero comes along, only training for the better half of a year, only met his deva just tonight, and he's the one to save the day while you were licking your wounds under water somewhere. I mean, that has got to be a blow to the ego."

Sensei's eyes narrowed, then he smiled and jostled Peter by the shoulder. "If I weren't so proud of you, I'd toss you in the river. Let's get back to the studio. I want a play by play. Tell me everything."

"Okay. But first, how was your little swim? Refreshing?"

When they got back to the dojo, Peter's adrenaline had him almost hopping. "Now that I have my powers, and they aren't flower-sparkle powers, are we going to spar? Air versus water!"

"That would be fun," Sensei laughed, "but no. These powers are not ours, but the devas'. They're on loan to us to use solely for the protection of the asuras' victims. They're not for our own benefit."

"But don't we need to practice them? Hone our skills?"

Rob shook his head. "The devas' powers don't need honing. Only our compatibility with them."

"Does that mean more meditating?" Peter asked, disappointed.

"And the eight-fold path and accumulating good karma."

"That's not like any superhero story I know," Peter grumbled.

"That's because we aren't superheroes, kid. We're exorcists."

Charlie came out of the office with an excited expression. "Did Peter meet his guardian spirit?" she asked eagerly. "How exciting! We should celebrate! Robby, why are you wet?"

"He took a swim while I saved the day," Peter bragged. "Can we get a cake? I really want a cake."

"Cake it is!" Charlie laughed. "So tell me. What was it like?"

"It was awesome!" Peter exclaimed. "I mean, I felt like all my senses were heightened. And I still feel so energetic, like I could do anything! There's just so much energy! I bet I could stay up for three days straight!"

Then he passed out.

When he started to stir, he was aware of Rob and Charlie sitting next to him on the benches. He couldn't open his eyes. His whole body felt lighter than air, but he couldn't move it.

"He's so cute when he's sleeping," Charlie said.

"But I'm cuter, right?" Rob countered.

She laughed. "Of course. It's just that sometimes I feel like he's our little guy." She smoothed Peter's hair back. "Like the studio mascot."

"Yeah. Like a monkey or something," Rob agreed.

Peter didn't know how he felt about being compared to a monkey twice in one night.

"Is he going to be alright?" Charlie asked.

"Yeah, this is just his system adjusting to the positivity of the deva," Rob explained. "The first time I met mine, the world became polarized. It was like coming inside after being in the bright sun and everything looks darker. Anything positive was beautiful and amazing and anything even slightly negative was just depressing. I saw a mom scolding her child for running in the street and I started sobbing." Charlie laughed. "You even out after the initial shock, though. The best part is: the more you interact with the deva, the easier it is to be virtuous."

"Does this mean he's reached enlightenment?" she asked in awe. "Have you reached enlightenment?"

"No. Just means that we're closer than we were before."

Peter passed out again.

Chapter 27: Claiming the City

A few days later, Sensei Rob took Peter to the top of one of the tallest hills in the city. They sat on the ground and Sensei placed a book of chants and a bowl with a hammer in between them both.

Then Peter read a discourse:

"'Whatever beings are assembled here, terrestrial or celestial, may they all have peace of mind, and may they listen attentively to these words. O beings, listen closely.'"

As he read, Sensei grazed the hammer on the edge of the empty bowl. It rang like a bell. The vibrations empowered Peter's reading.

He tuned in to all the wind that swept through the city. He could feel the innumerable asuras, rakshasas, pretas, pishachas, and various other spirits that tormented the people on every street.

He envisioned all their negativity as a gray-black smoke that peeled away from the humans below and traveled, swept by the wind, to their hill. In his mind's eye, he saw the smoke rise and dissipate into the atmosphere.

"'Whatever beings are assembled here, terrestrial or celestial, come let us salute the Buddha, the perfect one, honored by gods and men. May there be happiness. Come let us salute the perfect Dharma, the teaching honored by gods and men. May there be happiness. Come let us salute the perfect Sangha, the holy community honored by gods and men. May there be happiness.'"

Then Sensei nodded and turned the pages of the book.

"I will abstain from killing," Peter recited. "I will abstain from stealing…"

One by one, he took the vows the Buddha had instructed for his followers. Peter laughed to himself when he remembered that when Sensei had first started teaching him about the eightfold path, he had proclaimed that he would never be a monk. Now he took the vows and agreed with them whole-heartedly.

He finished with a prayer, "May I become at all times a protector for those without protection. A guide for those who have lost their way. A ship for those with oceans to cross. A bridge for those with rivers to cross. A sanctuary for those in danger. A lamp for those without light. A place of refuge for those who lack shelter. And a servant to all in need."

"Peter Hunter," Sensei said seriously, "you have now taken upon yourself the responsibility to protect the people of this city." Sensei placed one hand with his fingertips just touching the earth and the other hand with the palm facing Peter. Then he recited a blessing:

"May you be filled with loving-kindness. May you be safe from inner and outer dangers. May you be healthy in body and mind. May you find peace and be truly happy." Then Sensei Rob smiled. "Welcome to the front lines, kid," he said. "Get ready for your life to get a whole lot better. And a whole lot worse."

A week later, Peter, Rob, Charlie, and a few other representatives from the studio met at a convention center downtown for the city Tae Kwon Do competition. As Rob gathered the younger kids around for a last minute pep talk, Peter found a quiet spot to meditate. Almost immediately, he felt a wave of peace rush over him.

He saw his vision swell and swirl. He waited eagerly to hear some word of wisdom from Anuvata. He had meditated many times after their initial meeting, but had not heard or seen the spirit since.

"I may not listen well," he told the spirit within his mind, *"but if there's anything you want to tell me, I'm here."*

Then he felt a tug at his gut and couldn't stop thinking of Sensei Charlie. He looked around for her and recalled that she had left for the restroom long before he had started his meditation.

He rose and asked Sensei Rob where she was.

"Hm," Rob looked around. "She should have been back by now. Why do you…" he stopped and became very serious. He looked at his bandaged hand, then grabbed Peter's arm with his good hand. "I have to stay with the kids. Please go look for her. If anything happens…"

"I'll do what I can," he assured Rob before rushing off.

Peter ran to the lobby area and searched the crowd for any sign of Sensei Charlie. He looked over a banister down to the lower level and spotted her standing against a column with a young female competitor.

The young girl, who happened to have a very dark aura, was trembling as Charlie attempted to persuade her to drink some water.

Peter could tell that the girl didn't want to be exorcised. He wasn't sure what to do, but he started down the stairs.

"What you're doing is harming your body," Sensei Charlie told her.

The girl shook her head. "No, I'm fat. I need to lose more."

Charlie put a hand on the girl's shoulder. "If you don't eat and drink, your body will eat away at the muscles you've worked so hard to build up. You can't let all your effort go to waste. Especially when we still have a lot of discrimination to fight against in this sport. Think of all the girls out there who need good examples like you and me."

Peter saw the girl's aura vibrate in dissonance with the asura. "Okay," she nodded. "Okay. I'll drink."

Peter stopped halfway to them. The girl was ready to be free all because of what Charlie had said.

Then, as the girl reached for the water bottle, she started to shake as the asura took control. Peter started running. The girl got a corkscrew grin on her lips and pulled out a serrated knife from within her uniform.

"Look out!" Peter shouted desperately.

The asura didn't stand a chance. Charlie moved faster than Peter had ever seen her move before. She caught the girl's wrist, twisted the knife out and took her down to her back.

He saw the girl whisper something with a laugh. Charlie tightened her grip and pinned the girl down with an elbow to her neck.

"I will not be your victim!" Charlie shouted, a little too loud.

Peter finally reached them and quickly placed his hand on the girl's forehead. "Be swept clean," he declared.

The girl fell as the asura slipped away from her and hung in the air like a poisonous cloud. Before it could gather itself into some hideous form, Peter punched the air, conjuring a wind that blew it away.

"Is she okay?" Sensei Charlie asked hurriedly. "Did I hurt her?"

"She'll be fine," Peter assured her. "Look, she's waking up."

The girl's eyes fluttered open and Charlie breathed a sigh of relief.

"What happened?" the girl asked.

"You fainted," Charlie explained. "Do you see now? If you don't eat, your body won't be able to keep up."

"You're right," the girl said. "Thanks for talking sense into me. I'll go get something to eat."

"Good luck in the competition," Charlie told her as she walked off.

"You okay?" Peter asked Charlie tentatively.

She nodded. "Sorry you had to see that."

He raised an eyebrow. "Sorry I had to see you take down a possessed girl with nothing but martial arts? Because that was pretty cool."

"Thanks. No, I'm talking about the part where I *lost* my cool."

"They have a way of saying just the right thing," Peter said.

"How did she know?" Charlie looked into the distance and hugged herself. "She, or it, or whatever said, 'I bet this is how Jessie looked.'"

"Jessie who now?" Peter asked.

"My best friend. When we were in high school, some," she paused, choosing her words, "*jerk* took advantage of her."

"Oh," Peter reacted awkwardly.

"A lot of people assumed that she was at the wrong party, hung out with the wrong guys, or dressed immodestly. None of which was true. And even if she had done all those things, the boy was the one who singled her out, followed her home, and attacked her. No matter what the circumstances, he was the one who made that choice. Not Jessie."

"I bet that scarred you, almost as much as it did her," Peter said sympathetically.

Charlie nodded. "It totally shook me up. I just wish I had been with her. I could've protected her."

Peter wanted to comfort her, to offer some platitude, but he didn't know what he could say.

"I had been taking martial arts since I was a little kid," Charlie continued, "and if I had been there, I probably could have taken the guy."

Her shoulders seemed to get heavier.

"Geez, that's a lot of guilt to walk around with," Peter commented.

"It's not exactly something you get over." She sighed and shivered all at once. "I've channeled a lot of my guilt into athletics. That's why I teach classes at the gym and the dojo. So I can teach people how to handle themselves and so I can protect them whenever I have to."

Peter thought of how similar he was to Sensei Charlie. Even without a traumatic experience, he also wanted to save people from suffering however he could.

"Like today," Peter said. "Seriously, you protected that girl from some pretty horrible karma. That was awesome."

"You too," she looked him over. "How do you and Rob deal with it all the time? I imagine those demons must say things to you guys, too. I mean, if they knew my most painful memory, I'm sure they say even worse stuff to you."

"Pretty much," Peter said, "but they haven't said anything I couldn't handle yet."

They spent a few moments in somber thought.

Then Charlie smiled. "What do you say we go fight some regular, boring humans now?" she suggested. "Are you nervous?"

Chapter 28: In the Moment

A week later, Peter and his mom enjoyed a hike through the woods at a city park. Peter took a deep breath of the forest air and tuned in to the wind currents all around him.

"You're smirking you know," his mom complained while they trekked up a hill. "You're feeling pretty proud of yourself, huh?"

"Of course I am," he smiled brightly. "Last week, I proved myself to be the best thirteen-to-fifteen-year-old Tae Kwon Do fighter in the whole city. And in a few months, I'll take district, and someday the Olympics! What's not to feel proud about?"

His mom shook her head. "I'm your biggest fan, but hasn't anyone ever told you that 'pride goes before the fall?'"

He jogged ahead. "Ah, but see, that's a Christian saying." He turned around and gave her a charming smile. "And I'm a Buddhist."

"I'm pretty sure it still applies."

As they continued, Peter thought back to a horrid asura-inspired dream he had had the previous night. Although there were many reasons to feel proud, there were also the nightmares that still beat against his confidence.

"So hey," his mom interrupted the silence. "Even though you seem on top of the world lately, every now and then you look troubled. Everything okay?"

Peter eyed her. He wasn't counting on his mom being that perceptive.

He had thought about telling her the truth like Sensei Rob had suggested countless times, but he was afraid of her reaction. His dad was still struggling to find a job, and his mom might think it was his fault. He still remembered the asura's face in the dream as it asked him, *"Should I tell him? That he's only suffering because of you."*

"Yeah. Everything's great," he lied.

His mom laughed derisively. "Please, Peter," she said. "I'm your mom. I can tell you're worried about something."

"Nothing gets past you, huh?" Peter said nervously. "Alright," he decided, "I've been having weird dreams lately."

She stopped in her tracks and made a weird face. "Uh-oh. Is this a conversation you need to have with your father?"

"Gross, mom!" he complained. "It's not like that!"

"Okay. Go on," she encouraged him.

He struggled with his words. "Sometimes I have dreams where I do something awful," he confessed. "Like hurting someone I care about." Peter's heart sank in his chest as he came clean. "And I haven't done anything bad, but I wake up feeling like I did. And then I can't shake the feelings."

Mrs. Hunter paused and sat on a rock for a rest. "Dreams are funny," she said in between drinks from her water bottle. "I can't tell you how many times I've had dreams of your father cheating on me. And even though I know it's just a dream, I wake up and yell at him for what his dream-self did."

"That's not very fair," Peter said, sitting on the rock with her.

"Just like it's not fair to blame yourself for what dream-Peter did." She nudged his shoulder. "You're in charge of the choices you make. You're not in control of your dreams."

"But dreams are like wandering thoughts, right?" he argued. "They come out of the heart?"

She shrugged. "Maybe. But they don't have to come from desires. I don't *desire* that your father would cheat on me. I *fear* that he would. Maybe you're dreaming these things because you're afraid you might be capable of them."

"That makes me feel a little better, but I still feel all this guilt."

She gave him a sideways smile. "Well, take it from someone who deals with many emotions every day, emotions and feelings come and go. Sometimes you just have to wait and they'll leave on their own. But maybe they have something to teach you about yourself in the meantime. I think your guilt and shame show you the kind of person you want to be. You can't stand even the thought of hurting someone. And that's a very good thing. But also remember that guilt and shame accomplish nothing. Trust me."

"What do you mean?" he asked.

"My mom used to be really good at guilt trips," she complained. "She'd use them to manipulate me all the time. You're lucky I don't give you guilt trips."

"Right. Never," Peter said sarcastically.

She laughed. "I'm not as bad as your grandma," she asserted. "Trust me. But whenever she'd try to guilt me into something, all I heard was that I wasn't good enough. And that's really the thing about guilt, right? It's all about me, me, me. *I'm* not good enough. *I'm* awful. So I think it's more productive to focus on others when you're tempted to feel guilty.

When you have a bad dream, maybe choose to focus on helping someone instead."

Peter nodded as he considered her words.

"You know," she suggested, "You can always focus on doing the laundry, dishes, vacuuming, making someone breakfast in bed…"

"Mom!" he groaned.

"But another thing to think about is that the Buddha once said," she stuck her finger into the air and preached, "*'Do not dwell on the past, do not dream of the future, concentrate the mind on the present moment.'* Maybe after you have those dreams, you should focus on the present moment instead of the guilt of some false past or worries of what you might do in the future."

Peter considered her. "Are you Buddhist now, too?" he asked.

She smirked and revealed the phone she had been hiding in her lap. The screen displayed an app for a daily Buddhist quote with the saying she had just recited.

Then she threw her arm around him, messed up his hair, and pulled his face close to hers. "Quick, mom and son selfie!"

The next day, Peter thought about what his mom had said while he relaxed at the front desk of the dojo. He determined to focus on helping other people instead of stressing over his dreams.

But he was already helping out around the house, working at the Nasir's restaurant, and, of course, helping to free victims of demonic possession. He didn't know what he should do next.

"See ya, boys," Sensei Charlie called Peter from his thoughts as she walked for the door. "I've got to go help my friend through a nasty breakup. You might not see me for a while. We're talking days of pajama-wearing, chick-flick-watching, cookie-dough-eating revelry."

Rob met her at the door and gave her a long hug while he said, "Just promise me she won't give you any ideas."

Charlie laughed, "She couldn't if she tried."

Then she waved over her shoulder as she left.

Peter turned his attention back to his summer reading just as Rob smacked both his hands on the desk with a look of desperation.

"You have to help me," he said. "I want to marry Charlene."

“Whoa,” Peter reacted. “You guys have been dating, what, nine months or something?”

Rob started pacing nervously. “I know it seems soon, but we’ve been working together almost every day for over a year now. And when it’s right, you just know. Plus we’re older. We both know what we’re looking for. And she’s wonderful. I never have to guess what she’s thinking. There are no games, no tension. Even our fights have been respectful and calm.” He stopped and sighed.

“That’s great,” Peter said slowly. “Sooo… what? You want my blessing or something? Want me to give you away at the wedding?”

“No, punk. I need help. How does she want me to propose?”

Peter’s eyes grew. “You know her better than I do.”

“I know all the important stuff, like what she does when she’s angry, what she needs when she’s sad. But it’s the little things, like if she cuts her hair or what her favorite food is. Oh god, what’s her eye color?” he panicked. “Brown? Hazel? I look at them every day and somehow I don’t know!” He took Peter by the shoulders and shook him. “I have no idea how to do this!”

“And you think I will?” Peter matched Rob’s emotion.

“No, but you know some girls, right?” Rob shook his finger in Peter’s face. “You could ask their opinions.”

“Why are you so panicked?” Peter asked. “You’ve fought the forces of evil and darkness for decades.”

“Yes, and *this* is terrifying!”

“Okay, look at me,” Peter said in mock seriousness. “It’s going to be fine. I’m your apprentice, your sidekick. We’ll get through this,” he paused dramatically, “together.”

Chapter 29: Nasir Restaurant

A few nights later, Peter and his parents attended the grand opening of the Nasir family's restaurant. He was happy to see that the place was packed.

As soon as they were seated, the Nasirs came out to great them.

"We cannot thank you enough for sharing your son with us," Mr. Nasir told them after kissing Mr. Hunter's cheeks. "This young man helped us move boxes, paint, and stock shelves all for free."

"Not for free," Peter corrected him. "For karma."

"This guy!" Mr. Nasir shook him by the shoulder. "Tonight, dinner is on the house!"

"Oh, that's too much!" Mrs. Hunter gasped.

Mrs. Nasir clicked her tongue. "Nonsense," she said. "Maybe we'd like some good karma, too."

As they continued their conversation, offering friendly services back and forth in free food and help with taxes, Peter felt a whisper of a breeze near his ear. He focused his thoughts and felt the tug at his gut, pulling him to the alley behind the restaurant.

Then he nearly jumped as he looked up. His third eye had been opened and now he could see that there were countless asuras in the restaurant, lurking behind people.

He saw one bat-like creature, sitting on a young woman's shoulders as she lectured the man across the table. The asura looked pleased as it dug its talons into the woman.

There were ones that looked like viruses and germs. Some that looked like humanoid aliens with spindly arms and legs. There were some that were small circular shapes with protruding legs, like some mutated arachnid.

One even landed on Zahid as he bussed a table. It whispered something in his ear and Peter saw his shoulders slouch. He got a look on his face that Peter often saw. It was a sad expression, as if he would cave in on himself at any moment.

Then with a shake of his head, Zahid was back on task, with his face set like stone in determination. The asura flew off.

Peter wanted to stay and defeat all the asuras, but he felt a tug on his gut again. He hoped his family and friends would be safe from temptations as he excused himself and snuck out of the restaurant while his parents were distracted.

Peter circled the building to the alleyway, where he found Sensei Rob arriving on the scene with a splash of celestial energy crashing around him. A homeless man with a dark aura was at the other end of the alley, looking behind dumpsters and trashcans.

Peter was about to ask what was happening when the man pulled a squealing rat out of its hiding place and bit right into it. Peter had to fight the urge to throw up. He couldn't decide which preta had been more disgusting: this one or the one in the bowling alley.

"Well, Mr. I-just-met-my-deva," Rob said, "how about I sit back this time?"

"Is this really just so you can rest your hand?" Peter challenged.

Rob chuckled and motioned for him to focus on the possessed homeless man.

Peter started chanting. The homeless man dropped the rat and grasped his ears while screaming. Peter stepped closer, still chanting, until he was close enough to touch the man's forehead.

"Be swept clean."

He felt a surge of energy swirl in and around him before blasting into the man. A darkness emerged from his back and disappeared into the shadows.

The man slumped forward and fell onto the pavement.

"That was easy," Peter said, feeling a slight disappointment.

"Sometimes it's that easy," Sensei shrugged as he crouched down and rolled the man to a more comfortable position. "Some spirits are weaker than others."

Suddenly, the trashcans and dumpster burst into flames.

"And sometimes, they just haven't started fighting back yet," Rob explained dryly.

Peter started chanting, "OM MANI PADME HUM," as the flames spread to the trash that littered the space and smoke filled the air.

He fought to keep his focus while the smoke irritated his contacts. He closed his eyes and kept chanting, but the spirit tempted him with an echoing, disembodied voice.

"We don't have to fight," it told Peter. *"We can do you favors. We have so many powers over this world. We could get you all the money you could ever wish for. All you have to do is walk away from this foolish life of self-denial. Don't you deserve a reward for all your sacrifices?"*

Peter thought that having all the money he could ever wish for sounded great, but he knew the conditions were too steep.

He took in a deep breath and felt the wind swell and spiral around him. A tremendous gust of wind blasted through the alleyway, extinguishing the flames all at once. At the same time, a gut-wrenching howl pierced his ears and faded into oblivion.

"Boom!" Peter punched the air. "Who's awesome?"

He turned around, expecting praise, but saw that the homeless man was encased in a bubble of Sensei's sea green water. He had completely forgotten about the victim. If Sensei hadn't made that move, the man would've been roasted by the fire.

"It's okay," Sensei assured him gently as the water and glow faded. "That's why I'm here. Next time, you'll remember to protect the victim, right?"

Peter nodded sincerely.

"That was pretty good for your first official exorcism," Sensei Rob said, clapping his good hand on Peter's shoulder. "Just remember that the victim is always your first priority."

Peter nodded again. "Now that this one is done, we should take care of all the asuras infesting this place." He pointed with his thumb to the Nasir's restaurant.

"What are you talking about?" Rob asked.

"There are, like, twenty of them hopping around in there."

"Oh. This is the first time you've been in a crowd," Rob realized. "That's normal. In fact, I'm surprised there are only that many. The truth is, these things are almost always around us, whispering in our ears, trying to amplify our negative emotions. It's just that you can't see them all the time."

Peter shivered. "But… That's *not* normal."

"Not desirable," Sensei clarified, "but normal. See ya."

In a swirl of sea green, sparkly energy, Sensei Rob disappeared from the alley.

Peter walked back into the restaurant and almost ran into Zahid as he carried a bin of used plates and silverware.

"Everything okay?" Zahid asked.

"Yeah, just…" Peter thought about the asura that had been trying to depress him earlier. "Don't be sad, okay?"

Zahid gave him a strange look as Peter rejoined his family at their table. His spiritual sight was gone, but he could still imagine all the spirits lurking beneath visibility.

At the end of the evening, the Nasirs packed up their dinner and had even added more food to the boxes.

"What an amazing family," his mom commented as they walked toward their car. "We should eat here all the time."

Peter looked back at the alleyway and caught a glimpse of the homeless man. He was staring at the brick wall as if in a trance. Peter took one of the boxes of food and jogged over to him.

"Hey, we had some leftovers," Peter told the man as he handed him the box. He held his hand up and muttered a quick prayer of blessing: "May you be filled with loving-kindness. May you be well. May you be peaceful and at ease. May you be happy."

The man looked confused, but grateful.

"What was that?" his dad asked when he rejoined them.

"Oh, you know…" Peter started.

"Good karma," his mom laughed as she finished his sentence.

As Peter was about to get into the backseat of the car, something green caught his eye from behind the tire of the car next to theirs. It was a roll of cash, at least an inch thick and the bills he could see were hundred dollar bills. He remembered the temptation of the asura: *"We could get you all the money you could ever wish for."*

He knew it was more than a coincidence that the money was just sitting there. There was enough to solve at least of few of his family's problems. But he also knew it was an offering from the asuras. This money would do nothing but create new problems.

Peter got into the car and closed the door.

"Hey, do we have any soup kitchens near us?" he asked his parents as they drove away.

Chapter 30: Summer Festival

Peter dreamt that he and Zahid were walking out of school together. Zahid studied a book while Peter stretched and yawned.

Then Zahid pointed to a fast food restaurant across the street. "Oh, look," he said casually. "They're hiring. Maybe you should inquire within."

He got a goofy smile on his face and chuckled. Peter smiled back politely, hiding his anger. Then he raised his fist and punched Zahid hard in the face.

"You don't have to keep helping us," Zahid told Peter the next day as they unpacked boxes in the storage pantry of the restaurant.

Peter shuddered as he remembered the dream from the previous night. He was pretty sure he did have to keep helping them.

Mrs. Nasir came in and barked at Zahid, "If the boy wants to do free labor for us, let the boy do free labor!"

"Thanks, Mrs. Nasir," Peter chuckled. "Hey, after this, there's that festival at the park," he told Zahid. "Wanna go? I'll pay."

Zahid considered it. "I'd have to bring Yara and the boys."

"I'll pay for everyone," Peter offered. Zahid eyed him suspiciously. "I just need to…"

"Accumulate good karma," Zahid finished his sentence. "Fine. But sometimes I feel like you're just using me for karma."

When they got to the festival, Ahmed and Hassan ran off, promising to meet up in an hour.

"Do you want to go with them, Yara?" Zahid asked.

She shook her head. He smiled at her and squeezed her hand a little tighter.

Across the way, the crowd parted and Peter caught sight of Alicia with Gina and another girl named Hazel. His heart rate immediately picked up. Then he noticed that there was a rectangular boy pestering them. Jeremy.

"Geez, that guy doesn't even take summers off?" Peter scoffed. "I'd better go save those girls."

"Do we have to?" Zahid groaned.

"If I'm here, Jeremy won't hurt you," Peter assured him.

"Jeremy's not the one I'm afraid of." He nodded at Gina.

Peter laughed and pushed Zahid's shoulder playfully. "If I can get over my fear of libraries, you can get over your fear of girls."

"Not all girls," Zahid said. "Just the one. We'll wait here."

As Peter jogged over, he noticed that he smelled something off. Carnivals and festivals often had a particular smell, but this was different. It reminded him of the smell of the pishacha at the nursing home. He wondered if there was a spirit nearby.

"Peter!" Alicia's eyes seemed to brighten when she saw him. "I had no idea you'd be here."

Jeremy shoved him. "Back off, Hunter. I was here first."

"I don't understand," Peter said innocently. "I'm just saying hi. How's your summer, Jeremy? Are you enjoying my comic books?"

He looked disoriented by Peter's pleasant attitude. "Yeah, I…"

"Ugh, no one wants to hear about you," Alicia turned her back on him. "I want to hear about your summer, Peter. Didn't you have a tournament or something?"

"You remembered?" Peter smiled. "Yeah, got the gold and qualified for district in October. How's your summer going?"

Alicia smiled. "I've been kind of missing certain people."

"Yeah?" he gave her a sideways smile. "I thought I was the only one. Hey, I never got a chance to ask you. Are you going to Eastville High in the fall?"

"I am," she said excitedly. "Are you, too?"

Peter nodded. "Then maybe we'll see each other around." Peter noticed that Jeremy had stomped off. "I guess he took the hint."

"You're always protecting me," Alicia noted.

He shrugged. "Just doing what anyone would do."

They spent a few moments smiling at each other. He was pretty sure Gina and Hazel were rolling their eyes, but he didn't care. He could look at her smile all day.

Alicia hooked a strand of her long golden hair behind her ear and asked, "So, did anything else interesting happen this summer?"

He struggled with how to tell her that he had met an invisible spirit of positivity that helped him control the wind to fight evil spirits.

Gina studied him. "You look different," she said pensively. "I know. You don't look as short as you did in the spring."

"Thanks, Gina," Peter said dryly.

"Zahid!" Gina greeted as he and Yara walked up.

Peter figured they must have gotten bored waiting for him.

"And who's this?" Gina asked, bending down to smile at Yara. "Are you Zahid's girlfriend?" she asked playfully.

"No!" Yara giggled. "I'm his sister, Yara."

"What a pretty name. I'm Gina. And I want you to remember me. You think you can do that?"

Yara giggled again and nodded. Zahid was making a face like he had stepped in something nasty.

"Hey, now that I think about it, I'm glad I ran into you," Peter told Alicia. "There's something big I need to ask you."

Alicia smiled coyly. "Oh, really?"

"Yeah, can I buy you a funnel cake?" She nodded. "You guys, too?" Peter asked the other girls. "Free funnel cake for everyone. I could use as much help as I can get."

Peter couldn't tell if it was his imagination, but Alicia seemed suddenly mad about something.

"You were going somewhere, right?" she asked her friends.

"But he said free funnel cake," Hazel whined.

"Is Zahid coming?" Gina asked quickly.

"You don't have to," Peter whispered to Zahid. "It'll only take maybe thirty minutes. Just wait for me…"

"What's funnel cake?" Yara asked eagerly.

Zahid looked defeated. Peter knew he would never deny Yara.

"I'll buy you one," he told Yara. He turned back to Gina. "Yeah, Zahid's coming."

They all sat at a picnic table eating together. Alicia barely touched the food and sat with her arms crossed.

"This reminds me of something mama makes," Yara said.

"Fun fact," Gina told her. "Funnel cake is one of the oldest treats in history and actually originated in the Arabic culture." Hazel snickered. Gina looked embarrassed. "What? My nerdy cousin said it once," she shrugged. "I just remembered it."

"Do you know a lot about Syria?" Yara asked innocently.

"Not as much as I'd like to," she said with a telling smile.

Zahid sighed dismally.

"You wanted to ask us something?" Alicia asked Peter bitterly.

"Yeah," he dusted his hands off and leaned forward. "I have this friend who really likes this girl," Peter started.

"Oh, really?" Alicia smirked.

The girls exchanged looks and giggles.

"Yeah, I mean he's totally in love," Peter continued.

"And what's the boy's name?" Alicia asked.

He didn't know why she wanted to know. "Rob."

"That's a very common name," she laughed.

"I guess," he shrugged. He didn't understand why she found that funny. "Anyway, he wants to propose."

Alicia looked taken aback. "It's kind of soon for that, don't you think? I mean, they are way too young to be thinking about marriage."

"They're both thirty-something," he answered. "And they've been dating for a while."

"Thirty-something?" she looked disappointed. "Oh, so this is, like, an actual guy?"

Peter laughed awkwardly. "What did you think I was talking about?"

"Nothing," she grumbled. Then she waved her hand. "Go on."

"So Rob is trying to come up with the perfect proposal and he asked me to talk to every girl I know about it. But I only know the girls from our class, and since it's summer, I don't see any of them."

"I guess you get points for that," Alicia mumbled.

"For what? Points?" Peter was starting to feel like he needed a Girl-to-English language dictionary to follow this conversation.

"Nothing," she groaned. "Anyway, this Rob," she said the name like it was a piece of rotten food, "he just needs to show her that he likes her more than any other girl out there. And he has to put effort and time into planning it. As long as he does that, she'll most likely say yes."

"Does that work even if you're just asking a girl out?" Peter asked before he could stop himself.

"As long as you're not an absolute dork or creep," she said.

"Guess I'm out of luck, then," Peter joked.

"You're an idiot," she corrected him, "but not a creep or a dork. Why? Are you planning on asking someone out?"

Peter stared at her like a deer in the headlights. Alicia Lisowski probably didn't think much of someone as apparently 'idiotic' as him. And she seemed mad about something at the moment, so his chances were probably nonexistent.

“Nah,” he dismissed the idea. “I think the girl I like is pretty much out of my league no matter what tricks I pull.”

Alicia stared him down. “Maybe you ought to ask her, just to be sure.”

“Does Zahid have a crush on anyone,” Gina interrupted. “Ow!”

Peter didn’t see how Gina got hurt, but he imagined it had something to do with how Alicia was glaring at her.

“So, Peter,” Alicia turned back with a gaze so intense, he was starting to feel very hot. “I think you ought to go ahead and ask this mystery crush out on a date. She’s worth the risk, isn’t she?”

Peter gulped. Her gaze was sucking him in. He was afraid the next words out of his mouth would be too revealing.

Just then, he felt a whisper in his ear. He stood up quickly, startling everyone. His divine eye was suddenly opened and he realized that they were in a sea of asuras.

“I am so sorry,” Peter said quickly. “I just… I have to go.”

“What? Where are you going?” Alicia asked angrily.

“I want more funnel cake!” Hazel whined.

Zahid grabbed his wrist and pleaded, “Don’t do this to me.”

“I’m sorry, Zahid,” he wrestled free. “I owe you big time.”

Peter ran away convinced that everyone at the table hated him. Except maybe Gina.

Chapter 31: A Rampaging Elephant

Peter followed the tug on his gut and raced through the crowd. He saw Sensei Rob appear out of nowhere. No one in the crowd seemed to notice his sudden appearance.

"Pete!" Rob greeted with a smile. "How'd you get here?"

"I just happened to be in the area," he shrugged.

"Funny how it works out like that, huh?"

"I said I wanted a mixture of every soda!" a voice boomed.

Peter saw Jeremy threatening the worker behind a food counter. The man stood head and shoulders above Jeremy, yet somehow he looked scared of the angry, rectangular boy in front of him.

Now that Peter's divine eye was open, he saw that Jeremy was filled with dark energy. He recognized the same rancid stench he had noticed earlier, too. The crowd was going out of its way to avoid the booth.

"It's not that difficult!" Jeremy berated the man. "I know you're an uneducated, trailer park reject, but you should be able to figure out how to put a little of each kind of soda into one cup!"

"Get to work," Sensei urged Peter.

Remember the victim. Remember the victim, Peter reminded himself.

He approached hesitantly. "Hey, Jeremy," he greeted.

Jeremy turned and startled Peter. His face looked different. His teeth came to points and his eyes were an icy blue. Peter couldn't remember what color they were usually, but he knew they weren't icy blue.

Jeremy screamed a sound that reminded Peter of an elephant trumpeting. Then he turned and started running. Peter was on his heels in a second.

They ran through the crowd until they came to the hammer challenge, the "high striker." Jeremy grabbed the mallet from the game and swung it suddenly at Peter.

Peter punched the air, sending a powerful blast of wind that knocked Jeremy backwards. Jeremy recovered and jumped into the air, covering an unnatural distance. Peter dodged just in time as Jeremy and the mallet crashed into the ground, creating a crater underneath them both.

In an instant, Peter jumped forward and placed his hand against Jeremy's forehead. "Be swept clean."

The asura howled as it was expelled from Jeremy's body. Peter was pushed backwards by the noise. His feet scraped along the grass.

When he looked up, the asura had formed itself into a gargantuan elephant shape. Peter gulped as he stared up at the towering asura.

"We will trample you!" the elephant-asura taunted him. *"Then we will drag you and this boy down to the depths of Naraka with us."*

Remember the victim, Peter told himself as he glanced at Jeremy's resting body.

The elephant-asura reared up on its hind legs and blasted a trumpeting sound that shook the earth. Peter rolled out of the way as the elephant-asura's feet came crashing down.

He backed up to lure it away from Jeremy, but he couldn't think of much beyond that. The elephant-asura stomped repeatedly, trying to squash Peter, and all Peter could think to do was scuttle backwards.

Then Peter fell and stared up as the elephant-asura foot lifted over him.

Thankfully, Sensei Rob's green water crested over and crashed onto the asura. Within moments, the dark form was washed away.

Rob offered Peter a hand and said, "Remember that they can take any shape. And it might scare or startle you, but their form never affects their power. You could've taken him easily."

"Oh," Peter said, realizing that he had fallen for a simple parlor trick.

"And chanting can help focus your thoughts," Sensei reminded him.

"Oh, yeah. That chanting thing," Peter said, feeling stupid.

"Don't worry," Rob said, reading his face. "This is why you have a mentor. And you kept the victim safe. That's priority number one."

Peter and Rob propped Jeremy up to a more comfortable position, against the wall of a booth. The area had started to become populated again, now that the spiritual threat had evaporated.

"So 'Jeremy'?" Sensei asked. "Is this *the* Jeremy?"

Peter nodded. "He's also the son of that husband and wife."

Sensei made a sympathetic face. "How sad they all must be," he said softly. "Can you imagine the amount of pain that family must live in?"

Peter felt guilty for every thought of ill will he had had for Jeremy.

"You think he's been possessed this whole time?" Peter asked.

"Probably not," Sensei speculated. "They were probably working on this boy for years, conditioning him. But there's still hope for this boy. One good influence can make all the difference." Rob eyed Peter emphatically.

"Me?" Peter laughed. "Yeah, right. I mean, I'd love to help the guy, but he hates me with a passion."

"If not you, we can only hope there's someone who will help him. The Buddha said, *'Friendship is the only cure for hatred and the only guarantee of peace.'*"

The thought weighed on Peter.

"Well, I have to get back to a date with a lovely woman." Rob winked as he disappeared.

Peter returned to the picnic tables to find Zahid, his brothers, and Yara waiting for him.

Peter braced himself for Zahid's anger.

"You owe me," Zahid grumbled. "She played with my hair." He said it like it was the cruelest, most sadistic form of torture.

"I really am sorry," Peter said.

"Why do you not like big sister, Gina?" Yara asked innocently.

Peter raised his eyebrows.

"Big sister Gina?" Hassan repeated. He and Ahmed started playfully punching their big brother and laughing.

Zahid groaned, "Please don't call her that, Yara." Then he explained to Peter, "They hit it off big time."

"She was nice," Yara said. "Why don't you like her?"

"American girls are just a little bolder than I'm comfortable with," Zahid explained to Yara. "Remember back in Syria how boys and girls don't touch in public? It's different here and I'm not used to it. Speaking of bold girls," he turned to Peter, "are you going to ask Alicia out?"

"What? No," Peter laughed. "Alicia wouldn't ever look my way."

Yara asked, "Is that the one Gina said likes Peter?"

"Gina said that?" Peter asked quickly. "Was she serious?"

Zahid shook his head. "I love you like a brother, but you're an idiot."

"Why does everyone keep calling me that?" he complained.

"And you will let me use your bike for a week," Zahid demanded, "to make up for leaving me alone with Gina."

"A bike!" Ahmed exclaimed. "Can we use it, too?"

Peter laughed. "You can have the bike for the rest of summer."

Hassan's mouth dropped. "Can you leave my brother alone with that girl more often?"

Chapter 32: Proposal

A few weeks later, Peter sat at the front desk of the dojo during a class. Charlie was in the middle of demonstrating a combination and Rob was watching her with admiration.

When she finished, she turned to him and asked, "Did you have anything to add, Sensei Rob?"

"Marry me," he said absent-mindedly.

The whole room froze. The moms who were waiting snapped their heads up in attention.

So much for planning, Peter thought.

He couldn't interpret Charlie's face, but it was clear that she wasn't happy. Rob stammered out a recovery and continued with the class, though there was a very awkward sense of tension in the entire dojo.

After class, Charlie ran to the office to collect her things. Rob was about to chase her when a parent stopped him with a question. He looked at Peter with desperate eyes.

Peter knocked on the open door. "Sensei Charlie? You okay?"

"Yeah, I just… Okay, no, I'm not okay," she admitted.

"It didn't make you happy?" Peter dared to ask.

She stopped her movement and closed her eyes painfully. "It was so embarrassing," she said.

"He's serious about you, though," Peter argued. "Even if it wasn't how you imagined it happening, I think he meant it."

"Then that's even worse!" she exclaimed.

"Why?"

"Because I'm insecure, okay? I love him so much it scares me. So I don't want to be some afterthought, or some random impulsive idea that just popped into his head. I need to know if I'm important to him. Or I might just fall apart."

"Wow. I always thought *he* was the idiot in love," Peter quipped.

She fixed him with a glare, then sighed as she collapsed in the office chair. "People like Rob love in an obvious way, and people like me love with a quiet intensity. But now I worry that his passion is just impulse."

"No. Look, go easy on him," Peter pleaded. "He probably blurted it out because it's been all he's talked about for weeks now."

She looked up hopefully. "What?"

"Don't tell him I told you," he whispered as he sat in the chair in front of the desk, "but he's been totally obsessed. Every other sentence: 'What kind of ring should I get?' 'You have to be calm to fight the rakshasas.' 'Where should I ask her?' 'If you eat too many chips, the asuras will use it against you.' 'Should I hire a flash mob?'" Sensei Charlie covered her mouth. "He even had me asking opinions from every girl I know."

She let out a combination sob and laugh. "Thanks," she said softly. "That changes everything. He'd still better propose appropriately," she added firmly, "but now I'll give him a chance." She rose from the chair. "I'd better get home. Too many emotions for one day."

"What should I tell Sensei?" Peter asked, rising from his chair.

She paused in the doorway and let a smile grow. "Tell him that some girls think sapphires are better than diamonds."

"Move that one a little to the left," Sensei instructed as they placed rocks in the woods, spelling out the words, "Will you marry me?" so as to be seen from the top of a nearby hill. "Man, I feel like my whole life shaped me into the person I was supposed to be for her, just like we're shaping these rocks."

"Save it for the proposal," Peter teased. "But hey, is she becoming a worldly attachment?" He meant it as a joke, but part of him was truly curious. "Didn't the Buddha say that the more attached you are to something in this life, the more it can cause you suffering?"

Rob set a heavy rock in place and massaged the hand that had been injured the night that Peter met his deva.

"There is a significant danger," he admitted. "She could easily make me suffer by ceasing to love me. But there's a spectrum to love. When I think of how she makes me feel, it's self-centered. It's loving her for the sake of myself. When I think like that, she's an attachment and love becomes lust."

"Isn't that what love is?" Peter asked.

"No," Rob shook his head. "Love, real love, is selfless. If I focus on helping her to be happy or virtuous, and if I focus on what's best for her, then that's a love that transforms and enlightens."

"So is that what your love for her is?" Peter challenged him. "All pure and perfect?"

Rob laughed as he straightened a few rocks with his foot. "No. Not at all. I struggle moment to moment choosing to have the right love for her. But that's everything in Buddhism. It's all about the present moment. We can become great monsters or great gurus with every choice we make. No, my love is not pure. But I want to spend the rest of my life trying to get it there."

Peter thought of his crush on Alicia. If he was being honest with himself, he really liked how she made him feel. When she wasn't angry with him, that is.

"How do you make sure your love is selfless?" he asked Rob.

"My personal trick is that I take it to meditation all the time." Rob stretched his back, causing it to pop. "I run through scenarios to prepare my reactions. I think of what would happen if she decided to love another guy or if I lost her. If I'm thinking of myself, those thoughts are unbearable. If I'm thinking of her, then I can choose to let her go if it's what she really wants."

SHOOOSH!

A gentle breeze tickled Peter's ears. He felt an indecipherable whisper and saw a vision of a cabin in the middle of the woods.

At the same time, Sensei Rob was overtaken by a massive shiver down his spine. "Looks like someone needs us," he said.

He slapped Peter on the shoulder and transported him through the woods. They came to a stop outside the cabin from Peter's vision. When no one answered their knock, they stepped inside.

The interior was clean and organized, decorated with rustic colors, animal hide rugs, and creature bones everywhere. They searched the house slowly, the floorboards creaking beneath their feet.

"Hello," Sensei called out, but received no answer.

Absent-mindedly, Peter opened the fridge in the small kitchen area and nearly jumped at the sight.

"Geeze," he exclaimed. "That is beyond…" he struggled to find a word powerful enough.

"What is it?" Rob asked, looking over his shoulder.

There were individual body parts, wrapped in plastic wrap, resting casually on the shelves. Peter was crestfallen when he noticed how small they were. He wished he could return to a time when he didn't know such a horrendous act was even possible.

"Rakshasa," Sensei hissed the name with disgust. "Every culture has stories of a creature that lives in the woods and demands human sacrifices or eats wayward children."

"That really happens?" Peter asked, wishing it weren't true.

They heard a scream and raced to a door. Sensei threw it open to reveal a burly, outdoorsy man with a big beard and belly who had paused on the steps from the basement, reaching for the doorknob.

Peter noticed a jagged knife in the man's hand, the tip of which had a smear of red. The man smiled darkly and brought the knife to his mouth, licking the blood off with quick, snake-like flick of his tongue.

Sensei Rob formed a whip of water that grabbed the knife from the man's hand and threw it across the room. Peter sprang to secure it while Sensei Rob fought the man.

As soon as Peter grasped the knife, it sent a paralyzing shudder through his body. He was overwhelmed by visions of hurting people, cutting them up, eating their flesh, and drinking their blood. And in all the visions, he had a smile on his face.

He felt the familiar tug at his gut, informing him: "It's the knife!" he yelled to Rob. "The spirit is in the knife!"

The possessed man ran straight for Peter, but Peter blasted him back with celestial wind.

Sensei cried out, "The Metta Sutta!" while he hit the man with a barrage of waves. *"This is what should be done by one who is skilled in goodness, and who seeks the path of peace..."*

They recited the sutta together while fending off attacks.

The rakshasa tried to distract Peter by whispering into his mind, *"Fighting us is pointless. Just one taste of blood and flesh and you'll know. You'll like it. It tastes like power."*

Peter was only disgusted. He employed all his mental energy to focus on thoughts of loving-kindness as the rakshasa's temptations bombarded his thoughts.

Finally, the possessed man fell unconscious and the dark thoughts left Peter. They both surveyed the cabin, feeling peace and relief.

Sensei picked up the knife as if it weighed fifty pounds. "This should be clean now," he said, "but just in case, we'll purify it back at the studio and destroy it."

"Shouldn't we leave it for the police to find?" Peter questioned.

Sensei shook his head emphatically. "These things have a way of returning to people," he warned. "You have to destroy them in a thorough way. I'll teach you when we get back."

Peter started for the basement door when Sensei held him back.

"You heard that scream," Peter reminded him. "Someone's still down there."

Rob sighed heavily. "That's for the cops to sort out."

"But…"

Peter felt tortured over the decision. It made sense that they shouldn't tamper with evidence unless they had to, like with the knife, but he could only imagine how terrified and hurt the child was.

"Geez, that's just not playing fair," Peter complained.

"I know," Sensei sighed. "We can watch from a safe distance to make sure the victim is safe, if it'll make you feel better."

After making a call from the house phone, they watched, hidden behind trees, as the police and medics ushered a small boy into an ambulance.

Then they left the scene to return to their project with the rocks.

"So why the Metta Sutta?" Peter asked at one point. "It's so long."

"And it's powerful," Rob told him. "Apparently one day, the Buddha's monks were scared by a group of yaksas, or demons, in the woods and the Buddha gave them that sutta to chant. It calmed the monks down and calmed the spirits, too. Now, monks use it all the time for regular practice and for exorcisms."

Rob inspected their finished work with satisfaction.

"Geez. How can you even think of something like proposing after a fight like that?" Peter asked him.

"In a way, I have to," Sensei said seriously. "After witnessing such darkness, I need to focus on all that is right in my life. The beauty and the goodness in people like Charlene, that's why I fight the asuras. If I didn't remember that, I think I'd go mad."

Peter entered the dojo a few days later to see Sensei Charlie showing off her ring to a few moms while they all congratulated her.

"She said yes?" Peter asked Sensei Rob, who looked like he was about to cry tears of joy.

"She said yes," he said.

"Are you going to start calling her Charlie now?"

Rob took in a deep breath, his eyes still fixed on her, and replied, "Never."

Chapter 33: Everything's "Fine"

When high school started, Peter was anxious to see Alicia. A new school brought many changes, but he was happy to find out that he was in the same homeroom with both Zahid and Alicia.

As he placed his books in his locker, however, he overheard Gina and Hazel talking across the way.

"Alicia needs to drop the act," Hazel said. "She pretends like she's annoyed, but it's so obvious that she really likes Jeremy."

Peter stopped still. He was sure that couldn't be true. She never showed an ounce of affection for Jeremy. Still, he knew he would never understand girls. Maybe he had fooled himself all this time. It really didn't make sense that one of the most popular and beautiful girls in school would like him.

"There's no way she'd be caught dead with him," Gina scoffed.

Peter suddenly realized that he had never been nice enough to Gina. She deserved more respect than he usually gave her.

"Everyone likes a bad boy," Hazel said.

"Not me," Gina argued.

"I'd bet money that they'll be dating in a few weeks."

"Shh," Gina said suddenly.

Peter could sense their eyes on him and they switched to inaudible whispers.

When he entered the classroom, Alicia was sitting on top of a desk and laughing with two boys. She didn't even look his way.

"No, I'm serious!" she was telling them. "West Africa grows most of the chocolate the world eats and they trap kids our age on farms where they risk their lives to work all day. Most of the time, they're beaten and starved, too. Think about that while you're enjoying your candy this Halloween. Some kid suffered just so you could get a couple of minutes of cheap chocolate."

The boys switched the topic to some movie they saw over the summer and Alicia laughed with them. She seemed carefree and happy as she giggled at their jokes.

Peter thought about his conversation on love and lust with Sensei. He resolved that it was fine as long as she was happy. He repeated the thought to himself multiple times that day as he tried not to watch her.

A couple weeks into the school year, Peter and his class went on a field trip to a museum. As soon as they arrived, the students were instructed to pair up and fill out worksheets while they walked through the exhibits.

Peter and Zahid naturally paired up. Then Peter noticed Alicia and Jeremy nearby.

"You and me, Lisowski," Jeremy ordered. "Partners. You know you want to."

She leaned away from him and said, "Go away, Jeremy."

"Drop the whole hard-to-get act. I can tell you feel the chemistry between us."

Peter wondered if maybe there was chemistry between them and he just didn't see it because he didn't want to.

"Get over yourself," Alicia rolled her eyes. "And I already have a partner. Right, Peter?"

Peter snapped his head to attention. "Yeah." He sprang forward and put a hand on Jeremy's shoulder. "Sorry, I know you're disappointed that you and I can't be partners, but maybe next time."

Jeremy glared a threat, and Peter just smiled at him until he walked away, griping.

"Thank you," she sighed. "You totally saved me."

"Anytime," he shrugged. "Enjoy the field trip."

"Wait." She grabbed his hand and he felt an electric shock all throughout his body. "Where are you going?"

"I figured that was all for show, right? Don't you want to partner with one of your friends?" Peter nodded at Gina and Hazel.

"But if he sees me with one of the girls, he's going to come back. Can you really be my partner?"

Peter looked back at Zahid apologetically. Zahid shook his head and rolled his eyes.

"Sure," he answered her. "If you, uh, need me."

As they started their assignment, Peter found that he couldn't make his voice or mind work. But after a few grueling minutes, he finally dared to ask, "So, you uh, that is, I heard… um, you're not interested in Jeremy?"

"Gross!" Alicia reacted. "Who told you that?"

"I just heard a rumor that you might actually like him."

"I'd never like a bully like him." Then she smiled sneakily. "Don't tell me you were worried about that."

"I just didn't want to jump in and save you if you, you know, had a thing for him."

"You can feel free to save me from him any time," she said. "And for the record, I really like the strong and heroic kind of guys."

Peter hoped that might mean him, but he didn't know what to say. They passed a few more moments in silence, filling out the worksheets.

"So," she said slowly, hooking her hair behind an ear, "we haven't talked since the night of the festival."

"That's right," Peter responded. "I never thanked you for your advice. My friends are getting married soon."

"Cool. But I was thinking about how we were having an interesting conversation and then you just got up and ran away. I was worried that maybe I said something that upset you."

"Oh, yeah that," he tried to sound casual. "No, it wasn't you. Just an emergency."

She blinked a few times in rapid succession. "That's it?" she asked sharply. "No explanation?"

I had to go and save Jeremy from demonic possession by using superpowers from an angelic spirit, he thought.

"It's kind of hard to explain," he shrugged again.

She took a quick turn away from him. "Fine. Like I care."

Peter had heard it said that girls were especially *not* fine whenever they actually said that word, but he had never experienced it until now.

As the field trip continued, she was so icy and silent that he was pretty sure he had ruined any chance he had of even a friendship.

As they passed into the next room, she avoided his eyes but said, "You could at least maybe tell me if you ever asked that girl out. The one you talked about having a crush on."

He rubbed the back of his neck. "Nah," he said. "I'm still convinced I'm way below her level."

She twirled her finger through the tips of her golden hair, still avoiding his eyes. "If you tell me who it is I could tell you if she likes you. Girls always know."

"Uh, thanks, for the offer, but I don't want to bother her with my one-sided crush. If I thought for even a second that she really liked me, I'd ask her out."

Her lips scrunched up and she turned an intense glare on him. "Has it ever occurred to you that she does like you, but you're just a big dumb idiot who can't read the signs?"

"Whoa, are you mad?" he stepped back. "Why are you mad?"

There was only one reason he could think of for why she would be mad at him, but Peter wouldn't let himself believe that she liked him. He was dorky, and apparently, a big dumb idiot, and he had seen her flirting with other guys.

SHOOOSH!

And just at that moment, Anuvata's wind whispered in his ear.

"Naraka!" Peter cursed under his breath.

"What? What does that mean?" Alicia asked.

He looked around, seeing all the asuras weaving through the crowd. He pulled her into a hidden spot behind a column.

"I didn't know you were this kind of boy," she teased.

"It's not like that. I have to go somewhere, right now."

"Like you did at the festival?" she asked. "What's going on?"

"I really can't tell you. It's too urgent."

"Is it the runs?" she asked, rolling her eyes.

"Gross. No. It's a life or death matter, no exaggeration. And I can't give you details. But I have to go *now*. Can you please cover for me? I should be back, I don't know, maybe fifteen or thirty minutes. Please. I'll owe you anything you want."

Her eyes narrowed. "Anything?"

"Yes. Just please do this for me."

She scrunched her lips to the side and replied sharply, "Fine."

Chapter 34: Evil Eye

Peter followed Anuvata's guiding to where another school was gathered at the museum. The group was huddled in a mass around a girl who had fainted. A boy with short, curly hair and dark skin was cradling her.

"Wake up, Rachel," the boy pleaded. "Just wake up, please!"

Peter thought of how lucky they were to have each other. He couldn't even get Alicia to be friendly with him.

"They deserve to suffer," the thought popped into Peter's head.

He dismissed the thought, realizing that it was not his own. Then he noticed a girl at the back of the group. She had long and straight red hair and a face covered in freckles. She was watching the boy and girl with a sneer on her face.

What made Peter notice her, however, was the dark cloudy mass beside her that was swirling in a winding path, weaving around the crowd, towards the unconscious girl.

SCHWOOORSH!

Rob appeared right next to Peter.

"What's going on?" Peter asked him.

"Oh, that? It's the evil eye," Rob responded plainly.

Peter remembered Gina Salvatore's story from half a year ago. "I thought that was an Italian thing," he scratched his head.

"It's an almost-every-culture thing. Intense jealousy and hatred can call down a curse on someone. All that negative energy is like the opposite of Tonglen."

Peter reached his hand out and played with the air, forming shifting currents and swirls that disrupted the dark cloudy trail.

While he did that, Rob pushed through the crowd and chanted softly, "OM MANI PADME HUM," while he slipped a bracelet of red string with a single bead onto the unconscious girl's wrist.

After only a few seconds, the girl stirred. The boyfriend kissed her forehead.

"Thank you," he told Rob. "If you hadn't been here to perform CPR, I don't know what we would've done."

Rob smiled brightly, "I do what I can."

He squeezed through the crowd again and met Peter.

"CPR?" Peter asked him.

Rob shrugged. "People see what they want to see. In fact, anyone who didn't think it was CPR will probably become convinced once everyone else repeats the story enough times."

Peter considered that with great effort. He didn't understand how someone could dismiss something that was right in front of their own eyes.

"What was with the bracelet?" he asked.

"Every culture has a different way of warding off the evil eye. In Tibet, they use a bead tied with a red string. I poured my good intent into that bracelet, to make it a powerful blessing. But hey, aren't you supposed to be in school? They usually only summon me during your school hours."

"You fight without me during the day?" Peter complained playfully. "I feel left out. I guess they called me since I was here anyway. Field trip. Gotta get back."

They parted and Peter ran back to rejoin his school. He found Gina and Hazel first. Hazel was giggling and Gina was trying not to.

"Hey, Peter," Gina greeted. "Feeling okay?"

"Yeah, I'm fine. Have you seen Alicia?"

Gina pointed her out and smiled. "Glad you're feeling better."

He was confused, but shook it off. Gina was always confusing.

"You're back," Alicia said with a blank face.

"Did anyone notice I was gone?" he asked, looking around. He noticed that a few people were watching him.

"I covered," she slapped the worksheets hard against his chest. "You can finish the rest since I did so much without you."

"You're the best," Peter thanked her, hoping for forgiveness.

"Don't thank me just yet," she mumbled.

She barely talked to him for the rest of the trip and as soon as they lined up for the bus, she joined Gina and Hazel without another word. People were still sniggering and asking if he was feeling okay as he made his way to the back of the bus with Zahid.

"What's that about?" Peter asked as they sat.

"Alicia announced to the teacher that you had diarrhea," Zahid explained. "Everyone overheard."

"Wow. If that isn't karma..."

He figured that proved she didn't have a crush on him.

After school, as he was about to leave the classroom, he heard a voice shout his name, "Peter Hunter!"

He turned slowly to see Alicia.

"I'm sure you didn't forget that you owe me," she said.

She was giving him a powerful glare that could have easily rivaled the glare of the redhead at the museum.

"No, I didn't forget," he replied.

I was just hoping you would.

"Come with me," she ordered.

She took him by the wrist and dragged him until they were behind the gym building. The only problem was that it was a designated make out spot for couples.

Peter gulped. "Uhhh, what are we doing here?" he asked.

She turned and glared at him. "The favor you owe me," she explained. "I want you to talk."

"Huh?"

"I think I deserve to know why I covered for you. What was this," she used exaggerated air quotations, "'life or death matter?' I told the teacher you had the runs, by the way."

"Oh, I heard. Thanks for that," Peter said sarcastically.

"Anytime," she threatened. "Believe me. So?"

She crossed her arms and scrunched her mouth to one side. It would have been cute if it weren't for the fact that she apparently despised him right now.

"Alright, look," he caved. "It's a big secret. Even Zahid and my parents don't know."

"What is it? Like a secret spy job?" she mocked.

"It's more of an internship where I, uh, help people. It usually doesn't happen during the day, but it is life or death. So when it does happen, I need to book it."

"What kind of help?" she asked.

"I, um, save people from bullies."

"Like abusive relationships?"

"Pretty much." Peter hoped he wasn't imagining things, but she didn't look so mad anymore. "But I didn't want anyone to know."

"I get it," she assured him. "My mom works with the woman's shelter sometimes. I know they have to keep everything secret to hide them from their abusers. I won't tell anyone. But, Peter, that's really cool."

He shrugged. "I'm just doing what anyone would."

"Don't sell yourself short." She studied him for a second. "I have an idea." She took out a pen. "If you ever need someone to cover for you again, let me know."

She grabbed his arm, pushing the sleeve up and started writing numbers. He was paralyzed by her proximity and touch.

"Here's my number in case you need it," she said with a sly smile. "You know, for that or for any other reason."

Then she jogged away, leaving him in a stunned silence.

Peter walked into his house in a stupor that afternoon.

"Hey, honey. How was the field trip?" his mom asked.

"Awesome," he said, not really talking about the museum.

"What is that?" She pointed to Peter's arm.

He shoved his sleeve down but his mom pulled his arm and pushed it back up. She let out a long gasp.

"Is this what I think it is?" she asked. "Who is she? Spill."

"She's just this girl from class."

"Is she cute?" his mom sang. Peter smiled despite himself. "Are you thinking of asking her out?"

He rubbed the back of his neck nervously. "I think she's been giving me hints that she likes me."

"Really?" his mom asked dryly. "What makes you so sure? The fact that she wrote her number on your arm?"

Peter laughed awkwardly. "Yeah, maybe I've been missing a lot of hints, now that I think about it."

"Well, then, it seems we need to have a serious discussion."

"No," Peter shook his head fearfully. "Anything but that."

She crossed her arms and threatened. "You can either have this discussion with me or your father."

"Him!" Peter said immediately. "I choose dad!"

Peter's dad took him out to dinner that night for the purpose of having the talk. Peter hoped he had chosen well and that his mild-mannered father would keep his words to a bare minimum.

"First," his dad said from across the restaurant table, "You're free to make your own choices, but remember that everything you do will have a consequence. It's easy to go with the flow and follow your instincts, but in romance, hormones sound a lot like instincts. So take time to consider every action or desire."

"Ugh. Do you have to say desire?" Peter complained.

"Second, remember that girls always deserve respect and honor. You'll have good karma," he smiled, "if you open doors, let them go first, and protect them from harm."

"Of course. I already knew that."

"And, something else you probably know, is that all women will seem crazy. Even after all these years, I'm no closer to understanding your mother than I ever was." Peter laughed. "They will always seem crazy, but here's the trick: you never tell them that. And I mean *never*."

"Because they'll eat us alive?" Peter speculated.

His dad chuckled. "That and because they're not actually crazy. It's easy to think that we know everything and anyone who thinks differently is crazy, but the truth is, they're just different. And if we take the time to understand them, we can learn a whole lot about life. So remember: actions have consequences, treat her with honor and respect, and never tell her she's crazy."

"I'll remember." Peter waited for the next part, but his dad resumed his meal. "Is that really it?"

"We can go into more detail if you want," Mr. Hunter offered.

Peter shook his head emphatically. "No, I'm okay."

His dad let out a single laugh. "Can you imagine how long that would've taken if you had this talk with your mom?"

Chapter 35: Battling a Dragon

Peter had thought of a million ways to ask Alicia out, but decided that he would just wing it. Then, as he approached the school on Monday morning, he saw Jeremy chasing after her.

"Hey, Ali! I'm talking here." He grabbed her arm and forced her to face him. "You think you're so special, don't you? You think the world owes you anything? You're not even that pretty."

"Let me go!" she struggled.

Peter stepped up next to them and said, "You realize that insulting a girl doesn't actually work as a pick up line, right?"

"Stay out of this, Hunter!"

Jeremy let go of Alicia and tried to shove Peter, but Peter stayed put, rooted to the ground.

"You need to leave her alone," he warned.

"Just because you have a crush on her doesn't mean you own her," Jeremy derided.

Peter rolled his eyes. "Why does everyone think you have to have a crush on a girl to stand up for her? Look, she obviously doesn't like what you're doing. Just back off."

Jeremy threw the first punch, right at Peter's eye. Peter let it hit. It stung, and his skin had split right above the eyebrow. Peter returned the blow with a confident smirk that sent Jeremy into a rage.

Jeremy attacked with blow after blow while Peter dodged effortlessly. Soon Jeremy was tripping over himself in exhaustion.

Finally, he ran away shouting, "This isn't over!"

"Are you okay?" Alicia asked, approaching Peter cautiously.

"Yeah. Sure. This?" he pointed to his eye. "Pfft. Barely felt it."

"Here, sit down."

Peter sat on a nearby bench with her while she went through her backpack and pulled out a bandage. She placed it on his eyebrow. It gave him shivers that she was so close and touching him.

"You didn't have to," he said softly.

She smiled shyly. "It was really brave, what you did."

"Nah. It's what any cool, strong, handsome guy would do."

She scrunched her lips to the side, hiding a smile. "Still, it's really nice that you'd do that even without having a crush on me."

Peter laughed awkwardly. "I, uh, only said I didn't *have* to have a crush to protect you. I never said I *didn't*."

Her head snapped up and she stared at him. Just stared. There wasn't even the hint of a smile or a blush on her face.

And now I just made a fool of myself, he figured.

"Uh, you, uh, don't have to say anything," he stumbled. "I kind of always figured you were out of my league. You don't even have to worry about letting me down easy or anything. I'll just, uh, go…"

She planted a quick kiss on his cheek.

He gaped at her in a stupor. "Yeah?" was all he could say.

In class, Peter couldn't stop staring and smiling at Alicia.

"What's with you?" Zahid asked. "You look goofy."

Peter leaned over and whispered, "I asked Alicia out."

"Finally," Zahid rolled his eyes.

"What should I do? Where would you go on a first date? Most people would do the movies, but I really want to impress her."

"I've never dated," Zahid shrugged. "But whatever you do, don't talk about martial arts or Buddhism the whole time. At least, not unless you want to bore her to death."

"I don't talk about martial arts and Buddhism all the time."

"Right. Only three-fourths of the time."

"Really?"

Zahid laughed. "All I'm saying is take her to a place where you won't be even tempted to bring it up."

"Where did you take that library card for your first date?" Peter teased.

"Aliyah and I are doing just fine, thank you."

Peter paused. "You named it?"

"I named *her*."

That evening, Peter and Rob left their private lesson and drove to an exorcism. When the car stopped its magical, spirit-powered traveling, they had arrived at a farm on the outskirts of town.

"So where should I take her?" Peter asked Rob as they got out of the car. "Where did you take Sensei Charlie on your first date?"

Rob stopped him with a smile and a hand on his shoulder. "I think we should focus on the powerful, hate-filled, evil spirit in front of us and talk about this later," he said firmly.

"Oh. Right." Peter felt embarrassed. "Yeah, I'll focus."

"Keep your head in the game," Rob wagged his finger. "They can use any emotion against you if you aren't being mindful."

Peter gulped. Maybe he should have stayed home.

They heard frantic animal noises from the barn and ran for the doors. Inside, they found a girl about six years old in overalls and a sloppy ponytail. She was holding a small knife and a pig was running away from her, squealing.

"Come back, bacon!" she sang. "I just wanna play with ya."

The pig hid behind Peter's legs. It was covered in cuts.

"Who're you?" the girl asked with a curious tilt to her head.

Even if Peter couldn't see the darkness swelling around her, he still would've been able to feel the dominating presence of the asura. It filled the barn and he felt frozen to the spot.

The animals must have felt it, as well. Each animal was crying and moving in panicked motions. The injured pig pressed against Peter's legs and grunted. Peter looked down and saw the pain and fear in its eyes.

"We're here to help you," Sensei told the girl.

The girl's voice had no inflection as she replied, "I don't want help. I want to eat." Then her voice changed to that of a much older woman. *"Maybe I'll just eat the both of you instead."*

Suddenly, a wild wind swept through the barn. The girl's face changed before Peter's eyes. She looked like a reptile with a long snout and scaly green skin.

All the equipment hanging on the barn walls rose into the air. The animals went crazy, trapped in their pens. Bacon, the pig, squealed and squirmed, but stayed behind Peter.

Sensei Rob started chanting and Peter joined him. Rob conjured a wave that swept all the equipment away and gathered them in a heap on the floor. At the same time, a water current stole the girl's knife from her hands.

The girl howled as her limbs twisted in unnatural positions, switching rapidly as if she were having a violent seizure.

Rob approached the girl, about to expel the demon when she looked up at him with a fiery anger in her eyes.

"You think you can defeat me?" the asura asked, now with the voice of a man. *"You are one of usss,"* it hissed. *"Once a sssoldier of the Kingdom, always a sssoldier. You cannot essscape your fate."*

Peter thought it was a ridiculous threat. Sensei had spent years fighting against the asuras, there was no way he could be considered a soldier for their side. However, Sensei suddenly looked very weak and heavy.

The girl's reptile face twisted in a grin and Rob was thrown through the air like a beanbag. He hit his head hard against a wall and fell limp to the ground.

The girl turned to Peter, hissed, and then slithered off with snakelike movements. He continued the chant while he chased her.

"And you." Its voice echoed off the walls. *"What doesss it even matter to you that I'm hurting these thingsss? They're only food. And if you leave now, I can help you. I know you like that little blond girl."*

Peter froze his face to control his reaction, but his heart rate picked up. All his previous fears were true. He had put Alicia in danger just by liking her. Nevertheless, he continued his search, following the voice that seemed to come from everywhere at once.

"I can make it ssso she'll never leave you," the creature tempted him. *"Wouldn't you like that? We could even make her your ssslave. You could do whatever you want with her."*

Peter didn't know much about girls or relationships yet, but he knew a slave wasn't something he wanted.

The asura must have sensed his choice. It sprang from its hiding spot with bared teeth, showing unnaturally long and pointy canines protruding from the girl's gums.

She held out her hand and the knife flew back into it. Peter was ready to defend the animals and himself from her knife when suddenly he got a premonition. He saw the girl thrusting it into herself.

He took in a sharp breath and punched the air, sending a battering ram of wind at the girl. She flew backwards into a bale of hay. He swirled the air currents around the knife and ripped it from her hands. He brought it to himself and held it tightly.

Then the girl howled and started scratching and biting at herself. Peter rushed to restrain her, but before he reached her, her body was caught in a whirlpool that pinned her arms to her side.

Peter turned and saw Rob standing and turning the water with his hands. Peter wasted no time and pressed his hand against the girl's forehead. "Be swept clean," he said.

Wind filled the barn, rattling the building. The asura emerged from the girl, dropping her body like a discarded jacket and rising into the air. It formed itself into a dragon shape with a long neck. Its eyes were large jewels of darkness that held all the world's hatred.

The dragon loosed an ear-piercing cry. Together, Peter and Rob blasted wind and water as the dragon dodged, rolling over itself in the air with amazing speed and snakelike agility.

"You'll never win!" it taunted above the chanting. *"We'll tear you apart, ripping your pathetic livesss to shredsss!"*

It continued with more threats and insults, aimed at Peter and Rob, but also Charlie, Alicia, and Peter's parents. But Peter kept his mind focused on the chant and the battle.

As the dragon continued to dodge their attacks, Peter got an idea.

While Sensei Rob blasted the dragon with attempted blows, Peter formed Anuvata's wind into a small, thin stream that slipped undetected into the dragon's mouth and nose.

"You are nothing but disssgusting beastsss!" it continued to deride them. *"Full of disssgusting fluidsss: pusss, blood, and excrement! You are beneath usss! You were made to be our food and our play thingsss!"*

Then Peter clapped and the air within the dragon blasted in all directions, tearing the asura apart from the inside. The crushing presence of darkness was lifted and the animals settled. The pig came running and grunting to Peter.

"Good job, kid," Sensei praised him.

Peter looked down at the gashes and blood on the pig.

"I wish one of us had healing powers," he said, bending down to place a calm hand on the pig's head.

"Yeah, that sure would come in handy," Sensei chortled, examining his own injuries.

They guided the pig back to its pen and made sure the girl was in a comfortable position on the hay. Then they started walking to Sensei's car. Peter couldn't forget the look in the pig's eyes.

"I never realized how vulnerable animals are," Peter said. "I wish there were more we could do for them." He buckled himself in and studied the dark night out the windows.

Rob started the engine with a sigh. "*'All beings tremble before violence,'*" he quoted the Buddha. "*'All fear death, all love life. See yourself in others. Then whom can you hurt?'* Honestly, that's why I'm a vegetarian. I can't imagine having the heart to kill an animal, so why should I make someone else do it for me? I feel bad for these animals, but maybe we can offer up some good karma for them."

Then Peter remembered the temptation of the asura:

"We could even make her your ssslave. You could do whatever you want with her."

"Hey, are they really going to try to hurt Alicia?"

"I don't know," Rob said pensively. "They've threatened Charlene before. But you have to realize, these things have layers of plans and temptations. Maybe they really would hurt them and maybe they only want us to think they would. It's almost impossible to figure out their real game."

"Then how do we win," Peter asked, "if we can't figure out their real game?"

"We win by not playing. Let them make their choices, let us make our choices regardless of their threats and manipulations. Forget their games and just strive for loving-kindness in everything you do."

Somehow, Peter didn't feel satisfied by that answer.

Chapter 36: Peter Becomes a Vegetarian

“Good morning!” his mom sang as Peter entered the kitchen.

He nodded and feigned a smile. He was groggy and emotionally beat from the night before.

“Sleep well?” his dad asked from across the table.

“Just one nightmare,” he responded truthfully.

His mom slid a plate of bacon and eggs towards him. He stared at the bacon and suddenly all he could think of was the pig.

“Come back, Bacon! I just want to play with ya!”

“What’s wrong?” his mom asked. “Is there a bug on the plate?”

“No, it’s not that.” He paused a beat. “Thanks for cooking, but I just don’t think I can eat meat right now.”

His mom looked like she was anticipating a joke. “What?” she asked. “All meat? What about hamburgers? Tacos? Steak?”

Peter cringed at the thought of the animals being tortured by the little girl. “I just can’t right now.”

“What is this about?” Mr. Hunter asked.

He thought a moment about how to answer. “I saw something about the treatment of animals on farms. I just don’t think I can stomach meat right now. Literally.”

“You cannot be a vegetarian,” his mom asserted. “Where are you going to get your protein and iron?”

“I… don’t know,” Peter replied.

“Well, I’m not changing the way I cook,” she declared.

“Mom, I’m not trying to start a fight. I just wouldn’t want to kill an animal, so why should I make someone else do it for me?”

“Then are we monsters for eating bacon?” she challenged him.

“I didn’t mean that,” he defended quickly.

“No,” she slammed her spatula on the countertop. “You will eat the food I cook and that is final.”

“Jody,” Peter’s father chided.

“No, you know what? If my cooking isn’t good enough for you, then don’t eat it. You can eat a banana.” She took off her apron and threw it. “You can eat lots of bananas!” Then she stormed off down the hall.

“Why’d she go all psycho?” Peter asked his dad.

“She’s not crazy,” Mr. Hunter cautioned.

“Am I wrong for not wanting to eat meat? Lots of people are vegetarians, right?”

“I wouldn’t say you’re wrong,” his dad assuaged him.

“And how is it an insult? I didn’t even ask her to make me something different. And I said thanks, right? I said thanks.”

“You said thanks,” his dad nodded. “Why don’t you take a few minutes to think it over? I’ll talk to your mom.”

Peter huffed out the door and took a walk to his favorite park where he usually did his workouts and meditation. He sat on a bench and settled his mind until he felt Anuvata’s presence.

Why is my mom so crazy about this? He complained to the spirit in his thoughts. *It’s not like I’m hurting anyone!*

The spirit didn’t speak, but his dad’s words echoed in his mind, *“She’s not crazy. She just thinks differently.”*

Then what is she thinking? Peter questioned. *Why is she so angry?*

Suddenly, Peter had an image in his mind’s eye of his mom cheerfully cooking and putting the food on plates in whimsical designs. He remembered her reading countless books on nutrition over the years. He recalled the many times she had imposed new diets or food fads after much research. Sometimes that would drive him crazy, but Peter now realized that it was how she expressed her love.

His desire to stop eating meat was an insult in a way. It was equivalent to him telling her that all her work wasn’t good enough.

He felt his anger soften at the thought.

Peter was chopping vegetables in the kitchen when his mom came in, finally calmed.

“What’s going on here?” she asked.

“This is a thank you,” Peter answered. “And a peace offering.”

She sighed as she sat down on the counter stool. “You don’t have to…”

“Look, I get it mom,” he interrupted. “You’re always taking care of us and you love it. I’m grateful for that, but I really have to do this. So I’m going to make it easy on you. That’s why I’m making this vegetarian chili.”

“You really don’t have to do this,” she said.

“I want to. I promise to cook once a week and I’ll make enough to eat the leftovers all week if I need to. I’ll buy the food with my allowance and I’ll take care of my school lunches, too.”

"I'll buy the food," she assured him. "And I'll help. I just felt like you were saying my cooking wasn't good enough for you."

"I didn't mean it like that," he told her sincerely.

"You cooking once a week sounds fun, though," she said warmly. "Can I help?"

Peter smiled. "Sure. Can you get the beans?"

They worked together, laughing and joking as they prepared the meal. Peter thought it was amazing that his spirit was there to help him fight evil, save his life, and tell him how to handle his mom.

Then his mom drew in a sharp breath. "What's that?" she said, grabbing his hand quickly.

"What is it?" he asked. He thought back to the fight in the barn, but couldn't remember getting an injury on his hand.

"It's two new freckles," she said with wonder.

Peter rolled his eyes. "We're still playing that game?"

She studied the freckles more closely. "Ooh, they're special Buddhist freckles. From what I can tell, this one is for being non-violent, and this one is for being patient with your crazy mom."

Peter laughed as she let go. "You're not crazy," he assured her.

"Are you sure?" she asked with a forced smile.

He chuckled.

He was glad to be able to go meatless. He felt like he was helping in a small way to protect the animals who couldn't protect themselves.

At the same time, it wasn't enough. He needed to do something that took his uncomfortable feeling of negativity away. He stopped still when a thought came to him.

"Everything ok?" his mom asked.

"I just got an awesome idea for a first date."

As Peter waited outside the animal shelter, he tried to compose himself. He had stayed calm in plenty of life and death situations.

So I can handle a date, right? He asked himself.

His palms started sweating when Alicia arrived. She waved as her mom drove off.

"Hey," he said, smiling awkwardly.

"Hey," she returned.

Brilliant conversation, he scolded himself.

"So are you picking out a puppy or something?" she asked.

He smiled. "I'll show you."

He led her to a room of chairs where a few strangers waited.

"Is this a class or something?" she asked nervously. "Because it's a Saturday. We're not required to think today."

He chuckled. "Just wait. I promise it'll be worth it."

A worker came in and walked them through rules regarding the proper interaction with the dogs and cats. Alicia started to look excited. Then the worker led them to a hallway of walk in cages where they were allowed to play with any of the animals.

Alicia squealed and ran straight to a white fluffy dog.

For an hour, they played with the shelter pets, brushed them, helped to wash a few of them, and played games in the backyard.

By the end of the hour, neither of them could stop smiling.

"I was so worried when I saw the tables and chairs," she confessed as they walked out to the parking lot.

"Yeah, you looked kind of mad," he laughed.

"If it had been a class, I would've called my mom."

Peter gulped. "The ice is that thin, huh?"

She giggled. "You survived this round."

He stopped in front of her eagerly. "Does that mean there might be a second date?"

She laughed. "You're like a puppy!" she joked.

"A really handsome and awesome puppy, though, right?"

She scrunched her mouth to one side in a pretend pensive look. "I won't get rid of you just yet."

Alicia's mom pulled up and they both looked at each other. It seemed like she didn't want to say goodbye either.

"What do I say when my mom asks why I smell like wet dog?" she asked.

"New perfume?" Peter shrugged.

Alicia giggled. "Today was fun," she told him.

She smiled all the way to her car and he smiled as he watched.

Chapter 37: Message From the Boss

The next day, Zahid asked Peter to accompany him and his siblings to a museum downtown.

"You're always the one paying for things," Zahid told him, as they neared the entrance, "but today is on me."

Peter smirked, "Isn't today one of those free admission days?"

Zahid smiled broadly. "So, how did your date go?" He switched the topic.

Peter smiled automatically. "I think it went well. She seemed happy. And she said she'd be willing to have another one."

"What are you going to do for the second one?" Zahid asked. "I assume you have to top the first."

"Shoot. You're right," Peter sobered. "What do I do?"

"You could always take her here," Zahid suggested, "and show her your extensive scientific knowledge."

Zahid knew that Peter's science grades were his lowest.

"Ha, ha," he pretended to laugh.

Zahid thought a moment while Hassan, Ahmed, and Yara ran straight for the dinosaur exhibit.

"How about you start with what you like about her," he suggested. "Is it for shallow reasons like because she's pretty and popular?"

"Of course not," Peter attested. "I like how she's confident."

"You could challenge her to a competition," Zahid joked.

"I like when she smiles," Peter continued.

"Bring her to a dentist!"

"I like how she's always thinking about people in need. Oh, hey, that might work." They both stopped in front of a fossil encased in glass. "So what are we looking at here?" Peter asked.

"This is the *Anchiornis huxelyi*," Zahid answered plainly.

"You say that like I should know…"

"They used this fossil to extract the color of its feathers using a new method," he explained. "Now they're trying to find the color of other feathered dinosaurs. It revolutionized paleontology."

"Oh," Peter nodded. "And here I thought it was a rock with a picture of a bird on it."

Zahid held onto Peter's shoulder. "Repeat after me," he told Peter, "'Welcome to Value Mart. Can I help you with anything?'"

Peter pushed him playfully. As they were laughing, Peter's phone buzzed. He saw it was Sensei Rob and excused himself.

"Hey, Sensei," he greeted. "What's up?"

"Peter!" Rob sounded frantic. "Where are you?"

"Downtown," Peter answered. "Is everything okay?"

"I'm hurt. Really hurt. It was an asura. I need your help."

"Why didn't my deva call me?" Peter wondered.

"This asura was too strong for either of us," Rob answered. "I don't know if I'm going to make it. I've lost a lot of blood."

Peter pictured Sensei Rob passed out in some alley. He imagined Charlie's reaction if he died. The entire studio would be devastated and the whole town would be overrun with asuras without Rob.

"Calm down," he told Sensei and himself. "Where are you?"

"A couple blocks away. In the alley at thirteenth and Sunvale."

Peter excused himself from Zahid and rushed off.

His desperation gave him an idea. He centered his thoughts until he felt Anuvata's presence. Then he applied a blast of wind behind him, thrusting himself forward, faster than he could normally run. The people around him seemed shocked, but he imagined their minds would explain it away.

He had a sense of urgency in his gut from Anuvata. He knew he needed to have his guard up, but he blasted forward with no plan. He didn't know what to expect, but he had to protect Sensei Rob.

He arrived at the alley and looked all around. Sensei was nowhere. Peter started panicking, wondering if the asura had come to finish him off.

Then he felt a disturbance in the wind from behind him. He dodged, just missing a brick that smashed into dust against a wall.

Behind him stood three people, all possessed. The first was a woman in a business suit. Her hair was pulled into a bun and she looked like she was about to give a presentation or fire someone.

The second person was a young man with rock star style. He wore ripped jeans and a tight sleeveless shirt. His hair was long and wild and his sunglasses looked very expensive. He was holding a second brick.

The third person was an older man who wore an expensive suit with a handkerchief in the pocket, jewelry, and slicked silver hair. It seemed that this man had no problems in the money department.

Peter remembered the trick with the phone call from the pishacha at the nursing home.

"Sensei's not here, is he?" Peter realized.

The asuras laughed through their victims.

Peter started thinking quickly. He couldn't exorcise them if they didn't want it. He had to figure out how to run away or trap them.

"Relax," the older man said in an asura's gravelly voice. *"We're here with a peace offering from the boss."*

"What boss?" Peter asked.

"The head honcho. Mara, the King of the Desire Realm."

"We come to offer power," the female said. *"Power, fame, and money beyond your wildest dreams. And our gifts would be at your disposal whenever you wanted. You wouldn't have to worry about doing the bidding of some boring spirit. You wouldn't have to meditate or read or always make the 'right' choices."*

Peter had to admit that sounded tempting.

"We've helped lowly people achieve their own powers countless times," the rock star guy lectured. *"We can give you the gift of flight, withstanding fire, healing, or psychic powers."*

"And all I'd have to do is fight on your side," Peter finished.

"No," the older man said. *"You'd be free to do whatever you want with the powers. They'd be yours to command."*

"Nice try," Peter said sarcastically, "but you really expect me to believe you're such Good Samaritans? I'll stick with the spirit I've got."

"Maybe you need a demonstration," the rock star guy snickered.

Chapter 38: Peter Tries to Tell the Truth

The rock star guy slammed the brick into the concrete, shattering it and leaving a crater. He kept his hand on the pavement and the ground started shaking. At the same time, the older man breathed fire.

While all this happened, the businesswoman was staring intently at him. To an outsider, it would have looked as if she were doing nothing, but Peter felt forceful thoughts within his mind that attempted to take him over.

The thoughts rambled nonsensical logic:

"Up is down. Black is white. All is a dream concocted by your mind. Your mind exists, but it doesn't exist. Good is evil and evil is good."

On an on, the thoughts prattled. All the while Peter struggled to hang on to some semblance of logic while dodging the blasts of fire in the quaking alleyway. It was similar to hearing someone recite random digits while you tried to memorize a phone number.

Peter held out both hands and conjured a blast of wind that knocked all three of them back. The ground stopped shaking and he leapt into the air, flipping over them. He ran from the alley.

The woman, old man, and rocker guy were behind him in an instant. Peter dodged the people on the streets, but the asuras simply held out their hands and the people were thrown back by invisible forces.

Peter bent the wind behind him to propel him upwards. He jumped onto a trashcan, then an awning, and sprang to the narrow ledge beneath the second story windows. He ran along the ledge and the asuras followed, climbing up the building like spiders.

People gasped at the sight, and Peter wondered what they would convince themselves they were seeing.

He ran out of ledge and jumped back to the sidewalk. Again, the asuras were right behind him.

He ran into the street, thinking they wouldn't follow for the danger, but he was wrong. His heart skipped a beat when he saw an oncoming compact car. It honked, but couldn't stop in time. He ran towards it and flipped into the air, using the currents to make sure he stayed airborne over it. People nearby cheered.

The asuras tried to dodge the car, but the older man's body was hit. He rolled on the pavement. The car screeched to a stop and people all around rushed to help him. Peter's heart ached.

He continued to run, hoping that the man would recover. He had to get the other asuras away from innocent bystanders. He had to think of a way to stop them, preferably without hurting them.

The other two asuras caught up with Peter in a large flat field at a downtown park. The businesswoman ran straight at him. He ran towards her at the same time, bent low and grabbed her around the waist while rotating around to her back. Using his momentum, he flipped her backwards up and over him. She landed a few feet away, unharmed. A crowd had gathered and was applauding the impressive move.

The rock star guy and the woman ran at Peter. He jumped and flipped over the woman. They ran into each other. The crowd laughed.

They stumbled backwards, but recovered quickly. They ran towards him again. This time, Peter ran at the rock star guy, dropped his shoulder into the man and flipped him over and towards the woman.

A chorus of approvals rang out from the crowd.

So far, he had been able to fight them while inflicting minimal harm, but his adrenaline and stamina were dropping. He didn't know how much longer he could go on.

He surveyed his surroundings and saw the outside of the museum had a series of windows, drain spouts, and ledges. He raced towards the building and, using Anuvata's wind, propelled himself from foothold to handhold until he reached the flat roof. He bent over to catch his breath. He was at the tail end of his endurance.

Just as the two possessed people were coming over the edge, Peter used all his strength to shoot Anuvata's wind underneath him. He hovered in the air, out of their reach.

"This isn't over yet!" the asura in the businesswoman threatened.

Then both asuras shed their borrowed bodies like snakes shedding skin. The man and woman fell to the ground and two dark clouds of smoke rose towards Peter.

Before he could figure out his next move, they both shaped themselves into abnormally large crow shapes. Peter dodged one, but the other grabbed his arms and lifted him higher into the air. His arms were punctured by its massive talons. Then it dropped him. At the last moment, he summoned a wind that cushioned his fall.

He recovered and spun the air around him in a huge whirlwind. The bird-asuras tried to get through, but the wind forced them back.

Then, in one final effort, he let go of the whirlwind, letting it blast in all directions. The asuras were blown away.

After using the roof entrance and finding his way back to the ground floor, Peter cleaned off his wounds in the bathroom. After that, he stopped in the gift shop and bought a hoodie to cover his injuries.

"Where were you?" Zahid asked when they met up.

Peter avoided the answer by saying, "I bought a hoodie."

He thought was getting good at avoiding the truth without lying.

"Tell me the truth, Peter," Zahid said sternly. Peter lost his breath. "All this nerdy stuff was too much for you, huh? You had to go and cry over your inferiority complex?"

He slapped Peter on his shoulder, right where the bird-asura had scratched into him. Peter controlled his reaction.

"Believe whatever you want, man," he forced a laugh.

Yara tugged on her brother's shirt. "Can I have a hoodie, too?"

"Me, too! Me, too!" Hassan and Ahmed shouted at once.

Peter stumbled into his house that evening, anxious to bandage his wounds. He kept worrying about the victims he had left on the roof and the one on the street. He hoped their injuries would heal quickly.

"Hey, honey!" his mom greeted. "How was the museum?"

She and his dad were watching the evening news on the couch.

"I saw a bird fossil that was apparently important," he replied.

"Did you see the street performance?" his mom asked.

"The what now?"

Peter looked at the TV where shaky and blurry phone cameras depicted much of his fight in the city.

"It was the coolest flash mob!" an eyewitness was raving. "Or maybe it was a promotion or something? I'm not sure, but it was really cool."

"Hm. Interesting." His dad scratched his chin and pointed at Peter. "That brown-haired kid kind of reminds me of you."

Peter froze. Maybe it was the exhaustion and stress of having to fight three supernaturally-powered humans, but he suddenly regretted the numerous times he had deceived his parents. Even if he had done it without technically lying, he still knew that he ought to tell them the truth.

"Mom, dad?" he said. "That is me."

Chapter 39: Adventures of Candy Boy

They turned their heads slowly and looked at him over the back of the couch. His muscles were all tense, but he kept going.

"I should've told you months ago, but Sensei Rob recruited me as an apprentice exorcist and we free people from demonic possession. It was just so weird I didn't know how to say it."

"Ha, ha, ha," his mom pretended to laugh. "Now go get cleaned up. We're going out for dinner."

"No, it's not a joke." Peter shook his head. "That's why Sensei was teaching me all that Buddhist stuff. See, there's this good spirit who chose me as a vessel or a partner and it helps me fight against Mara, who's the devil, and his minions, who are the asuras. When I was at the museum, three of the asuras ambushed me. But everyone just saw what they wanted to see and thought it was a performance."

"Someone's been reading too many comic books," his mom laughed.

"I'm telling the truth here!" Peter attested.

"That would make a very interesting superhero story," his dad pondered. "I had no idea you were this creative."

"You should write a book!" his mom encouraged. "You could call it Peter Hunter and the Minions of Mara!"

"That has a nice ring to it," his dad assessed.

"Why don't you believe me?"

"Get your sarcastic butt up those stairs, mister," his mom ordered. "We leave in ten minutes."

Peter surrendered. He figured people also heard what they wanted to hear.

That night, Peter woke up from a horrible, asura-inspired dream where he was beating the old talkative man, Martin, from the nursing home that was once plagued by a Pishacha.

After beating Martin, Peter pushed him into a street where he was hit by a car. Martin rolled on the pavement, shocking Peter out of his dream.

As he stared into the darkness and tried to ignore the lingering images of the nightmare, he struggled with feelings of guilt and shame.

I won't let them win, he told himself.

A couple weekends later, the doorbell rang and set Peter's heart into double speed. His mom got there first, but Peter raced around her.

"Hey," he greeted Alicia. "Ok, thanks, mom. Bye now."

"Hold your horses, young man," his mom complained.

He cringed. "Ok, mom, this is Alicia. Alicia, my mom."

"Slow down," his mom stopped him. "Hi Alicia." She smiled brightly. "Is Peter being respectful?"

"Always," Alicia assured her.

"If he ever isn't," Mrs. Hunter conspired, "you tell me and I'll ground him forever, okay?"

"Yes, ma'am," Alicia nodded.

"Oh, and I can't let this opportunity pass without telling you an embarrassing story," his mom clapped her hands together while her eyes danced mischievously.

"No. Mom, please," Peter pleaded.

"It's my job as your mom. When I was potty training him…"

"No," he groaned. "Anything but this."

"We used to reward him with colored candies. I kept them in the cabinet behind the toilet. So this one time…"

Peter resisted the urge to bang his head against the wall.

"…he went, I flushed and all that, and when I gave him his reward, I accidentally dropped one in the potty…"

"Can we at least not call it the potty?" he complained.

"Anyway, he looks down and he sees it, I think it was red, and he goes, 'I poop candy?'" Alicia and his mom laughed together. "He thought he was magical or something!"

"That is the best thing I have ever heard," Alicia proclaimed.

"How could you do this to me?" Peter questioned his mother. "Your own flesh and blood, your only son and heir."

"It's my sacred right and duty as your mom." She let out a laugh. "Hah. 'Duty.'"

"Mom, please!"

"It was nice to meet you, Alicia," his mom said. "I hope I see you again soon." Then, to Peter's horror, his mom winked before she left the room.

Peter turned slowly to Alicia who was grinning superiorly.

"Can we please just wipe those last few minutes out of existence?" he begged her.

"'Wipe?'" Alicia started laughing.

"Please don't use this against me."

"Your secret's safe with me, Candy Boy. So what are we doing today?"

He led her to the kitchen where he had all the ingredients laid out for chocolate chip cookies.

"Cookies?" she noted. "Should I call you Cookie Boy instead?"

"Why not Handsome Boy?" he complained. "Or Cool Boy?"

She giggled playfully. "So you know how to make cookies?"

"Yeah. Doesn't everyone?"

She bit her bottom lip and scrunched her nose. "Don't tell anyone, but I've never cooked or baked anything."

"Then I'll have to teach you. It's a really difficult family recipe, handed down from generation to generation," he bragged.

"The one on the back of the chocolate chip bag?" she asked.

"I didn't say it was *my* family's recipe."

When the cookies were finished, Alicia waited as Peter cleaned up.

"So cookies are in a box," she said. "Are we taking them somewhere?"

"Yep. On a walk."

They walked a few blocks away to the nearby nursing home where Rob had exorcised the Pishacha.

"An old folks' home?" Alicia asked. "Do you have a grandparent here?"

"Nope. I started doing some community service here recently. I thought it'd be fun to do it together."

"So… stranger old folks?" She didn't look excited.

He nudged her with his shoulder and said, "Give it a chance."

Peter and Alicia handed out the cookies to the residents while listening to their stories and sharing smiles. Peter was amazed by how simple it was to lift their spirits.

At one point, Martin stopped Peter and asked, "Is she your sweetheart?" He pointed to Alicia who was listening to another resident.

Peter smiled as he watched her and said, "I hope so."

Due to either old age or the same forgetfulness that seemed to plague everyone, Martin had forgotten the details of how he and Peter had first met. He only remembered that they knew each other.

"You remind me of myself and my Delores," Martin told him.

"Your wife, right?" Peter asked.

"It was love at first sight," Martin told him. "The first day of high school, I looked at her smile and," he made a sound that seemed to say she took his breath away.

"You just knew, huh?" Peter asked.

"You know that first day of spring sunshine after a long winter?" Martin waxed poetically. "The one that melts all the ice and snow? That's what it felt like. I married her as soon as I could. We had fifty years together and they were the best years a man could ask for. When you find a girl with a smile like that, a smile that melts your ice and snow, you do everything you can to keep her smiling."

As they walked back, Peter felt a high from the joy they had spread. He figured that this was what positive karma felt like.

"That guy Martin had some great war stories, too," he told Alicia. "If you come back, you should ask him to tell you one."

"Great," Alicia responded blandly.

"Hold up." Peter stopped and faced her. "You're not smiling."

"It's fine," she lied. "It's just that today was weird."

"I'm an idiot," he scolded himself. "I was just stressing about topping the first date. I thought you liked community service stuff."

"I do, but part of the fun of a date is telling your friends about it afterwards. There's nothing romantic about hanging out with a bunch of smelly old people."

"Aw, geez. I messed up."

"It's ok," Alicia said. "Just let me choose the next one."

His heart skipped a beat. "Next one?"

She smiled and looked at her feet. "Yeah." Then she fixed him with a stern gaze and a finger aimed at his nose. "But you'd better play your cards right and do just what I tell you to, Candy Boy."

Chapter 40: Grasping at Attachments

The next weekend, Peter and Alicia met at a movie theater. Peter laughed to himself that he had been so worried about impressing her with interesting dates when apparently, her choice was a movie.

"What do you want to see?" he asked her. "There's that new Nocturnal Ninja movie out."

"No, we're seeing that one." She pointed to the poster for a romantic comedy. Peter grimaced. "Don't make that face, Hunter. You made me go to an old folks' home. Now, we are seeing this movie and you will be cute and romantic with me whether you like it or not."

He laughed. "Is that an order?"

She nodded seriously. "It's an order, soldier."

"Ma'am, yes ma'am!" he joked.

After buying her ticket, he figured he would play up the game.

"What are your orders now, miss?" he saluted.

She raised an eyebrow. "Really?"

He shifted awkwardly, suddenly feeling stupid. "You said I had to be romantic, but honestly, I'm pretty clueless in that area."

"More like an idiot," she agreed.

"Gee, thanks."

"You could start with a compliment," she suggested.

"So you get to call me an idiot and I have to compliment you?"

"You *get* to compliment me," she corrected. "And yes. That's exactly how this works."

"Okay," he studied her. "Um, wow," his mind was suddenly blank. "I am not good at this."

"There must be something you like about me." She twirled.

"There's a lot," he confessed. "I just can't think of what they are right now. I'm finding it hard to think about a lot of things."

"My hair," she suggested, "my eyes, my stunning intellect."

"You seem to be doing just fine on your own," he laughed. "Um," he scratched the back of his neck nervously. "I guess I like how you're always trying to help people. And you always know just what to say. And I really like when you smile. Is that enough?"

She scrunched up her nose. "For now."

"Are you going to compliment me, now?" Peter asked.

"You're so funny," she giggled. "No, now, you buy me some popcorn."

"Ma'am, yes, Ma'am."

The movie was mind-numbingly boring, but he was too busy enjoying orders like, "pretend to like this part," "repeat that line to me some time," and "hold my hand."

After the movie, they sat and talked until her mom pulled up.

"Any last orders?" he asked her.

"Hm. Let's see," she tapped her chin playfully. "You will tell me you had the best time ever."

"I did," he said sincerely.

She smiled. "You will text me before the weekend's over. And as I drive away, you will watch after me with the saddest puppy dog eyes ever."

"Orders received, princess."

"Goodnight. I mean, at ease, soldier!"

The next Monday, as Peter entered the classroom, he smiled when he saw Alicia at her desk. She smiled back and he felt a flurry of butterflies. Then Jeremy ruined it all by tugging on her hair.

"Ow. What was that for?" she complained.

"For ignoring me," Jeremy informed her.

Peter's butterflies were replaced by rage.

"Maybe I don't want to talk to you," Alicia sneered.

"You're so stuck up. Why can't you just get over yourself?"

"Hey, Jeremy!" Peter sprang to Alicia's desk. He got in Jeremy's face and warned him clearly, "Leave my girlfriend alone."

"Girlfriend?" Jeremy shot gazes back and forth at the two of them.

"Girlfriend?" Alicia also asked, jumping to her feet.

Peter felt the burn of the entire class watching and waiting.

"Did I just say that?" he said quickly. He turned to Alicia apologetically. "I was going to ask you in a better way, I promise…"

She gave him a quick peck on the cheek, right there in front of everyone. "You heard the man," she told Jeremy as she laced her fingers into Peter's. "Leave his girlfriend alone!"

Peter felt like his feet weren't even touching the ground when he entered the dojo that afternoon. He tried to control his giddy smile. He saw Charlie at the front desk and Rob in his office, leaning back in his chair with his hands behind his head.

"Someone looks happy," Charlie studied Peter.

Peter was about to tell her when Sensei Rob interrupted, "He got a girlfriend today."

Charlie gasped.

Peter turned to Sensei, shocked. "What? How did you…" Then he dropped his bag in frustration. "What the Naraka! Don't tell me we're back to this again! Why didn't Anuvata just talk to me about this?"

Rob shrugged. "My deva said you weren't listening."

"You're devas talk to each other?" Charlie asked, appalled. "Behind your backs? That must be incredibly annoying."

"It sure is," he agreed. "So? Am I not allowed to have a girlfriend?"

"I'm merely supposed to point out that after all your training and meditation you got a bit mindless around this girl. Apparently," he filled Charlie in, "he just blurted out that she was his girlfriend without even asking her. Do we need to review Right Mindfulness and Right Speech?"

Peter glared at Sensei. "I don't see how it's that much different from blurting out a marriage proposal during class," he challenged.

Charlie cleared her throat emphatically in agreement.

Sensei sat up calmly. "I've never said I was perfect. My deva and I had a long talk about that when it happened. Now it's your turn." Sensei stood and walked to the front desk. "It's easy to lose your head with romance, but it is rarely ever more important to keep your head."

"So what exactly do I have to do?" Peter grumbled.

"I am sure your deva will have some ideas," Rob said. "Remember what I told you about how I take my love for Charlene to meditation every day? I challenge myself to make sure I'm always focusing my love on her, not on how her love makes me feel."

"You really do that?" Charlie asked, apparently touched.

They shared a sickening moment of blissful smiles.

"That's what I do," Rob continued to Peter. "Sometimes it can be difficult or mentally exhausting..."

"As mentally exhausting as this conversation?" Peter griped.

Sensei's eyes narrowed. "But it's important to make sure we're loving selflessly, without unnecessary attachment. The Buddha said, *'In the end, only three things matter: how much you loved, how gently you lived, and how gracefully you let go of things not meant for you.'"*

"But I still get to date her, right?" Peter asked grumpily. "Or are you going to tell me she's an unnecessary attachment?"

"That's what your deva is for, but you have to listen to it. In fact, that's the lesson for today." He pointed to the dojo mats. "Go talk to your spirit."

"Is this really just because you have some wedding planning to do?" Peter challenged.

Charlie sniggered.

"Just sit," Sensei ordered.

Peter rolled his eyes and slumped his shoulders as he trudged over to the dojo area. "Geez, I've been crushing on her forever," he complained. "Can't we just be happy like normal people?"

"I'm not normal and neither are you, kid," Rob declared.

"You said it," Charlie agreed under her breath.

Peter sat in a corner and closed his eyes while complaining within his mind. All his excitement had been robbed of him, now.

But he knew that Sensei was right. If Peter had been more in control of his thoughts and words, he could have asked Alicia to be his girlfriend in a much less embarrassing way.

He took deep breaths, evening them out, and tried to settle his thoughts. After a few minutes, he felt Anuvata's presence within him.

Sorry for not being more mindful, he told the spirit.

Peter felt no blame or accusations in return, but a sense of caution washed over him.

He saw a vision within his mind of himself and Alicia walking side by side, talking, and laughing. Without warning, she leaned in and kissed him. He smiled as she pulled away and giggled. Then, as he leaned in to kiss her back, he changed into Jeremy.

The sight of the two of them kissing jolted him from his peaceful state. He felt his heart beating erratically. His wandering thoughts jumped to anger, resentment, and retribution.

Then he realized that Anuvata had used an inciting image to remind Peter that Alicia was not his. She did not belong to him. He did not own her or her affections. She was subject to change just like everything else. She could not be the source of his lasting happiness.

If he cared about Alicia and not just himself, he should be able to be happy for her, even if she did choose Jeremy over him one day.

He knew that sense of detachment was ideal, but it would take a lot of meditation to internalize, considering that the thought only made him feel sick at the present.

On the following weekend, Peter and Alicia rode their bikes to a nearby park. After sharing a picnic, they held hands and walked the paths while they talked. Peter felt proud of himself for memorizing questions to keep the conversation flowing.

"If you could be famous, what would you want to be famous for?" he asked.

She didn't even have to think. "I'd want to be famous for some great humanitarian work, saving poor starving children or something."

"I could see that," he chuckled. "And why are you friends with Gina and Stacey?"

"Ugh. Stacey," she rolled her eyes. "We are not friends."

Peter suddenly realized that he hadn't seen Stacey hanging out with them since high school had started.

"Yeah, things were cool and all," Alicia explained, "and then one day she said that she liked Mr. Feretti's English class."

"Wow. She's evil," Peter said sarcastically.

"No, you don't understand. She was going on and on about how fun and easy it was and everyone knew that Gina didn't do well in the class and that Mr. F totally picked on her."

"But she didn't mean to insult her, right?" Peter asked.

"She meant it. There's this whole other language girls speak."

"I knew it!" Peter congratulated himself.

"Anyway, it was like a declaration of war. We couldn't be friends with someone who insults one of us like that."

"Ah," Peter said, not sure of what else to say. He and Zahid often said worse things to each other, but neither of them meant any harm. He was convinced that he would never understand girls.

"It was for the best," Alicia continued. "She was horrible about Zahid."

"What? Why?" Peter asked.

"She was afraid of him. Didn't you ever realize that she never came with us when Gina and I talked to you guys?"

"Hm. Now that you mention it…"

"But anyway, Gina's a great friend. She's always honest, and passionate, and loyal. What do you like about Zahid?"

"He's smart, and a good person."

"Do you think he'll ever like Gina back?" Alicia giggled.

Peter laughed. "He's mentioned a few times that he doesn't like how forward and bold American girls are," Peter explained.

Alicia stopped and stood very close to him. "And what do *you* think about forward and bold American girls?" she asked.

Peter felt locked into her eyes and gulped.

SHOOOSH!

"Naraka!" he grumbled.

"What does that mean?" she questioned.

"I am so sorry, Alicia…" he apologized.

"What? Your job?" she realized. "How do you even know?"

"I'll come back as soon as I can," he promised.

"You expect me to wait?" Her eyes were huge in indignation.

"I'll make it up to you, I promise!" he started running off.

"Peter Hunter!" she hollered after him. "You get back here!"

Peter was sure that he was digging the grave for his short-lived first relationship, but an exorcism could mean life or death.

He met Rob under a bridge at the park where a teenaged boy held a knife to a girl's stomach. She had tears streaming down her terrified face and Peter could smell the alcohol on the boy from where he was standing.

"Shh," the boy chided her. "One noise is all it'll take." He stroked her cheek with his other hand. "This will all be over soon."

"It'll be over sooner than you think," Sensei answered.

The boy turned around and barred his teeth. Sensei formed a whip that tore the knife from the boy's hand.

"Get the girl," Sensei instructed before starting a chant.

Peter led the girl out from under the bridge and down the path until she pulled him to a stop and started sobbing. Peter figured she was in shock so he gave her his jacket.

"Are you ok?" he asked softly.

"He wasn't always like that," she said. "When he started drinking…"

She was overwhelmed by her tears and buried her head into his chest. He put his hands on her shoulders awkwardly, trying to calm her down.

"You're safe now," he told her.

"Peter?" Alicia's voice sent shivers up his spine. He let go of the girl, jumped back, and turned to see her standing a few feet away.

Chapter 41: Fire and Water

"I can explain," he said quickly.

Alicia was fuming. "You can explain how you ditched me on our date to double-cross me with this floozy?"

"You don't know what she's been through," Peter defended the girl.

"Oh, this is rich," Alicia put her hands on her hips and huffed. "Do you have any idea what *I've* been through?"

"It's not what you think," the girl stopped her, stepping forward. "He and his friend, they just saved me." She started crying again and Alicia looked shocked into silence. "I was… this guy, he was… he was going to hurt me and your boyfriend saved me. If he hadn't been there…" she shook her head and choked on the words.

Alicia hugged her while giving Peter a look over the girl's shoulder.

"I took care of it and got the cops called," Sensei Rob said as he came around the corner. "Uh, who's this?"

"My girlfriend," Peter told him. "Alicia, this is my Sensei, Rob. He's my mentor with the whole *part-time job thing*."

"You told her about our work?" Sensei asked, "but not your parents?"

"Don't worry, mister sensei," Alicia explained. "I know I'm not supposed to talk about it."

"Why don't you two run back to your date?" Rob suggested. "I'll wrap up the details here."

"Thanks," Peter said. "I owe you."

Alicia looked up at him while they walked back together. "I'm sorry I doubted you," she said in a whisper.

"Sorry for the confusion," he told her sincerely. "I promise I'd never date anyone behind your back. Or to your face. It's just you."

She slipped her hand into his. "You're amazing."

"Nah. I'm just doing what anyone would do."

Alicia stopped him and studied him for a second.

"What?" he asked nervously.

She raised herself on her toes and planted a quick kiss on his lips.

"You really are a superhero," she said.

Peter studied Alicia laughing with her friends across the lunchroom. She caught his eye and smiled back.

"You seem happy," Zahid noted sarcastically. "I wonder why."

Peter laughed. "It's not just her. I mean, a lot has to do with her, but I have that district competition coming up soon, and my dad finally has a new job. I feel like things are falling into place."

"I don't care if there's no more pudding here," they heard Jeremy yelling at a lunch lady. "Go to the back and get more. That's your job!"

Peter shook his head and sighed. "Is that guy ever nice?"

Zahid said something in Arabic.

"What does that mean?" Peter asked.

"'He who has his hand in water is not like he who has his hand in fire.'"

"Uh, what now?"

"That's right. I forgot who I was talking to," Zahid teased. "Let me see if I can simplify it. You and Jeremy come from different places. You have kind and loving parents. Maybe Jeremy's home is not the same."

Peter had the extreme privilege of knowing Jeremy's parents.

"You're right," he realized. "He does seem angrier than usual."

Peter thought of what Sensei had told him over the summer: Jeremy needed a positive influence.

"I'm going to go talk to him," Peter decided.

He got up from the table and Zahid followed.

Jeremy was still waiting for the lunch lady to return with more pudding when Peter and Zahid approached him.

"Hey, Jeremy," Peter called his attention.

"What do you want, Hunter?" Jeremy barked.

"Um," Peter paused awkwardly, "are you okay?"

Jeremy looked like a volcano about to explode. "You wanna know if I'm okay?" he seethed.

Peter and Zahid exchanged a scared glance.

"You seem really upset lately," Peter said slowly. "We thought we'd see if you needed to talk or something."

"You and me. Outside," Jeremy bellowed. "NOW!"

Jeremy started pushing Peter to the courtyard, to a spot around a corner. Zahid followed while Jeremy spewed insults.

Then as soon as they got around the corner, Jeremy lowered his voice. "Alright, who told you?" he demanded.

"Uhhh," Peter exchanged an apprehensive look with Zahid. "Who told us what?"

Jeremy sneered. "You expect me to believe you care about my mood?"

Again, Peter and Zahid exchanged a look.

"We do," Zahid said sincerely.

Jeremy's face looked furious, then confused, then his bottom lip stuck out and started quivering. He looked away. "I'm just going through some stuff, okay?"

Peter could see how vulnerable and small he looked.

"Well, you know, in Buddhism…" Peter started to say.

Jeremy suddenly threw a punch at the wall in between Peter and Zahid. His face returned to its usual rectangular stiffness.

"You tell anyone and I'll kill you," he warned.

Then he stormed off, back to the cafeteria.

The next weekend, Peter's mom drove him up to a large, two story house with a circular drive. There was a meticulously trimmed garden in the front and two large lanterns by the stately front door.

"Daaang," Mrs. Hunter said. "Are you dating royalty?"

"Mom," Peter rolled his eyes.

"I should've coached you on salad and dinner forks." Her eyes got bigger. "Wait. Do I know the difference?"

"Mom."

"Okay." She grabbed Peter by the shoulders. "Look them in the eye, say 'yes ma'am' and 'yes sir.' And if they ask you about your investment portfolio, tell them your servants handle it. No, your servants' servants."

"Bye, mom," Peter said as he unbuckled and opened the door.

"I'll pick you up at the stroke of midnight!" she declared dramatically.

"See you at eight," he called back.

He waited until his mom had driven away to ring the doorbell. Alicia threw the door open almost immediately.

"Thank you so much for this," she told him with a cute wrinkle to her forehead. "It's going to be weird and awkward, I know. But my dad said he had to meet you if we're going to keep dating."

Peter smiled and assured her, "No problem. I'm looking forward to this." She gave him a doubtful look. "I'm going to hear some of your potty training stories tonight, right?"

She giggled. "Sorry, but I've already coached my parents against it. Alright, let's get this over with."

She led him into the house, which was just as fancy as the outside. Peter could only imagine what his mom would say if she saw the winding staircase, and the statues. The actual statues.

They met Mrs. Lisowski in the kitchen as she was setting out trays of food. "Nice to meet you, Peter," she greeted. "I've heard a lot about you."

"Mom," Alicia complained.

"Oh, yeah?" Peter smirked. "What have you heard exactly?"

Alicia's mom smiled and ignored the question. "Make yourself at home," she told him. "We'll start dinner as soon as Mr. Lisowski arrives. But can I interest you in an appetizer?"

Mrs. Lisowski presented a few options that were laid out neatly on the countertop. They all had meat in them, but Peter didn't want to be rude, so he picked one and took a bite.

"Thank you," he said. "So what do you do, ma'am?"

"I do grant writing for non-profits and charities," she told him.

"Wow," Peter marveled. "I bet you help a lot of people."

There was a sound of a door closing and Alicia nearly jumped.

"Oh, no. Here's daddy," she exhaled. "Okay look, he's a scary lawyer, and super protective and I'm his little princess."

"I'll be on my best behavior," Peter promised. "Our relationship is on the line, right?"

"Not completely, but close," she admitted.

Mr. Lisowski arrived in the kitchen with a dominating presence. He immediately fixed a stern gaze on Peter.

"Daddy," Alicia straightened her back. "This is Peter."

"Hello, sir. Nice to meet you," Peter said politely.

Mr. Lisowski shook Peter's hand but eyed him critically. "What kind of grades do you get?" he asked, plunging into the grilling process right away.

"Almost all B's," Peter answered.

"Tell me about your friends," Mr. Lisowski continued.

"I hang out mostly with my best friend, Zahid."

"He's from Syria," Alicia supplemented. "Peter was friends with him before anyone else welcomed him."

Mr. Lisowski scratched his chin. "What does your father do?"

"Sales for a computer engineering group."

"Ugh. A salesman?" Mr. Lisowski complained.

"He's an honest one," Peter argued. "He had to change companies recently because he refused to lie to a customer."

Mr. Lisowski nodded. "I've always said it doesn't matter what work you do, as long as you do it with integrity. What are your hobbies?"

"Martial arts."

He looked impressed. "That takes a lot of self-discipline."

"Yes, sir. I've been doing it since I was five. And I hear you and Mrs. Lisowski do a lot of humans' rights stuff. Alicia's always keeping people informed about the issues."

"Yes," Mrs. Lisowski answered. "We're involved in a number of outreach programs and charities."

"Peter does a lot of community service," Alicia said quickly.

"Really?" her dad asked.

As Peter listed his usual activities, Mr. Lisowski warmed up and started calling him, 'my boy'. Peter thought that was a good sign.

Then he ushered Peter into the dining room while talking his ear off about ethics and human rights and asking him all about karate.

By the time the evening was over, Peter had barely talked to Alicia. She walked him to the door and waited with him on the front porch.

"You know, sometimes it's annoying how perfect you are," she bemoaned.

"Only sometimes, right?" he asked. "I mean, I was supposed to get your dad's approval."

She kissed his cheek. "You were great."

Peter remembered the last kiss she gave him was not on the cheek. He wondered if he could initiate it this time. She looked like she might be expecting it.

Does she want a kiss? he wondered. *Would it be okay to kiss her?*

Then his mom pulled up and he lost his moment.

"Well, there's my mom," he stated the obvious.

"That would be her," Alicia said with an annoyed look.

"Tonight was fun. Thanks." He kissed her cheek and waved as he got into his mom's car.

He regretted not kissing her, but hoped he'd have another chance soon.

"So how'd it go?" his mom asked in a singsong voice.

"Good. I think they liked me."

"Wow. My son's going to be a prince!" she marveled. "Quick, let's get home before the car turns into a pumpkin!"

Chapter 42: The Lust Curse

A few nights later, Rob drove Peter to a nearby cemetery where they found two girls spreading out salt in a wide circle. Peter could see two tall and lanky asuras watching over the girls from behind.

Then Peter realized that both girls looked familiar. The one with long straight red hair was the jealous girl from the museum and the one with dark hair was the girl who had tried to sacrifice her cat.

"They aren't possessed," Peter noted from where he and Sensei Rob were hiding behind gravestones. "Why are we here?"

"Just wait," Rob instructed pensively.

"I don't get it," The red-haired one said. "We've been doing it for weeks and nothing has changed."

"Patience, Crystal," the other girl chided. "Sometimes you have to repeat a spell a few times before..."

"Crystal? Is that you?" a boy's voice called. It was the curly-haired boy who had been in the museum with the victim of the evil eye.

"Eddy?" Crystal gasped, standing to meet him. Then she twirled her red hair in her fingers. "What are you doing here?"

Peter could see a bat-like asura riding on the boy's shoulder.

"I don't know," Eddy said, studying his surroundings with a confused look. "I… you're going to think I'm weird, but I've been dreaming about this place for weeks. Like, I just had to come here."

"I don't think it's weird," Crystal told the boy.

"Um, I've been thinking a lot about you, too," he confessed.

"Really?" Crystal smiled.

"For some reason, I just can't get you off of my mind."

"I'll let you two be alone," the girl with dark hair said. Then she pulled Crystal aside and said, "Remember how to complete the spell?"

Crystal nodded as her friend walked away. "Now what were you saying about having me on your mind?" she asked Eddy.

She took his hands and led him to the center of the salt circle. The boy was stammering through an explanation while the asuras moved around them with excited energy.

"It's about to possess the boy," Rob said.

"I'm on it," Peter said as he played with the air currents and shaped them into an arrow.

"Whoa. Look at you!" Rob marveled.

Peter shot the arrow straight at the boy's asura and pinned it in place. It howled as Peter turned the arrow into a circlet of air that tore it apart.

Eddy shook his head as if waking up from a trance. "Did you hear that?" he asked Crystal.

"It's probably just a cat or something," she said quickly. "Now what were you saying about my eyes?"

"No, that was no cat." He looked scared and tried to let go of Crystal's hands. "It sounded really close."

"Shh," Crystal lulled him with a hand caressing his cheek tenderly. "All that matters right now is you and me."

"Wait, what?" He looked all around and wrenched his hands from hers with a look of disgust. "What is this?" he demanded as he studied the salt circle. "What am I doing here?"

"Eddy," Crystal pleaded, "We're meant to be. You and me…"

"No," he started backing away, out of the circle. "I don't want this. I'm dating Rachel."

"She doesn't love you like I do!" Crystal declared.

He shook his head while backing away.

"Leave me alone," he said with a punctuated tone.

He stormed off in the direction he had come from and Crystal ran off, sobbing, in the other direction.

Rob and Peter stood and examined the calm and peaceful graveyard.

"I've seen this before," Rob explained. "People just don't understand love. It's not something you can force. See, they call it a love spell, but it's really a lust curse. They attached an asura to the boy, giving him weird dreams and thoughts. She wasn't thinking about what was best for him, she only wanted control."

Peter looked at the salt circle of the failed curse and resolved never to try to force anything on Alicia.

A few days later, Peter and Alicia met at the park. As they fed ducks and talked, Peter soaked up every warm detail of being with her.

"So there's this competition in Cratersville," he was telling her as he tossed breadcrumbs. "And if I place there, then I go to the national competition over the summer. We're driving there for just a day. And I was thinking maybe you might want to come and see me in action."

"Hm. That's cool," she replied absent-mindedly.

"Oh no. Am I talking too much?" he worried.

She turned and faced him with a serious expression. "Peter? When are you going to kiss me?" she asked plainly.

"Uhhh…" His mind went blank.

"A couple weeks ago, I kissed you," she reminded him. "I thought maybe you'd want to start kissing, you know, regularly."

"I didn't know if you wanted that, too," he explained.

"Well, duh, we're dating. That's the whole point."

"I didn't want to force it. Sooo… can I kiss you now?"

She rolled her eyes. "Did you seriously just ask permission?"

"What? Am I not supposed to? I thought that was respectful."

She sighed. "I want you to have, you know, passion. I want you to be so overcome that you can't control yourself."

"If I couldn't control myself, bad things could happen," he argued.

"I'm not saying I want you to attack me. Just a kiss."

"Sorry, I'm just still so nervous around you," he apologized. "You're really pretty, and smart, and… opinionated."

"None of that matters if you aren't attracted to me. I mean, do you even want to kiss me? You haven't even tried and we've been dating officially for a month now! What's the point of being together unless…"

He interrupted her with a sloppy and quick kiss. They looked at each other and laughed. He kissed her again. It was longer, and less sloppy.

As they walked back to their bikes, hand in hand, they didn't talk too much, but smiled and laughed any time their eyes met.

When they arrived, she stopped him. "So, Gina's throwing a big Halloween party."

Peter grimaced. "A party? I'm not really a big fan of parties."

She played with her hands. "But everyone's going and I don't want to go without my boyfriend. I think it could be a lot of fun."

Peter looked reluctant.

"Okay, how about this," Alicia suggested as she slipped her arms around his neck. "If you come to Gina's party with me, then I'll come to Cratersville to watch you compete."

"Sounds like a good deal," Peter agreed. "Should we, uh, kiss on it?"

She rolled her eyes and laughed at him. "Oh, my god, you are such a dork! But kiss me anyway."

Chapter 43: Lessons from Brown-Belt-Man-Crush Kid

The day of the competition, Alicia arrived at Peter's house before the sun rose. He brought her to the kitchen where his mom was gathering things for their trip.

She greeted Alicia with a smile. "It's good to see you again."

"You, too," Alicia returned. "Any more embarrassing stories?"

His mom laughed. "Not today. We have to make sure Peter's pumped up instead of torn down. So ask me next time."

"By the way, I didn't tell you how much I love your house," Alicia told her. "It's so quaint and… cozy."

Peter wasn't sure why, but his mom seemed upset.

"Thank you," she said while blinking excessively.

"So what kind of work do you do?" Alicia asked pleasantly.

"Oh, I stay at home," his mom answered.

"In this day and age?" Alicia gawked. "Women can be anything they want now."

His mom looked at her and blinked again. "Yes, and I *want* to be a dedicated wife and mother. I work hard to make our home a place free of worry and stress for my boys."

"So you're living for men?" Alicia asked slowly.

Mrs. Hunter took a deep breath and gave her a tight smile. "I'm living a life of love and selflessness for my family."

Alicia thought a moment and shrugged. "I guess that's okay, as long as you aren't selling yourself short."

DING!

The doorbell rang.

"Hey!" Peter diverted their attention. "Zahid's here!"

Alicia followed Peter to the door. "Zahid's coming, too?" she asked. "Isn't it going to be cramped in a small car for three hours?"

Peter shrugged. "Two and a half with how my mom drives. And you know, the Buddha said that *'patience is the greatest prayer.'*"

Alicia glared. "You know, sometimes the whole Buddhism thing is kind of annoying."

"Alicia," Mrs. Hunter said sharply, "I hope you don't get carsick. I don't want to *sell myself short*, but I tend to swerve a lot."

Peter rethought inviting Alicia while they rode. She and his mom didn't seem to be getting along. Besides that, there were many uncomfortable lulls in the conversation.

Then Alicia laughed, breaking one of the uncomfortable lulls as they started approaching the city.

"What's funny?" Peter asked.

She showed him a picture of Gina in a new outfit. "Can you believe her clothes?"

"I don't get it. What's wrong?" Peter asked.

"She's wearing brown shorts over black leggings," she explained. "That's the biggest fashion mistake ever."

He shrugged. "It looks fine to me."

She patted his cheek. "You're so cute when you're stupid."

"Jody, Jody, Jody!" Mr. Hunter yelled. "You're sliding over the line." The car swerved back into place. "Want me to drive?"

"No," she sighed. "I won't do it again. I just got a bit," she glared through the rear view mirror, "distracted."

Alicia texted back to Gina and laughed to herself.

"What's the street I'm looking for again?" Mrs. Hunter asked Mr. Hunter. "Laurel? Or was it Lorris?"

Mr. Hunter looked at the directions on his phone. "Third Street."

"Third?" she questioned. "I could've sworn it was Lorris."

Peter's dad thought a moment. "I think you're thinking of that other street. Norris Street."

"Norris? I don't remember that one."

"You know, the one they named after Chuck Norris."

"There's a street named after him?" Peter asked excitedly.

"It didn't last long," his dad said plainly. "They had to change the name because there were too many deaths. You know," he paused, "because no one crosses Chuck Norris and lives."

Peter chuckled. Alicia rolled her eyes.

"I don't get it," Zahid said. "Who's Chuck Norris?"

"He's a famous martial artist," Mrs. Hunter told Zahid. "And an astronaut. He's been to Mars, you know." Zahid looked like he was about to challenge it. "That's why there're no signs of life."

"There are lots of jokes about Chuck Norris," Peter explained. "But there're no jokes about Bruce Lee because Bruce Lee is no joke."

“That may be true,” his dad said in a pensive tone, “but no one fights Jackie Chan in a room full of furniture and lives to tell the tale.”

Peter and his parents laughed together.

“Seriously,” Zahid asked, “who are all these people?”

Peter’s first few competitions ended swiftly and without any challenges. Then, while they were waiting for a bout, Peter and Sensei both got a summons to an exorcism.

They left Charlie and found their way to a merchandise stall where the chipper sales worker was taking care of business with a smile and a dark aura.

“Your change,” she told a customer. Then she fixed the woman with deadly serious eyes and her voice changed. *“And your mother heard what you said at her funeral. What an ungrateful brat you are.”*

The customer stood still for a moment, shocked, then hurried away with a look of shame and horror. The woman licked her lips in satisfaction.

Peter noticed a katana mounted on the wall behind the register that was glowing with darkness. He pointed to it and Sensei nodded.

“That’ll be twenty-four sixteen,” the cashier told the next customer. She fixed the man with the same deadly stare. *“And Cathy cheated on you because you’re as annoying as you are ugly.”* The man stumbled off with a stunned expression. “Wow, that shame tastes so good. And you,” she fixed her eyes on Rob as he stepped up. *“The man who’s always trying to pay for his sins. But never will.”*

Peter snuck around behind the woman and started chanting softly:

“OM MANI PADME HUM.”

The merchant turned quickly and tackled Peter. Sensei Rob pulled her up while she twisted like a snake. She hissed and spat at Peter. A spray of something hit him in the eyes. It burned.

Peter heard Sensei cry out and imagined he was suffering from the same attack. Peter couldn’t force his eyes open. The spirit cackled wildly.

He tried to think of some way of attacking the strong, flexible, and poison-spitting opponent while blind. He came up short.

THUP! THUP! SCHOOOP!

Before Peter could think of a move, he heard the asura stop laughing as someone attacked it.

"No one hurts my friends!" Charlie's voice threatened.

A number of people whooped and hollered nearby. Peter felt around until he reached the katana displayed on the wall.

"Be swept clean," he ordered.

The poison evaporated as quickly as it had come and he was able to open his eyes just in time to see a small cloud of darkness emerge from the sword. He conjured a quick tornado that tore it apart. The saleswoman fell limp within Sensei Charlie's headlock.

Charlie sat the merchant in a chair and waved as the spectators clapped. Peter helped Rob up and they both watched Charlie, smiling and waving as the crowd dispersed.

"Boys, boys, boys," she said as she threw her arms around their necks, "how did you ever survive without me?"

Peter blasted through his last competitions and took the gold for his age group. Afterwards, his father patted him on the back affectionately.

"We'll check for new freckles at home," his mom told him with a wink. "I won't embarrass you in front of your," she looked less cheerful, "charming girlfriend."

Zahid slapped his hand and shook it. "That was amazing!" he raved. "I knew you were good, but I didn't know how good."

"Is that an actual compliment?" Peter marveled.

Zahid laughed. "I don't give them out often," he told Peter. "Only when they're truly deserved."

Alicia stepped up. "Is it my turn?" she complained playfully.

Peter laughed and hugged her.

"That was so cool," she told him. "Thank you for inviting me."

"You sure?" he asked. "You weren't bored?"

"Only when I wasn't watching my amazing boyfriend."

Peter looked at her smile and realized that it had a magical ability to erase all his tension and stress. Then he saw his mom behind Alicia, glaring at her. The magic was short-lived.

"It's such a long walk back to the car," Alicia complained as they started to the parking garage. "I'm still sore from the walk here."

Peter saw his mom make another angry face.

"Mom," he interjected before she could react, "can you come and pick us up? Please?" Then he leaned in and whispered, "I'll do some extra chores to make up for it."

"Okay," she agreed reluctantly. "But only because you won."

She forced a smile at Alicia before walking off.

"By the way, Zahid," Peter's dad asked as they walked off, "have you ever heard that you shouldn't eat too many chickpeas?"

"No, sir," Zahid looked worried. "Why not?"

"Because you'll *falafel*," Peter's dad smirked.

Peter let out a sigh. "So how bored were you?" he asked Alicia.

"I wasn't bored," she denied. "It was cool. You won, right?"

He could hear the insincerity in her voice. He was about to press her when she pulled out her phone and started texting.

"Oh, and I think your mom hates me," she said.

Peter felt the sting of annoyance. He didn't understand why Alicia and his mom weren't getting along. A wave of negative emotions washed over him and he found himself focusing on all the things he didn't like about his relationship with Alicia.

Since she was pretty much ignoring him, Peter decided to take the opportunity to meditate. He evened his breaths and felt Anuvata's presence. But before he could ask the spirit for advice, Peter became distracted by a group of kids who were waiting nearby.

"Shh. See that kid?" a boy Peter's age was whispering. "That's the guy that got the gold for the thirteen-to-fifteen boys and he's only our age. He was so cool, like the Nocturnal Ninja."

Peter couldn't help but smile. Then he realized that he was getting more praise from strangers than from his own girlfriend.

He heard another boy from the group mumble.

"What was that?" the first boy asked aggressively.

"I said it sounds like you have man crush."

"It's not a man crush! I'm just saying he was cool."

"He was amazing," said a girl with wavy brown hair.

"Someone else crushing?" the second boy asked.

"No, I don't… I'm not…" she stammered and turned bright red.

Peter smiled smugly.

"I mean he's cute, but he obviously has a girlfriend, and probably from out of town, and it's not like I even know him..." She took a breath.

"I was just saying that maybe you should say something. Everyone likes compliments."

"Nah, he wouldn't waste time on a lowly brown belt," the first boy said. "Anyway, thanks for coming with me today. I know you were probably bored out of your minds."

"It was awesome!" a girl with a deep voice responded. "I recorded a bunch of the fights so I could use them for my stories."

"I loved it, too!" a third girl added. "The drama, the suspense!"

"The physics, too," the second boy said. "Fascinating that the original masters, I suppose, had very little scientific knowledge, but discovered the most efficient and powerful moves through practice."

"Whoa," brown-belt-man-crush kid reacted. "Don't tell me Science Boy actually admitted to learning something here."

"I knew I shouldn't have said anything," Science Boy sighed.

"Anyway, thanks again for coming," brown-belt-man-crush kid repeated. "It means more to me than if you were into all this."

Peter looked back at Alicia, still focused on her phone. He realized that what brown-belt-man-crush kid had said was true. Her presence meant more because she didn't want to be there. She had sacrificed a whole Saturday for a boring road trip just for him.

He had been thinking only of himself and what he wanted. He had missed what a great gift it was that she was here. He wondered if Anuvata had orchestrated it so that the group of kids was walking by just at that moment.

"Thanks for coming," Peter told Alicia. "It really meant a lot."

"Of course," she smiled and kissed his cheek. "You were amazing. And you're going to the party with me tomorrow, right?"

Chapter 44: Gina's Awesome Party

A few nights later, Alicia's mom dropped her and Peter off at Gina's house for the Halloween party.

"Alicia!" Gina squealed as soon as they entered the house packed with kids and no parents in sight. "I'm so glad you could come! I love your Native American dress."

"I wore it with a purpose," Alicia declared. "Did you hear about that oil spill by the Reservation?"

"No!" Gina gasped. "What Reservation?"

"I can't remember what tribe it was," Alicia said. "But it was enormous and there's, like, no media coverage at all."

"Hey, Peter," Gina said with a forced smile, "How cute. You're a ninja," she added insincerely. "But where's Zahid? I only invited you because I thought you'd bring him."

"Thanks, Gina. Nice to see you, too," Peter smiled pleasantly.

"He's my boyfriend now," Alicia scolded her. "You have to be nice."

Gina rolled her eyes. "Alright, alright. Just don't talk about martial arts and Buddhism all night."

"Do I really talk that much?" Peter asked.

"You might be a little long-winded," Alicia admitted. "But you're also totally cute. Now come on, let's have some fun!"

They walked through the party, which was everything Peter had thought it would be. The music was so loud he had to shout to be heard. Kids were laughing like hyenas at the stupidest jokes and playing pointless games. On top of that, they were all talking about music and TV shows that Peter had given up months ago.

"I've got to be honest," Peter shouted over the music. "I feel really awkward. I never know what to do at parties."

"Well, there's talking and hanging out," Alicia suggested, as if it were obvious.

"Yeah, but I can't talk about martial arts, right?"

"Right," she confirmed.

"Even though I just proved myself to be the strongest male age thirteen-to-fifteen in four states?"

"Is that what happened?" she asked.

"Yeah. That was the whole point of the trip," he laughed.

"Sorry. I was just thinking of how cool you looked. I guess I wasn't paying attention to other things. Look, just keep it to school. What teachers you hate, what subjects you hate, what lunches you hate."

Peter realized that he'd be at a disadvantage considering that he had spent the last year trying to eradicate hate from his vocabulary and thoughts.

"But I don't really hate a lot of things," he voiced his concerns.

"Come on, idiot," she linked her arm in his.

"Why does everyone call me that?" he complained. "That's not going to be your pet name for me, is it?"

"Just stick with me. I'll teach you everything."

He followed her lead and made casual conversation with a few friends as they wandered through the party. Peter was almost enjoying himself when Jeremy showed up and ruined it all.

He walked by with a drink in his hand and a flushed face. Peter guessed that he had snuck in his own drinks.

"Hey, Ali," he slurred. "Did you wear that short skirt just for me?" Then he slapped her rear.

Peter instantly grabbed his wrist in a lock. "I'm going to need you to apologize to my girlfriend right now," he warned.

"You gonna make me?" Jeremy spat.

"It's not about making you," Peter said calmly as he let go of Jeremy's hand. "It's about being respectful and honorable."

"Whatever. I could take you," Jeremy challenged. "Right now. Let's go outside, loser."

"I think that's a great idea," Peter agreed.

He dragged Jeremy out to the backyard and Alicia followed.

"You wanna go at it?" Jeremy challenged. "Fine. Put 'em up!"

Peter faced him with a stern expression and crossed arms. "What's this really about?" he demanded.

"This is about me kicking your butt," Jeremy thundered.

"Look around," Peter said. "No one's watching. It's just you, me, and Alicia. I know you're going through something, but this is a horrible way to deal with it."

To his surprise, Jeremy started crying. He collapsed on the steps of the back patio and held his knees. Peter and Alicia exchanged a confused look.

"My mom left a few months ago, okay?" he confessed. "Just up and disappeared. My dad can't find her anywhere." He seemed to grow smaller and younger. "Why didn't she take me with her?" He sniffed.

"That's rough, man," Peter said slowly. "You know, if you need someone to talk to, I'm here. And I bet a lot more people would feel the same way if you opened up and told them about it."

"No," Jeremy stuck out his rectangular bottom lip. "This is weak. Nobody likes a weak guy."

"Sure they do," Peter argued. "People love weak and vulnerable. Think of a puppy. Who doesn't love a puppy? But have you ever heard of karma? That there are consequences to every choice you make. When you say things like you did to Alicia and when you touch them without permission, well, people don't usually like that."

Jeremy sniffed and turned to look at Alicia. "I'm sorry, Ali."

She crossed her arms, looking very impatient. "Just don't do it again," she glowered.

"Oh, god," he choked. "Do you think that's why my mom left? She really doesn't love me, does she?"

"Whoa. Hold up." Peter sat on the step next to him. "Maybe it wasn't about you. Maybe she had some other reason."

"My dad," Jeremy nodded sullenly. Then his bottom lip stuck out even farther. "And I act just like him. I'm so messed up."

He buried his head into his knees and shook.

"You know, in Buddhism, there's this idea that life is always in the state of changing and evolving. If we base our happiness on things that change, then our happiness will change. But if we base our happiness on things that don't change, like truth and virtue, then you can find peace."

Jeremy nodded and then, without warning, puked on Peter's foot.

"I feel a lot better now," he said as he wiped his mouth. "Thanks, man."

He stumbled back into the house, leaving Peter to wipe his shoe off in the grass. "Geez, I might have to throw these away," he complained, trying not to look down.

"What was that about?" Alicia asked sharply. "Are you and Jeremy best buddies now?"

"I don't know if he'll even remember this tomorrow," Peter chuckled. "But I'm trying to understand him better, rather than judging."

Alicia stood on the steps, glaring down at him. "After everything he's said and done to me, you helped him?"

Peter suddenly realized that he was in trouble, but he had no idea why. "Yeah," he said hesitantly. "I mean, I don't like what he did, but he's still human. Shouldn't we help others?"

"Not when they're Neanderthals!" she yelled. "Not when they're monsters! You should've beaten him up!"

"I don't do that. Look, the Buddha said, *'Hatred does not cease by hatred, but only by love; this is the eternal rule.'*"

"Can you stop it with the stupid Buddhist wisdom?" she shouted. "It's so annoying! So what? Are you in love with Jeremy?"

"Not like that. But it's not going to solve anything if I beat him up. He's going through a painful time. He needs a little kindness."

She threw her hands up in frustration. "What is everyone going to think? They're going to say that I'm some desperate girl and you don't like me enough to defend me."

Peter sprang up the steps to meet her. "I did defend you. I just did it without violence. Does it really matter how I stop the fight as long as it's stopped?"

She shook her head. "You're not even listening to me. I can't take this anymore."

SHOOOSH!

A whisper of wind tickled Peter's ear.

"Aw geez," he rolled his whole head, not just his eyes. "Alicia, I swear I wouldn't do this unless I had to…"

"You have got to be kidding me," she said when she understood. "Now? How convenient. Sure, Peter, dodge this bullet." She threw her hand out to the dark night. "Go save someone else." Then she pointed her finger directly at his nose. "But don't bother coming back to the party."

Chapter 45: The Joys of Being and Exorcist on Halloween Night

Peter used the back gate and wandered out to the streets filled with trick-or-treaters running from house to house with no thoughts of anything other than candy.

Those were the days, Peter thought.

A few houses away, Peter spotted Rob as he appeared suddenly, surrounded by a rush of glowing water that no one else could see.

"Are you ready for a long night?" Rob asked as he approached. Then he sniffed. "Did you get sick? You smell funky."

Peter sighed. "Long story. So what's going to make tonight long? Is Halloween really a night of evil spirits like all the movies say?"

"Any day is only what you make of it," Rob explained. "But enough people believe Halloween is a dark night that they tend to do crazy things. The spirits have come to expect it."

They passed a group of trick-or-treaters leaving a house and Rob took the candy out of one child's hand.

"Trust me, kid, you do not want this." Rob replaced it with a couple chocolates he had in his pocket. "Spread the word that this house's candy is poisoned." After the kid left, he sighed. "Man, that was my slave-free chocolate."

"Slave free?" Peter asked.

"Yeah, most of the major chocolate companies get their cocoa from West African farms that imprison children into slave labor."

Peter remembered that Alicia had talked about that before.

"The candy was poisoned?" Peter asked. "Who does that?"

They rang the doorbell and a man answered with a monster mask on his face and a dark spirit inside him.

Rob smiled brightly, "Trick-or-treat," he said.

The man howled like an animal and slammed his door in their face.

After a grueling fight, Peter went home and climbed into bed. He sent Alicia a text but heard nothing in return. He wondered if he should go back to the party, or follow her orders and stay away. He figured she'd be mad at him either way. Sometimes, he thought that fighting the asuras was easier than trying to figure out what she was thinking.

When he finally fell asleep, he only got about an hour before Anuvata woke him up. He had a strong sense in his gut that he needed to leave his house and travel east.

He opened his window and peered east. He had always relied on Sensei's traveling or coincidentally being in the area already, but it seemed like he would have to get there on his own this time.

He leapt from his window, landing in a roll. Then he wrapped the wind currents behind him, propelling himself forward at an unnatural speed. The world blurred around him.

He came to a stop at a field near a suburban neighborhood and Sensei Rob appeared next him.

"Hey, how'd you get here?" Sensei asked.

Before he could answer, they both became distracted by a large flame and a screeching cat. Three teenaged boys and a girl were smoking something that smelled awful. And they were all laughing uncontrollably at the cat trapped inside a ring of fire.

Rob and Peter extinguished the fire, freed the cat, and exorcised the teens.

"That was a gaggle," Rob instructed. "They're spirits that work in groups. I'm sure you've seen cases where each person is worse when they're in the group. Gaggles create gangs and mafias, too."

"Hm," Peter nodded sleepily. "Good to know. I'm going back to bed."

He barely slept when Anuvata woke him up again. He started to run with the wind propelling him. Then he had another idea.

He saw a strong current of wind right next to him, going in the same direction. He leapt into the air and let it blow him from behind. When that current finished, he found another and got high enough to surf on it. He surrendered to the current and let it take him where he needed to go.

Peter looked down from the sky and saw Rob in front of a house where he was staring up at a Halloween decoration. It was a zombie of an elderly woman that hung from the tree.

"Hey!" Peter called as he dropped from the sky.

Rob jumped. "Where'd you come from?"

"I just learned to ride the wind tonight," Peter bragged. "No big deal."

"You learned to break wind?" Rob asked with a smile.

"No! *Ride* the wind! *Ride* the wind. It's totally cool."

Rob smiled and laughed. "Good for you."

"So what's the story behind this exorcism?" Peter asked.

Rob nodded grimly to the decorative zombie and Peter looked closer. He lost his breath. It was a real old woman, painted and dressed as a zombie, swaying stiffly in the breeze.

They both looked at an open window of the house and saw a woman inside, bringing a drink to a stuffed strawman on a couch.

"Yes, mother," the woman said to the strawman in a hollow voice. "Here's your drink, mother." Suddenly, the woman's voice grew sharper. "You always have to have your drink! Yes, mother. No, mother. Whatever you say, mother!"

Rob and Peter exchanged a disturbed look before racing to the house.

Hours later, Peter jumped from his bedroom window, following yet another summons. He rode the wind until he arrived at the same cemetery where he had witnessed the lust curse. To Peter's great annoyance, he found the same girls performing another ritual. This time, they were digging up a grave.

"Are you sure this will work?" Crystal asked the other girl. "I don't want to hurt him."

"Trust me. It won't hurt a hair on his head unless we tell it to. As long as we establish control. We'll tell it to scare him, and then you'll rush in and save the day. He'll have to fall in love with you."

Rob appeared next to Peter and crouched behind a tombstone.

"How do we know this is the body we need?" Crystal asked.

The other girl shrugged. "The spirits told me."

"They were wrong last time," Crystal grumbled.

"They weren't wrong. They said there was interference."

"Like someone working against us?" Crystal asked.

Peter and Rob exchanged a nervous look.

The other girl nodded. "Okay, ready?"

"Yuck," Crystal complained, "this thing smells."

They lifted a stiff corpse out of the ground and laid it on the grass. Then they held hands and started chanting in another language.

"They're trying to raise a vetala, right?" Peter asked Rob in a hush. "A spirit that inhabits a corpse that hasn't had the proper burial rights and drinks human blood?"

Rob raised an impressed eyebrow. "Someone's been studying."

"Man," Peter shook his head, "if you tried to tell me a year ago that vampires were real, I would've called you crazy."

"Every culture has some version of vampires," Rob said. "The stories are based on something."

When the chant was finished, the girls held a dagger together and thrust it into the corpse. The wind swirled around them and Peter saw an asura enter into the dead body.

The ground shook as the corpse started convulsing. Before Peter's eyes, the body was rejuvenated. Wounds healed, skin reformed, hair regained its luster until it looked like a fully alive human being. But its eyes were solid black, darker than dark.

The girls jumped up and down, holding hands and squealing.

"I told you it was real!" the girl with dark hair said. "Didn't I tell you it was real?" She turned to the vetala and said in a dramatic voice, "I, Vida, the one who created thee, charge thee. We charge thee to seek out the one named Eddy and scare him."

The vetala looked at them with a blank expression.

"We charge thee…" Vida attempted again.

Before she could finish, the creature let out a howl and the girls jumped back in fear. Then the creature lunged and snapped its teeth at them. They turned and ran off with panicked screams.

Peter and Rob raced in to stop the vetala. Rob held the creature's arms at its sides and Peter exorcised it.

"Be swept clean," he commanded.

The asura emerged and the body immediately fell with a cracking sound as it became a rotted corpse again. The asura faded away without a fight.

Rob and Peter looked at the scene of the freshly dug grave, rotting corpse, and salt designs.

"What a perfect ending to a delightful night," Peter remarked.

Chapter 46: Conquering Anger

"Good morning, sleeping beauty," his mother sang when Peter stumbled into the kitchen, scratching his belly. "You going through a growth spurt or something?"

"Just a long night," he slumped onto the counter.

She looked up skeptically, paused in her task. "You fell asleep at ten and I never heard a peep out of you. Rough dreams?"

"Nightmares," he confessed. "Can I help?"

"Sure." She handed him a spatula. "Someday, when you meet the girl of your dreams, you can woo her with a meal like this."

"Mom, I'm still dating Alicia," he reminded her.

"Aw, I'm sorry," she pitied him.

Peter gave her a look. "Give her a chance. She was really intimidated by you on the road trip."

"Intimidating?" she pretended surprise. "Moi?"

"Seriously, Alicia's a good person." He stared off to the side.

"Seems like you're trying to convince yourself as well as me."

Peter sighed and confessed, "We had a fight last night."

"I knew it. She's bad news. Where is she? Let me at her."

"Come on, mom. You and dad have disagreements all the time. That doesn't mean you stop loving each other, right?"

His mom groaned. "Please tell me you haven't used the 'l' word."

"I haven't," he assured her. Then he told her the story.

Mrs. Hunter added the vegetables to the pot then rested her backside against the counter while thinking. "I wonder if there's something else going on," she speculated. "Some undercurrent issue that's making other issues seem bigger than they are. Like when everyone annoys the crud out of you because you have a headache or didn't sleep well."

"You think she's upset about something?" Peter asked.

She nodded. "And as much as I don't think she's good enough for you, or a good influence, or pleasant to be around…"

"Mom. I get it," Peter complained.

"But still, maybe you ought to try talking to her about it. You're right, you don't end a relationship over just any disagreement. You have to try to make a mutual compromise. That's why relationships are so great. If you walk away without giving it a chance, you never learn anything."

"My two favorite people," Mr. Hunter greeted as he entered from the garage and kissed Mrs. Hunter's cheek. "What are you talking about?"

Peter sighed heavily again. "Alicia's mad at me and I…"

"Say no more," Mr. Hunter stopped him. "Let me tell you the secret to dealing with a woman." He wrapped his arms around his wife from behind and held her tight. "She's right."

"But what if she's not?" Peter challenged.

"Then she's probably still right," his dad said.

"I married the smartest man in the universe," Mrs. Hunter praised him.

His dad set his things on the counter while loosening his tie and explaining, "Sometimes you do need to struggle over right and wrong, but you, Peter, you tend to see a right and wrong in everything. You think there's a right and wrong way to eat a hamburger."

"But onions are gross and they make your breath stink."

"The point is," his dad chuckled, "sometimes, you need to let it go and let them eat their hamburger however they want to."

"Listen to the man," his mom gushed. "That's the secret to a happy marriage and a happy life right there."

Peter raised an eyebrow. "The secret to a happy life is onion breath?"

On Monday, Gina came to visit Peter at his locker.

"Thanks for ruining my party," she said.

"Sorry for not beating someone up in your backyard."

She rolled her eyes. "Alicia's still mad at you."

"Thanks, Gina. But I figured that out already."

"Since you're not the smartest, I'll give you some advice. You need to do something awesome to get on her good side again."

"I appreciate it," he said, "but this is between me and Alicia."

"I don't think you understand," she warned him. "There might not be a you-and-Alicia anymore. You have to do some big apology if you want to keep her."

"What do I need to apologize for?" he asked, exasperated.

"Idiot," she said as she rolled her eyes again. "Good luck. You need it."

As Peter watched her walk away, he realized that he would never understand girl-logic.

"Hey, Hunter!" Jeremy boomed from behind him. "You and me, behind the cafeteria, *now,*" he gnarled.

Peter slumped along, following him until they turned a corner and found themselves alone. “What did I do now?” Peter asked wearily, putting up an unenthusiastic guard.

Jeremy looked over his shoulders while he declared, “I am going to beat you into next week, idiot!” Then he lowered his voice, “Dude, I heard you and Alicia are fighting and it’s all because of me.”

“What now?” Peter let his arms drop.

“I didn’t mean to start any problems. I just wasn’t thinking clearly. And now I messed it up. It’s like I’m cursed. I just ruin everything! Look, I want you to hit me. We’ll stage a fight in front of everyone. Pretend to beat me up, I’ll go down easy. Just this once.”

Peter thought that he didn’t need Jeremy to “go down easy.” Still, it was a generous offer. “Are you serious?” he asked.

“You do this sort of thing for friends,” Jeremy responded.

Peter wasn’t sure when they had become friends, but he was still taken aback. “Thanks, but I didn’t want to hit you then and I don’t want to now. I’ll figure things out with Alicia.”

After Alicia ignored him all morning, Peter went to her locker before lunch. As he came around the corner, he saw Jeremy again.

Peter started worrying that Jeremy had put on a friendly act just to get Peter’s defenses down. Then he heard what Jeremy was saying.

“No, listen. Peter is the coolest guy ever. Don’t tell anyone I said that. But you should give him a chance.”

“It’s none of your business,” Alicia griped.

Jeremy gave up and banged into Peter’s shoulder as he passed. “Outta my way, loser.” Then he leaned in to whisper. “I did what I could.”

“Hey, can we talk?” Peter said when he reached Alicia.

“I am not in the mood,” she menaced. “No, you know, what?” She turned on him fiercely. “You’ve got some nerve sending Jeremy…”

Peter put his hands up. “I didn’t. He did that all on his own.”

“Just leave me alone. I’ll let you know when I’m ready to talk.”

She huffed away. Peter didn’t want to leave things unresolved. She’d probably talk to Gina at lunch and decide to break up with him by the end of the day. He needed to fix things before that happened.

He caught up with her and held her at her elbow. “Come on,” he pleaded. “You know I care about you. Can we please talk?”

She let out a harsh breath. "Sometimes a girl needs to fume a little so the guy can feel desperate and realize how wrong he was."

"That's craz…" he stopped himself. "I mean, unnecessary."

"It is my right as the girlfriend," she attested. "And if you want to stay my boyfriend, well then, you had better start feeling desperate."

She started off again, but he caught up with her. "Wait, Ali…"

She turned around and stomped her foot. "Come on! Would you let me storm off already? I'm trying to make a strong and dramatic end to the conversation and you are just not getting it."

He tried to understand, but gave up. He conceded. "Go ahead."

"Are you sure?" she challenged him. "You don't have anything else you want to say? No sarcasm, no stupid Buddhist wisdom?" He shook his head. "Good." She thought a moment. "Dangit! Now I don't have any dramatic last words. You made me use them all up."

"You want to just repeat a sentence you said earlier?" he suggested as he tried to conceal a chuckle.

"I can't do that, idiot. And stop smirking! It's really annoying! Argh! Sometimes you make me so crazy!"

You said it, he thought, *not me.*

"Ooh, got one." She turned her glare back on. "If you really care about us, you'll think long and hard about what I mean to you."

She stormed off and this time Peter let her.

Peter and Zahid took their lunches outside that day. They had just finished praying and meditating when they jumped at the sight of Jeremy looming in front of them.

"We speak English here!" he told Zahid in a loud voice.

Peter and Zahid just waited. Then his voice became friendlier. "What was with that weird singing?" he asked Zahid.

"It's just prayers," Zahid answered.

"Oh. Interesting." He plopped down on the bench and grabbed a falafel from Zahid's box. He took a bite. "Hey, these are good."

"Thanks," Zahid said dryly.

"So is Alicia still mad?" Jeremy asked Peter.

"I didn't do anything wrong," Peter complained. "I shouldn't have to apologize for not beating someone up. It would be bad karma."

"He's Buddhist," Zahid explained to Jeremy.

“Right,” Jeremy said. “He only talks about it all the time.”

Peter sighed. “I should just swallow my pride and say I’m sorry.”

Zahid raised an eyebrow. “Have you ever looked in the mirror?” he said. “It’s going to be obvious what you’re really thinking.”

Peter realized he was right. “I’m done for.”

“I know!” Jeremy said excitedly. “Maybe you can ‘apologize’ without saying, ‘sorry.’ Like some big gesture.”

“Hey, that could work,” Peter agreed.

“My dad used to do it all the time,” Jeremy continued. “He’d do something awful to my mom and never apologize, but he’d buy her something special or treat her to a fancy date night to make her *think* he was apologizing.” His eager smile fell. “Now that I say it out loud, it sounds like a horrible plan. No wonder she left us!”

“It could still work,” Zahid encouraged, “with an appropriate amount of sincerity. You could leave a gift and a note in her locker.”

“But I don’t know her locker combination,” Peter complained.

“How are you dating and you don’t know her combination?” Jeremy questioned. “Even Gina knows her combo.”

Peter and Jeremy immediately gasped and looked at Zahid.

Zahid’s eyes widened. “No,” he whined.

“Please?” Peter begged. “I’ll make it up to you, I promise.”

He gritted his teeth. “If she touches my hair, you owe me.”

When Peter got to school in the morning, he, Zahid, and Jeremy met in the courtyard. Zahid had already gotten the locker combination, and was not cheerful about it.

“You owe me for this,” he glowered.

“The hair?” Peter asked.

“The hair,” he said.

“So what did you get her?” Jeremy asked Peter.

Peter opened his backpack and showed a small box of candy.

“For a first fight, that’s okay,” Jeremy assessed. “And the note?”

“Didn’t write it yet. I figured I’d just write something simple.”

“Please tell me you’re not planning on writing it in one sitting.”

“Uhhh… what’s wrong with that?” Peter asked.

Jeremy sighed and massaged his temples. “Don’t you know how girls work? She thinks you don’t like her enough. Writing a note on the fly is not going to prove her wrong.”

“But I suck at poetry and stuff,” Peter worried.

“Get a notebook,” Jeremy ordered. “Let’s start brainstorming.”

They spent about fifteen minutes arguing over words and phrases. When they were finished, Peter examined the note in his hands. It definitely wasn’t his style, but he had a feeling Alicia would like it.

“I don’t know what I’d do without your help,” Peter told them both.

“Fail miserably,” Zahid answered with a smile.

When Alicia entered the classroom, she rushed over and surprised Peter with a kiss on the cheek. “You’re forgiven,” she declared.

Peter bit his tongue from saying that he didn’t need to be forgiven.

Instead he smiled. “I meant everything in the note,” he told her.

“This was our first fight,” she said. “It’s worth celebrating. We should have a fancy date. I want to get all dressed up and stuff.”

“How about the dance?” Peter asked. “You wanna go to that thing?”

She looked at him with what he now called her “angry eyes.”

“What?” he asked nervously. “What’d I do now?”

“Really?” she blinked. “You just… really? That’s how you ask me?”

“Uhhh…”

“There are guys who have been singing and dancing to ask their girlfriends to the dance,” she reminded him.

“And making a fool out of themselves,” he added.

“Exactly!” Alicia said. “They’re willing to embarrass themselves if it means that one special girl might go to the dance with them.”

Peter did not find the idea an attractive one.

“So I’m confused,” Peter said slowly. “Are we going or not going?”

“Oh, we’re going,” she told him. “But you are going to ask me in a special way.”

Chapter 47: Peter Meets A God

Peter saw his dad sitting at a business meeting, presenting to his coworkers at his new job.

The boss leaned back, pyramiding his hands thoughtfully. "I want it done in four months," he declared.

"Uh, sir, the team won't be able to complete it in that time," Peter's dad argued. "We need at least six months."

"What will it take to get it done in four?" the boss asked.

Mr. Hunter thought a moment. "Well, we could simplify it and remove some of the functions, but we'd have to cut out the things that the customer specifically asked for."

"No problem. We'll sell it, tell them it's a bug when they complain, then give it an update later."

"I don't feel comfortable lying to the customer."

"You won't have to. Someone else will. Moving on..."

Peter's dad looked troubled, but powerless.

Suddenly, the workers all faded into thin air and the boss looked directly at Peter. "Time for the fun part," he said.

The boss' appearance changed. He had dark hair styled flawlessly, thick eyebrows, and a strong, cleft chin. His eyes were brown, but in them, Peter saw all the fierce power and hatred of an asura.

His clothes became a fancy well-tailored suit and the office room transformed into a swanky penthouse with chandeliers, expensive art, and statues. The place was filled with people in nice clothes with drinks and food in their hands.

"Welcome, welcome!" the boss slapped Peter on the back and led him through the party. "Have you ever had Indian food?" he asked Peter, pointing to a buffet table. "Maybe you don't like Indian food. That's okay. We have hamburgers, chicken nuggets, and just for you, since I knew you were coming," the man motioned to the table where a single tray lay stacked with strips of bacon, perfectly curled and crunchy. "Go ahead. It's all free. Eat your heart out."

Peter studied the man's face. He remembered seeing it before, but he couldn't place him. "Do I know you?" Peter asked.

"No, no, no," the man laughed. "Not yet. But I've been watching you for a long time, kid. And I gotta say, I like what I see." The man swirled his hand in the air and a glass of red wine appeared out of nowhere. He

swirled his free hand and produced another glass of wine, which he gave to Peter. Peter looked at it nervously.

"Oh, it's just a dream," the man told him. "Live a little."

When Peter gave him a questioning look, the man sighed and waved his hand again, transforming the drink into a cold can of soda.

"You're funny," the man continued after a sip of his wine. "You want to know my favorite thing you've done so far?" He smiled, revealing sparkling, straight teeth. "When you first met your deva and you made that sarcastic remark about it not tattling on you anymore!" The man was seized by an uncontrollable bout of laughter. "That was hilarious! I thought it would've torn your head off!"

Peter set the soda can on the buffet table and studied the man. "I'm sorry, who exactly are you?"

"Oh, right," the man composed himself. "Haven't introduced myself yet." After another sip, he waved his hand, causing the wine glass to disappear. "I've had tons of names over the centuries," he flashed his charming smile, "but you can call me Mara."

"Mara?" Peter gulped. "As in the *Mara?"*

"In the flesh." He winked. "Or the mind. Or an emanation of consciousness. Whatever you want to believe I am. Point is, I'm the life of the party."

Peter narrowed his eyes and smirked. "The guy that the Buddha turned into flowers and sparkles?"

"He didn't turn me into anything," Mara growled. Then his smile returned as he straightened his jacket. "That was a long time ago."

"I think I'll be going now."

Peter took a step backwards, but Mara caught him, throwing an arm around his shoulders. He ushered Peter deeper into the party.

"Now wait a second," Mara chided. "Are you the kind of closed-minded guy who'd write off a god without meeting him first? You've never even heard my side of the story."

"You have a side to the story?" Peter asked with a raised eyebrow.

"There's the smart open-minded kid I noticed. You know, when they all first told me about you, they kept saying 'he's just an idiot.' But I didn't believe them for a second."

"Thanks," Peter said dryly.

Mara grabbed a couple plates of bacon-wrapped shrimp from a waiter's tray and handed one to Peter.

"I knew you were just so much smarter than the average person that they couldn't understand you," Mara praised him.

"So what is this?" Peter asked. "Some sort of deal with the devil?"

"Whoa, whoa, whoa," Mara said with a mouth full of shrimp. "We don't use the 'd' word here. It's pretty insensitive. Really, labels. Who needs 'em? I prefer titles like," he waved his hand dramatically, "the King of the Desire Realm! And that's what I'm here to offer you: all your heart desires. You see, you got pulled into this fight without knowing all your options. Aren't you sick and tired of that boring deva of yours? What did it tell you to call it? Anuvata? Funny story: in Palī, that means favorable wind. Basically, its saying even its farts smell good."

Mara took a few moments to laugh about that. Peter imagined he might have found it funny if someone else had said it.

"Anyway, think of every problem that's been popping up lately," Mara continued. "Every time you talk to your deva, Mr. Favorable Farts, what does it say? It tells you to sacrifice your own needs or desires. Hah. You can really tell it cares, huh?"

"Anuvata's just trying to teach me discipline," Peter asserted.

Mara flouted. "More like servitude. You know what I'd offer you?" He swept his arms out. "The world. You could eat and drink whatever you want. I'd fix all your dad's problems. You could have a million-dollars and he'd never have to work again. You could be in the lap of luxury. And what's that cute blonde girl's name?"

Mara waved his hand and Alicia appeared at Peter's side wearing a sparkly teal dress and her usual gorgeous smile. Peter's heart picked up as she took his arm in her hands.

"Bam! She's yours forever," Mara promised. "Or as long as you want. If you get bored, I'll get you another one." Mara waved his hand and Alicia was gone in smoke. "I could give you good grades. I could help you win the Olympics. Anything you want and you wouldn't have to work at it. Name your price."

"So you want me on your team?" Peter asked incredulously.

Mara fixed his powerful, dark eyes on Peter. "I want you at my side as my right hand man. I have big plans for this world and you'd be a great help." He held out a hand for Peter to shake. "What'dya say, Peter Hunter?" He smiled. "Do we have a deal?"

"Name my price?" Peter repeated, studying Mara carefully. "Anything I say?"

Mara's smile broadened. "Anything."

"Alright," Peter agreed.

"Yes!" Mara rejoiced.

"For starters, I want to achieve true enlightenment. The real thing. With selflessness and virtue out the wazoo."

Mara looked disappointed, but indulged Peter. "Okay. A bit boring in my opinion, but sure."

"I want you to stop your minions from bothering humans. No possession, no obsession. No accidents leading to suffering or death."

Mara's smile became forced. "That's not really…"

"Oh, and one more thing. I want you and all the asuras, rakshasas, pishachas, pretas, every negative spirit to practice Buddhism wholeheartedly. What'dya say, Mara?" Peter held out his hand and smirked. "Do we have a deal?"

Mara was barely smiling. His eyes darkened. "You should think carefully about your choice," he told Peter sternly. "I'm offering you an everlasting party here, kid."

Peter shrugged, "I've never really been into parties."

Suddenly the room dissolved into a fiery pit. The guests started screaming and morphed into shadowy figures crying out in pain and torment as flames danced around them.

Mara changed, too. His skin turned a sickly yellow, with thick and curly red hair and mustache that looked like flames. His eyes became bulging red and golden spheres, with a third eye in the middle of his forehead. His teeth looked like something between vampire fangs and boar tusks. He wore a crown of human skulls and had green snakes dangling from his hair.

As Mara grew at least three times in height, Peter instantly regretted mocking him.

"I'm not an enemy you want to make!" Mara bellowed. The light from the fire of his tortured victims illumined his face from below. "I'm also the King of Destruction. You're going to regret this when you see the suffering I can cause you."

In a flash of fire, the dream dissolved into darkness.

Peter awoke with a start and caught his breath. He desperately wanted to convince himself that it had only been a dream, but he had seen firsthand how real his dreams could be.

Chapter 48: Stupid Buddhist Wisdom

A couple weeks later, Peter was getting ready for the school dance when he was summoned for an exorcism. He and Rob arrived simultaneously at a house in the suburbs and rang the doorbell. As they waited, Peter felt a tug at his gut and saw a telephone in his mind's eye.

A man answered with two young sons peeking in from another room. "Can I help you?" the man asked, studying Peter and Rob.

"Hello, sir," Rob greeted with a smile. "We're here about the phone."

Peter wondered what their telephone problems could be, but it must have been serious. The man paled and stared at Rob agape.

A woman walked around the corner and called, "Honey? Who is it?"

The man turned slowly and told his wife, "He says he's here about the phone."

As if on cue, the phone started ringing. The dad, mom, and the two sons all jumped and stared at a phone on the counter in the kitchen, just visible through a doorway.

"You going to answer that?" Peter asked.

The two boys started talking at the same time:

"It's the man. He calls every night," the older son said.

"It'll keep ringing until we answer it," the younger one added.

"He knows where we go and what we do."

"The police say the call is coming inside the house."

"He said he's going to kill us in our sleep!"

The mom and dad tried to hush their sons while Rob tried to ask them questions. All the while, the phone kept ringing. Peter looked at the clock and realized that he was going to be late to the dance. There was no telling how mad Alicia would be.

In the confusion, Peter walked into the kitchen and picked up the phone. "Hello? Who is this?"

"Are you ready to play a game, little monkey?" a spirit responded.

Doors started slamming all over the house. Lights flickered. The kids and their parents started screaming. Then impish asuras appeared out of nowhere, grabbed each of the family members, and dragged them away into different rooms.

The doors slammed behind them and the family members were all trapped, screaming on the other side.

Rob turned a scolding gaze at Peter.

"What?" Peter contested.

Rob ran for the basement door to try to free the dad and Peter went for the hallway closet, where the younger son had been trapped.

He tugged on the door, but it would budge. All the while, Peter was preoccupied with a tug at his gut, pulling him back to the phone.

He returned to the kitchen and picked up the receiver. "What do you want?" he asked the spirit.

The voice laughed. *"What do you think we want? We want to feast on your suffering. And it looks like we're winning."*

Then Peter figured it out. He felt like an idiot. Anuvata had given him the answer before he had even entered the house.

I seriously need to work on my listening skills.

He started chanting over the phone from the Metta Sutta:

"This is what should be done by one who is skilled in goodness, and who seeks the path of peace." The lights became more erratic and the noises increased. He continued. *"Those living near and far away, those born and to be born, may all beings be at ease!"*

FSSST! CRACK!

Everything went still as the phone snapped in half and sparked at the connection to the wall. The lights stopped flickering and Rob turned to look at Peter.

"Oh. Good job, kid," he praised Peter.

The family stopped screaming. The doors opened slowly and they all spilled back into the room.

"Okay. Your problems should be solved now," Peter said quickly.

"Was it an electrical problem?" the father asked.

"You should get a new phone," Rob told them as he took the broken one. "And here's my card in case something happens again."

"Wait, it's really done?" the mom asked with grateful tears in her eyes. "Can we pay you or something?"

Rob shook his head and was about to respond when Peter interrupted. "You can wrap this up, right?" he asked Rob anxiously. "Girlfriend's waiting." He looked at the clock and paled. "And she's probably furious."

"You're afraid of *your girlfriend?*" one of the boys gawked. "She must be terrifying."

"Please, please, please!" he pleaded as he raced towards the school, riding the air currents.

He hoped she wouldn't be mad at him. He was only fifteen minutes late. But then again, he was fifteen minutes late.

When he entered the school gym, he spotted her in the middle of the dance floor with Gina and another girl named Jessica. He didn't know what had happened to Hazel, but it was probably something complicated that he'd never understand.

He wove through the crowd to get to her. She looked stunning. He wanted to burn her smile into his memory so he would always have it.

Then her eyes met his and her face melted into an intense glare.

Oh no, he gulped.

She turned and huffed away.

"Oh, you are in so much trouble," Gina sang.

Peter exhaled. "Yeah, thanks, Gina."

He chased after her.

"Alicia," he called out while she clicked and clacked down the school hallway towards the front doors. He caught up to her as she shoved the doors open and walked to the football fields toward the street. "I'm really sorry," he said desperately. "You know my job..."

"Oh, right." She didn't slow down. "This mysterious unpaid internship that's more important than your girlfriend."

"Please hear me out," he begged.

She turned suddenly with a force that startled him. "No. I'm done hearing you out," she said. "I'm done with all the lies."

"What lies?" he worried.

"Do you really think I'm stupid enough to believe all that nonsense about your job?" She put her hands on her hips and glared even deeper. "What's her name?" she demanded.

"Uhhh… Who's name?" Peter asked.

"The girl you're cheating on me with."

Peter was utterly confused. "Hold up. Where is this coming from? You know I would never…"

"Is that really why you're late?" she interrupted him. "Did your other girlfriend have her school dance tonight, too?"

"How can you even say that? You know I would never do that. I mean, I can barely handle one girlfriend, how could I handle two…"

He had meant it as a joke to dispel the tension, but one look at her face told him that he was an idiot.

Smooth, Pete, he mocked himself. *Real smooth.*

"You want a shovel for that grave you're digging?" she heckled.

"Look, you gotta know how I feel about you," he said. She avoided his eyes, but he continued before she could argue back. "You're the only girl in my life. I'm not good at saying the right things or being on time, but I really do care about you."

She suddenly started crying. Peter stood frozen for a moment, not knowing what to do. Her sobs came out as little hamster squeaks and she rested her head against his chest. He wrapped his arms around her. He figured it was a good sign that she didn't push him away.

"What's wrong?" he asked. "Is it just that I'm an idiot or is there something else?"

"My dad," she sniffled. "He's…" she choked a sob. "He's leaving. After twenty years of what I thought was a happy marriage. My mom found out a few months ago that he's been cheating on her for years."

"Geez, Alicia, I am so sorry." He squeezed her tighter.

"They've been trying to do counseling for months, but he said he's fed up and he's leaving. How could he do that?" Alicia squeaked a sob. "Didn't he love her? Didn't he love me?"

Peter took a deep breath. "The Buddha said…"

"NO!" she barked, causing him to jump. "No stupid Buddhist wisdom." Then she sniffled. "Just hold me and tell me I'm pretty."

He held her even tighter and rested his head against the top of hers. "You're beautiful and I'll hold you forever if you want."

"You're so good," she told him. "Even if you were twenty minutes late and we didn't get to dance. You're just so good."

Then he got an idea. He asked for her phone, opened her music player, and turned on a slow song. There on the dark football field, under the stars, he held her while they swayed. Her tears calmed into a somber sadness and she pressed her cheek against his shoulder.

When the song was over, Peter gave her his suit jacket to keep her warm. They lay on the ground next to each other, looking at the stars and holding hands.

"Give me some stupid Buddhist wisdom," she asked.

"You sure?" he asked. She nodded. "Well, Buddhism is based on these four noble truths. The first one is that suffering is a part of life."

"I believe that one," she said, dispirited.

"The second is that suffering exists because we want something that we won't get or that we don't need. The third is that if we let go of that desire, we can find peace and true happiness."

She rolled over and settled her head onto his chest. "What's the fourth truth?" she asked.

"We can let go of our desires through meditation and self-discipline."

"That's why you meditate all the time?" she asked.

"Yeah. I could teach you sometime if you want," he offered.

"Maybe." She lifted her head up and made a pouty face. "I should probably get home, though. I'll send my mom a text to come get me."

"You don't want to go back to the dance?" he asked while she texted.

She picked at her curls. "With my hair like this? And my makeup all ruined? I probably smell like grass."

He sat up on his elbows and studied her. "You're beautiful."

She smiled dimly. "Thank you for tonight, Peter," she said softly. "I don't know what I'd do without you."

"You'll never have to know. I'll always be there for you." He promised. "Alicia, I love you." He said it before he could stop himself.

She nearly dropped her phone. "Really?" she whispered.

He nodded and held her cheek in his hand.

"I, I love you, too," she returned.

They shared a long kiss.

Chapter 49: Aunt Edna

Peter had a dream that his dad was in the middle of another meeting. He and a coworker stood in front of the boss' desk.

"Sam knowingly sacrificed the project just to get it out earlier," the coworker accused him.

"But..." Mr. Hunter looked confused. "You were both there when I..."

"It's too late to save yourself," the boss shook his head. Then he addressed the coworker. "I'm glad you caught this so early. Obviously, you should've been in charge the whole time." He turned back to Mr. Hunter. "I hate to tell you, Sam, but this is strike two. One more and you're out."

Then the boss turned to look at Peter with the face of Mara. "I could mess with your people for the rest of eternity. And I plan to."

The next day, Peter and his parents picked up Alicia to go to Rob and Charlie's wedding. Peter marveled at her as she walked to the car. She was wearing a teal dress and had curled her hair. He could barely believe someone so amazing had agreed to be his girlfriend.

The conversation between Alicia and his mom still seemed forced, but as he studied her smile, everything else melted away.

When they entered the wedding venue, Peter became distracted by an older woman with dark skin and gray hair. She was wearing a skirt and jacket with an elaborate flowered hat, all the same light blue color.

"I got it at a garage sale," she bragged as she showed a ring to the woman next to her. "Only paid ten dollars, but it's a genuine stone. Just because I'm almost seventy doesn't mean I have to look almost seventy!" the woman laughed.

Peter thought he saw a strange wisp of darkness swirling around the ring, but he blinked and it was gone.

Alicia and Peter held hands during the ceremony, stealing smiles at each other. Then Peter became distracted again. As the sermon was starting, the woman with the ring looked like she had an unreachable itch.

She scratched at her neck and grunted. The people nearby gave her furtive glances. She grabbed at the golden cross necklace around her neck and ripped it off, throwing it on the ground and backing away from it.

She became immediately calmer as a sinister grin blossomed.

SHOOOSH!

A breezed tickled Peter's ear.

Like you had to tell me, he joked to his spirit.

Immediately, his eyes were opened and he saw the dark energy that flowed from the ring and through the woman. She started walking for the back doors. Peter excused himself and followed her out to the garden area.

The night was cold, but the garden had been set up for overflow from the party. There were a few tables with appetizers under silver covers, a walking path surrounded by shrubbery, and a large stone fountain in the middle of the area, adding ambient noise.

Peter thought this would be a great place to take Alicia, but that idea was all but ruined by the current situation. The old woman was paused in the middle of the area.

"Hello ma'am," a young and well-dressed coordinator greeted her kindly. "I think the ceremony is still going on. Would you like me to escort you back inside?"

"I'm hungry. I want food," the woman in blue responded.

"Sorry, but we can't start serving the food until after the ceremony. You'll have to…"

"I said I want food!" the woman in blue interrupted.

She grabbed the coordinator around the waist. With absurd asura strength, she carried the woman to the fountain and tipped her face first into the icy water. Then she held the woman's head down, under the water.

"Be swept clean," Peter said quickly, pressing his hand against the back of her head. The old woman fell limp and the coordinator sprang upwards, sprinkling water everywhere. Her hair and outfit were soaked and her makeup was running. "What the hell?" she panted.

Peter said, "Why don't you go get warm? I'll take care of her."

"Yeah… I just… thanks," she stammered. "What the hell…"

Peter watched as she walked towards the hall.

Then the asura slammed into Peter's side in the form of a massive bull. The force threw him into the bushes. He held his side, worrying about his ribs as the bull-asura started charging again.

This time, Peter dodged by leaping into the air in a flip.

The spirit pawed at the ground threateningly. It charged him and he spun out of the way while generating a whirlwind that trapped the asura in place. Then he reached down and took the ring from the woman's hand.

He set the ring on the stone of the fountain. He found a large rock and pounded with full force, shattering the stone into dust and fragments. Finally, the asura disappeared into thin air.

Peter held his side again, massaging the bruise. He swept the ring into his pocket to purify and dispose of later.

Then the woman in blue started stirring and he sprang to her side.

"Hey, are you okay?" he asked as he helped her up.

"Lordy," she declared. "When did I come out here?"

Peter just smiled. "Can I escort you back inside?"

He offered his elbow as she came to her feet.

"Well, aren't you a fine young gentlemen," she grinned.

"Careful," he warned her jokingly, "I'm already taken."

At the reception, Rob pulled Peter aside. "I saw you run out," he said. "Now, I know you wouldn't skip out for a bathroom break during the wedding of the century. Everything okay?"

Peter told him the story and even pointed out the old woman.

Charlie, who had overheard, looked personally wounded. "Aunt Edna?" she asked in a hushed voice. "*My* Aunt Edna?"

"She's better now," Peter assured her. "Anyway, I guess they let you have the day off, considering," he told Rob.

"It would have been hard to explain," he joked as he wrapped an arm around Charlie's waist. "Thanks, kid. Best wedding present ever."

"It's what I do," Peter bragged. "Pick up your slack."

Rob shook him by the shoulder. "Don't press your luck, punk."

During the reception, Peter asked Alicia to dance. She rested her head on his shoulder and he breathed in her vanilla scent.

"You look beautiful," he told her. "This is a great color on you."

"I know," she said, flashing him a confident smile. "It's my color."

"You have a color?" Peter chuckled.

"All girls do. That's why I'm not talking to Hazel anymore."

He realized he hadn't seen Hazel since the night of the school dance.

"Why? What did she do?" he asked.

"You didn't see? She wore teal to the dance. She knew it was the color I look best in."

"I think you look great in everything," he said.

"You're sweet," she told him. "But it was a very intentional insult."

“Hm,” Peter considered it. “I guess it’s a good thing my teal suit was at the cleaners.”

She giggled. “So these were the friends you talked about that night at the festival, right?” she asked. He nodded. “It’s a funny memory now,” Alicia said, “but I was so mad at you at the time.”

“What’d I do?”

“The way you talked, I thought you were trying to ask me out. Then you just ran off. It was so disappointing.”

“You liked me back then, huh?” he smirked.

“Maybe,” she tried to hide a smile. “I always thought you were cute and nice, but I think it was field day that made me really notice you.”

“I’m just that awesome, huh?”

“What about you?” she asked.

“Oh, now this is embarrassing,” he rubbed the back of his neck. “Remember that day you walked me to the nurse’s office after I fought Jeremy? I think I started liking you then.”

She studied him a moment, then kissed him passionately.

He pulled back. “Whoa, my parents are right there,” he complained.

“So?” she asked with a mischievous smile.

“It feels weird. Can we keep the kissing more private?”

She gave him her angry eyes. “Are you telling me I can’t kiss my own boyfriend when I want to? Urgh!” She pulled away from him. “This night is just not going the way I wanted.”

He noticed that she had caught the attention of other guests, but he couldn’t get a word in edgewise as she continued her rant.

“First it’s awkward because it’s like a double date with your parents. I mean, that is just weird!”

Peter led her off the dance floor.

“Then you leave halfway through the ceremony and I have to sit with your mom and it’s so obvious that she still doesn’t like me!”

Peter took her hand and walked her out to the garden area where he had fought the bull-asura earlier. The night was crisp and the stars were bright. Still, Alicia complained the whole way.

“And then we finally have a romantic moment and you tell me I can’t kiss you? Do you even want to kiss me? What am I to you?”

Before she could go on, he kissed her. All her anger and unhappiness seemed to melt away as they spent a quiet moment together under the stars.

Chapter 50: Mara's Messages

That night, Peter dreamt of Zahid's family. He was helping to set up the tables at the restaurant, getting ready for the dinner rush.

He spread linens, lit candles, and placed rolls of silverware. Then, instead of lighting a candle, he held a match against the tablecloth. There was a satisfaction in watching it spread and burn.

"Peter?" Yara's voice called him. She was watching with a confused and horrified look.

He grinned sadistically.

"Yara, go get mom and dad!" Hassan ordered.

"What are you doing," Ahmed demanded.

"What you deserve," Peter answered.

He laughed as the fire spread.

Peter woke in a sweat as the clock changed to three in the morning.

SHOOOSH!

He would have to worry about his dream later.

He rode the wind, enjoying the currents. Then his heart stopped as he reached his destination: the Nasir Family Restaurant.

He pulled the door open quickly to find the place bustling. He didn't see the Nasirs anywhere, but the place was packed. He was about to wonder why the Nasirs kept the place open at three in the morning when he spotted a familiar face. There was one chair open, at a table for two. The man in the other chair waved.

He had dark hair styled flawlessly, thick eyebrows, and a strong, cleft chin. His eyes held all the fierce power and hatred of an asura.

Peter's jaw locked. "What do you want?" he asked coldly.

"No need for that," Mara turned on his charm. He waved and the plate in front of Peter filled with food. "Sit, sit!" Mara instructed as he started cutting into his steak.

Peter sat with a tired sigh and ignored the food. "If you think I'm going to change my mind, you're crazy. You and your minions have been nothing but annoying. There's nothing you could say to convince me to stop fighting you."

Mara studied Peter. "I admire your confidence, boy, but do you really think you can win? I've existed for untold ages. And you're what, fourteen?" He smiled sneakily. "You're playing with fire."

"If I'm no threat, then why are you here?" Peter smirked.

Mara laughed. "You know, that smirk really is one of the most annoying things about you." Then Mara leaned forward with his arms resting on the table. "I'm here to see if you got my messages."

"What messages?" Peter quipped.

"You know, your dad's trouble at work. Alicia's parents getting divorced."

Peter stiffened. "Are you saying that was you?"

Mara relaxed in his chair. "I'm just getting started."

Peter stood suddenly and slammed his palms on the table as he shouted, "Stay away from them!"

The restaurant quieted in an instant and all heads turned, but Peter didn't take his eyes from Mara. Now it was Mara's turn to smirk. He waved his hand and the people continued talking, laughing, and eating.

Mara locked eyes with Peter and told him, "I do what I want. I'm the king."

"This is your last warning," Peter threatened.

"Warning?" Mara thundered as he stood up. "Who are you to warn me? You think you can work against my plans and get away with it?"

"I will never join your side," Peter vowed.

"That deal's off the table," Mara laughed. "You had your chance."

"Then why are you here?" Peter repeated.

"I already told you. I'm here to see the look on your face when you realize that I'm. Just. Getting. Started."

In a flash of fire, Mara and all the other apparitions were gone. Peter would've let out a sigh of relief, but the restaurant was on fire.

He immediately called on Anuvata for help. He swirled a wind throughout the restaurant, but only managed to spread the flames until the smoke got under his contacts and he could barely keep his eyes open. Then he remembered that fire needed oxygen. He raced from table to table and formed a vacuum over the fires until they were all extinguished.

In the end, he had won the battle, but looking at the damage done to the Nasir's restaurant, he felt like Mara had won the war.

Peter and his parents helped the Nasirs sift through the damage the next day. Mrs. Hunter sat at a table with Mrs. Nasir comforting her while she cried. Peter's dad explained the insurance paperwork to Mr. Nasir. And Peter helped Zahid and his siblings by making piles of damaged and undamaged items.

Peter felt fully responsible for each and every damaged item. He knew dwelling on the guilt would get him nowhere, however. That was what Mara wanted. He knew the only way to fight back would be to accumulate good karma.

"Is there anything else?" Peter asked Zahid. "Anything at all?"

"No, Peter, you've done enough," Zahid told him. "Without you, none of this would have happened."

Zahid indicated the organized piles, but Peter couldn't help but interpret his words another way.

Chapter 51: A Kick in the Bhuta

In early December, Peter, his dad, and Rob flew up to New York for the national Tae Kwon Do competition. Peter was defeated by one of his first opponents.

Afterwards, as they walked to meet Peter's dad, Rob tried to console Peter in his own special, Buddhist way.

"Are you disappointed?" Rob asked.

"Well, we flew all the way up here and I didn't win."

"Did you need to win?" Rob asked.

Peter rolled his eyes. "No. I just wanted to."

"Why did you want to?" Rob asked.

Peter shrugged. "I guess I'd feel good about myself."

"You don't have enough to feel good about?" Rob asked.

After the horrid dreams and the guilt over Mara's machinations, Peter had felt that he did need a win. However, he knew where Rob was going.

"You know, wanting is a slippery slope," Rob told him. "I'm generally happy. I live very simply with few possessions, but every month, after the bills, I look at the extra money and think of how I'm going to use it. And suddenly, I realize that I don't have enough of anything. I don't have enough food. I don't have enough clothes. But before all that, before I thought I needed something, I was happy."

"I get it," Peter agreed unenthusiastically. "I don't need victories and medals to boost my self-esteem. There is no 'I' in team."

"Actually, there is no 'I' at all," Rob corrected him. "Another great lesson in Buddhism is the concept of the non-self or anatta. It's hard to explain, but I guess you could say that we're all parts of one grand consciousness. The idea is that the essence of who you are, –when you strip away circumstances, choices, and the body– all that's left is a piece of that pure consciousness that looks very similar to everyone else's piece of pure consciousness. We're all intimately connected. Interdependent."

Peter raised an eyebrow. "Are you saying I'm not a unique little snowflake? Because that goes against everything my mom ever told me."

"But that's another type of clinging and attachment, when you think of it," Rob lectured. "The truth is, without your sarcasm, without your tournament winnings, without your strong sense of justice, you're still equal to everyone else. The Buddha said, '*The foolish man conceives the idea of "self." The wise man sees there is no ground on which to build the idea of "self"'.*"

Peter realized it would take him a while to reconcile with this concept. He liked who he was and it was difficult to wrap his head around the idea that there was no individuality.

"So what you're saying," Peter said thoughtfully, "is that there is no 'I' in *consciousness*."

"Yes! That's exactly…" Sensei Rob stopped when he realized what Peter was doing. His eyes narrowed.

"There's no 'I' in *mind*," Peter continued the joke. "There's no 'I' in *equality*."

Rob glared. "I bet your pure consciousness is still a sarcastic punk."

That night, Peter and his dad settled into their hotel beds.

"Thanks for bringing me," Peter said. "I know things are crazy at work, so it's probably a huge sacrifice to take time off."

"Actually," his dad sighed, "I could use the break. I've been thinking of looking for another job."

"You didn't get fired again, did you?" Peter worried.

"Nothing like that. Things are just tense. I'm looking for something else just in case. So don't worry about work. This is a welcomed break."

His dad turned off the light, leaving Peter wide awake with his thoughts.

When Peter finally slept, it wasn't long before he was awoken with a sense of urgency. He left his snoring dad, walked up a few flights of stairs, and found Sensei waiting at the door of a hotel room.

"What's this?" Peter asked, rubbing the sleep out of one eye.

"Not sure," Sensei said, staring at the door. "I can sense…"

"Hey, what are you two doing?"

They both turned and saw a tall, pot-bellied hotel worker in blue coveralls walking towards them.

"Don't tell me you heard the noises, too," he asked them. "You both can go back to your rooms. I'll take care of this."

Peter was about to ask for details when a bloodcurdling scream rang out from the other side of the door.

The hotel worker banged on the door. "Maintenance. Is everything okay in there?" The screaming continued. "I'm coming in!"

The man used his card key and thrust the door open. The screams stopped immediately. The room was dark and empty. The worker turned to Peter and Rob with a look between scared and confused. A sudden, cold, and strong wind buffeted them.

"Did you feel that?" the worker asked them both in a hush.

Sensei nodded grimly.

The worker tried the lights, but they were inoperable. He raised a flashlight high and entered with Sensei and Peter right behind him.

"Hello? Anyone in here?" the worker asked.

Sensei started chanting softly, *"Homage to the Buddha, possessed of the eye of wisdom and splendor. Homage to the Buddha, compassionate towards all beings..."*

"What's that?" the worker asked.

"Just a prayer," Sensei answered.

"Well, it's creepy. Cut it out."

They heard a noise and all turned to see a woman in a white gown by the window. She held her head in her hands as if she were crying.

She looked up with a face of pure terror and screamed the same horrible sound they had heard earlier. They braced themselves as she ran right through them and out the door.

"Tell me you guys saw that," the worker said, obviously shaking.

"She was running from something," Peter observed. "What could scare a ghost?"

"The thing that killed her," Sensei answered, turning to the worker who had started convulsing in the telltale signs of possession.

As soon as the asura took over, Sensei thrust his hand against the man's head and declared, "May you be washed clean."

THUD!

The man fell to the floor and in his place stood a human form made of asura smoke. Sensei summoned a curl of water and directed it at the asura, but the spirit dispersed before the wave hit.

Peter and Sensei turned in all directions, looking for the asura. Peter felt his heart rate pick up.

Suddenly, something slammed into Sensei from behind. He stumbled from the force and sent a splash of water into the empty air. Then his knees buckled as something hit his legs.

Again, he turned to attack, but found only shadows. As he stood, something raised him into the air and threw him against the wall.

Peter tried to find the invisible assailant, turning around and searching the darkness. He didn't understand why they were only attacking Sensei Rob, but then he realized:

"What if this is a trap set by Mara? What if Rob dies because of me?"

Peering into the intense blackness, Peter noticed a smoke creeping towards them from all directions. They were completely surrounded.

He and Rob backed up, pressing their backs to each other as they braced themselves for the attack. Peter tried summoning Anuvata's wind, but he couldn't clear his mind.

"It's all my fault," he told Sensei quickly. "When Mara offered me anything I wanted, I refused. Now he's tormenting me and I can't stop it. What if he kills you? What would Charlie do? It's all my fault!"

Sensei stared at Peter with a blank look. "You really thought the best time to get into this was while we're trapped by an evil spirit in a haunted hotel room hours away in another state?"

Peter paused. "When you say it like that… Look, I understand if you hate me because of this. But please know that I never meant to hurt you."

Sensei startled chuckling. Soon, laughter was bubbling out of him. Peter felt like he had missed some tremendous joke.

Our lives are in danger! he thought. *Why is he laughing?*

Then Sensei conjured a wave that washed the smoke away and left the room in a quiet calm. Sensei wiped a tear as his laughter settled.

"Alright, that bhuta ought to be able to find her way back to the bardo now," Sensei said as he clapped his hands.

"Ah. So… are you still talking to me?" Peter asked tentatively. "Even though I put you in danger?"

"Come here, you little punk," Sensei Rob gave him an earnest noogie. "I know you'd never harm me or anyone else."

"But Mara…"

"That's a dangerous thought," Rob stopped him. "Think about it. What is Mara's ultimate goal?"

"To make me suffer," Peter answered.

"And what is the best weapon we have against him and all his underlings?"

"Loving-kindness."

"Exactly," Rob nodded. "What they want is for you to stop loving people. They can't do it by making you hate. You're too strong for that. But they can still drive you away from the people you love the most."

"But then how do I stop Mara?"

"Honestly, I don't think it's all Mara. Look, yes, they're watching us all the time, and yes, they like to mess with us. But they can't control everything. Sometimes they orchestrate situations to work against us, and sometimes, bad things just happen and you can't control it. Suffering is just a natural part of life in this realm."

"So you think Mara's not controlling everything?" Peter asked.

"He's probably doing something. And he's probably taking credit for everything. The spirits can influence people, but they can't make anyone do anything."

"How can I tell the difference?" Peter asked desperately. "How do I know when it's Mara and when it isn't?"

"Nope. Wrong question," Rob shook his head. "Mara and his minions are going to play their games and mess with our minds. Trying to figure out their plan is almost impossible. It's best just to ignore them. Instead of asking, 'how can I tell the difference?' or 'how can I stop them?' we should be thinking, 'how can I increase my loving-kindness for everyone.' As the Buddha said, *'Radiate boundless love towards the entire world above, below, and across, unhindered, without ill will, without enmity.'*"

Peter knew that Sensei Rob was right, but he still wanted to protect everyone. There had to be a way to stop Mara.

"What happened?" the worker asked in a daze as he started stirring. "I had the strangest dream."

Chapter 52: Going Solo

Over the holiday break, in early January, Peter met Alicia at the movies for a date. It was another horribly boring and unrealistic movie, but Alicia seemed to enjoy it. And Peter got to put his arm around her while she leaned against him. So he wasn't complaining.

SHOOOSH!

A breeze tickled his ears in the middle of the movie.

"Naraka!" he grumbled.

Alicia sat up. "You only say that when you're about to run."

He gave her an apologetic look. "I have to."

"No, you don't," she retorted. "That's what your Sensei's for. He's strong enough to handle it all on his own, isn't he?"

Peter thought it over a moment. "I think so," he considered. "I mean, he's been doing it for years."

"See? It's settled. I'm your first priority."

It didn't feel right, but he just wanted to enjoy a peaceful, romantic moment. He settled down, but felt another summons.

SHOOOSH!

Then another.

SHOOOSH!

"I have to go," he resigned.

"No, you don't," she argued.

"They wouldn't keep calling me unless I was needed."

She glared at him. "If you go, there will be consequences."

"I know. I'm sorry." He kissed her cheek and ran off.

He rode the wind to an apartment building across town and used his spirit's power to open the main door. He heard a woman yelling and followed the noise down the hall.

"Izzy, I'm not trying to tell you what to do," a man's voice answered with an exasperated tone. "But you're drinking at the clubs every night! You're so hungover that you go to work late. You have to stop this."

"Blah, blah, blah!" the female voice complained. "All I hear is you judging me! You're saying you don't accept me the way I am!"

"I'm not trying to judge you! I'm trying to save you from your destructive behavior."

"I'll do whatever I want and you can't stop me!"

"No, Izzy, wait…"

BAM!

Peter heard a gunshot. His heart stopped.

"What have I done?" the woman's voice squeaked.

BAM!

He heard another.

"No!" Peter screamed as he opened the door.

Two bodies were on the floor with pools of blood beneath them. The gun lay in the hand of a woman with bright red hair.

A haunting laugh echoed through the apartment, *"Too late, little monkey. You're too late!"*

Peter felt the full weight of crushing guilt. If he had listened to the first summons and ignored Alicia, he would've been there in time. Two people would still be alive.

Then he had a chilling realization. Sensei Rob wasn't there. He had only ignored the summons because he knew that Rob would be there.

Peter rode the wind to Sensei's house and knocked frantically.

Sensei opened the door in an apron and a huge smile. "Hey, Pete!" he greeted cheerfully. "Charlene! Pete's here. Come on in. Come on in. I was just finishing some sautéed veggies. Want some?"

"I don't get it…" Peter shook his head.

"Don't get what?" Rob asked. "You doing okay?"

"Sensei, I just came from a… why weren't you there?"

Sensei's face fell. "Here, sit down and tell me what happened."

Peter related the story while Sensei listened with somber attention.

"Why didn't they call me?" Rob scratched his chin. "You know this isn't your fault, though, right?"

Peter shook his head. "But it is. If I had just listened…"

Sensei was pensive for a while. "It's not just one thing that leads to a victim's downfall. Lots of people, lots of circumstances all come together. You may have been able to change the outcome if you had answered the first summons, but it wasn't you who pulled the trigger. It wasn't you who invited the spirit in. It wasn't you whose actions provoked anger. It's easy to assign blame when something bad happens, but it's pointless."

"Right," Peter said. "No matter who's to blame, they're still dead."

"But this regret," Rob told him. "It can fuel your training and your resolve. You can use it to make sure you never miss a summons again."

Peter nodded. "But why didn't they call you?"

"Hey, Peter!" Charlene greeted cheerfully when she came into the kitchen. "I'd hug you, but I have some kind of stomach bug."

"Everything okay?" he asked.

"I think it's just a case of the *Kung Flu*," she said with a smile.

Peter feigned a laugh, but nothing could lighten his mood.

That night, Peter was interrupted from his studying by a summons. This time, he sprang into action immediately. He jumped from his window and surfed on the air currents until he arrived at the city coroner's office.

The building was dark and empty. He didn't see Rob anywhere, but he followed his instincts to a cold hallway of lab rooms with steel tables and drawers in the walls.

"Hey, kid!" a voice startled him.

Peter turned slowly to see a large, muscular man with a security guard's uniform. Peter held up his hand to shield his eyes from the blinding flashlight and read the man's nametag: Larry.

"You're trespassing," Larry told him.

"Uhhh…" Peter struggled to come up with an answer.

CLANG! CLANG! CLANG!

The sound came from one of the rooms off the hallway. Peter and the guard both turned slowly to look.

"Kid, you should go," the guard told him. "You get a free pass, just get out of here."

"No, I'll stick with you," Peter said.

"Your choice," the guard shrugged.

CLANG! CLANG! CLANG!

The sound rang out again. They walked slowly toward the source, with Larry leading the way.

"'Work the night shift,' they said," Larry grumbled under his breath. "'You'll make more money,' they said."

CLANG! CLANG! CLANG!

The noise came from a particular drawer and Larry reached out slowly to grab the handle. Peter could see dark energy swirling from the edges of the drawer, but didn't know how to warn Larry.

Hey, this is obviously a case of demonic possession. Why don't you let me take care of it? You're older, stronger, and you have a gun while I'm only a trespassing teenager, but trust me. I got this.

Larry slid the drawer open slowly to find a corpse, toe tag and all, lying still and breathless under the undisturbed white cover.

Larry laughed at himself. "Knew it. Just scaring myself."

The body sprang to life in an instant, clamping its hand around Larry's neck. He choked and sputtered while the body lifted him off the ground with unnatural strength.

The woman with bright red hair and pale skin looked just the same as when Peter had seen her earlier that day. There was no sign of decay on her body but her eyes were solid black.

The vetala turned a twisted grin at Peter.

"Hello again, sad little monkey," it taunted.

Larry threw a confused and disturbed look at Peter.

"Some hero," the vetala continued. *"It's funny how you thought you were so cool when you defied Mara, and yet here you are, failing miserably. At least if you had accepted his offer, you could've enjoyed job benefits. But now your failure is pointless."*

Peter created a current that smacked the vetala from behind. It grunted and let go of Larry. He scrambled away and towards Peter.

"What's going on?" Larry screamed.

"Go," Peter told him.

Larry took off running while Peter started chanting.

The vetala sprang towards him. *"You stole my meal!"*

The creature caught his arm and bit into his shoulder. He felt it suck the blood from him, draining his energy.

He tore it from his shoulder and backed away. It laughed maniacally with blood on the woman's face.

Then he twirled around her and caught the vetala from behind, pinning the arms down while it twisted the head around, trying to bite him again. "Be swept clean," he declared.

As the darkness left the woman's body, he blasted the asura cloud into nothingness with a punch of wind.

He looked around.

This fight never should have happened, he thought, *but at least I was able to finish it.*

He picked up the body, placed it back in the drawer, and prayed:

"May you be filled with loving-kindness. May you be peaceful and at ease. May you be happy."

Peter rode his bike to see Alicia the next day. He knew her smile would be like a medicine after all the negativity he had experienced. But when she opened her door, he was reminded by her deep scowl that she was insanely mad at him.

"Hey," he said awkwardly.

She glared and told him, "For the record, I am not happy."

"I know," he chuckled nervously.

She wants to be my first priority. And she deserves just that.

"Look," he said, avoiding her eyes, "this isn't easy, so I'm just going to say it. You deserve someone who'll always be there, but I can't…"

"Wait," she stopped him. "Are you breaking up with me?"

"I don't want to." He met her eyes. "But I'm giving you the chance to break up with me. This job is important and if you don't like how I'm always late and leave suddenly, that's something I just can't change."

"If this is some arrogant ultimatum…"

"Alicia, two people are dead now…" Alicia gasped and covered her mouth. "I can't take even a minute next time," he told her. "You deserve someone who's always going to be there and drop everything for you. But that's not something I can give you."

She placed her hand on his arm. "I had no idea. Are you okay?"

He shook his head dismally. "I could've saved them."

She hugged him. "It wasn't your fault," she assured him. "You would never hurt anyone."

He breathed in her comfort. "But I still could've prevented it. Do you see what I'm talking about?" He pulled back, holding her shoulders. "I really like being your boyfriend, but I can't make you the first priority."

"I guess I don't need to be your absolute first priority," she compromised. "But maybe just make sure I'm up there near the top."

He nodded. "But I'll understand if you change your mind about us."

"Peter!" she stopped him. "Do you want to break up?" He shook his head. "Then drop it." She smiled dimly and softened her tone. "You're stuck with me." She leaned in and kissed him.

Chapter 53: Peter's Greatest Weakness

After visiting Alicia, Peter rode his bike to the studio to talk to Rob.

"Hey, Pete, how are you doing today?" Rob greeted brightly.

"Hm, let's see," Peter responded. "I fought a vetala last night. Again, without you. It bit me, so now I'm worried about becoming one. And just now, I almost begged my girlfriend to break up with me."

Rob leaned against the front desk and took on a philosophical look. "That sounds rough. Well, at least I can tell you that Vetala bites aren't contagious. And remember, all suffering is caused by craving. Are you maybe craving justice and praise for your good work when the karma should be enough?"

Peter glared at him. He suddenly understood why Alicia always called it "stupid Buddhist wisdom."

"Right," he agreed quickly, hoping to spare himself a deeper lesson. "Who needs praise?"

Then Peter realized that Sensei looked oddly cheerful.

"Where's Sensei Charlie today?" Peter asked.

"She's at home with that Kung Flu," Rob said, holding back a smile.

"I hope she feels better soon," Peter said, trying to keep the conversation normal.

"I think it's going to last a while. Maybe a few months."

"Wait, is Kung Flu an actual thing? I thought she was kidding."

"What Charlene has, it's real," Sensei chuckled. "And I think it's something only women get."

"Is this a joke or something?" Peter asked. "Why are you laughing about your wife being sick?"

"Pete!" Rob exclaimed. "She's pregnant!"

"Whoa!" he stood up.

"I'm gonna be a dad!"

"Geez, congratulations!"

"She's only a few weeks along," Rob explained. "But man, I'm reeling. There were so many times I wondered if I was even allowed to have a family. But now I met the most amazing woman and we're starting a family. This whole last year has been like a dream."

"But what if something happens to you during a fight?" Peter worried. "You have two people depending on you now."

"That's why we don't fight on our own." Sensei Rob gripped Peter on his bad shoulder and Peter winced. "Sorry." Sensei switched to the other shoulder. "As long as we stay connected to the devas, they'll protect us if it's too dangerous."

Peter was struck by a sudden realization. "Wait a minute," he said. "What if that's why they only called me out the last couple of times."

"No," Rob dismissed the thought. "I have a feeling it was just a fluke."

SHOOOSH!

At that moment, Peter received a vision and Rob started dancing from a shiver down his back.

"See?" Rob said with a smile. "What did I tell you? Race you there!"

They arrived on the scene at the same time. Outside a fast food restaurant, a woman in the drive through lane had gotten out of her car and was yelling through the window.

"I don't care if it's too late to get breakfast!" she screamed at the cowering workers. "I want hash browns and you're going to get me what I want! You filthy vermin are meant to serve me!"

Peter and Rob started chanting and the woman turned and screamed at them. The scream was so powerful that they were pushed backwards, as if by a strong gust of wind.

While they adjusted, the woman ran into a wooded area next to the restaurant. Rob and Peter followed.

It had been a bright sunny, winter's day, but as soon as Peter entered the woods, the world dimmed. The forest was as dark as night and a strange silver mist swirled through the gaps in the trees.

Peter turned around and realized that he was alone. The woods seemed to go on forever. He couldn't see the road or Sensei Rob.

He felt Anuvata lead him deeper into the eerie forest. He stopped when he found the woman they had been chasing. She was face down on the ground and passed out. Peter felt along her neck. Her pulse was active and the woman was clean.

Sensei must have exorcised her, Peter speculated, *but where is he?*

He finally found Rob crouched in a ball next to a tree with the dark aura of possession. He was mumbling to himself and looking around with erratic jerks of his head.

"Sensei?" Peter asked nervously.

Rob didn't seem to hear him. His mumbling grew louder. Then he roared in pain before collapsing in a fetal position on his side. His body snapped repeatedly as if something were attacking him. Peter could see dark energy spilling out of his ears and nose.

Then Sensei sat up, howling like an animal and tore off his jacket. Peter saw red stains on his shirt from wounds underneath. Peter didn't understand how he had gotten the wounds when his jacket and shirt showed no damage, but the blood formed into letters, spelling out:

DIE

"Be swept clean," Peter declared.

With an earth-shaking howl, the spirit exploded from Rob and disappeared into the shadows of the forest. Peter helped Rob up.

"Are you okay?" he asked, utterly disturbed by Rob's state.

"I was trapped," Rob whispered. "It was telling me everything I'd ever done wrong and why I'll be a horrible husband and father."

"That's not true," Peter countered. "You're going to be the best dad."

"The same one," Rob started to cry. "It was the same one."

Peter didn't understand, but didn't care. He knew he had to get Rob out of the forest and into clean air and sunshine. He had never seen Rob cry.

Suddenly, Peter felt a blow against his knees. He and Rob fell to the ground. Peter sprang to his feet and looked in all directions.

"You think you've won," a voice echoed from the mist, *"But I will have him again. He was marked as mine ages ago."*

Sensei Rob collapsed onto the forest floor. Peter suddenly understood. This was the same spirit who had possessed him years before.

"Well, too bad," Peter argued. "He's not yours anymore."

The asura voice laughed. *"Once a soldier for the Kingdom, always a soldier for the Kingdom."*

Rob slapped his hands against his ears and cried out.

Peter closed his eyes to focus his thoughts and started to chant. He conjured a breeze to blow the mist away, but it fought against his wind. He could feel it creeping along the air currents, reaching out for him.

Despite resisting, the mist entered through his eyes, nose, and ears. Peter's thoughts were flooded with the spirit's voice:

"Cold are the monkey's ears and toes."

Before Peter could figure out what that meant, all his senses switched. He tasted sounds and saw scents. He felt sights and smelled sensations against his skin. The result was intense confusion.

"Wishes are hopping," a voice in his head continued. *"And the trees are dripping with fire. Friends are just baskets and hats. Food is sitting with weather lying."*

The voice continued speaking nonsensical statements. He barely had time to process one statement before another one began. He could understand how the nagging voice could drive someone crazy.

But then he realized that this was how his brain felt whenever Zahid was trying to explain confusing homework, or whenever he heard a science lecture. He started laughing. The confusion made him taste his laughter, but still he laughed.

Anuvata's wind grew stronger and ripped through the mist. Peter's thoughts and senses returned to normal.

Then, above the wind, he heard the asura's livid voice:

"Think of all you've sacrificed for this annoying hobby!" it blustered. *"You're not allowed to be a normal kid. Your parents would be furious if they knew the truth. And you think that silly girl cares about you? She'll reject you as soon as someone better comes along."*

"Fine," he yelled as Anuvata's wind continued to sweep through the forest. "I don't care what sacrifices I have to make. As long as I can protect people from you!"

With one final burst of energy, Anuvata's wind swirled in all directions, eliminating the asura and its illusions. Streams of sunlight pierced the scene, returning the world to normal.

Peter felt like a king, but when he helped Sensei up off the ground, he saw that Sensei looked horribly sad.

"Peter, what were you thinking?" Sensei asked dismally.

"Uhhh… I think I just saved your butt," Peter replied. "You're welcome very much."

Rob studied him regretfully. "You did," he said. "And I'm grateful. But Peter, you just spelled it out for them."

Peter didn't understand, but he started to feel like an idiot. "What do you mean?" he asked.

"Now they know exactly how to attack you. You told them."

Peter searched his thoughts. "What did I tell them?"

"You're greatest weakness," Rob revealed, "is wanting to protect the people you care about."

The weight of the statement settled onto Peter's stomach. He had just doomed everyone that he loved.

Chapter 54: Mara Attacks

Despite Peter's initial worries, months passed without a significant attack from Mara. The spirits had stopped summoning Rob for exorcisms, but Peter was grateful for that. The only problem was Alicia's stress over her parents' divorce.

"How is everything?" he dared to ask one weekend in March as they were cloud watching in a park.

She sighed heavily. "It's almost final. I'm just ready for it to be over. But Peter," she sat up to look at him, "I can't thank you enough. You've been the best boyfriend ever. If it hadn't been for you, I couldn't have gotten through any of it. I owe you so much."

"I'd do anything just to see you smile," he assured her.

"So speaking of anything," she said slowly, "there's this huge St. Patrick's Day party tomorrow." Peter made a grimace. "Gina knows this girl whose older brother is a sophomore, so it'll be a great way to meet people from the higher grades."

"I don't know. Things have been pretty crazy with the job lately since my Sensei retired," Peter told her. "Everything usually picks up in the evenings. I don't want to commit to something and then disappoint you. Gina will be with you, right? So you don't really need me."

"I guess," she pouted. "But you owe me a really romantic date."

"Anything you say, beautiful."

SHOOOSH!

He felt a tug at his gut and a whisper in his ear. He turned to tell Alicia, but she must have read his face.

"Gotta go save someone, huh?" she smiled sweetly.

He nodded, grateful that she was more understanding about his work.

"Take care of yourself, superhero," she told him with a kiss.

The following Monday, Peter held Alicia's hand while they walked through the hallway in between the classes.

"It's weird since Zahid's parents made him join band," Peter was telling her. "I was thinking of joining the volunteer club. It'd be fun to do something like that together. What do you say?" Alicia didn't answer. Her forehead wrinkled as she studied the crowd. "Everything okay?" he asked.

"Can't you tell?" she whispered. "Everyone's looking at us."

"You're just that beautiful," he told her. "And I'm not so bad myself."

She forced a smile, then stopped as she heard a girl nearby whisper, "She's still with Peter? Doesn't he know she's cheating on him?"

Peter's heart dropped. He looked at Alicia. She looked terrified.

"I swear, I didn't…" she shook her head.

"What are they talking about?" he questioned.

She shook her head again, eyes full of tears, and ran away.

He tried to chase her, but he didn't get far before Jeremy tackled him.

"I didn't do it," he told Peter desperately. "It's just a stupid rumor."

It took a moment for Peter to understand what he was saying. "Hold up. You?" Peter laughed. "The rumors are about *you* and Alicia?"

"I promise I didn't," Jeremy repeated.

"It's okay," Peter interrupted him, suddenly feeling lighter. "I trust you. And you're the last person I'd imagine her going for."

Jeremy looked angry. "Hey!" he complained.

"No, you're cool," Peter assured him. "I'm just saying that Alicia hasn't always been your biggest fan."

"Yeah. Good point," he conceded.

Peter ran off, trying to find Alicia, and saw Zahid at his locker. "Hey, have you seen…" he started.

"Is it about those rumors?" Zahid asked with a grimace.

"Has everyone heard them?" Peter complained.

"I think you should be careful," Zahid cautioned.

"Alicia wouldn't cheat on me," Peter asserted before running off.

He finally found Alicia behind the gym, crying.

"Hey, are you okay?" he asked her softly.

She looked up. "You aren't mad at me?" she asked, shocked.

He smiled warmly and sat next to her. "I'm sure if you were sick of me, you'd let me know instead of sneaking around behind my back."

She nodded. "I would."

"Plus with everything that happened with your parents, I know you wouldn't do that to someone else. You know what it feels like."

"Right," she nodded. "I would never. Thank you for believing in me."

"Of course." He clasped her hand. "I'm sure these rumors will fade soon. And I'll be there to defend your honor until they do," he promised.

"Then we're still dating?" She barely made it through the sentence before she was sobbing.

He laughed and pulled her to a hug. "As long as you'll put up with me," he soothed her. "I wouldn't break up with you over a rumor."

"I don't deserve you," she said as she buried herself into him.

He kissed her forehead. "Then we don't deserve each other."

He was grateful that he was able to comfort her, but then he started wondering if Mara had something to do with the rumors.

Over the next few weeks, the rumors died down, but Alicia started acting distant and distracted. Peter worried that Mara was messing with her in a way he couldn't see.

One day, Peter was called out to an exorcism where two men in suits were arguing at a restaurant over who got to pay the bill. Somehow, their fight had escalated to an all-out brawl in the fancy restaurant.

Peter exorcised one man from behind. "Be swept clean," he declared.

He fell to the ground and Peter turned to fight the second man. Before he could anticipate it, the man spewed a green smoke from his mouth, right into Peter's face.

The smoke smelled awful and stung beneath Peter's contacts. His eyes forced shut. Then he felt a chair slam into the side of his head.

The man tried to punch Peter, but he felt the motion in the air. He grabbed the man's arm and flipped him over his shoulder and to the floor.

"Be swept clean," he pronounced.

He was finally able to open his stinging eyes as the asura left the man and flew out of the restaurant. Peter followed it to the streets.

As soon as he turned a corner to the alley where the asura had fled, he was hit with a blast of the same green gas. As Peter's eyes shut tight again, he heard two asuras laughing.

"We can't wait to see the look on your face," one asura taunted. *"We've been preparing our traps and now they're ready to spring."*

"What traps?" Peter asked defiantly, feeling along the wind currents for the asuras' locations.

"Be prepared to lose everything," the second asura warned.

"And everyone," the first one added with a cackle.

Peter could tell that they were only going to continue speaking in riddles. He abandoned trying to find their location and conjured a windstorm massive enough to fill the entire alleyway.

He was able to open his eyes again as the asuras' faded.

Peter trudged to school the next morning rubbing his eyes beneath glasses. He was lost in a world of thought as he tried to anticipate what traps the asuras had been planning.

He entered the cafeteria and paused when he saw Alicia, Gina, and their new friends. In the past few weeks, they had made three new friends, all of whom were loud, crass, and prone to gossip. Peter hoped they would all settle down soon or that they would start wearing teal.

"Hey," he greeted as he kissed Alicia's cheek and sat down next to her. Then he realized that they were all staring at him. "What?" he asked.

"Since when do you wear glasses?" Alicia asked worriedly.

"Since I was a kid," he said. "My contacts were bothering me."

"Oh," Alicia said.

Peter thought that "Oh," seemed a lot like "Fine."

"Is that okay?" he asked tentatively.

"It's fine," she answered insincerely. "You can't help it, I'm sure."

"She's trying to be nice," Gina interjected impatiently. "But glasses don't really help your whole dorky, boring guy look."

"Thanks, Gina," Peter said dryly.

"Anyway, do you have to sit with us all the time?" Gina complained. "The least you could do is bring Zahid with you."

"Zahid's got band friends now," Peter responded.

"It's for the best," Alicia said. "He's more than a little dorky."

Peter couldn't tell if he or Gina was more offended.

"Zahid's great," Alicia assured him. "I'm just saying that sometimes, certain people can ruin your reputation."

"I don't really care about my reputation," Peter said.

"Right. I forgot," she spurned. "You're perfect and Buddhist."

"Is there something wrong with Buddhism?" he asked.

"You're just always so flat line. You don't care about anything."

"I'm just controlled. It's a good thing to be self-controlled, right?"

She scoffed. "Are you calling us uncontrolled and emotional?"

"No, I never said that," he retorted quickly. "Did I say that?"

The other girls stared at their phones.

"Is there something else going on?" he asked Alicia. "Something that's making everything else seem worse than it is?"

She flashed angry eyes. "Did you just ask if it's my time of the month?"

"Whoa. No, I did not," he reacted quickly. "Look, can we start this conversation over? I feel like we're talking two different languages."

"Aren't we always?" she rolled her eyes.

BRIIING!

Luckily for Peter, the bell rang. Alicia walked off, laughing with her friends. He felt like he was missing something big. Then he caught Gina looking at him sympathetically before rushing off.

After school, Peter went to find Zahid at his locker and saw Gina, arguing with him. They stopped when they noticed Peter.

"Hey, guys. What's up?" he asked slowly.

"Just flirting with Zahid," Gina answered nonchalantly. "Think about what I said, handsome." Then she rushed off.

"She wants you break up with Alicia," Zahid explained with a sigh.

"What? I thought they were friends." Peter felt like his head was swimming from trying to understand girls.

Zahid shrugged. "So what are you going to do?"

Peter laughed. "I'm not going to break up with Alicia just because Gina Salvatore told me to."

"Are you going to break up with her, though?" Zahid asked.

"What? No. Where did you hear that?"

"I didn't. But you look confused whenever you mention her."

Peter pushed air through his cheeks. "I don't know. Sometimes I think getting a girlfriend is easier than keeping a girlfriend."

Zahid gave him a skeptical look. "Peter, it took you a year to work up the courage to ask her out."

"I know!" he said.

Zahid laughed. "Every step forward is a step out of balance," he philosophized. "Maybe you two need to sit down and have a discussion about what needs to change in your relationship."

"That's a great idea," Peter agreed. "Thanks, man."

Peter went in search of Alicia and found her as she and her friends were leaving school. He pulled her away from the group.

"Hey, I feel like things have been weird between us," he said. "Can we take some time just to ourselves tomorrow?"

"Sure," she smiled. "What did you have in mind?"

"How about the duck pond? You know, where I first kissed you. Meet me there around noon and I'll bring lunch." She nodded eagerly. "Love you." He kissed her cheek and ran off.

Chapter 55: The Sun, the Moon, and the Truth

That morning, Peter had everything ready for a romantic picnic in the park when Anuvata called him out to an exorcism. He found a normal looking woman on the patio of a restaurant, ordering food.

"I'll have the Cobb salad, but without the egg. And with poppy seed dressing instead of ranch. I want the dressing on the side, but can I get two containers? And leave the tomatoes out as well."

"Susan!" the woman beside her exclaimed. "Can't you just order a simple salad?"

"That's what I'm doing," Susan protested. "Oh! On second thought, I'd like the eggs in the salad, but still no tomatoes. And a diet cook to drink."

The waiter winced, "Is diet popsi okay?"

Susan's face twisted and she leapt at the waiter, snarling like a beast. The other people on the patio all reacted by pulling out their cell phones.

Peter sprang over the patio fence and placed his hand on the back of her head. "Be swept clean."

The woman fell unconscious into the waiter and the asura flew off into the crowded streets. Peter chased it through the oblivious crowd. Finally, he got a clean shot and trapped the asura in a whirlwind.

"It's time for you to leave," he panted when he caught up.

"And it's time for you to wake up," the asura mocked as it struggled. *"How's your girlfriend? Have you checked up on her today?"*

Peter was incensed, "You don't get to lay a finger on her!"

"You can't even see it?" it cackled. *"The trap we've laid."*

"What did you do to her?" he asked quickly.

The spirit just laughed in reply. Peter figured he wouldn't get any more answers. He ripped the asura's form apart with Anuvata's wind and raced, riding on the wind, back to his house.

He picked up his phone and tried texting and calling Alicia as he hurried to the park on his bike. She wouldn't respond. He was starting to feel desperate.

He was only five minutes late to their date, but he couldn't find her anywhere. Not knowing where else to look, he raced to her house and pounded on the door.

She answered and stepped onto the porch with him.

"I was so worried." He leaned his head onto her shoulder and breathed a sigh of relief. "When you weren't at the park, I panicked."

She pulled away from him and folded her arms. "Peter, I think we should break up."

Peter's heart fell. "Hold up. What did I do?"

"You didn't do anything," she said. "You never do anything wrong. It's just that," she paused, "you can't control the heart."

"But… why?" Peter struggled to understand.

"There's not always a reason. It's like a book sometimes. This is just the end of a chapter. You're a great guy and I'm really grateful for all our time together. You're so nice and good. But I need you to just let me go."

Peter spent the rest of the weekend trying to process the breakup. He ran to his favorite park to meditate and asked Anuvata for advice, but the only message he received was a Buddhist quote:

"Three things cannot be long hidden: the sun, the moon, and the truth."

Peter didn't know what that meant, but he hoped that if he spoke with Alicia in depth, he'd be able to discover the real reason she had pushed him away. And, of course, he hoped that he could change her mind.

He arrived at school early on Monday morning, planning to find Alicia and talk. As he rounded a corner, he heard Alicia and her new group of friends laughing.

He was just in time to hear her say, "He's a really good guy, but he's just an idiot, you know? I was trying to get him to break up with me for weeks and in the end, I still had to be the one to do it."

Peter stopped dead in his tracks.

"At least now, after weeks of torture, you can finally be with Jeremy in public," one friend said. Then she noticed Peter, staring wide-eyed at her revelation. "Oops."

Alicia turned and blanched when she saw him. The other girls made quick excuses for leaving.

"Don't make this harder than it needs to be," Alicia scolded.

Peter felt like raging. He had been constantly sacrificing and compromising for their relationship while she had always been stubborn and dramatic. For the first time in years, he wanted to lose his temper. He wanted to smash in lockers and punch walls.

Alicia scoffed at his silence. "Come off your high horse," she said. "You would've done it, too."

Peter forced his voice to sound calm. "No, I wouldn't. When I said I loved you, I meant it," he told her. "I thought you did, too."

She rolled her eyes. "What was I supposed to say? 'Gee, thanks, buddy'? If I didn't say it back, I'd have looked like a jerk."

His heart broke when he realized she had been lying to him every time she had said it. "I would've been patient," he said softly.

She laughed bitterly. "Patient! You're always so patient! Can't you just once, lose it and yell or something?"

"Like Jeremy?" Peter asked sarcastically.

"He might not be perfect, or noble, or disciplined, but at least I know he cares about me. His passions are always on the surface, but even now, you found out I cheated on you and you're just calm."

"I'm *controlled*," he stressed. "But hey, if you wanted me to insult you and treat you like garbage, you should've said something."

"Jeremy doesn't do that anymore," she defended him. "And anyway, you can control your emotions because they're not that strong, but Jeremy's so passionate, that he can't. He loves me more than you ever did. You were always nice, and respectful, and boring."

"Boring?" he gibed. "Is that you talking or Gina?"

"You know what? I don't have to explain myself anymore. We're done. I owe you nothing."

She walked away and high-fived a friend.

At lunch, Peter was interrupted from his much-needed meditation when Jeremy came to sit next to him.

"I told her to tell you right away," he explained desperately. "But she said her plan was better."

Peter collected the last dregs of his self-control. "Jeremy," he exhaled, "right now, everything is raw. If we talk, I might end up hurting you."

"You should. Hit me," Jeremy suggested. "Here. In front of everyone. Knock out a tooth, give me a black eye. I deserve it."

It was tempting, but Peter knew he would only reap negative karma.

"That won't solve anything," he told Jeremy.

"It might."

"Just let me cool down," Peter ordered.

Jeremy looked like he wanted to say more, but gave up and walked away just as Zahid came to sit with Peter.

They passed a few moments in silence until Zahid said, "Wanna talk?"

"No," Peter replied.

"Everything okay, Pete?" Rob asked when Peter walked into the dojo that evening. "You look down."

"I don't know many people that would just bounce back from getting cheated on, dumped, and mocked," he quipped.

"All that happened? I'm sorry to hear that." Rob sat on the bench next to Peter. "It'll take time, but trust me, one day you'll meet someone who will make all these experiences make sense. That someone will heal your heart. And your world will feel bright and alive and you'll be able to laugh even when nothing's funny."

Peter narrowed his eyes at Sensei. "You know you're really annoying right now, right?"

"Yes, I do," he clapped his hand on Peter's shoulder. "And one day, you'll be just as annoying."

"Robert, leave the boy alone," Sensei Charlie came out of the office.

"I just thought if he saw how happy we are, he would…"

"Honey," she in an angry-parent tone. "Why don't you take care of tuition?"

"You're right. You're always right," he said as he kissed her cheek and patted her growing belly.

Peter rolled his eyes as Rob hurried away. "Thanks for saving me," he told Charlie.

"That's my job," she smiled. "If you do ever need to talk about it, I can promise I won't be as annoying."

"I think I'm mostly upset by the injustice," Peter admitted. "I mean, I was a great boyfriend. I was the kind of guy I thought all girls wanted. I was calm, respectful, kind, and gentle. I defended her from the jerk and she ends up dumping me for the jerk."

"Wait. She dumped you for that Jeremy kid?" Charlie asked.

"She was always complaining about him and insulting him and bickering with him. How could I have seen it coming?"

"Oh," Charlie said long and slow. "I think I see what's going on."

"What?"

"Didn't you get together after you defended her from him?" Charlie reminded him. "And she got mad at you for not beating him up that one time, right?"

"Yeah, but what does that…"

"Peter," Charlie said, "I think she may have always liked Jeremy."

"But he was always so mean to her," Peter argued.

"And she thought she could change him. When she dated you, she may have been trying to send him the message to clean up his act. She may have been trying to tell him that she would like him if he were nicer to her like you were. I'd bet money on it."

Suddenly he realized how much sense that made. She always seemed to be more flirtatious when Jeremy was watching.

"She played me?" he asked, even more broken-hearted.

"It's a crummy thing to do to someone," Charlie agreed, "but she probably didn't do it intentionally. I'm sure she did have feelings for you, too. She probably felt conflicted and didn't know which way her heart was pointing. Most people your age aren't as self-aware as you are."

"Are all girls like that?" Peter grumbled.

"Some. But not all. There are girls who are more mature and self-aware. They just don't always stand out as much as someone like Alicia does."

"I feel like I wasted my time with her," Peter said.

"I wouldn't say that," Charlie consoled him. "With any relationship there will be some good and some bad. It's never a waste if you learned from your experience. And I think everyone gets an allowance for one stupid crush. Some choose to have more, but I think one is excusable. Want to hear about mine?"

"I already know about Sensei Rob," Peter responded plainly.

"I heard that!" Rob griped from the office.

Charlie laughed and Peter smiled as he picked up his ringing phone. "Hey, dad, what's up?"

"Peter, it's your mom."

Chapter 56: Losing Yourself

Peter arrived at his mom's hospital room as his dad was talking to a doctor in the hallway.

"We still have a few tests to run," the doctor explained. "If they're inconclusive, we'll refer you to a few specialists. But she should be able to go home tonight."

"Thank you for your time," Mr. Hunter said sincerely. "I know you're all working hard."

"We'll let you know as soon as we find anything."

The doctor departed and Mr. Hunter gave Peter a sad look.

"What happened?" Peter asked.

"She had been complaining about a headache for a while," he explained. "Then out of nowhere, today, she collapsed. They've given her medicine for the pain and she's getting some rest."

Peter looked through the open door at her, sleeping on the hospital bed, and felt miserable.

"It's okay," his father reassured him. "We'll get through this together. What's important is that we have each other."

Peter wasn't so sure about that last part. He was starting to think everyone would be better off without him.

His mom's sickness offered a great distraction from his other worries. His problems with Alicia and Jeremy seemed miniscule compared to the medical mystery that was his mom.

She came home from the hospital that night after a myriad of inconclusive tests. All weekend, Peter offered chants and Tonglen for her. He also took on all her housework, hoping he could accumulate good karma for her.

On Sunday, he came into the kitchen and found her trying to cook. Her hands quivered as she held the knife over an onion.

"Here, let me…" he offered.

"No!" she contested passionately. "I can do this."

Peter touched her arm. "I know you *can*. I just want to do it for you."

She studied him before giving in. "Okay. But I'm not crying," she sniffed. "It's just the onion."

Peter took over and tried not to move too quickly or skillfully. His mom sat at the counter staring out the window.

"I wish I knew what was wrong with me," she said. "I want to fight it, but you can't fight unless you know who your enemy is."

Peter stopped still. He knew who the enemy was. This was no random sickness. In fact, Mara had probably planned this. Peter had thought it was weird that the asuras only seemed to be attacking his dad, while nothing bad happened to his mom.

Peter had said chants and offered karma for his dad this whole time, while they were probably setting up the sickness within his mom. He hadn't seen it coming, but maybe now that he realized their game, maybe he could still find a way to fight back.

He looked at his mom across the counter, consumed by her own worries as she stared out the window. "Uh oh," he put down the knife and moved to her. He smoothed back the hair on her forehead.

"What is it?" she asked quickly. "What now?"

"A new freckle," he whispered. She laughed bitterly. "But hey, this is a special one. It's a freckle that marks the love of a son who's going to help you through everything. No matter how scary it is."

She started crying and pulled Peter to a hug. "I don't know what I'd do without you."

Peter thought that without him, she probably wouldn't be sick at all.

That afternoon, Peter meditated at his favorite park. One by one, he confronted and acknowledged each of his negative feelings.

I am angry and sad that my mother is suffering, he admitted. *I feel guilt for being a part of her suffering. I am angry with Jeremy and Alicia. I feel embarrassed and betrayed.*

He thought of how Alicia had accused him of being capable of the same actions and felt bitterness swell in his heart.

Then he thought of Sensei's teaching on anatta, the non-self. Peter liked to think he was special and unique. He had a sense of loyalty and justice. But when he thought of why, it had a lot to do with all that Sensei and his parents had taught him.

Maybe, he realized, *if you take away all my circumstances and replaced them with Alicia's, maybe I would've done the same.*

Maybe if he had grown up in Jeremy's household, he would have been just as confused and conflicted. Maybe that was the idea of anatta. Stripped down of all choices, emotions, and circumstances, maybe all humans, all beings were the same, connected through their identical nature.

Peter wasn't sure he understood or accepted the idea yet, but he was sure about one thing: it was certainly harder to be angry with them when he thought like that.

That Monday, at lunchtime, Peter found a quiet spot outside and took in a few mindful moments while he ate. Then Jeremy ruined it all by sitting next to him. Peter sighed.

"I don't know if you're ready to talk," Jeremy said, "but I wanted to say I'm sorry. Again. And I'll keep on saying it until you forgive me."

"Look, I forgive you," Peter told him. "But it still hurts. I can't just act like it didn't happen."

"You're right." Jeremy's lower lip stuck out. "I feel like such a scumbag. I never meant to make a move on her." Peter raised an eyebrow. "At least, not since we've been friends. It just happened."

"The St. Patrick's Day party?" Peter realized.

Jeremy nodded. "I wasn't," he cleared his throat, "thinking clearly. And she was talking about her parents and how sad she was and I couldn't control myself. I just wanted her to stop crying. So I kissed her. And I immediately regretted it. But after that, it was like there was this craving, this pull that neither of us could stop."

Peter had to hold himself back from giving a brilliant Buddhist lecture on the many ways he could have stopped or controlled his cravings.

Zahid came and sat down with them. Luckily, Zahid didn't say much. They all sat in silence until Gina came. Peter wondered if he had some sign on his forehead or something.

"How's it going?" she asked. "Are you still heart-broken and sad?"

"I can honestly say I'm not thinking about Alicia much right now," Peter told her.

He thought about telling them about his mom, but he was already receiving more attention and pity than he wanted.

"Good," she nodded. "I mean, you're still totally boring..."

"Thanks, Gina."

"But you're a good guy. I think the way that she played you and cheated on you, lied, dumped you, talked smack about you…"

"Gina," Zahid said emphatically.

"I think what she did was stupid," Gina summarized. "No offense, Jeremy."

"No, I agree," Jeremy stuck out his lip again. "I'm a monster."

Gina rolled her eyes. "Anyway. You deserve better. Hang in there."

"Thanks, Gina," Peter said sincerely.

Peter lost himself in his part time job. It was easy to forget his own problems when he was battling the forces of evil.

It seemed like the asuras were helping, too. All week long, they gave him plenty of opportunities. He caught a man trying to kidnap unescorted children from their routes home from school. He saved a group of kids touring a haunted house in their neighborhood in the middle of the night. They were there for thrills, but the asuras wanted to follow them home. He saved a group of teens when the wrong kind of spirit tried to communicate with them through a Ouija board.

Then one night, he arrived at a cemetery at three o'clock in the morning where he found two familiar faces.

"I can't take it anymore, Vida," Crystal complained. "They do things to me, horrible things. They're in my room at night. Sometimes, they throw things at me or try to pull me from my bed. I'm terrified. Why would my spirit guides treat me like this?"

"Calm down," Vida attempted to soothe her. "Sometimes you have to make sacrifices for what really matters."

Crystal looked hysterical and weak with dark circles under her eyes and hollow cheeks. Peter could see the dark energy swirling all around her.

"You know what matters to me now?" she defied her friend. "Sleep. I just want to sleep. And I want to be in control of myself."

"This is what you signed up for," Vida reminded her. "Sometimes you have to lose yourself in order to gain something."

Crystal shook her head. "If you can't help me, I'll find someone who can. I'm done, Vida. Done."

Crystal started to storm off and Vida yelled after her, "You can never leave him! You signed up for this for life!"

Crystal stopped in her tracks as the asura took over. She started convulsing and foaming at the mouth. The energy pulsated at strange disharmonious intervals.

"Crystal?" Vida asked nervously.

The spirit inside of Crystal cackled in a high-pitched voice and she started levitating. Vida took a few steps backwards in astonishment.

Peter rushed out of his hiding spot and surprised the girl with a quick exorcism. "Be swept clean."

Crystal fell in a heap and Peter conjured a cyclone that chased the asura away immediately.

"You!" Vida blustered at Peter. "You're the one who keeps messing things up!"

He turned slowly to face her.

"You stopped our spells!" she exclaimed. "I'll make you pay."

"Or you can thank me," Peter suggested with a forced smile.

Vida started chanting. Peter saw three asuras swirling through the air in a whirlwind around her. He took an instinctive step back and watched as the spirits entered into her body.

Then, before he could react, she produced a dagger from her belt and stabbed it into her stomach. She cried out in pain and pulled it upwards. To Peter's great surprise, no blood emerged.

But he saw the moment that the girl's eyes changed. Suddenly, her presence was simply gone and the only thing left inside was the asuras. Darkness took over like ink or dye until her entire eye, iris, pupil, and cornea, was black.

The asuras seemed to test the body by moving the head and limbs, stretching them out. Then the vetala's black eyes fixed on Peter.

"Aren't you tired of fighting us?" it lulled Peter. *"Don't you just want to give up and sleep?"*

Peter felt a sway to the world around him. He was so tired. Its words were hypnotic.

"Just give in and sleep. Why do you have to be the one to fight us, anyway? Really, if the humans just resisted us, you wouldn't have to pick up their slack and fight. They're just getting what they asked for. Give up and go to sleep, Peter Hunter."

Peter fought against the weariness with every ounce of his will. He used Anuvata's wind to raise the vetala off the ground, he swirled it in a circle until she should have been dizzy, chanting the whole time.

He lost energy and dropped the vetala. He fell to one knee and tried to summon more strength.

Crystal woke slowly and looked around, bleary-eyed. The vetala grabbed her by the arms and chomped down onto her shoulder. Crystal screamed out in horror and pain.

Peter held his hand to the back of the vetala's head and solemnly said, "Be swept clean."

The body fell forwards with a mess of blood around the mouth and more spilling from the stomach. There was an emptiness in its eyes now.

Crystal held her shoulder and stared at her friend. "No! Vida!" She leaned over her friend and almost touched her. She started sobbing.

Peter started to say, "I'm sorry for your…"

"You!" She turned on him with fierce anger. "What did you do to her?"

"Uhhh…"

Crystal stood. "She was right. There was someone stopping our spells. Everything would've worked out if you hadn't messed it all up! I'd be with Eddy and Vida would still be alive! Where do you get off ruining people's lives like that?"

Peter felt a surge of anger. From his perspective, Vida and Crystal were the ones ruining people's lives while he was the one fixing everything. The least he could get was a "thank you."

Then he let that feeling go. He didn't need her praise or thanks. That was not why he was exorcising spirits. He realized that the girl was speaking through intense grief, pain, and confusion. She didn't need him to add to her problems with his own anger.

"The foolish man conceives the idea of 'self,'" he remembered.

She and Peter were actually similar. They had both been betrayed by someone or something they trusted. She had lost her friend and Peter was in danger of losing his mom. They were both losing their lives to the dark spirits' machinations.

"I am sorry for all the pain you've been through," Peter told her sincerely. "I wish I could take it all away for you."

She sneered. "Stay the hell away from me!" she growled.

She stomped off and Peter didn't follow.

Chapter 57: Nothing is Lost

By May, Peter's mom had been in and out of specialists, but still no one had been able to pinpoint what was wrong with her. Then, one day after school, Peter arrived at home to find his dad on the couch with his head in his hands.

Peter's heart felt as heavy as lead. "What's wrong?" he asked.

"Pete, I need to tell you about today's appointment."

The condition was so obscure that Peter had never heard of it. It was a complicated disease with no apparent cure.

"They said it'll be a matter of months," his dad explained. Peter could see the tears in his father's eyes. "We could have a year if we're lucky."

His father went on to explain all the details from the doctor, the pamphlet on hospice and grief counselling, and the process of deterioration his mother would have to endure.

Peter barely heard any of it. As soon as his dad was finished, he said he was going for a bike ride and raced to the dojo.

"Hey, Pete!" Rob greeted cheerily. "How's it going?"

"They said she's going to die," Peter blurted out.

"Oh."

"I've been doing Tonglen for months now," Peter vented. "I haven't gotten so much as a cold and she's only getting worse. And now the doctors say she's going to die within the year. You have to help me. There has to be something else I can do."

"I don't know," Rob said regretfully. "But Peter, you may have to accept that people get sick and sometimes there's nothing we can do."

Peter shook his head. "No. Not this time. It's my fault. Mara's going to kill her because of me. Can he even do that? Can he take a life? And if it's because of him, I can fix it, right?"

"I'm not sure, but I'll help. We'll try everything we can. But Peter, the Buddha said, *'Even death is not to be feared by one who has lived wisely.'*"

"Geez!" he fumed. "I can't just give up! She's my mom."

"But you need to prepare yourself for the worst. If she dies, she dies whether or not you're ready for it. And in the meantime, the asuras can use this against you."

"I don't care anymore!" Peter exploded. "I hope they all burn or freeze in Naraka for the rest of eternity. I'm sick of dealing with them."

"Peter…" Sensei Rob chided.

"No," he interrupted. "I can't deal with this right now."

Peter took off running out of the dojo and into the wooded area that bordered the nearby street. He ran until he was lost deep in the woods and out of breath. Thick clouds rolled in, making it darker. But Peter didn't care. He sat on the ground next to a tree and cried.

He thought about Rob's words, *"If she dies, she'll die whether you're ready for it or not."*

He didn't understand how Sensei could give up so easily. Peter wasn't ready to give up.

It started raining but Peter didn't care.

His mom was so full of life and love. When they had started targeting his dad, he had thought it was unfair that they were attacking the calm and easy parent, but now he felt guilty for thinking that.

The rain turned into a downpour, and he let it wash over him as he cried. But as his grief dulled, he realized that he was in danger. The ground had become soggy and his hands and feet were starting to sink into the thick mud.

He examined his surroundings. He didn't know which way he had come or how to get back. A nearby creek was overflowing with all the drainage from the surrounding hills.

BOOM!

Lightning struck and put a chill in Peter's heart. It was close. The crack shattered the air around him. He felt it vibrate through the ground. He was filled with a sense of dread from the storm.

No, he thought. *It's not the storm, is it?*

Lightning flashed again and he saw that he wasn't alone. The flash illumined three creatures standing just a few yards away. Two rakshasas towered above Peter, as tall as trees. When the light faded, their red eyes glowed, piercing the darkness.

Another lightning flash revealed the character sitting on top of a huge elephant in between the rakshasas. Mara.

He laughed with the force of the thunder.

Peter panicked. He was in no shape to fight. He needed to run.

SCHLOOOP!

He popped one foot up from the mud, causing the other to sink even deeper. The mud, dread, and despair were all sucking him down.

"What a pathetic, hairless monkey," Mara smirked. *"To think I bothered to show myself to you."*

Peter was overcome with hatred and fury. Mara was the cause of all his suffering. He was the one to blame for his mom's pain.

As the lightning flashed, Peter saw the rakshasas get closer and closer. He struggled in the mud while Mara laughed atop his perch, unaffected by the wind and the rain.

One rakshasa grabbed Peter around the neck, threatening to choke him. Peter quickly thought of all the defensive moves he knew, but he only had moves that worked against humans. Although the rakshasa's hands were material enough to close his windpipe, Peter's hands passed right through its smoky limbs.

The second rakshasa pinned his arms to his side.

"Just give up, boy," Mara taunted gleefully. *"You've worked hard every day, sacrificing and training yourself, and I still beat you."*

The rakshasa's grip on Peter's throat tightened, restricting Peter's ability to speak. He was being forced to listen.

"It's all an illusion anyway," Mara argued. *"Love, nobility, and virtue, it's all a dream. Nothing is real. It's all impermanent. And I'll let you in on a little secret. Guess what happens after this life? Nothing."*

The words seemed to slam into Peter with a force. His breath was becoming short and he could see stars.

"That's right," Mara continued. *"No shining, bright heaven. No compassionate god or unified consciousness. No rebirth into another incarnation. You just fade into nothingness, because that is all you are: nothing. Your mom is nothing."*

Peter struggled. He could feel his consciousness fading as anger consumed him.

Mara held his hands out in a grand gesture. *"The great secret to the universe, the entire cosmos is...* nothing.*"* In another lightning flash, Peter thought he could see three sets of arms on Mara. *"There is no meaning or purpose. No right and wrong. Think of all that effort meditating and perfecting yourself. It was all for* nothing.*"*

Peter was on the verge of collapsing. Mara's words were like arrows, piercing his heart. He felt the weight of nothingness dragging his soul down like the mud swallowing his feet.

Then, when he was just about to give into despair, something snapped within him. He felt utterly empty. He had no strength, no clever ideas, and in his emotional state, he couldn't connect to Anuvata. He had nothing to cling to.

And in this moment of emptiness, he let go of all his emotions. He surrendered to his emptiness. Then he felt a miraculous wind fill his very being. He suddenly saw the interconnectedness of all life. Everything was subject to change and death, but that's what made it precious.

The realization filled him and he knew it was true. He didn't care what Mara said. He didn't care about deciphering what was true and false about his speech. He had found deep satisfaction in meditation and self-discipline. He knew in his gut that love and kindness were true. And he trusted his gut and Anuvata more than he would ever trust Mara.

The rakshasas holding him dissipated into sparkles, as if they were merely the stars he had been seeing in his breathlessness. He laughed triumphantly as he levitated out of the mud.

He was now eye level with the King of the Desire Realm, the Evil One, the King of Destruction.

"Sorry," Peter told Mara as laughter bubbled out of him. "Were you saying something? I've been told I'm a terrible listener."

Peter laughed at his own joke as the tempestuous winds of the storm wrapped around him, protecting him. Mara now struggled to hold his own against the wind.

"This isn't over, boy!" Mara howled. *"I'll still destroy everything you hold dear!"*

"You'll have to speak louder," Peter hollered back. "I can't hear you over all this wind!"

With a roar of frustration, Mara dissipated into sparkles just as the rakshasas had. The rain washed the layers of mud from his clothes and skin and the wind whooshed around him. He looked around and realized that he was higher in the air than he had ever been and he wasn't riding an air current.

His body lifted higher into the air, above the tree line, and he could see the lights of the houses in his neighborhood glowing in the dark storm.

Peter willed himself toward his home. The flight was exhilarating, the rush of the wind and rain in his face, the turns of his stomach. He felt as if he were made of the wind.

He touched down right in front of his house and reached for the doorknob just as his dad opened it. They both stared at each other for a few moments in shock. Then his father pulled him to a hug.

“I didn’t know where you were,” his father explained. “I thought…” his voice wavered. “I didn’t want to lose you, too.”

Peter hurt with his father, but he realized that he also had a certain optimism now. He still didn’t want his mom to die, and he would do all he could to cure her, but he saw every moment filled to the brim with purpose and meaning. Even the saddest experiences could hold great beauty.

And he knew that he would never truly lose her. She was a part of everything, as was Peter. They would always be interconnected. Nothing was lost.

Chapter 58: The Deal With Demons

When he arrived at the dojo the next day for deskwork, Peter apologized for his behavior and Rob comforted him in his own way.

"I want you to think of a fish," Rob told him.

"Still with the water analogies?" Peter asked warily.

"The fish is a symbol of mindful wisdom in the Tibetan culture, because its eyes are always open. Even in the throes of death, caught in some animal's mouth, its eyes are open and watching."

"Uhhh… creepy," Peter responded.

"Maybe. But also inspirational. See, when a little kid is afraid of monsters in their bedroom, they close their eyes and pull the covers up over their heads. That wouldn't actually save them from a threat, and at the same time, if they were to open their eyes and observe their surroundings, they'd see that there's nothing to be afraid of. If you open your eyes and observe what's going on, you'll find you have nothing to fear."

On the weekend of his birthday, Peter answered his door to find Jeremy and Zahid with a cookie cake from the store.

"If you didn't invite us to your party, you're dead," Jeremy warned.

He didn't understand how Jeremy could pretend like nothing had happened between them. He figured, however, that it might have been an attempt to apologize without saying, "sorry."

"No party this year," Peter said with a sigh.

They sat on the front porch and Peter told them the whole story of his mom's condition. After that, they ate the cookie cake in silence.

"You just can't catch a break," Jeremy said. "I stole your girlfriend, then this happens. Your life just sucks, dude."

"Thanks, Jeremy," Peter said dryly.

"But I know how you feel," Jeremy went on. "My mom took a part of me with her when she left. It's like they have this spot inside your heart and if they leave, that piece goes, too, and you can never replace it or fill it. You'll just have to live with the emptiness and misery."

"Jeremy, you're failing at this," Zahid scolded him. "Look, Peter, we care about you. That's what Jeremy's trying to say. Let us know if there's anything you need from us, but otherwise, we'll just keep being your friends through your suffering."

"Geez, that's pretty much exactly what I needed to hear," Peter told him. "How did you know?"

"Safera," Zahid said softly. The single word seemed to be charged with some deep hidden meaning.

"What does that mean?" Peter asked, thinking it was some proverb.

Zahid got his usual faraway look. "It's a name."

"Pretty name," Jeremy said.

"Pretty girl, but it was in her genes," he cracked an unenthusiastic smile. "My older sister. She was annoyingly smart and bossy. She was like a second –and very annoying– mom. But I loved her."

"Loved?" Peter asked.

Zahid's eyes glossed over as he told them, "Our school was hit by a bomb. I made it, she didn't."

"Zahid," Peter exhaled, not knowing what else he could say.

"I don't like to talk about it," he wiped his eyes on his sleeve.

Peter, Jeremy, and Zahid sat there teary-eyed, not talking anymore, but enjoying each other's understanding.

That night, after dinner and cake with his parents, Peter was called out to an exorcism. He dropped down from the sky in front of a familiar cabin in the woods. He shuddered with a flashback to the rakshasa-possessed knife that had inspired a man to cannibalism.

He started for the door when he felt a disturbance in the air behind him. He dodged as a thin sword pierced a tree behind him.

"Remember me?" the asura voice hissed.

Peter turned to see a young man who looked like an average college student, but filled with the darkness of an asura.

SHIIINK!

The sword unsheathed from the tree and flew to the man's hand.

Then Peter recognized the sword as the katana from the fight in Cratersville. He and Sensei had forgotten to purify and dispose of it, and now it had found its way into the hands of the man in front of him.

The man swung the sword while Peter dodged desperately. Then, as the man prepared for a strike, Peter twirled inside the attack. He stood with his back to the man and his hands secured on the man's arm.

In a few clean moves, he peeled the sword out of the man's hand while simultaneously throwing the man over his shoulder.

As soon as he touched the hilt of the sword, Peter felt he could see the world so clearly. He could tell the most intimate secrets of the man before him, just by looking at him.

He could see into his own soul, too. All of his weakest and most painful moments flooded his mind.

He saw how much Alicia and Jeremy's betrayal had hurt him. His heart burned with anger. He felt embarrassed that Gina and Zahid had had their suspicions. They probably thought Peter was an idiot for falling for Alicia.

He felt abandoned when he thought of how Zahid had been spending all his time with his new band friends and how Sensei Rob had chosen Charlie and left Peter on his own to fight the evil spirits.

He relived the day he rushed to the hospital to find his mom and the day his father had told him that his mom was dying.

His head swam with the knowledge and the pain, but he still managed to say, "Be swept clean."

The man fell unconscious and the asura emerged from the sword and took on a snakelike shape. It spit into Peter's eyes. As his eyes slammed shut against the poison, the asura wrapped around his ankles, then hung him upside down. Peter struggled and the asura wrapped around his arms and torso.

"I have an offer," the asura hissed. *"Let thisss one human go free."*

Peter struggled in vain, but laughed. "Yeah, right."

"Let usss torture him to death. If you do, we'll let Jody Hunter live."

Peter's heart stopped.

"*Shouldn't he be dragged to Naraka?"* the asura tempted. *"He has used this sword for unspeakable evils. Doesn't she dessserve to live more than this beassst?"*

The asura's words stung more than the poison in his eyes. Still, in his gut, he knew it was too good to be true.

Peter jerked his head and the wind responded, tearing the asura away from him. He fell with a clunk and rolled. His eyes were still shut, but he felt the wind currents for any sign of the spirit.

"Idiot!" the asura hissed. Its voice seemed to echo from multiple locations. *"You could sssave her."*

Peter's heart hurt. He wanted to take the deal. More than anything, he wanted to save his mom. But he knew that it wouldn't work out the way he expected. He'd be ushering in a whole new set of problems if he accepted.

Peter raised his arms. "Here's a new deal," he said as he gathered innumerable wind currents towards himself. "I defeat you. Period."

He clapped and sent the air out in a ring-shaped explosion. The asura howled as it faded and the sting in Peter's eyes receded.

He picked up the katana, wishing that he and Sensei had remembered to destroy it back in Cratersville. As he flew home, he tried not to think of the deal he had been offered.

The next afternoon, Peter sat in a chair reading a book from this summer reading list while his mom slept on the sofa. He was still haunted by his conversation with the asura the night before.

Then he jumped when he realized his mom was watching him. "When did you wake up?" he asked.

She squinted at him. "I was trying to figure out who you are and where my real son is." She pointed to the book.

"It's required reading," he chuckled.

"And it's still June. Usually, you don't get serious about that until the last week of August when I start nagging you."

"How are you feeling?" he asked. "Do you need anything?"

"I do actually," she said seriously. "Can you get that paper and pen? I need you to write something down for me."

"Sure. What is it?" he asked as he reached for a notepad.

"A list. Number one," she dictated, "I love you forever."

Peter's heart tightened. "What is this about?"

"Just write. Number two: I'm proud to be your mom."

"If this is what I think it is, I'm not doing it," he protested.

"It's just a list. There's nothing final about this."

They stared each other down, but Peter knew in a battle of stubborn wills, his mom had the advantage of years of experience.

"Okay," he started writing. "Proud to be my mom. Number three?"

"Always protect girls and women. Not because you think they're weak and need your protection, but because you know they deserve to be treated with honor and respect."

"Honor and respect," he wrote.

"And here's what to look for in a future girlfriend. Don't you roll your eyes at me," she scolded. "You didn't listen to me about Alicia, you'll listen to me next time."

"Alright, fine," he surrendered. "Future girlfriend. Go."

"She needs to be a positive force. Always kind, even to people she doesn't like. No talking badly about people behind their backs."

"Is this really necessary?" he asked.

"Don't stop writing. How many times do I have to tell you? Geez, you were never good at listening."

"I think I heard that somewhere before," Peter smirked.

"Look for someone who'll be a good friend," she continued. "The only way your dad and I suffered living together for so many years is because we're best friends. Romance comes and goes in waves. Friendship lasts."

"Good friend. Got it."

"You need someone who couldn't lie if she tried. And make sure she makes you laugh. Alicia never did."

He rolled his eyes. "Yeah, yeah, you told me so."

"Which brings me to my last piece of advice. It's a magic spell that guarantees any girl will fall madly in love with you. It's so powerful that you can *only* use it on the right person. When you do find the right girl and you're one hundred percent sure, don't be afraid to say the three words that solve every problem and heal any wound."

"I love you?" Peter guessed. She shook her head. "I am sorry?"

"No." She counted the words on her fingers as she said, "'You. Were. Right.' Sure-fire way into a girl's heart. Magic spell."

"I'll remember that one," he chuckled. He looked up from the list with a serious expression. "But how do I know when it's the right girl?"

"I think you'll just know. You might not even need the list. But just in case, I'll cross over from heaven or the collective consciousness or wherever I end up and I'll give you a sign."

Peter grew silent and stared out the window. Listening to her talk about the finality of her death hit him hard.

"Peter," she took his hand. "I know this is hard."

He smiled dimly at her. Here she was trying to comfort him when she was the one dying.

"I'm sure it's a lot harder on you," he said.

"It's hard for all of us. You want to talk about it?"

"No," he shook his head. "I just want you to stay."

He blinked back tears. He wanted to be strong for her.

"I'm sorry," she said sincerely.

He let out a bitter laugh. "It's not like it's your choice."

"It's not *your* choice, Peter. I know you're thinking it's your fault for not being strong enough to protect me or some other nonsense. But it's not your responsibility to save me."

Her gaze was steady. He knew she meant it.

But would she mean it if she knew the truth about me?

"What if I could've stopped this with one simple choice?" he posited.

"You know it doesn't work like that," she said forcefully. "Don't trust deals with demons, they always lie."

He studied her. "What does that mean?"

"Just an expression," she waved her hand dismissively. "Point is, there's no choice you can make to save me. Sometimes sucky things happen and, well, it sucks. And you can spend all your energy fighting it, but the sucky thing is going to happen anyway. So you should just accept it and find other less-sucky things to focus on."

"The Buddha said something like that," Peter joked. "Though I think you're paraphrasing."

"Well, here's some more Buddhist wisdom. Let yourself be angry. Let yourself cry. I don't need you to try to be strong for me."

"Nah. Don't worry about me," he denied.

"You want to know one of my favorite parts of being your mom? It's being needed. It sounds wrong, but I used to love when you'd get hurt as a kid. You'd come running straight for me," she smiled and let out a victorious laugh, "right past your dad, and I'd hold you as you cried. I used to think there was no greater feeling than holding you and being your comfort. Then you grew up and got all strong and self-sufficient." She laughed. "Do you know, when you were just two years old, I offered to kiss a boo-boo and you said, 'Nope, I got it.' And you kissed it yourself. You never needed my kisses after that. You have no idea how much I miss those moments," her voice choked. "So you know, if you broke down and cried right now, you'd actually be doing me a favor."

He gave in. He collapsed into her arms and they held each other while they both cried.

Chapter 59: Loser Festival

In early September, right after school started again, Peter received a message from Sensei that Charlie had gone into labor overnight and had had a baby girl. Peter immediately rushed off to the hospital.

"I can't believe you did this to me!" Peter heard Sensei Charlie's voice from down the hallway. "When did this even happen?"

"You were sleeping…" Rob answered, sounding like a timid child.

Peter peeked in and saw Charlie in tears.

"I am exhausted, drugged, and hormonal! And you took advantage of me for some little joke? I bet you planned this for months, didn't you?"

Peter couldn't imagine what Sensei Rob had done.

"We can change it if you really feel that strongly," Rob tried to assuage her. "It'll just mean paperwork, but if it's that important to my beautiful, patient, loving wife… Oh, look! It's Pete! Come in, buddy!"

"Oh, you are not getting out of this," Charlie growled.

"What on earth did you do?" Peter asked apprehensively.

"I just filled out the birth certificate while she was sleeping," Rob said.

"Suzy!" Charlie cried out as if he had just betrayed her somehow. "We agreed on the name Suzy."

"And Suzy is short for Suzanne just like Charlie is short for…"

She covered her face in her hands.

"Seriously?" Peter asked Rob.

"It seemed like a funny idea at the time," Sensei shrugged. "I didn't account for the horm…" he stopped when he noticed the look in her eyes. "For Charlene's feelings," he corrected himself.

Peter shook his head. "I don't know whether to smack you or be impressed by your bravery."

"Smack him, please," Charlie said.

Peter punched Sensei's shoulder.

"Ow!"

"Karma," Peter said plainly.

"I love your name," Rob told Charlie. "Just think, if you didn't have that name, we might never have fallen in love with each other."

"Really?" she asked with heavy eyes. "That's why you married me? You wouldn't love me if my name were Denise?"

Rob smiled. "I just want to honor her mother by giving her a similarly beautiful name."

Charlie took a breath. "Promise to call her Suzy?"

"I promise to try."

She rolled her eyes and grumbled as the nurse came in, wheeling a cart with the baby girl wrapped up tightly in blankets.

"There she is!" Rob rushed over. "Here's our little Suzan… Suzy."

"Wow! They make people this tiny?" Peter asked.

"Thank god she was that small," Charlie mumbled.

"Want to hold her?" Sensei Rob asked. "It's okay. I trust you."

Peter looked to Charlie who nodded in agreement. Peter scooped her up very carefully. She felt as light as a pillow.

"Make sure you support the back and neck," Rob instructed.

Peter stared at her sleeping face, tucked in by a tiny cap and blankets. He was overcome with the need to protect her. She couldn't do anything for herself. Her existence demanded responsibility and loving care from others, as if her beginning in the world necessitated loving-kindness and gentleness from those around her.

"She reminds me of a quote," Rob said softly. "*'Every child is the little Buddha that helps his parents grow up.'*"

Peter thought of all the circumstances and coincidences that had led to Rob and Charlie starting their family. He thought of the day Charlie had witnessed the rakshasas attacking Rob in the dojo. He thought of the day Rob had been trapped by the spirit that had possessed him years ago. They were all lucky Peter had been there to help.

Then he realized something. It just clicked. She was important. Sensei Rob and Charlie were important. So important that maybe the devas had arranged everything.

Peter wondered what the chances were that he just happened to take classes at Sensei Rob's dojo. He wondered what the chances were that the devas wanted him to start training as an exorcist just after Sensei Rob and Charlie met.

What if everything was set up just so I'd be ready to take over full-time when they started their family?

"Peter, you okay?" Rob asked.

Peter realized that he had a tear on his cheek. He wiped it on his shoulder. "Yeah, I just… Oh, god, why did you let me hold her? She's so important."

Rob and Charlie shared a glance. "So would now be a good time to ask you for a favor?" Sensei Rob asked.

"Sure, what do you need?"

"Well, Suzy needs a godfather."

"What? Me?" he protested. "I'm just some kid."

"You are so much more than just some kid," Charlie laughed.

"You don't have to do much more than love her and be there for her if we're not for some reason."

"Absolutely," Peter agreed. "I mean, I imagine you guys have thought this through. If you're really asking me, then yes. Wow. I have a goddaughter." Then he whispered, "Hey, little Suzy. Welcome to the world of the breathing. I promise to always protect you and love you almost as much as your parents do."

Charlie started sniffling again. Then Suzy squirmed and used her whole body to push out a little blast of gas. They all chuckled.

Sensei placed his hand on Peter's shoulder. "I think that means she likes you, Uncle Peter."

"But godfathers don't have to change diapers, right?" Peter joked.

Months passed quickly as his mom's health gradually deteriorated. When the semester started up again, Peter and Zahid hung out occasionally, but Peter mostly focused on meditating and offering up karma for his ever-weakening mom.

After Thanksgiving, when he realized the end was near, he requested to stay home. His parents and the school agreed.

During the Christmas holidays, Peter took a break from his daily routine to visit Rob, Charlie, and Suzy with some baked goods.

"So how are you doing?" Sensei asked him while Charlie took Suzy to her room for a nap.

"It's been relaxing, actually," Peter told him. "I finish my schoolwork early, do chores, exercise, and meditate every day. It's kind of like I'm on retreat or something."

Rob chuckled. "Remember when you said you'd never be a monk? You basically are one now."

"It's not as bad as I thought it'd be," he admitted. "Anyway, I still feel guilt for my part in all this, but I know I'd never choose for my mom to suffer, so I guess I'm coming to terms with it."

"Funny you should say that. Merry Christmas," Rob handed him a wrapped book.

Peter took it and opened it. "The Tibetan Book of the Dead? Seriously?" Peter complained. "Salt in the wound, Sensei."

"No, it's good," Rob promised. "See, in our culture, we're terrified of death. We spend our energy and money avoiding it. And when it happens, our first instinct is to declare that it's unfair. We shouldn't *have* to die. But where do we even get that idea? Every living thing dies. And maybe it's not actually a bad thing. Death is a transition, like being born. Sure it's different, and unknown, but it's a necessary part of life. Tibetan Buddhists, instead of avoiding thoughts of death, they use their whole lives to prepare for it. Death is not to be feared. It is to be embraced and prepared for."

"I just want my mom to be okay," Peter said somberly.

"Read the book," Sensei urged. "If you're brave enough to try it, read it to your mom to help her have peace with the transition. Oh," he brightened, "and I wanted to invite you to something. In February, Charlene and I are having a Losar Festival and I want you to be there."

Peter raised an eyebrow. "A loser festival?"

"Lo-sar," Sensei corrected him. "It's the Tibetan new year."

"Will there be loser food and loser activities?"

"There will be awesome food and awesome activities," Rob returned. "And anyway, this year's animal is the monkey, so you're like the mascot."

"Alright, fine," Peter caved. "I'll come to your loser festival."

Peter joined Rob and Charlie in early February for the celebration. As soon as he arrived, Sensei gave him a broom and told him to use it.

Peter raised an eyebrow. "Was the whole loser festival just an excuse for free cleaning service?" he challenged.

"No," Rob laughed. "It's symbolic. We're sweeping away the dust and the grime of the past year. Trust me. It'll be good for you."

As Peter swept their kitchen and living room, Rob cleaned the windows and Charlie dusted the whole house. Peter thought it would be convenient if he could just wipe away the filth of the past year.

As he cleaned, he imagined the dust being Alicia and Jeremy's betrayal, his dad's work troubles, his mom's sickness, and Mara's machinations.

When they were finished, they all sat down at the table to eat a bean soup with two dumplings in the middle of each bowl. Peter aimed for the dumplings with his spoon.

"No! Don't!" Rob stopped him before he could bite down. "They're not cooked."

"So you make me clean your house then offer me uncooked food?" Peter complained. "This really is a loser festival!"

"They're like fortune cookies," Charlie explained with a chuckle. "When we're finished with the soup, we all open them and read our fortunes for the upcoming year."

Rob opened his dumplings first. He held up a little red chili pepper and a pebble. "This one means that I'm hot and spicy," he explained. "And the rock means I'm strong and determined."

"I knew you'd do this!" Charlie caught him. "I looked up the symbols ahead of time to hold you accountable." She explained to Peter, "The chili pepper means he's quick-tempered and the rock means he's stubborn and hard to get along with."

Peter laughed. "Wow, I didn't know these would be so accurate."

When Peter opened his first one, it was an intricate interwoven network of lines in the shape of a diamond. "What does it mean?" he asked.

"It's the symbol of death and rebirth," Rob answered solemnly. "The symbol actually has some deep meaning," Rob explained. "Look. There are lots of twists and turns, but there's no beginning and no end. In Buddhism, we believe that life continues. Death is nothing more than a transition to the next phase."

Peter held up his second fortune. "And what's the sun mean?"

Rob looked pensive. "The sun is a powerful symbol in every culture. It's a symbol of warmth, kindness, healing, and knowledge. Maybe it means you'll reach enlightenment this year."

After the meal, they molded dough into shapes representing whatever they wanted to leave behind of the previous year. They mostly laughed at each other's crude designs.

Then, with candles, they went into the backyard and burned the dough on the barbeque pit. Peter liked the idea of all his problems burning away and disappearing into smoke, blown away by the wind.

By the end of the evening, Peter had a sense of hope for the future. The festivities had left him thinking that maybe he wasn't a complete loser.

Chapter 60: Nobly Born, Jody Hunter

The next morning, Peter's mom seemed even weaker. Her eyes were sunken and her cheeks were hollow. She was a shadow of herself.

Peter sat in a chair next to her bed, wanting to be close to her. He had a gut feeling that he needed to pay attention and stay with her. While he waited, he read the Tibetan Book of the Dead and found it more comforting than he had initially suspected.

"What are you reading?" she asked when she woke up.

"It's this cheerful, uplifting book Sensei got me," Peter said. "It's the Tibetan Book of the Dead. It's supposed to help us with the transition."

"You've been holding out on me?" she smirked.

"You want me to read it to you?" he asked, surprised.

She nodded and adjusted herself with great difficulty.

He started reading, "*'O nobly born, Jody Hunter...'*"

"Nobly born. I like that," she interrupted.

He smiled. "I think you're supposed to listen."

She gave him a sideways look. "You ever follow that advice?"

He continued reading. "*'...The time has come for you to see the path. You will be set before the clear light. And you will experience it in its reality in the bardo.'*"

"What's a bardo?" she interrupted again.

"It's like an in between place," he explained, "between this life and the next. Anyway. *'In the bardo, all things are like the void and cloudless sky and the naked spotless intellect is like a transparent vacuum without circumference or center. At this moment, know yourself and abide in that state. I, too, at this time, will sit with you face to face.'*"

"What's that 'clear light' and 'spotless intellect'?"

"You know how everyone talks about seeing a light at death? It's supposedly pure consciousness or intellect, like if you were stripped of everything except for the energy that's you. Anyway, the light is pure consciousness. *'Jody Hunter...'*"

"Wait, am I not nobly born anymore?"

Peter rolled his eyes. "*'O nobly born, Jody Hunter, resolve thus: O this now is the hour of death. By taking advantage of this death, I will act for the good of all sentient beings peopling the illimitable expanse of the heavens, as to obtain the Perfect Buddhahood, by resolving on love and compassion towards all and by directing my entire effort to the Sole Perfection.'*"

She became relaxed as she listened. Peter continued for about ten minutes. She was so still, he was afraid she had fallen asleep or worse.

When he was finished, she took a long and slow breath. "That was wonderful," she whispered with her eyes closed in reverie.

"I don't know how much I believe of what happens in the afterlife," Peter confessed, "but it's fun to try to think about, huh?"

"Tell me about the realms of existence. Any travel brochures?"

"There's Naraka," he told her, "which are supposedly these super cold and hot caverns of hellish torment."

"I'll just cross that one off the list," she decided quickly.

"It's for those who've earned a lot of negative karma," he assuaged her. "And even if you did end up there, you could pass on to another realm once your evil karma runs out."

"Hm. So it's like a cosmic jail?" she speculated.

He smiled. "Then there's the realm of hungry ghosts."

"Is that the realm where I can haunt you?" she asked eagerly.

"Trust me, you don't want to be a hungry ghost. They chase things they think will make them happy, but they're never satisfied. Plus they're really ugly and can breathe fire."

"Are all the realms this bad?" she griped.

"The animal one is next," he said cheerfully.

"Ooh. I always wondered what it would be like to fly like a bird."

"It's exhil…" Peter caught himself. "It's fun to think about. The next one is the realm of the asuras. And they suck."

"That bad, huh?" she asked.

"Yeah, they're spirits full of anger and hatred. They battle the good spirits, and try to mess with our lives here. They cause a lot of trouble."

"I wouldn't want to cause you any more trouble," she joked.

Peter continued. "You could be another human. Apparently, you may even have some choice over who your next parents will be."

She made a face. "I think that would be weird. Imagine ten years from now, you're married with kids and a little ten-year-old shows up on your doorstep and orders you to do your homework."

"You'd hunt me down like that?" he asked.

"Absolutely," she threatened. "You'd have to adopt me. And that would just be beyond strange. Oh. What if your father's still alive and remarried?" She had a look of horror on her face. "Nope. Not that one. Only one more option left. It'd better be a good one."

"The celestial realm," Peter told her, "with the devas, or divinities, or whatever you want to call them. There's even one section that sounds like heaven. It's called the Pure Land. You don't have to work and you have all the luxuries you can think of. It's easier to reach nirvana from there, too."

"That's the one!" she decided. "But can I watch over you from there?"

"I don't know for sure, but I do know that the devas interact with our world just like the asuras. So I imagine you can find a way. Though you should be trying to let go of your earthly attachments."

"You and your father are not earthly attachments," she argued. "You're just people that I love dearly and want to see again."

"I'd like that, too," he smiled dimly.

"Then it's settled," she decided. "I'll go there and wait for you both. And if I get tired of waiting, I'll come down and haunt your dreams!"

"Hey, my dreams are off limits," he complained. He had had enough dreams to last a few lifetimes.

"What do I do if I have to tell you something?" she complained.

"Leave a message in someone else's dreams," he proposed.

"What if they don't want me in their dreams either?"

"I'm sure you'll find a way," he chuckled. "There aren't many people who have told Jody Hunter 'no' and lived to tell the tale."

"You *Buddha* believe it," she smirked.

Peter shook his head and laughed at her.

"Oh, and hey, I have something for you." She picked up a small gift from the side table drawer and handed it to him.

"What's this?" he asked.

"It's something I want you to have. To remember me."

"Oh, good," he joked. "I'd forget you otherwise."

She laughed and it made her cough.

He opened the gift and found a framed picture of the two of them in the woods. It was the selfie she had taken the summer before his freshman year when they had talked about his nightmares.

"It's one of my favorite pictures of us," she explained. "I need you to promise me that you'll keep this," she said seriously. "I don't want it in a drawer, but somewhere you'll see it every day."

"Okay," he nodded.

"Promise me," she demanded emphatically.

"I promise," he agreed.

Chapter 61: Fish Eyes

A few days later, all the extended family brought food for a massive potluck that promised to leave the Hunters with plenty of leftovers.

While they were all eating and laughing, his dad went to check on his mom and called the family in. He explained that she said she wanted to see everyone.

Then she started her goodbyes, one by one. Peter started crying immediately.

Peter and his dad held her hands on either side of the bed.

"I'm not afraid," she told Peter with tears in her eyes. She looked like she wanted to say more, but settled for, "This is for you and your father."

He didn't understand, but wondered if maybe she was delirious.

"I love you, mom," he assured her. "That will never change."

Then she turned to his dad. "Sam, the years I knew you were the best of my life. Thank you for sharing them with me.

"Jody," he said, "nothing and no one could ever..." he couldn't finish.

She seemed to understand. She held his hand and smiled at him through her tears.

Then she glanced up and her face and body relaxed. It looked like she was gazing at a sunset and her lips parted in awe. "I see…" she whispered in awe. "Peter, I see it! It's beautiful."

Peter followed her gaze and was astonished to find that he could see it, too. He saw a bright light, as if he were staring into the sun, but even brighter. It emanated peace and kindness. He turned back to tell her that he could see it, but she was already gone. Her eyes were wide open and empty and her body was completely still.

Peter's father reached out and closed her eyes as the light faded from Peter's view.

The funeral fell on the same weekend as Valentine's Day, which Peter thought was just wrong. But his dad worked it into her eulogy, saying that she lived for love of others.

The ceremony passed too quickly for Peter. He thought it was strange to wrap up his mom's entire lifetime in less than an hour.

At the reception afterwards, there was a non-stop stream of family and friends who tried their hardest to give condolences.

Peter appreciated when people shared special memories, but more often than not, they offered common sayings that felt empty.

"She's in a better place," many said. Peter hoped she was, but he couldn't think of a place that was better than being with him and his dad.

"I know how you feel," many said. Peter was sure they didn't.

"You should be grateful for the time you had with her," a few others instructed. As if Peter wasn't grateful already.

He didn't enjoy listening to the empty platitudes, but he realized that almost everyone was terrified and confused by death.

The Nasirs offered prayers and food instead of condolences. Peter figured that they had probably heard many of the same phrases over the years.

Zahid simply told him, "We're brothers in grief now."

"Does it ever get easier?" Peter asked.

Zahid shook his head. "But you learn to focus on the good stuff."

After the Nasirs came Charlie and Rob. Charlie wrapped Peter in a hug. She looked like she couldn't have said anything if she tried.

"How are you holding up?" Rob asked when Charlie went to comfort Mr. Hunter.

Peter shrugged. "The Book of the Dead actually helped."

"Good," Rob clapped him on the shoulder. "If you've read through it, you know that Tibetans believe that the consciousness sticks around for forty or fifty days. If you read the book aloud, your mom might hear and it might help her with the transition."

Peter nodded. "I imagine it'll help me, too."

"I bet it will," Rob agreed.

"You know," Peter stared at the crowd to avoid Rob's eye contact, "I get what you were saying about death, that we don't have to fear it. I've accepted that, but I still feel guilty. If it weren't for me..."

He couldn't finish the thought.

"I wish I had wisdom for you," Rob said. "The only thing I can say is that this right here," he wagged his finger, "that's what Mara and the asuras were trying to accomplish. But maybe your deva has some wisdom for you. It's there to help."

When he went back home, Peter meditated in his room, but couldn't hear any wisdom from Anuvata. Instead, he was reminded of the framed picture his mom had given him. It tugged at his thoughts.

He opened his eyes and studied the picture. She had spoken that day of guilt being an unproductive emotion. She had said that when he felt guilt, he should try to do some act of service for someone else.

Maybe that would help him overcome his negative feelings even now.

That night, in his dreams, Peter found himself in the throne room of an enormous castle. Towering white columns opened to lush gardens as far as the eye could see. There were tables laid out with piles of food and drink, musicians playing strange instruments, and people dressed in elaborate Indian robes talking and laughing.

And on the throne, Mara sat in his human form, studying Peter with a smug, evil smile.

"Well, well, well," Mara sang. "The little monkey has come to visit me in my palace. You thought you were so clever and funny that day in the woods. You thought you had won." His smile turned devilishly wicked. "But I still got your mom."

Peter's heart rate picked up as all the rage he had felt for months took over his mind. He ran straight for the throne, ready to wring Mara's neck.

Mara quickly held out his hand and Peter was stopped, held midair by some invisible force.

"This is my realm," Mara chuckled. "You really think you can attack a king in his own realm?"

Mara constricted his hand into a fist and Peter hollered in pain, feeling crushed from all sides.

Mara laughed and his subjects joined him, jeering and pointing at Peter.

"You've lost, boy," Mara told him with a victorious grin. "You lost the battles, you lost the war, and you lost your mom. She's all mine now."

"You're lying," Peter yelled through gritted teeth. "She was going to die eventually. We all are. You never had any control over her death and you definitely never had control over how she lived."

"You despicable creature!" Mara snarled. "I'm still not done with you! I'll tear your father down and leave you orphaned. I'll destroy that

friend of yours and his whole family. I'll ruin anyone you ever care about!"

Peter felt the knots as they twisted his stomach. He hated how the anger felt. It was the same way he used to feel whenever he thought of Jeremy. In essence, Mara was just like him: a bully.

Then, like a burst of wind, Peter's mind cleared. He remembered Sensei Rob's advice from long ago for how to deal with Jeremy: a bully gets his power from the victim's reaction.

"Hold up," Peter said. "You want me mad. You want me to hate you."

Mara tightened his hand again, but this time, Peter didn't feel any pain.

"No," Mara contradicted. "I want to destroy you," he growled. "I want to torture you for all..."

"You're trying to make me angry," Peter interrupted him, suddenly dropping to the ground, out of Mara's control. "Because you know that anger and hatred are their own torture," he thought aloud. "Well, sorry to disappoint you, Mara, but I choose to have thoughts of loving-kindness for everyone. Even you. I only wish you could be transformed by the right thoughts and actions. I wish you could find the peace that I've found."

Mara loosed a roar that rattled his entire castle as he transformed into a red and yellow ogre. Peter only smiled back.

The dream ended with Mara screaming insults at Peter, but Peter no longer cared. In the end, Mara, the Evil One, the King of the Desire Realm, the King of Destruction, had no power over him.

When Peter returned to school, he almost regretted it. He had enjoyed his days at home, focusing on his parents and his training. He had felt so much peace. He hoped he could retain some of that peace now that his routine would fill up with mundane things again.

As he approached the school, he heard a voice. "Peter?"

He turned and saw Alicia standing a few steps away. He could tell by her face that she had heard the news.

"Hey, long time no see," he attempted a normal conversation.

"I heard," she said. "I'm sorry. She's in a better place. It was her time."

Peter didn't think it was her time. Her time should have been when she was eighty-something, but Peter's choices had cut her life short.

He nodded. "Thanks, Alicia," he said.

She rolled her eyes. "God, you are still as stone-faced as ever. Please tell me you at least cried at her funeral."

Peter just stared at her.

"Alicia!" Gina barked from behind Peter. She had approached when Peter was focused on Alicia. "After everything you put him through, now this? Go easy on him."

Alicia scoffed. "You know what? I don't even know why I tried."

She stormed off and Gina and Peter watched her go in silence.

"Yeesh, someone went full on drama queen," Gina said at last.

"It's really okay," Peter smiled dimly. "Death confuses and scares people. I don't think anyone really knows what to say."

"Tell me about it," Gina agreed. "My Nonno passed away like a year ago and I still remember the stupid things people said. 'He was such a good person, God wanted to be near him,'" she quoted.

"'There's a reason for everything,'" Peter repeated. "'You should look for the silver lining.'"

"'It's God's will and you shouldn't question it.'"

"Geez. That's harsh," Peter reacted. "If this is God's will, I don't want to have anything to do with him."

"I never believed that one," she said as they started walking into the school, side by side. "But you know what I do believe? I believe life does go on somehow. Think of the first law of thermodynamics. Energy is neither created nor destroyed. It can only be converted. I truly believe that the energy that was my Nonno is out there somewhere, just transformed."

Peter studied her. "That's pretty brilliant."

"My nerdy cousin," she smiled. "Anyway, if you need anything, just know I'm there for you."

"Thanks, Gina," he said with sincerity.

"I mean, not, like, in a romantic way," she amended. "You're a nice guy and all, but you're still pretty boring."

"Thanks, Gina."

Chapter 62: Subject to Change

The rest of the semester went by quickly. Peter spent most of his time at school alone. Zahid had invited him to sit at his new lunch table many times, but now that the asuras had shown how far they were willing to go, Peter was afraid of letting anyone get too close.

At the same time, he was grateful for the opportunity for solitude. He had started craving meditation. Every day at lunch, he finished his food quickly and found a quiet spot to meditate.

Then, in May, his dad dropped life-changing news at dinner.

"I need to talk to you," he said seriously.

"Is it work?" Peter worried. "Are you still having trouble?"

Peter hadn't had a dream about his father or Mara in months. He had thought the asuras had realized that they had done enough to hurt him for the time being.

"I'm just tired," his dad sighed. "I'm tired of the business world. People only care about money. I get punished for making the right decisions. I've been thinking about changing to a different job."

"What else could you do?" Peter asked.

"I applied to a few universities to see if they'd hire me. My hours would be more flexible. I might be able to get off when you do so we could spend more time together."

"That sounds great," Peter told him.

"It wouldn't pay as much," his dad cautioned.

"You think I care about that?"

"We'd have to live tight for a while."

"We don't need as much as we have."

"I heard back from one university," his dad confessed.

"Oh, yeah? Which one?"

"It's a small school just outside of Cratersville."

"Cratersville?" Peter felt heavy. "So we're moving?"

"I won't take it if you need to stay here," his dad promised.

Peter thought a moment. He remembered Sensei had once said that the spirits move their vessels around as needed.

Is this the devas' work? Or would I be abandoning this town if we moved?

He searched within himself and felt a familiar tug at his gut. Somehow, he just knew that this was Anuvata's doing. And after all this time, he knew better than to question it.

"Take it," Peter decided.

A couple weeks later, Peter and his dad sat in the kitchen eating a large cake for Peter's birthday.

"You got all this cake just for us?"

His dad smiled. "We'll have to eat it all week."

"But that's against the rules," Peter joked.

They both became quiet, thinking of how she wasn't there to enforce the rules anymore.

Then the doorbell rang. Peter opened the door to see Gina, Alicia, Zahid, and Jeremy. They cheerfully sang him happy birthday and helped Peter and his dad finish off the cake.

After a few moments of laughing and joking in the family room, Peter decided to bite the bullet and tell them the news. Everyone stopped and stared at him.

"You're moving?" Zahid asked sadly.

He nodded. "Before the summer is over."

"And you weren't going to tell us?" Jeremy asked aggressively.

"I was. I just…" he rubbed the back of his neck.

"You'll come back for holidays, right?" Zahid asked.

"Yeah, I got family here."

"Then you'll stay in touch," Jeremy decided.

"You said it was a small town outside of Cratersville?" Gina inquired. "Which one?"

"Crescent City," he answered.

"No way," she breathed. "I have family in Crescent City. I'll have to check up on you when I go visit."

Alicia sat on the couch next to him. He felt uncomfortable being near her now. He wasn't sure what she would do or say.

She reached out and placed a hand on his arm. He looked at it and realized that her touch no longer worked any magic on him.

"I know things aren't great between us," she said, "but know that you'll be missed. You're such a good person. Even though things didn't work out, between us, I hope you have a good life."

"Thanks," he nodded. "I wish you and Jeremy the best."

"Really?" she asked dubiously.

"Yeah. What? Is that not okay?"

She rolled her eyes. "Just take care of yourself, idiot."

He was grateful that he didn't have to stress about figuring her out anymore. That was all Jeremy's problem now.

"You're still my brother," Zahid told him. "Now and forever. Don't forget about me and call me sometime, okay?"

"Me, too!" Jeremy demanded. "I want updates on everything. Make sure to call me when you get a crush, too. You need all the help you can get in that department."

Peter chuckled politely but thought that he'd never again trust Jeremy to help him with a crush.

"Whatever you do, don't call me," Gina told him. "I mean, I'll miss you and junk, but I don't need updates."

"Thanks, Gina," Peter said.

A couple months later, Peter and his dad went through all his mom's possessions as they prepared for the move.

"Look at this," his dad held up a crude green statue. "I think you made this in first grade for a Mother's Day present."

"What is it even supposed to be?" Peter laughed.

"My guess is a frog?"

"And she kept it?"

"She kept nearly every present you ever gave her." He lifted up a shoebox next and looked like he might cry when he opened it.

"What's that?" Peter asked.

"Remember when we went to that marriage workshop a few years ago? They made us write letters to each other. It was torture," he chuckled. "I wrote one sentence for each letter while she wrote three pages. And apparently she saved them."

"So you're keeping those?" Peter asked.

He nodded. "What about you? What are you keeping?"

"That picture she gave me and a list she made me write. I think that's all I need."

After a few moments, Peter's dad said, "Hey, we need to talk about your school."

"Is there a problem?" Peter worried.

"The public school system isn't that great where we're going," his dad revealed.

“That’s alright,” Peter said. “I’ve never been that great at school anyway.”

“Well, there’s a local Christian school that’s supposed to be good. The academics are top notch.”

“Won’t it be expensive?” Peter asked.

“They have a good scholarship program.”

“A Buddhist going to a Christian school?” Peter laughed. “That sounds like the setup for a joke or something. What do you think?”

“I think you should go,” his dad said.

The doorbell rang and the Nasirs came in. Mr. Hunter guided Mr. and Mrs. Nasir to piles of unwanted items. Zahid’s younger siblings started playing all over the house.

“Hey, man, thanks for coming by,” Peter greeted Zahid.

Zahid raised one eyebrow. “You’re thanking me for taking free stuff from you?”

“Well, it just makes it easier on us,” Peter explained.

“Peter, I’m really going to miss you,” Zahid divulged. “You were my first friend here. If it hadn’t been for you, I don’t think I would’ve been able to adjust.”

“Nah. You’re stronger than anyone,” Peter told him. “After all you’ve been through, how you manage to smile is amazing.”

“You have more to do with that than you realize,” Zahid confessed. “I didn’t want to say this in front of everyone at your birthday, but I need to tell you. When,” he paused, “when everything happened, I went to a dark place, spiritually and mentally. I just couldn’t believe that Allah would let something like that happen when we had always been faithful.” He got his usual sad look, but it didn’t last as long as it usually did. “I was angry and broken. And I stayed that way for years.”

“That seems pretty normal to me,” Peter said. “I can only imagine going through what you did.”

“But when I met you,” Zahid continued, “your friendship was the first good thing that happened to me in years. Your dedication to Buddhism really inspired me to be more dedicated to my own faith, too. I still don’t understand the reason why things had to happen the way they did, but your friendship helped me realize that maybe I shouldn’t be blaming Allah for what evil beings did. And maybe He can still make good things happen after the bad.”

“I taught you that?” Peter joked awkwardly. “Funny, because the whole time, you were inspiring me by dealing with all that.”

They passed a few moments, not knowing what to say.

Then Zahid shook his finger at Peter. "Keep in touch," he ordered. "And I'll pray that someone in your new town welcomes you as you welcomed me."

Peter smiled and nodded.

He watched from his doorstep as Zahid and his family drove away. He thought of how much sadness and pain the Nasirs had been through. He thought about the fire that almost destroyed their restaurant because of him.

It was one thing to keep in touch with Sensei, who could protect himself from the asuras. But it was another thing to put Zahid in danger when Peter would be hours away, unable to protect him.

The choice was clear. In a decisive moment, he deleted all the contacts from his phone. He was a poison. He was a contagion. And he wouldn't spread this disease to anyone else.

Chapter 63: Saying Goodbye

"Do you really have to go?" Charlie bemoaned when Peter joined them for a farewell dinner a few nights before his move.

Peter shrugged regretfully. "I promise I'll come back to visit," he said. "I've got to check up on my goddaughter."

Rob took a break from cooing at Suzy in his arms to tell Peter, "As much as we'll miss you, I have a feeling the devas orchestrated this."

"But what about the spirits in this town?" Peter asked.

"They might be calling me out again," Rob speculated, "or they might call someone new. I'm sure they have it figured out. You remember the ceremony for establishing authority in the new town?"

Peter nodded. "I'll be fine."

"But how will you be emotionally?" Charlie asked him. "I know you've stopped hanging out with people. Tell me the truth. Are we the only people you talk to?"

"I talk to people," he argued. "Sometimes."

"Peter," she sounded disappointed. "You need people."

He forced a smile. "I hurt people."

"No," Rob corrected him, "the asuras hurt people. You help people. You can't let them win."

"I'm not letting them win," Peter attested. "Look, tons of people have been hermits and lived. In fact, most hermits spend their days offering up compassionate thoughts for everyone on the planet. I don't have to take the risk of hurting people just to love them."

Rob studied Peter. "Still, you should make friends in your new town. If the asuras target them, we can figure it out together."

Take the risk of caring about people only to put them in danger? Peter thought. *Yeah, right.*

"I'll think about it," he promised.

"Well, that's the last of the boxes sorted," Peter's dad commented as he set a box down in the kitchen area of their new apartment in Crescent City. "Now we just have to unpack them all."

SHOOOSH!

Peter felt the telltale whisper of wind next to his ear.

Wow, didn't take long, he thought.

“Hey, I’m going to go for a walk,” Peter told his dad. “You know, get to know the place.”

His dad looked like he wanted to say more, but settled for, “Stay safe.”

Peter followed his instincts deep into the woods behind his apartment complex and found a man in tattered clothing. He wore what used to be a white shirt, now stained with old blood and untold other things. He was covered in festering, gangrenous wounds and had unshaven, ratty red and white hair. He smelled awful.

He was curled into a crouching position, holding his head and mumbling. It reminded Peter of the spirit that had trapped Sensei Rob.

He approached slowly, trying not to make a noise. The man sputtered something that could have been a laugh and looked at Peter from under his forehead, not blinking. His tremors stopped.

“So the new victim has arrived,” a hollow voice said. The man smiled, revealing pointed teeth that were stained red. *“We’ve already planned your downfall. We already know your weaknesses,”* the presence taunted. *“And we’ve laid the traps accordingly. We will feast on your flesh!”*

The man regained control, trembling. “You don’t belong here!” he yelled. At first, Peter thought the man had addressed him, but then he banged on his head. “This is my body. You are not welcome.”

“Do you see what awaits you, little monkey?” the asura interrupted. *“This hollow shell is the man you will replace in more ways than one.”*

Peter crouched and stared directly at the man’s eyes, now holding another consciousness. The asura snarled, and barked but Peter remained calm.

“I see what awaits all your kind,” he said over the asura’s low growl. “I can see that this exorcist has been giving you lots of trouble. I can see how weak his fighting has made you.”

“You are weak!” the asura snapped. *“You’re nothing but weaknesses!”*

“Maybe, but we don’t give up. So go ahead. Tell your brethren about me, discover my secrets, lay your traps. But you know what? I’ll never stop fighting you just like this man here.” He placed a hand on the man’s forehead. “Be swept clean,” Peter pronounced.

The asura's cry caused the earth to quake as it peeled away from the man. The asura evaporated without a struggle and the man collapsed.

"Hey, are you still with me?" Peter asked, slightly shaking the man's shoulder. "We need to get you to a doctor. I can fly you…"

"No, it's too late." the man croaked. "The spirit was keeping me alive for torture. I should have died days ago."

"Don't give up. Here, I can carry you. Do you have family looking for you?"

"No," he said plainly, "there's no one. I'm alone."

The words hit Peter hard. He couldn't help compare this scene with the memory of his mom's passing.

Then the man grabbed him by the shirt collar and got a frantic look in his eyes.

"The spirits in this town are clever," he warned. "Don't let them win. Confront your weaknesses, because they are ruthless." He let go, but Peter still felt a phantom pressure around his neck.

Then he saw a cloud of light peel away from the man's body. His muscles went slack and Peter felt the cold that had already been there.

Chapter 64: Peter Ruins Dinner

Late that night, Peter flew from his window and found a spot near the center of town on the highest hill, which happened to be at the University where his dad would be teaching. He sat down for a long chant.

"Whatever beings are assembled here, terrestrial or celestial, may they all have peace of mind, and may they listen attentively to these words. O beings, listen closely. May you all radiate loving-kindness..."

As he chanted, he felt his wind sweep through the entire city, reaching every corner and telling the story of the town. He saw the crimes most frequently committed and the pains most frequently experienced. He felt a surge of powerful devas, too, some that seemed as powerful as Anuvata.

He imagined all the town's negativity floating into the atmosphere and dissipating as he said, "By the power of the truth of these words, may this town ever be well."

The next evening, Peter arrived at a suburban home where the back door to the kitchen was wide open revealing a woman preparing dinner. She looked like the epitome of a suburban stay-at-home wife, except for the aura of darkness.

"There you are," she smiled graciously as he approached the door.

"Do we know each other?" he asked as he stepped inside. He wasn't sure if he was talking to the asura or the woman.

"We've never met before," she, or it, answered. "But of course, we know all about you, Peter Hunter."

"Is that so?" he asked dryly.

"We know about Alicia and how she betrayed you and dumped you for Jeremy. We know about Zahid and how you almost destroyed his family with that restaurant fire."

"You can stop right there." He tried to sound bored instead of angry.

"But I haven't even mentioned your mom," the asura pouted.

"Is there a point to all this?"

"We saw that little ceremony you did last night and thought it would be nice to give you a fair warning that you don't belong here. It would be much safer for you and your dad if you gave up. This town belongs to us."

"So what, you're like the demonic mayor or something?"

The woman laughed. "The human mayor is demonic enough. But I am one of the strongest demons here. Even your predecessor never caught me. Wow, he was smelly at the end. I was surprised you were even able to touch him. Michael Moss, his name. He was a strong fighter. Stronger than you, that's for sure. And, well, you saw where it got him."

"Can we just get this over with?" Peter said, rubbing his eyes wearily.

"How about, instead of fighting, I make a peace offering?" She ladled some soup into a bowl. "Just a goodwill gesture, no strings attached. What'dya say? I make a mean dinner."

She placed the bowl in front of Peter.

"There's a hair in your soup," he pointed out.

"Many hairs, actually," she confirmed. "You didn't expect me to pluck out all the little follicles, did you? Such a tedious job. And this lady's husband was quite the hairy man."

Peter backed away instinctively, staring at the soup as a severed finger floated to the top.

"You could argue that he deserved it," the asura said, still smiling through its vessel. "Well, we argue that you all deserve it. But you should see the bruises this young lady has all over. And do you want to know the funniest part? He wasn't even possessed. Everything he did was his own choice." The asura grinned sadistically. "Oh, sure, we gave him suggestions, but he ran with those suggestions right away. Sad, really, that we had to kill him before he could realize his full potential."

Peter was about to strike the first blow when the asura chucked a knife at him. Peter dodged quickly and it lodged in the wall behind him with a:

CLANG!

Knives lifted from drawers, pots and pans all hovered. With a flash of the asura's smile, all the objects darted at Peter.

Using Anuvata's wind to give him more speed, he dodged each item. Ceramic and glass shattered against the wall behind him. Then the asura caught him in a headlock while it bent him over and breathed in his face. The smell stung his lungs.

"You smell that?" it asked. *"That's the smell of all your anger. Anger at that cute girl and your friend cheating on you. Anger at your sensei for choosing a family and leaving you to fight alone. Anger at Zahid for choosing his band friends over you. But mostly, you're angry with yourself, aren't you? Angry that you just keep giving up."*

Peter struggled against the hold, but the poison was making him cough and wheeze.

"You could've fought for all the things you wanted, but you retreated like a coward. You could've struck a deal for your mom, but instead you let her die. You could've challenged your father and stayed in Eastville. But instead you gave up."

Peter could barely breathe and was about to pass out. His entire head and torso burned. He wrapped his arms around her neck and tipped her forward, landing her onto her back. He held her down with an elbow pressing into her neck.

"Oh, dear," the asura mocked. *"You've just ruined my dinner."*

He placed his hand against her forehead. "Be swept clean."

The asura exited the woman's mouth in a dark cloud and fled into the woods behind the house. Peter followed.

He lost sight of it quickly. Then out of nowhere, it spread over him. The cloud burned his eyes and throat. His lungs felt a stinging that weakened his entire body. He coughed, desperate for clean air, but only took in greater amounts of the poison. He fell to his knees.

At the same time, anger flooded over him. All that the asura had tried to tempt him with suddenly swelled within his mind. He was angry. At everyone and at himself. And he was angry with the asuras.

But he wouldn't hold on to it. "I am angry," he wheezed. "But I can choose what to do with these feelings."

He called on Anuvata's wind and swiped at the air, pulling the currents into a mini tornado that dispersed the poison cloud.

He choked in fresh breaths as the air was purified. Then, he looked up and realized that he was surrounded.

Chapter 65: The Welcoming Committee

Behind Peter stood a middle-aged man with a potbelly, scraggly facial hair, and a rat-like appearance. He looked like the kind of guy that hit on twelve-year-olds at bus stops.

To Peter's right was an attractive blond girl who looked like she was late for cheerleading practice.

To his left was a large, overweight man in a gamer shirt. His cheeks and neck were so thick that he looked like a blob.

And in front of him was a little dark-skinned girl who couldn't have been more than ten. She had thick hair in a ponytail that stuck out in all directions and a smile that stretched to the edges of her cheeks. He felt like he was looking at Suzy all grown up.

They were each possessed, but there were no indications that they wanted to be freed.

"What do you want?" he asked, eyeing them all carefully.

The little black girl had her arms crossed with the air of a leader. *"Consider us the welcoming committee,"* she said.

"So what?" Peter asked with an exhausted sigh. "Are you going to try and kill me or just stand there talking?"

The small girl started laughing. Peter's stomach twisted at the deceptive sound of pure joy.

"Kill you?" the girl giggled with one hand resting comfortably on her hip. *"After all this time, you still know nothing about us."*

"What an idiot among idiots!" the cheerleader scoffed. *"Why are we even talking to this fool?"*

"We don't want to kill you, little boy," the sleazy rat-man said in a raspy voice.

"We want you to suffer," the Suzy look-alike explained. *"How can we make you suffer if we kill you?"*

FWOMP!

The overweight man moved in a flash. He grabbed Peter in a bear hug. Immediately, Peter felt his strength leaving him like it was being sucked away by a vacuum cleaner.

In a swift movement, Peter head-butted the man, dropped out of his hold, and twirled away.

"You can tell Mara that his tricks are pointless," Peter said. "He has no control over me."

"Mara?" the little girl threw her head back and laughed. *"We don't work for Mara. He's fun compared to our master."*

The cheerleader put her hands out and Peter felt a wall of energy push him backwards. He smashed into the rat-man. The rat-man cackled and grabbed Peter's head as the man's hands became unnaturally hot. Peter smelled something burning. Quickly, he ducked and slipped out of the hold.

The rat-man's hands burst into flames. He threw the fire at Peter. As he dodged, the cheerleader jumped high in an acrobatic move and kicked.

As he dodged her, the blob slammed into him and knocked him to the ground. They all pummeled him and Peter felt the last vestiges of his strength wane.

"Let go of being strong," he heard Anuvata's windy whisper in his ear. *"I will be your strength instead."*

Suddenly, Anuvata's energy felt stronger and more electric within him. At the same time, a blast of wind disoriented the asuras. Peter stood, feeling energy flood his entire system.

He realized that he had always been holding back a part of himself, afraid that Anuvata would take over completely. But now, weakened, he entrusted everything to his deva.

A strong wind picked up all around him, pushing the possessed victims back.

"*'This is what should be done by one who is skilled in goodness,'*" Peter started chanting from memory. "*'And who knows the path of peace: let them be able and upright, straightforward and gentle in speech…'*"

"You think your stupid chanting will do anything?" The Suzy-asura leapt towards him.

Peter stopped the girl with a wall of wind as he started levitating. He continued to chant, pouring all his love and compassion into the passage. And apparently it was working.

The cheerleader, rat-man, and blob all shed their victims' bodies and reshaped into smoky forms. There was an elephant, a giant rat, and a tiger. But his wall of wind turned into a whirlwind, rotating around his body in a ten foot radius.

"You think you can win against us?" the Suzy-asura mocked. *"Know this, Peter Hunter: you are not safe. Ever. No one is safe. We will destroy you and everyone you care about."*

Peter ignored her and continued, "*'Whatever living beings there may be, whether they are weak or strong, omitting none, the great or the mighty, medium, short or small, the seen and the unseen, those living near and far away, those born and to be born. May all beings be at ease!'*"

"Stop it!" the Suzy-asura screamed. *"Or I will kill this little girl."*

He opened his eyes and saw her holding a large rock over her head. His heart swelled with righteous anger. As he continued the chant, his wind moved according to his will. It slammed into the rock, blasting it from the girl's hands.

"*'Let none deceive another, or despise any being in any state. Let none through anger or ill-will wish harm upon another. Even as a mother protects with her life her child, her only child,'*" Peter choked on the words, but continued. "*'So with a boundless heart should one cherish all living beings; radiating kindness over the entire world: spreading upwards to the skies, and downwards to the depths; outwards and unbounded, Freed from hatred and ill-will.'*"

Then the Suzy-asura gave up. It left the girl's body and, along with the other asuras, darted off into the forest.

That night, Peter and his dad ate a quiet meal of Chinese takeout amidst empty boxes and an almost-organized apartment.

"So, are you ready for school tomorrow?" his dad asked.

Peter returned the question with a smirk. "Are you ready for school tomorrow?"

Mr. Hunter chuckled. "I think we both have a lot to look forward to."

"We already know your weaknesses," the asura's threat repeated in Peter's mind, *"and we've laid the traps accordingly."*

He knew he could try to figure out their schemes, but beneath everything, he was tired. He was tired of worrying. He was tired of playing their mind games.

Forget their plans, he decided.

Instead, he resolved to live a life of loving-kindness, no matter what they did. He didn't want to die like Michael Moss, alone. He wanted to die like his mom had, surrounded by love.

"The Buddha said, *'Just as a mother would protect her only child with her life, even so let one cultivate a boundless love towards all beings,'*" his dad recited.

Peter studied him with wide eyes.

His dad held up the little slip of paper. "Fortune cookie."

Chapter 66: Peter Sees the Light

The next morning, Peter watched all the students flooding into his new school. They had no idea the monsters that threatened them. He couldn't help but want to be like them. He wouldn't change any of his choices, but he wished for their carefree existence.

He wove through the crowds on his way to the school office.

SHOOOSH!

He was stopped by a vision of an asura as it snapped a light fixture that fell from the ceiling, crashing onto an unsuspecting girl.

That's new, he thought.

He had always protected people from obsession and possession, but had never seen the asuras causing accidents to target their victims.

He looked up and saw that all the lights looked the same. He searched the crowd, looking for the asura, but now that his third eye was open, he could see them everywhere in dark and shadowy forms. It would be hard to discover which one would be causing the accident.

Then he spotted the girl from the vision. She was hurrying through the hallway looking for something. Her dark brown hair was up in a twist with a pen holding it in place.

Cute, Peter thought to himself.

He saw her bump into people and offer apologies. He thought if he delayed her, he might be able to save her from the asura. He had to admit that he could probably try harder to find the spirit, but talking to the girl seemed much more appealing.

No, it's efficient, he told himself. *I'm just being efficient.*

He approached, unsure of what he would say. She didn't see him, as she was still searching the crowd for something. He figured he should call her attention, but couldn't think of any words.

Before he could decide, she bumped straight into him.

He smiled, holding in a laugh at the awkwardness. "Excuse me," he managed to say.

She looked up at him and he nearly froze. It was as if she radiated sunlight. Her eyes were bright, innocent, and honest.

"No, excuse me," she said.

"Hey, as long as I have you," he tried to think of an excuse to keep her safe from the asura, "do you, uh, know where the office is?"

The office we happen to be standing right in front of, he scolded himself. *Smooth, Pete, real smooth.*

Then she smiled. It wasn't a mocking smile. It was a sweet and gentle smile, like he had just cracked a joke. It reminded him of the first warm day of spring, melting the winter ice.

"Yep," she nodded to the door. "Right there."

He smiled back, letting out a slight laugh. "Ah. So it is. Thanks." He hoped that was enough to protect her, because he couldn't think of anything else to say. He took slow backwards steps towards the office and told her, "And, hey, stay safe."

He turned around and let out a breath. He hoped she hadn't noticed him staring at her eyes.

"Hi, I'm Peter Hunter," he greeted the receptionist. "I'm new."

"Hello," she smiled. "Let me get you all the..."

CRASH!

Peter turned to look as students hopped out of the way of a light fixture that had fallen in the hallway.

"Oh my!" the receptionist took in a breath.

She picked up the phone to make a call to the janitor.

Peter could see from the office windows that no one had gotten hurt. He was especially happy to see that the girl was safe.

She stared at the broken glass scattered everywhere. Then she slowly looked at him in the office. Her mouth was hanging open and her eyes were wide. He smiled and waved and she gave him a tentative wave back with her mouth still hanging open.

Peter laughed to himself that it was almost as if he could read her thoughts. He figured she must be an honest person, because her expressive face would give away any thought in an instant.

"Okay, Mr. Hunter," the receptionist called his attention and placed a stack of papers on the counter in front of him. "Here's a copy of your class schedule, a map with your classrooms highlighted, and a copy of the school handbook. Welcome to Sacred Heart Academy. I hope you make lots of new friends."

"Thanks. Me, too."

He walked into the hallway again and smiled to himself as he saw the girl being tackled into a group hug by two other girls.

Maybe making new friends won't be such a bad thing after all.

The Metta Sutta

This is what should be done by one who is skilled in goodness, and who knows the path of peace: Let them be able and upright, straightforward and gentle in speech, humble and not conceited, contented and easily satisfied, unburdened with duties and frugal in their ways. Peaceful and calm and wise and skillful, not proud or demanding in nature.

Let them not do the slightest thing that the wise would later reprove. Wishing: In gladness and in safety, may all beings be at ease. Whatever living beings there may be; Whether they are weak or strong, omitting none, The great or the mighty, medium, short or small, the seen and the unseen, those living near and far away, those born and to-be-born —May all beings be at ease!

Let none deceive another, or despise any being in any state. Let none through anger or ill-will wish harm upon another. Even as a mother protects with her life, her child, her only child, so with a boundless heart should one cherish all living beings; Radiating kindness over the entire world:

Spreading upwards to the skies, and downwards to the depths; outwards and unbounded, freed from hatred and ill-will. Whether standing or walking, seated or lying down, free from drowsiness, one should sustain this recollection. This is said to be the sublime abiding. By not holding to fixed views, the pure-hearted one, having clarity of vision, being freed from all sense desires, is not born again into this world.

Preview of Book Two

"So get this!" Zeke exploded as Chiara sat at the table.

"Buckle your utility belts," Mac warned everyone.

"Did you know," Zeke said, punctuating his consonants, "that there are real life superheroes out there?"

Chiara perked up. She watched Peter as he took his seat next to Zeke. She was disappointed that his muscles didn't even tense.

"There are all these normal, everyday people who dress up and do vigilante work in their cities," Zeke explained.

Chiara had –of course– come across this information in her extensive research. She had never found any information on people like Peter, however.

"That is so exciting!" Mac exclaimed.

"Cool," Peter nodded.

Chiara studied his reaction or lack thereof. She would be blushing and nervously avoiding the topic if she were in his place. Maybe he had forgotten the previous night's events just like the man he had fought.

"I'm sure there are some that have actual super powers," Zeke speculated. "Mainly because I *want* to be sure of that." Cosmo rolled his eyes. Zeke ignored him. "But most are just average Joes and Janes that use their normal talents. Like one guy's a researcher like Chiara, but for supernatural things. There's another guy who's an EMT."

"Dude, we should do this," Mac bounced in the chair.

"Peter and I already do martial arts," Zeke fed off Mac's excitement. "And Chiara could be like the researcher guy. Cosmo could, I don't know, use science to make weapons and stuff."

Cosmo sighed. "I don't know about mechanics," he complained. "I know mostly about the brain and physics."

"Maybe you could hypnotize people!" Zeke said with wide eyes. "Mac too, since your mom's a psychiatrist."

Chiara caught Peter yawning. He noticed and smiled at her.

While the group continued their conversation, Chiara leaned over and whispered, "You look like you stayed up late fighting monsters or something."

"That's not too far off," Peter gave her a half smile.

"So you admit it then?" she prodded eagerly.

He shook his head, laughing it off and Chiara conceded. If he ever did reveal his secret, it wouldn't be in the middle of a packed cafeteria.

Look forward to the next title from the
FREELANCE EXORCISTS **series:**

Chiara Marino and the Demons of Darkness
Coming in winter, 2017

For more information, visit:

freelanceexorcistsbooks.blogspot.com

Or find us on Facebook: Freelance Exorcists Book Series

Made in the USA
Columbia, SC
08 July 2017